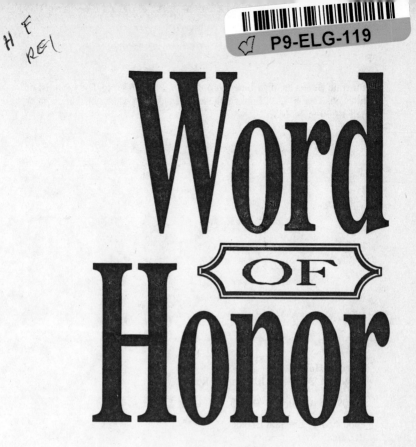

Word OF Honor

T. Elizabeth Renich

Emerald
Books

P.O. Box 635
Lynnwood, Washington 98046

Emerald Books are distributed through YWAM Publishing. For a full list of titles, visit the YWAM Publishing web site at www.ywampublishing.com or call 1-800-922-2143.

Dedication

*T*o Carol Elizabeth Renich—thank you, Momma, for putting up with me. You've been a trooper through the many battlefields, libraries, museums, graveyards and re-enactments, along with the rental cars, airline flights, train rides, and ferry boats. One day, I'm going to teach you how to read a road map properly so we won't have to backtrack. *I love you!*

*T*o my niece, Jessica Elizabeth Renich—maybe someday you'll read this when you're old enough.

*T*o Mrs. Jan Palmer, my Advanced Composition teacher at Saddleback High School in 1982— for helping me develop my own style of writing, and for teaching me that there are many other words to use besides "said."

*T*o Jerry Witte, Head Football Coach/History teacher—who instilled a fondness for the two things that have come to be my livelihood and hobby—football and history.

and

*T*o the memory of my great-great-grandfather, Private Frederick Renich, Company L, 9th Illinois Cavalry— who was awarded his American citizenship for fighting to preserve the Union.

Acknowledgments

I never thought I'd see the day when I had a manuscript published, let alone a work of historical fiction. I am in no way attempting to re-write history—it is merely my intent to tell a fictitious story set in a rich, vivid historical era. Accuracy and facts are very important to me, for I want to do this right. In my story are places that will never be found on any map, events that never actually occurred, and characters that are purely figments of my imagination. I've enjoyed weaving the historic details to enhance my tale, and giving my characters a chance to mingle with some of those who played vital roles in American history and ultimately the outcome of the Civil War—or War Between the States, depending on how you choose to interpret it.

Early on I found that writing such a story is work that cannot be done alone. It takes constant support, prayer, encouragement, and assistance on all sides, and I know there are *many* to whom I owe a debt of deep gratitude, including: Dick and Joanie Bridgman; Joyce Byas; Steve Crumbacher; Daddy; Molly Daniel; Shirley Davis; Laura-Leigh Fenstermacher; Patty Harter; Janet Hoffman; Anna and Don Isbell; Nancy Proclivo; Joe Reich; Elizabeth Renich; Fred Renich; all of the San Diego Chargers family, coaches, staff and players; Mark (Segovia) from Tulsa; Patty Seleski; Linda Shimamoto; Auntie Jan (Tornell); Warren Walsh; and the Wisners-Jahnsens-Johnsons.

Special thanks goes to all of those who have assisted with my research, including: the clerks and reference librarians at Carlsbad Library; Sal and Joan Chandon, Doubleday Inn; Carol Coile, Fairfax Court House; Tina Fair, Civil War Institute; Cal and Betty Fairbourne, Inn at Antietam; Carol Drake Friedman, Author/Historian (Northern Virginia); Jim Heuting, Licensed Battlefield Tour Guide/Gettysburg; Doug Knapp, Museum of the Confederacy; Patty Melton, Gettysburg College; Donnie Ross, Tour Guide/Richmond; the Park Rangers-Tour Guides at Alcatraz Island; Chatham Mansion; Hugh Mercer's Apothecary Shop; Stonewall Jackson Shrine; Sully Plantation, the Visitor's Centers of the Antietam, Chancellorsville, Fredericksburg, and Manassas Battlefields; and Walney.

Most importantly, my desire is to give the praise and glory to Jesus Christ, my Lord and my Savior. I thank Him for giving me *"a way with words"* and for being my constant source of inspiration.

T. Elizabeth Renich

Other Books by T. Elizabeth Renich

Word of Honor
Matter of Trust
Not without Courage
Strength and Glory

Chapter One

Northern Virginia, Near Chantilly
August, 1862

*F*rom her room, Salina Hastings could distinctly hear the grandfather clock downstairs in the parlour. The endless tick-tock, tick-tock, tick-tock was punctuated by three resonant chimes. During the daylight, the sounds of the old clock faded, but at nighttime, each sway of the pendulum echoed throughout the still house.

Restless and unable to sleep, Salina pushed aside the muslin sheet and slipped out of her high four-poster bed. Softly she crossed to the washstand and poured well water from the pitcher into the porcelain basin. She dipped a corner of a towel into the water and then wiped her face and neck. She sighed. The coolness was indeed welcome, especially in the sticky heat of the darkness, yet she found herself more awake than before.

At the window seat, Salina pulled a lacy curtain aside for a glimpse outdoors. The moon and stars shone brightly enough to make out the barn, the dairy, and the covered well. The trees surrounding the house cast long, black shadows across the yard below, and she knew that dawn was still a ways off yet.

Something was out there. She could feel it in the pit of her stomach. Salina let the lace drapery fall back into place. From the bureau drawer she pulled out a pair of britches that once belonged to her older brother, Ethan, along with one of the work shirts he had outgrown. Quickly she changed from her nightgown into Ethan's old clothes and pulled on a pair of riding boots. She tied her thick, dark hair back with a satin ribbon and set a cap over her curls.

Quietly, cautiously, Salina moved the rocking chair away from the wall and lifted the needlework tapestry from its place. She ran her fingers along the paneling until she touched the spring catch and pushed it. Without a sound, the panel slid open, and Salina stepped into a secret passage. Pushing another such catch, the door slid silently closed behind her, and Salina proceeded to make her way down the narrow space between the walls of the house. This concealed tunnel, which slanted downward and ran beneath the ground floor, had its opening in a dense grove of trees beyond the dairy, near the bank of the stream.

Salina exited the passageway and started toward the woods where the horses were corralled. They never kept the horses in the barn anymore. They hid their animals instead, to avoid tempting any patrolling Union soldiers who might be likely to confiscate the horses should they be discovered. Since the war began, Salina's family — as well as many others in the area — had learned to hide what they didn't want the Northern armies to take away from them.

"Starfire," Salina softly called into the night. The horse, answering to his name, nudged Salina's shoulder with his nose, whinnying in her ear. "Come on, boy, let's you and I go for a little ride." She didn't bother to saddle up Starfire; she merely used a nearby stump as a boost to swing up onto his bare back. Threading her fingers through Starfire's coarse mane, she clucked twice, then gave the command, "Giddy-up, boy."

Intuitively, Salina rode along through the trees to the clearing where the schoolhouse stood. It was here that the edges of her family's estate, Shadowcreek, bordered Ivywood, the Armstrong plantation lands.

Here at the schoolhouse Salina had learned lessons under the guidance of a co-op teacher. Several of the neighboring families had pitched in to raise the teacher's salary; therefore, the local children — boys and girls together — were provided an opportunity to receive a basic education. The teacher had boarded with the Armstrongs at Ivywood until the war came, and then the idealistic young man deserted his pupils in order to fight for the Confederacy. That was well over a year ago.

Since that time, Mamma tutored Salina herself. There had been little talk of finishing school, and Salina was glad that she hadn't had to go away. She hadn't wanted to leave Shadowcreek, and Mamma had been reluctant to send her. Instead, Mamma took great care to instruct Salina not only in standard bookwork, but also in practical lessons — such as how to manage the Shadowcreek estate. There was much work to be done just to keep the place up, especially in Daddy's absence.

Daddy. He was the reason Salina had ridden out to the schoolhouse. She felt that he was close by, and she'd never been wrong when she'd had this feeling before. For reasons beyond Salina's comprehension, she could correctly sense when Daddy was near. She was beginning to put more trust in her instincts as of late, and she had yet to be proven wrong. She dismounted and rubbed her arms to ward away the goosebumps rising on her arms. *Was he truly here?*

Captain Garrett Hastings sat perfectly still, his pistol trained on the schoolhouse door. Having heard the stealthy sounds of a rider's approach, every muscle in his body was tense with anticipation when the door opened, ever so slightly. He heard a soft, melodious voice whisper, "Daddy, are you here?"

The Captain sighed in relief and put the safety lock back on his revolver. "Sally-girl, *what* do you think you're doing out here in the middle of the night?" he demanded roughly but couldn't contain a proud grin.

Salina pitched herself into his strong arms, landing on his lap. "Oh, Daddy! I just *knew* you were here. Oh, I'm so glad to see you!" She buried her face in the hollow between his shoulder and his jaw, laying her cheek alongside his neck. "Daddy, I've missed you so!"

The Captain's reply was a fierce bear hug full of love. "My little darlin'!" His chuckle rumbled deep inside his chest. "Let me take a look at you!" He held her by the shoulders, at arm's length, and questioned, "Ethan's clothes?"

Salina grinned. "He outgrew them. He's getting taller and taller every day. I expect he'll be as tall as you are soon — if he's not already."

The Captain nodded in agreement. "I expect so. How is he?"

"Fine," Salina answered. "Although I'm sure he regrets promising that he'd stay at Shadowcreek to look after Mamma and me. He hasn't come right out and said as much, but I know he wants to join the army very badly so that he can defend Virginia, like you do."

The Captain shook his dark head. "We've had that argument many times before. Your brother looks at the war as some glorious, romantic adventure — fighting in the name of the Cause. Well, let me assure you, it is not all bugle blowing and gallant pageantry. I, for one, don't want him getting himself killed. Besides, your Mamma would never forgive me if he did."

"Mamma's always worrying that you'll be getting *yourself* killed if you're not careful," Salina admitted. "I'm glad you're safe! I know she will be, too. We pray that God will keep you constantly in His hand, and thankfully He has. Can you come up to the house?"

"No, not this time," the Captain said. "I'm meeting...someone...here in a little while, and then I'm heading south to Richmond. I have reports to make to President Davis and to the War Department. I'll be back in a week, though, and I'll be able to see Mamma then."

"If you're going to Richmond, does that mean your assignment west was a success?" Salina questioned.

"It was," the Captain replied. "Now it will be the decision of the War Department whether or not they want to make another attempt to make a campaign for the Western territories and California. Did you get my letters?"

"Yes," Salina nodded. "One from San Diego and two from Santa Fe."

"Then you know I was able to make contacts everywhere I went during my scouting mission—not only in San Diego and Santa Fe, but in Tucson, Mesilla, Las Cruces, Carson City, Denver, and San Francisco. Now, all I've got to do is present to President Davis the maps and plans I've come up with, and we'll see if it can work. We will be much more organized this time and better prepared. We won't repeat the mistakes we made in the battles at Valverde and Glorieta Pass," the Captain declared. "There is need of more certain supply bases for food, ammunition, clothing, and horses. When I get to Richmond, I will begin an attempt to put the pieces of the puzzle together."

Before the Captain departed three months ago, in May, to follow his orders west, he had explained to Salina why the Confederacy wanted to capture New Mexico Territory and California. California could provide the Confederacy not only with unblockaded coastal ports but also with the wealth of the gold and silver that came from the mines. The Southern government and army was desperately in need of resources to fund the continuing war effort, and California could more than provide for the growing need.

The Captain had also heard rumors that some Southerners had hopes to annex the northern states of Mexico which, if a successful venture, might well extend the Confederacy beyond Texas all the way to the Pacific. Somewhere in the back of his mind, the Captain didn't know if that would be prudent or not. He understood that it would mean the perpetuation of slavery, and, personally, he did not condone the South's "peculiar institution," as it was often called. However, he was not in a position to question. It was merely his duty to carry out his assignments to the best of his ability for the sake of his country.

Salina remembered Daddy's account of those far western battles in New Mexico Territory — of the Confederate victory at Valverde, and of the Colorado volunteers who had marched 400 miles in thirteen days to help the Union forces stop the Confederates at Glorieta Pass. The defeated Confederate forces, comprised mostly of Texans, retreated from Santa Fe to San Antonio, leaving a trail of starvation, disease, and death. The fruitless campaign spanned approximately six months, ending in March of this year, and only half of the original 3500 Confederate soldiers had survived the ordeal.

"Daddy, if the South was able to capture the land between Texas and California, and California itself, then that means we would have seaports on both the Atlantic and the Pacific. Then it would relieve the pressure of the Northern blockade, wouldn't it?"

"Yes, I suppose, but I understand there are profiteers who have been rather successful at getting past the Yankees in spite of their blockade." The Captain confided, "Your Uncle Caleb outfits a rig that makes runs to England or Nassau every now and again. Amazing that money can wield such power and command such greed."

"If we had the gold and silver, it could be spent on things our soldiers need — food, horses, arms, and ammunition," Salina suggested.

"Yes, I realize that," the Captain nodded. "I am of the opinion that the key to overthrowing the current form of government in the West is to command separate Southern armies of volunteers to simultaneously attack at vital locations. The trick would be getting everyone to cooperate together. Communication between the volunteers would be absolutely essential and timing would be crucial. Do you understand what we're trying to accomplish, Sally?"

"I think so," she nodded.

For a moment the Captain studied his daughter's pretty face. *Why was he telling her all of this?* he wondered. But he knew the answer: It was because Salina was sharp and intelligent, and could be relied on to keep such knowledge to herself. She had always been a quick learner, and she had a keen sense of adventure, not unlike that he found in himself. And on occasion she could be impulsive, though not so much as he admittedly was. Salina was of slight build, like her Mamma, and possessed a similar strength of character and loyalty of heart. Even now the Captain could see the sparkle of brewing mischief reflected in Salina's green eyes — eyes that were replicas of his own.

The Captain was silent for a long moment. He had prayed all the way across Texas, New Mexico, and Arizona that God would answer his petitions by revealing to him two people — both loyal and willing to take risks — with whom he could work. It wasn't until this last trip to San Francisco that part of the answer to his prayers presented itself, and the Captain thanked God on a daily basis for the young man who was now his assistant. But the Captain was still in search of the second helper.

Suddenly, an idea startled him with almost frightening resolution. Could it be that *she* might very well be right under his own nose? *She'd be perfect,* he told himself, *because no one would suspect her capable of pulling it off — least of all the Yankees.* Yet uncertainty plagued him...

"Darlin', do you remember when you said you wanted me to find a way that you could help me with my work?" the Captain inquired.

Salina immediately nodded. "I remember well. Last time you were home we talked about it a little bit. Have you found something that I can do?" she asked anxiously.

The Captain hesitated. He had made Ethan promise to stay at Shadowcreek to look after things, to keep him from getting involved in the bloody conflict that raged all around them. The Captain figured Ethan would be free from harm. How could he keep his son from getting involved and then justify encouraging his daughter to do so?

There was another reason why the Captain hadn't wanted Ethan involved, one which until now the Captain had kept to himself. He had cause to believe that because certain Yankees considered him a traitor in their eyes, they would stop at nothing in order to prove his connection to the Confederate Secret Service. The Captain was confident that the Yankees, should they manage to catch him, would bring him up on charges of treason against the United States' government. He understood that these Yankees might not only suspect *him,* but probably *anyone* he was close to as well. By securing Ethan's word of honor that he would stay at home, the Captain had intended to shield Ethan from learning that he was under a cloud of constant suspicion merely because he was the Captain's son. The Captain knew his son well, could guess at what Ethan's reaction might be, and he didn't want Ethan to do anything rash.

Mamma was under suspicion also, because of her relationship to the Captain, but not to the same extent Ethan was, and that was because she was a woman. The Captain was fairly sure that the Yankees would overlook Salina altogether. Salina was clever and reliable. She could be trusted to carry out assignments without question and without drawing attention to herself. The Captain hesitantly contemplated a role for Salina within his Secret Service operations. He wasn't ready to tell her about it just yet, though. He wanted to be absolutely sure that bringing her into the Network was what he felt he should do. For the present time, the Captain needed his family's silence, along with their ability to make appearances at Shadowcreek seem as normal as they possibly could. The less they knew, he was convinced, the less likely they'd be in any real danger.

"I may have found something that you can do to help, Sally — if you are willing." The Captain would not force her into anything. He wanted her to have a choice.

"You know I will do what you ask of me, Daddy." Salina added, "You have my word."

The Captain smiled inwardly, pleased by his daughter's determined spirit. It was times like these when he saw much of himself in her. It both amused and alarmed him. "Very well," he nodded abruptly, then said lowly, "When I get back from Richmond, we'll have a long talk, you and I. Very serious. You're nearly sixteen, now, Sally. That's quite a grown-up age, I believe. If you should decide to help me, grown-up things will be required of you."

"I'll be sixteen in a week's time," Salina nodded. "I'll be waiting for you, Daddy. Shall I meet you here?"

"No. I'll seek you out when I think it's safe. Say nothing to Mamma of this," he ordered softly.

Salina smiled. "Rest assured, I won't. We both know Mamma'd skin you alive if she knew you were going to let me be involved in the Secret Service."

The Captain put his finger to his lips. "Sssshhh," he grinned. "You know your Mamma well enough to imagine the degree of her displeasure if she were to find out. Let's just keep this between the two of us. In the meantime, I want you to take this to Ethan." He handed her a note. "I'm giving him an order: to teach you how to shoot — straight. Ethan's a good teacher. He'll make sure you learn properly how to defend yourself."

Salina arched an eyebrow in question. "Will I *need* to defend myself?"

"I never want you to be caught unaware, Sally-girl. Even as we Rebels have eyes everywhere, so do the Yankees," the Captain cautioned her. "Learn well," he said and then kissed the top of her head. "Get on back up to the house."

"I'll see you in a week." Salina smiled radiantly.

"Yes," the Captain nodded. "One week. And I'll have a fine birthday present for you by then. You just wait and see."

Chapter Two

*C*aptain Duncan Grant held a pair of field glasses up to his eyes and carefully surveyed the land before him. It had been at least five years since he'd last been a guest here, but he easily recognized the peaceful farmlands.

Rose-colored dawn crept over the Shadowcreek estate, touching the main house and the outbuildings with pale pink light. Retreating into the cover of the trees on the far side of the gurgling creek, Captain Grant and his fellow Yankee scout, a lieutenant named Lance Colby, continued to observe the farm.

"No sign of him, Captain?" Lieutenant Colby asked, stifling a yawn.

"No," Captain Grant replied wearily. For the past two days they had traveled with little food and without sleep to reach this part of Virginia in hopes of tracking down an elusive Rebel Captain. "No sign of him."

"You're positive this is his land?" Colby asked.

"Yes, I'm certain." Captain Grant again looked through his field glasses. He spied wisps of smoke curling from the kitchen chimney. Two black slaves appeared in the barnyard, tending to the morning's chores.

A black-haired young man rode into the yard on a graceful golden horse with a cream-colored mane and tail. He dismounted quickly and signaled for the black man who joined him in front of the barn to hold the animal.

"That's his son, Ethan. Spitting image of Garrett Hastings, that one is," Captain Grant muttered. "All of this land belongs to Hastings: from the creek to the turnpike to over yonder, past those hills. If he's gone into hiding, there's many an acre for him to choose from here. Hastings knows every inch of this place blindfolded."

Lieutenant Colby poured himself a cup of cold coffee. "You suspect Hastings has hidden the information we're looking for here?"

"It would seem logical that he may have hidden some of the documents on the premises, but Hastings is too wily to have secreted them all here. I strongly believe he's working with someone—maybe his son or possibly even the local citizens. All I have to do is find Captain Hastings, and that'll put a stop to whatever it is that he's up to this time."

The lieutenant glanced at his captain. "Sir, may I ask a question?"

"Of course, Lieutenant. What is it?" Captain Grant asked.

"Does it bother you, sir, to have been assigned to the duty of tracking your best friend?" Colby inquired.

Duncan Grant's features turned to stone, and his gray eyes looked like cold granite. His lips formed words, but his throat went dry, rendering him unable to speak. Clearing his throat, he whispered hoarsely, "It bothers me very much, Lieutenant. More than anyone will ever know. My feelings, however, are not the issue. It is my duty to follow orders from the United States War Department. I'll not shirk my assignment. Garrett Hastings understands duty and honor better than most—it's what he's fighting for. In a sense, it's what we're all fighting for. Hastings and I simply ended up on opposite sides, which puts us at odds against each other. That is the part which is hardest to stomach."

Lieutenant Colby nodded silently.

"Come on," Duncan Grant said briskly, again in control of his traitorous feelings toward the man he'd come to Virginia to locate.

"Let's get some sleep. We'll come up with a plan, and maybe we'll force a move on his part."

☆☆☆☆☆☆☆

Salina was up early, in spite of being awake so late the previous night. She had watched the sunrise from the window seat in her second-story bedroom. Today was undoubtedly going to be a busy day. Ethan had told her, after she'd given him the note with Daddy's instructions, that they'd begin their shooting lessons prior to breakfast this very morning. Afterward, Salina would be occupied with the dressmaker that Aunt Priscilla was sending over from Ivywood, and Salina was not looking forward to having to stand absolutely still for the length of time it was bound to take for the fitting. But she had no choice. The dress must be finished before her cousin's wedding. Mary Edith was to be married to a Confederate naval officer named Randle Baxter, and she insisted that Salina be a bridesmaid for the ceremony. Salina had accepted the honor. This was to be her third time as a bridesmaid, and she'd probably hold the position again if and when Ethan ever got around to declaring his intentions of marrying Taylor Sue Carey. Most of the girls Salina's age were engaged if they weren't already married, but none of the boys particularly piqued Salina's interest—not since one special young man had gone west to seek his fortune.

Through the window, Salina saw Ethan dismount from his horse and hand the reins to Peter Tom. "Where has he been already this morning?" she said to no one. "Perhaps Dr. Phillips needed him on another visitation..." During the past year, the elderly doctor had taken her brother under his wing, and he had come to rely on Ethan's assistance and God-given gift of healing. When Dr. Phillips offered Ethan an apprenticeship, Ethan accepted without the slightest hesitation. Ethan took to accompanying Dr. Phillips on his rounds and helped out around the office with greater frequency. Ethan had read all the medical books he could lay his hands on at least twice. His studies helped keep him sane, Salina suspected, and perhaps preoccupied him enough so that the war wasn't always the first thing on his mind. Of course, Salina knew Taylor Sue Carey commanded a fair share of his thoughts as well.

Jubilee knocked lightly on Salina's bedroom door. "Missy Salina?"

"Come in," Salina called.

"Massah Ethan says fer ya ta meet him in da orchard," the tall, slender black-skinned woman informed Salina. "Ya gonna tell Jube what it is yer up ta?"

"Up to? Me?" Salina grinned at the faithful maidservant. "Why are you always so sure that I'm up to something, Jubilee?"

"Dat 'cause ah's known ya since da day ya cum inta dis here world wid a screech an' a holler. Ya've been mischief ever since, chile," Jubilee said fondly. "Ah knows ya through an' through."

"Don't tell Mamma just yet, because no doubt she won't like it," Salina confided. "But Ethan's going to teach me how to shoot."

Jubilee sighed. "Aye, Miz Annelise won't like it, but ah reckon she'll know dat in times like dese, it cain't hurt. Ah won't say nothin', but ah want ya ta tell her all 'bout it yersef. Hear?"

"All right," Salina agreed. She sat down at the vanity table, weaving her curls into a loose braid. "Jubilee, would you mind getting me a ribbon from the dresser?"

Jubilee opened the dresser drawer and selected a red satin ribbon from inside. She pulled on it, assuming it to be tangled with some of the other ribbons, but she quickly discovered that the red one was being used to bind several envelopes together. Jubilee gathered the envelopes in her hand. "What's dis now?"

Salina looked into the mirror and caught Jubilee's questioning glance. "They're...just some letters, Jubilee. Mostly from Daddy..." her sentence trailed off into silence.

"An' from who else?" Jubilee put on an expression of innocence and used one specific envelope to fan herself.

Salina quickly snatched the letter from Jubilee's hand. The maidservant chuckled heartily. "Still pinin' away fer dat Pony Express rider, ere ya?"

Salina stared down at the faded letter addressed to her in bold script: *Miss Salina Hastings of Shadowcreek, in care of Chantilly Post Office, Virginia.* The image of a certain long-legged, broad-shouldered, blue-eyed, sandy-haired young man she once knew came to mind. "I'm not pining away for anyone," Salina insisted in a hoarse whisper. Unfolding the single sheet of paper, Salina read to herself the two-year-old letter dated in 1860:

> *Miss Salina,*
> *You were right when you guessed that my uncle had beaten me again. Even though you're smart enough to piece it together, I was ashamed to admit it to you. But it doesn't matter anymore, for I am going away. I can't live*

*like this—especially not when Uncle John makes it no se-
cret that he'd like to kill me himself. It's been going on
ever since my father died and my mother went back to
England a few months ago. I'll tell you where I'm going
because I know you'll keep it a secret. I'm going to Missouri, perhaps even as far as California. I've found a
newspaper advertisement placed by Russell, Majors &
Waddell to recruit riders for their newfangled Pony Express. The ad says:* Wanted—skinny, wiry fellows not
over 18. Must be expert riders willing to risk death daily.
Orphans preferred. Wage: $25 per week. *I'm practically
an orphan, wouldn't you agree? As for risking death
daily, well, one of these days Uncle John just might make
good his threat to beat me to death—so why not? I have
nothing to lose, and Uncle John certainly won't miss another mouth to feed. Will you miss me, Salina? I pray that
you won't forget me. I wanted to tell you farewell before I
go, but I didn't know if I would have the opportunity to do
so. I'll write when I can.*

> *Ever your faithful friend,*
> *Jeremy Barnes*

Salina slipped the cherished page back into its envelope, sighing
wistfully. "Jeremy Barnes never wrote save for this one letter. I know
I was just fourteen when he went away, but he specifically asked me
not to forget him." She lowered her eyes and said softly, "I didn't—
couldn't—forget about him, Jubilee, although it's quite plain to tell
that he forgot all about me. Evidently, in Jeremy's eyes I was merely
Ethan's little sister. And since he's been gone for so long, I would
suppose that even if he were to come back to Shadowcreek this very
day his opinion would not change on that point."

"Humph," Jubilee crossed her arms over her ample chest. "Ah
don' know 'bout dat, Missy. If'n my memory serves me true, ah do
seem ta remember diff'rently. Ah recall clearly how da pair of ya used
ta walk ta-gether an' talk ta-gether fer hours on end down by da mill at
Carillon, an' y'all used to laugh and ride off together, not ta
mention da way he allays smiled whenever he'd give ya a fresh-
picked pink rose from Miz Annelise's garden..."

"Stop it, Jubilee," Salina ordered more gruffly than she'd intended. She also remembered those things, no matter how hard she
willed herself not to. She impetuously crumpled the letter, tossing it

into the grate to be burned next time a fire was built. "Jeremy's gone, and that's that. He's started a new life for himself far away from here. There isn't any reason for him to return, and there's never really been any use for me to pine for him."

Jubilee chose to hold her tongue. Instead of replying, she pulled a white ribbon from the drawer and used it to secure the end of Salina's braid. Salina muttered "Thank you," tied her bonnet under her chin, and stalked from the room without further comment.

With Salina out of the room, Jubilee retrieved the discarded letter, smoothed out the crinkles as best she could, and secretly tucked it back in the drawer with the others. "Mmmm-mmm—Dat girl needs ta learn ta think tings through afore reactin'," the maidservant shook her head sagaciously. "Dere are times when she jist acts an' reacts..."

Chapter Three

*E*than presented Salina with a handsome pearl-handled silver pistol. "You can consider this as an early birthday gift, little sister."

Salina held the gun well away from herself. "Thank you—I think." She tipped her head back to look up at her eighteen-year-old brother. "You'll really teach me how to use this to defend myself?"

"I said I would, didn't I? Don't hold it between your thumb and forefinger like that, Salina. That's dangerous, and you could drop it too easily. Get a good grip on the handle," Ethan instructed.

She held the pistol's pearl handle in her small palm, pointing the barrel away from herself and from Ethan.

He chuckled. "Don't be so prissy, Salina. Hold it like you mean business."

Salina gripped the gun more firmly. "Like this?"

"Much better," he nodded, his gray-green eyes dancing with unmasked amusement. "First, I'll teach you how to load the gun, and then I'll teach you how to shoot it properly," Ethan told her.

Salina was a quick study, and she picked up the procedures Ethan demonstrated for her quite easily. "Maybe this won't be so terribly difficult after all."

"Good," Ethan nodded encouragingly. "Now, let's try some target practice." Ethan hung half a dozen glass bottles on varying lengths of twine from the lower branches of a tree. He stepped back to where Salina was standing and helped her aim the pistol. "Take your choice of a target, then take your time and concentrate on your aim."

She closed one eye, aiming carefully, but before Salina could fire a single shot, one by one each of the six bottles shattered and fell to the ground.

Both Ethan and Salina spun around, wide-eyed, locating the source of the perfectly targeted shots. "Lord, have mercy on us all!" Ethan exclaimed. "Would you look who it is!"

The visitor was off his horse in a split second, and Salina froze on the spot, silently witnessing the reunion of two long lost friends. She stood tongue-tied in disbelief, her heart pounding almost painfully in her chest.

"Jeremy Barnes!" Ethan laughed as they clapped each other on the shoulder. "What a surprise to see you! Why didn't you let us know you were coming home?"

"I got here late last night," Jeremy answered with a wide grin. "The Armstrongs were kind enough to let me borrow a bed and feed me before I headed straight over here to Shadowcreek." He cast a curious glance at the dark-haired young lady standing a short distance away. Mistaking her for a lady-friend of Ethan's, Jeremy queried, "I haven't interrupted anything, have I?"

Ethan shook his head. "I was just teaching my little sister how to shoot—until you came along and shot up all the targets I wanted her to take aim at. Your fancy shooting probably scared the living daylights out of Salina."

Jeremy tethered the beautiful chestnut roan he called Comet and flashed a dazzling white-toothed smile. *"This* is little Miss Salina?" he asked, most certainly surprised. He stopped to stand directly in front of her, resting his hands on his lean hips. "Have I been away so long that you've gone and grown up while I wasn't looking?"

"Why? Do you think I've changed?" Salina asked evenly, thankful that her voice remained steady and did not betray the nervousness or the pleasure she felt at the mere sight of him.

"Yes, indeed you have, Salina. Changed for the better, if you'll permit me to say so," Jeremy grinned. "I declare you've grown even more lovely than you were when I left." He took her hand, the one not holding the gun, and pressed it to his lips. Mischief danced in his sapphire blue eyes. "Did you miss me?"

"Perhaps," was all Salina would allow. "Welcome home, Jeremy. That is if you consider yourself being home."

"Virginia's the only home I've ever known. I'm a native son, and I've obviously been away for far too long. Yes, I am home...and now I am even more glad of it. Mind if I join you?"

"You're welcome to stay here with Ethan, but I've an appointment with the dressmaker back up at the house," she said lightly, silently wishing she could stay in the orchard instead.

Ethan did not fail to notice the blush that stained Salina's cheeks. She coyly hid beneath the brim of her bonnet because she knew he could read her mind through her expressive eyes. He'd told her time and again a person could see her soul in their depths. Then he looked at Jeremy, who hadn't taken his eyes off Salina. "You've got a few minutes to spare yet, Salina," Ethan said, glancing at his pocket watch. "As long as you're here, Barnes, perhaps we can impose on you to share some of your skill with a gun? I seem to recall you being a fair marksman."

"*Fair* marksman?" Jeremy queried. His grin was positively contagious. "Miss Salina, do I need to remind your brother that I won the county's shooting contest two summers ago?"

"Jeremy could out-shoot you any day of the week, and you know it, Ethan," Salina said with certainty.

"Thanks for refreshing my memory," Ethan rolled his eyes. "I'll get some more bottles."

"And I'll gladly do anything I can to help, Salina," Jeremy glanced down at her, skimming her petite frame from head to toe and back. "Today, if you have time, or any other day, for that matter. You just let me know."

For another fifteen minutes, Ethan and Jeremy gave instructions and praised Salina when her aim started getting closer to the intended target. She still had plenty of room for improvement, but at least she was on her way.

Jeremy stood directly behind Salina, as Ethan had done, and whispered soft commands to her. Once she turned to look up at him, meeting his intense blue eyes without flinching. They stood silently gazing at each other, wordlessly beginning to reacquaint themselves.

Ethan audibly cleared his throat. "I thought I heard Jubilee calling out your name, Salina. Sounds like the dressmaker has arrived."

"Oh," she shook her head as though clearing cobwebs from the corners of her mind. "Yes, I really must go now. Thank you—both—for teaching me." She handed the gun back to Ethan.

"We're a long ways from being through, Salina. We'll be practicing every morning," Ethan warned her, "until you get it right."

"Then I'll look forward to the challenge," Salina nodded. She lifted her skirt and petticoats as she climbed the gentle slope back up to the main house.

Jeremy followed her with his eyes. "Ethan, she is...I'm stunned...I mean...How could I *not* have recognized your *sister* right off?"

Ethan shrugged nonchalantly. "I don't know...but then, I suppose to someone who's not seen her for two whole years there might be good reason to think she's changed a bit. Next week is her birthday. She'll be sixteen, you know."

"Sixteen?" Jeremy raised an eyebrow in question and rubbed his clean-shaven jaw. "Well, I suppose she's quite the proper young miss."

"To a degree. You know Salina. She still has her impulsive side." Ethan nodded. "But she's become reliable, too. She's already helping Mamma and me keep the estate going. She cooks and cans, sews and mends, tends to the household chores with Jubilee. She can read and write and balance the books. Mamma's teaching her well how to be a good wife for somebody someday."

"She's beautiful," Jeremy whispered. "Of course I knew that all along, but to see her now..."

"Now? What?" Ethan wanted to know.

"Surely you must remember that Salina and I spent a fair amount of time together before I went to California," Jeremy reminded himself as well as Ethan. "Perhaps we'll get reacquainted. She's not promised to anyone around these parts?"

"No, although there has been talk of late that she would be a rare prize. Fact is, though, that most of the eligible bachelors aren't around much anymore since the fighting started."

"I'll take that as a hint of good fortune for me," Jeremy drawled.

"I'm warning you, tread lightly, Barnes," Ethan cautioned. "Don't trifle with her. You'll answer to me if you do—just the same as anyone else who finds that they might fancy my sister. Salina's a young lady, not just a girl anymore, and she might see things differently now than she did then."

"I wouldn't toy with her affections, if that's what you mean," Jeremy assured Ethan. "Is she at all the same as she was before I went away?"

Ethan hesitated before answering. "Well, Salina can be nice and docile—as she was just now, or whenever it suits her purpose—but she can be a spitfire when her temper's riled. Underneath that Southern belle gentility Mamma and Jubilee are so bent on teaching her, Salina possesses a proud spirit. She's kind, tender, loving, giving, loyal, sensitive—yet she's determined and has a mind of her own."

"Does she still like to ride and sing and go fishing?" Jeremy asked, recalling the instances when he and Salina had done those things together.

"Certainly," Ethan replied. "And she'd probably still laugh at your idiotic jokes, too. She's not like some girls who can't keep a thought in their heads. She's intelligent and she's funny. I very much enjoy her company."

"I used to," Jeremy nodded, fond memories returning. "I've always thought she was very special."

"Yes, she is at that. And don't you forget it," Ethan said firmly, poking a finger at Jeremy's chest. "Enough about my sister. Tell me, what brings you back to Virginia?"

"Pony Express folded when the telegraph came into being. I stayed on in San Francisco for awhile. I worked in the express office, and I rode shotgun for a stage line that runs down to San Diego," Jeremy explained. "Once I had earned enough money to pay off all my father's gambling debts, I started to put away a tidy little fortune for myself. But I got bored, and I figured that I was missing out on the action back here. I've been considering trying my hand at fighting the Yankees. How is it that you're still here and not off serving the Confederacy?"

"I haven't gone to enlist because I gave my word to Daddy that I'd stay. I'm bound by duty and honor to protect Shadowcreek and all that is in it. Houses have been confiscated by the Yankees for headquarters, and food and supplies have been *requisitioned* by both sides. So far, we've been fortunate in the fact that Shadowcreek isn't easily seen from the road. Patrols have passed it because they don't know where to look," Ethan said. "It's not that I *don't* want to fight, because believe me, I do. Yet I gave my word."

"Your father's a wise man," Jeremy said knowingly, sensing he was dealing with a rather touchy subject as far as Ethan was concerned. "If he asked you to stay here, around Chantilly, trust that he believes that it's what he thinks is best."

Ethan nodded. "That's all I can do."

☆☆☆☆☆☆☆

"Why is it dat ya look like ya seen a ghost, Missy Salina?" Jubilee helped Salina out of her day dress. "Hold still while ah re-do dese stays."

Salina made a face. She hated her corset and confining stays almost as much as she hated her hoop skirts, but fashion dictated that these items be worn by ladies of good social standing. Jubilee tugged on the strings, tightening the corset until Salina complained she couldn't breathe.

"Please, Jubilee, loosen the stays just an inch," Salina begged.

"Oh, ah s'pose it'll be fine," Jubilee conceded. "Yer already slim as a reed, ah reckon dat ya don' gots ta be in pain ta wear dis new dress."

"Thank you." Salina breathed more easily.

"Now dat ya gots sum color back in yer cheeks, tell Jube why ya was pale an' shakin' like a leaf when ya first cum up here."

Salina knew that word of Jeremy's return would not remain a secret for long. Her emerald eyes danced, and she felt a rush of giddiness. *"He's* back, Jubilee. *Jeremy Barnes* is down in the orchard right now with Ethan. I wouldn't have believed it if I hadn't seen him with my own two eyes," she sighed. "He's taller than he was before and more handsome, if that's possible."

"So," Jubilee hid a smile, "ya've seen dat boy again, an' now dat liddle heart o' yers is flip-floppin' inside."

Salina whispered, "When he first rode up, I don't think he knew who I was. Have I changed so much in two years? Don't you think that it's odd how he just showed up like that..." Her mind drifted back to reading Jeremy's letter earlier.

"Almost like we was speakin' him into existence," Jubilee nodded, practically reading Salina's unspoken thoughts. "He be handsome, ya says?"

"Oh, yes. But what difference does that make?" Salina pouted. "Jubilee, you should have seen the look of pure disbelief on his face when Ethan mentioned my name..."

"Had ta look twice ta be sure, did he? Ah s'pose ya might have ta jog his memory jist a liddle bit, an remind dat boy who ya ere," Jubilee suggested.

"What makes you think I'd want to do that?" Salina asked, feigning innocence.

"Like ah's tole ya afore. Ah knows ya through an' through, Missy. An ah knows ya got yer cap set fer him—ya allays have. Ya've been dreamin' of him since ya was all o' twelve year old, an more'n likely even afore dat."

Salina's cheeks were turning crimson again, and she covered them with her hands. "I have not!" Salina protested profusely. "And it shouldn't matter to me that he's back. He never wrote like he promised. He went off without ever letting me know he'd reached his destination. Now he appears with no warning whatsoever and...and he barely recognized me!" she said indignantly.

"Ya've changed in dat time, Missy. I reckon he done changed sum, too. Both of ya ernt quite da same as ya was afore, but deep down ya know him, and he knows ya." Jubilee smiled this time, her white teeth bright in contrast to her dark black skin. "Let me say ta guard yer heart, Missy, but why not give da boy a chance?"

☆☆☆☆☆☆☆

Mamma was the one who insisted that Jeremy Barnes stay to have dinner with them when she learned of his return. "You look well, Jeremy. The west coast seems to have agreed with you. Come, eat with us. I want you to tell us all about San Francisco. Captain Hastings was stationed there years ago, and we lived there for a short time. My sister Genevieve lives there with her husband and their children, and they own a lumber mill, maybe you know of it—Dumont's Lumber Mill?"

"No, I'm afraid I don't." Jeremy held Salina's chair for her.

"Thank you," she nodded politely.

"Well, did you hear the ruckus this morning?" Mamma asked. Jubilee brought in the midday meal from the kitchen. "I'm sure there was another skirmish what with all the small-arms fire I heard."

Jubilee cleared her throat loudly and shot a meaningful glance at Salina.

"That wasn't a skirmish, Mamma," Salina said. "That was Ethan and Jeremy teaching me how to shoot."

"Shoot?" Mamma asked, holding a spoonful of green beans halfway between the serving dish and her plate. "What on earth for?"

"Because Salina should know how to protect herself," Jeremy replied. "You can protect yourself, can't you Mrs. Hastings? If not, we'd be happy to teach you, as well."

"I can shoot straight enough, thank you, anyway," Mamma reluctantly admitted. "I suppose you're right, though. Salina really should learn."

Salina bit back a smile and Jubilee winked as she inquired, "Y'all care fer more fried chicken anybody?"

"We're fine, Jubilee," Mamma dismissed the maidservant. "Will you see if the apricot cobbler will be ready for our dessert?"

"Yas, Miz Annelise, dat ah'll do." Jubilee headed toward the kitchen.

"So, you've just recently arrived." Mamma smiled at Jeremy. "I'm sure Ethan has told you all the news going on around here."

"Actually, I haven't had a chance," Ethan said.

"Anything exciting that I should know about?" asked Jeremy.

Ethan gave Jeremy details of local news, mingled with the news from the front lines. "In June, General Lee and his Army of Northern Virginia fought off McClellan's march on Richmond in the Seven Days' battle. The Yankees thought they were going to stroll right in and take the capital. Well, our troops stuck to their guns and let those Yankees have it."

Mamma explained that both armies had been taking turns occupying Centreville and Fairfax Court House. "And most of our servants ran off some time ago. Jubilee, Peter Tom, and Cromwell are the only ones who have stayed on."

"So the slaves are running away," Jeremy pondered.

"In time, I'd have freed them all myself," Ethan stated firmly. "Daddy might have done the same eventually, I think. He was never keen on the institution of slavery but saw it as a necessary evil. The Southern economy is founded on it. Daddy was a stern master and required disciplined work out of our people, yet he never mistreated them. In fact, Daddy had already made an agreement with Peter Tom allowing him to work off his purchase price in exchange for his freedom."

Jeremy nodded, knowing well the reputation of fairness that Garrett Hastings had. "There are those who are not like your father, however, and some have treated their slaves horribly. That's what got all those Northern abolitionists all riled up—combined with that novel by Harriet Beecher Stowe and John Brown's raid at Harper's Ferry a few years ago."

"Well, we Southerners are not all like the beastly characters in *Uncle Tom's Cabin,* as Mrs. Stowe might want the world to think!" exclaimed Ethan.

Mamma decided it was time to turn the topic of conversation to something more pleasant than the war or slavery. "Well, since you've already been at Ivywood with the Armstrongs, then I'm sure you've heard that there's going to be a wedding next week."

"Yes," Jeremy nodded. "Miss Lottie was telling me that Miss Mary Edith is about to become Mrs. Randle Baxter. It was news to me that Randle is serving with the Confederate Navy."

"He is. In fact, he served on that ironclad ship, the *Merrimack*—or rather, the *Virginia,* since they changed the ship's name—and saw action this past March at Hampton Roads against that Yankee ship they call the *Monitor.* The newspapers said it looked like a cheese box floating on a plank. Can you imagine that?" Mamma asked. "This is the first time Randle has been granted leave to come home to be married. I'm certain Mary Edith and Randle would be delighted to have you attend. Salina's going to be one of Mary Edith's bridesmaids, and Lottie the other," Mamma told Jeremy.

Jeremy arched a questioning eyebrow in Salina's direction. Lottie had somehow failed to mention to him that Salina, too, would be standing up with Mary Edith.

"That's why the dressmaker came, to do some alterations on my gown," Salina explained with a slight shrug. She lowered her eyes to avoid his inquisitive glance.

Ethan confided, "Uncle Caleb had the material smuggled right through the Yankee blockade. He has connections with quite a few of the blockade runners and privateers. He has the money, the connections, and the power to get almost anything the Armstrongs want or need."

Jeremy nodded. "I noticed that when I was there last night. Because of all their money, the war seems to have very little effect on Ivywood at all. The Armstrongs have extended an invitation for me to stay with them, and perhaps I'll go ahead and accept—at least until the wedding ceremony."

"And then you'll be leaving again?" Salina asked. He had just returned. Surely he couldn't just leave again so soon.

Jeremy shrugged. "I don't rightly know just yet. I think I'll just wait and see what happens before I make any definite plans." He had much to do, actually, and a short time to do it in. First of all, he had to see the Reverend Yates, and then he'd have a better idea of what was in store for the near future. But he wasn't at liberty to discuss it with the Hastings.

Instead Jeremy told them all about San Francisco, and he told them some comical stories from when he rode for the Pony Express between St. Joseph and Sacramento. To his pleasure, Salina's smile appeared every now and then, and her eyes seemed to glitter with the giggles indicating that his attempts at humor were successful.

Mamma, too, was smiling and laughing softly by the time they finished their meal. She stood up and said, "I'll go see what's keeping Jubilee from bringing in the cobbler..." She put a hand to her forehead and swayed on her feet. "Oh, my..." she whispered.

Jeremy and Ethan sprang from their chairs, catching Mamma just as she fainted away.

"Miz Annelise!" Jubilee cried out, rushing to set down the tray she carried before she dropped it altogether. "Take her inta da parlour an' let her lay on da sofa in dere," she quickly told the boys.

Salina pressed a cool cloth to Mamma's forehead while Ethan held her hand. Jeremy stood back, not wanting to be in the way but wanting to make sure Mrs. Hastings was all right.

Jubilee clucked like a nervous mother hen. When Mamma opened her eyes it was to see the black woman pacing back and forth, wringing her hands together.

"Stop your pacing, Jubilee," Mamma said softly. "Watching you makes me feel like the room is tilting."

"Miz Annelise, why ya go an' scare us all like dat?" Jubilee scolded.

Mamma was embarrassed. "I do apologize. I certainly didn't mean to..."

"Ya lay right down dere," Jubilee insisted as Mamma tried to sit up. "Yer white as a sheet."

Ethan's eyes were filled with concern. "Has this happened to you before, Mamma?"

"Oh, yas, Massah Ethan, it has at dat," Jubilee nodded her head.

"Jubilee, hush," Mamma said tiredly. "No need to worry the children."

"Dey's grown chillen, an' dey gots a right ta know," Jubilee argued insistently.

Jeremy took a step closer. "Is there anything we can do to make you more comfortable, Mrs. Hastings?"

"I'll be fine," Mamma shook her head. "Thank you for your kind offering."

"What aren't you telling us, Mamma?" Salina wanted to know.

Mamma's eyes flashed at Jubilee, but Jubilee ignored her mistress's look of displeasure. "I didn't say anything because I didn't want to worry either of you..." Mamma began.

Ethan grinned. He had worked with Dr. Phillips long enough to know the symptoms, but only this minute did he realize the diagnosis. "You haven't been feeling well in the mornings, and you're tired all the time. Some of your favorite foods you refuse to touch, and while you haven't been eating all that much, you've still been putting on weight..."

Mamma nodded slowly. "Yes, I'm going to have a baby. But please, I beg you both—and you, too, Jeremy—to keep quiet concerning this. I haven't always been successful in carrying a pregnancy to term. I haven't even told Daddy in any of the letters I've sent him lately. I guess I'm just afraid that something bad will happen, as it has so many times before." Mamma had miscarried several times, and there were graves of two stillborn babies in the small family cemetery.

Salina smiled encouragingly. "But to think of a new little brother or sister! Oh, Mamma, you've got to let Daddy know. He'll be so pleased!"

"You'll be showing by the time he manages to come home again," Ethan predicted. "He'll know one way or another by then."

"I just don't want him to worry about us here," Mamma tried to explain. "He's got enough to think about just trying to carry out his assignments for the War Department. I wouldn't want him to lose any of his concentration as he needs to be focused on what he's doing out there..."

"He thinks about all of you no matter where he is," Jeremy said matter-of-factly, then quickly added, "At least I know I'd always have my loved ones in the back of my mind—if I had any loved ones to think of." He mentally kicked himself for nearly slipping up. He couldn't afford to let them know that he was in communication with Captain Hastings—not yet, at least. "I reckon I should be heading out. Thank you, Mrs. Hastings, for the good food and the pleasant conversation. I do hope you're feeling much better soon. And rest assured, I'll keep quiet. Please accept my congratulations."

Mamma smiled weakly. "Come see us again soon, Jeremy. It's nice to have you back."

"Thank you, ma'am." Jeremy turned to Ethan, "What time do the shooting lessons resume?"

"Shall we say half past seven tomorrow morning?" Ethan looked to Salina for agreement.

She nodded. "Then we'll see you in the morning, Master Barnes?"

"I'll be here, Miss Salina," he bowed at the waist, "bright and early."

Chapter Four

Jeremy Barnes had shown up at Shadowcreek bright and early every morning of the week following his return to Northern Virginia. Each day Salina improved her skill, and each day he felt as though he was breaking through the cool facade she displayed whenever he was around.

Ethan was off working with Dr. Phillips on the morning of Salina's birthday—the twentieth of August—which was also the date set for Mary Edith's wedding. Jeremy was pleased to have the rare chance for some time alone with Salina.

"Mrs. Barclay's labor began shortly after midnight, and Ethan went with Dr. Phillips to assist with the delivery," Salina explained her brother's absence. "I guess that leaves just the two of us to carry on with target practice."

"If you like, or it gives us an opportunity to talk." Jeremy looked down at Ethan's sister. "I've been watching you, Salina, all week.

You're coolly polite, and you seem determined to keep me at a distance. Why?"

"Whatever do you mean?" Salina inquired, not quite meeting his sapphire eyes.

Jeremy hooked his finger under her chin and lifted her head slightly, forcing her to meet his eyes squarely. "I mean that you've been acting very reserved and proper ever since I came back. Before I left, you and I used to laugh and talk about everything under the sun. Back then I told you things I'd never shared with anyone else because I knew I could trust you. I'm not the stranger you've been treating me as. I just want to know why won't you open up so we can be friends again."

"Perhaps I've nothing much to say to you now," Salina replied.

"I think I know you better than that, Salina. It seems that you're upset with me for some reason, and I want to know what that reason is," Jeremy stated. "I can't make amends if I don't know what's wrong."

"You broke your word," Salina answered simply, saddened to learn that Jeremy hadn't had any idea as to what she meant. "I got your note telling me you were leaving—in which you promised you'd write. Nothing ever came, Jeremy, and it hurt to think that you'd forgotten me so quickly."

"It wasn't so much that I'd forgotten you, Salina. It's just that I was busy working for the Express. I was far away, and I struggled to put all of this out of my mind. I didn't set out to intentionally break my word. It just happened," Jeremy shrugged. "But seeing you again, Salina, I am sorry that I didn't write. How could I have been so blind?"

"Blind to what?" she asked.

"Blind to you," he murmured. "In all the miles I've traveled, Salina, there isn't anyone else like you anywhere."

"And this is news to you?" she asked coquettishly.

Jeremy tilted his sandy-blond head to one side. "Yes, I guess it is. It's something I've just figured out for myself. I like you very much, Salina Hastings, and I think I always have."

Salina wanted to believe him, but she did as Jubilee had advised: She was guarding her heart. "You wanted to talk. I'm here, and I'll listen. You can rely on me to keep everything spoken between us just between us. I won't tell a soul."

Jeremy studied her face for several moments. "I've got a lot to tell you, Salina. And I've got to trust you—with more than my life."

She looked puzzled.

Jeremy wasn't sure where to start, so he said, "I know where your father is, and I have been asked to tell you that he's coming back here to Shadowcreek tonight."

Salina already had Daddy's word that he would be home tonight, but she wanted to know how Jeremy knew. Her instincts told her to be wary. "How do you know this?"

"Because he and I have business to discuss. We're meeting each other not far from here, and then he's coming to see you, because he promised you a special birthday present," Jeremy replied.

Jeremy could only have known about the birthday present through what Daddy had told him, Salina decided. She asked, "What kind of business?"

"Secret Service business. Has he ever told you anything about his work?" Jeremy asked.

Salina nodded, still cautious. "A little bit. Why?"

Jeremy was satisfied that he could trust her, but it wasn't his place to tell her that the Captain had a notion to bring her into the Network. He had worked with the Captain for the past two months, and during the last week Jeremy was beginning to see how Salina might be a valuable link for the collection and forwarding of vital information. "I was just wondering if he did. You're the trustworthy sort, Salina. The Captain knows you'd keep his secrets."

"What makes you say that?" she inquired.

"Just a hunch," Jeremy lifted his broad shoulders in a shrug. "Speaking of birthday presents, I've got one for you, too." He tapped the end of her nose with his finger. "Stay right there." He went to where Comet was tethered and withdrew a wooden box from one of the saddlebags. "I hope you like it."

"Jeremy, I shouldn't accept this..." Salina began in half-hearted protest.

He grinned. "But I insist. Come on. Open it up."

Inside the wooden box was a silver brush, mirror, and ivory-toothed comb. Each had a rose design engraved on the handle. "Jeremy, these are lovely," Salina was pleased. "I truly do like them," she said, giving him a warm smile. "In fact, I'm going to ask Jubilee to use them when she dresses my hair for Mary Edith's wedding."

"Good, I'm pleased you like them. Taylor Sue Carey assured me you would. I asked her when I saw her in Fairfax yesterday," Jeremy explained. "She wanted me to tell you that she's looking forward to seeing you at Ivywood for the wedding, and she's looking forward to dancing with Ethan at the ball afterward."

"I haven't seen Taylor Sue in weeks," Salina said, "since the last Women's Assistance Guild meeting. Her mother is the director, and we do what we can by way of sewing and mending uniforms, gathering lint for the medics to use to treat the wounded, and things like that. Taylor Sue and I will have lots of catching up to do."

"Of that, I'm sure," Jeremy chuckled. "Still the best of friends?"

"But of course," Salina nodded. "I'm hoping that she'll end up as my sister-in-law, if Ethan ever gets around to asking her to be his wife."

Jeremy chuckled. "It's only a matter of time, I think."

"I think you might be right, but Ethan is slower than a snail sometimes." Salina shook her head, smiling. "Do you happen to know what time it is?"

Jeremy checked his pocket watch. "Don't want to be late for breakfast?"

"No, it's just that Jubilee has to help me get ready. It takes nearly half an hour to drive to Ivywood from Chantilly in the carriage. You'll be there, won't you?"

"Yes. Save a dance for me?" Jeremy asked, leaning close enough to whisper in her ear.

"We'll see," Salina said coyly. She picked up her box and retrieved her pistol. She stood on tiptoe and impulsively kissed Jeremy's cheek before she lost her nerve. "Thank you for the beautiful birthday gift."

Jeremy grinned from ear to ear. "Oh, you're quite welcome."

☆☆☆☆☆☆☆

"You look like you're feeling better today, Mamma," Salina breezed through the side door of the parlour. "Is the morning sickness going away?"

"It doesn't plague me as much this week as it did last," Mamma said, arranging fresh-cut flowers in a crystal vase on the harpsichord. "You've been out early again?"

Salina nodded, a sparkle in her green eyes. "Ethan went to assist Dr. Phillips, but Jeremy Barnes offered to step in as instructor so I wouldn't miss a lesson."

"Jeremy Barnes has been spending a good deal of time around here since his return," Mamma noted. "I can't decide if it's because he's here to see Ethan—or if he's here to see *you*."

Salina absently touched the keys of the harpsichord. She smiled. "Would you like to see what he brought me as a birthday gift?"

Mamma admired the silver brush set. "This is quite a gift from someone who proclaims to be merely a friend, Salina. I'm wondering if you ought to return it to him."

"But, Mamma, when I told him I really shouldn't accept such a present, he insisted. He said he wanted me to have it and refused to take it back," Salina explained.

Mamma nodded thoughtfully. "If you aren't sweet on him already, Salina, you will be very shortly."

"He's a fine young man, Mamma," Salina said, not knowing why she felt she had to defend him. "Don't you like Jeremy?"

"Oh, I like him fine, darling," Mamma assured Salina. "We've known his family for years and he is a good sort. It's just that..."

"It's just what, Mamma?" Salina prodded.

"It's just that I hope he remembers you're still young." Mamma touched Salina's cheek.

"I'm sixteen years old, and just yesterday you told me I was turning into a fine lady. How is it that I'm back to being so young again today? Mary Edith is sixteen, and she's marrying Randle in a few hours. Randle is *twenty-seven*. At least Jeremy is only nineteen. He's just a year older than Ethan."

"He's closer to twenty, and I wouldn't worry so much if Jeremy was *more* like Ethan," Mamma sighed. "The more time he spends around here, the more convinced I am that Jeremy Barnes is cut from the same type of cloth as your daddy."

"Then that's commendable, isn't it?" inquired Salina. "Daddy is every inch a Southern gentleman."

"Yes, he is," Mamma nodded. She loved Garrett Hastings very, very much. "Sweetheart, it's not that I object to you spending time with Jeremy Barnes so as long as he courts you properly and his intentions are true. I only meant that Jeremy and your father share a deep sense of loyalty, duty, and honor, which at times may be placed above all else because that's the way they were brought up to act as gentlemen. Beyond that, they are proud, stubborn, and can drive a woman mad if they have a mind to."

"Meaning they can be reckless when they stand for what they believe in," Salina surmised. "But you know as well as I do that Daddy has a tender, loving side to him, and I think Jeremy might as well. They are both God-fearing men."

"Well, *that* is the most important thing," Mamma nodded, "especially in times like these, when all of us need to draw nigh unto the Lord, to live in His strength and abide in His perfect love."

Mamma had a deep faith, and it was something that Salina had always admired and coveted for herself. No matter what happened, Mamma *always* seemed to possess an inner strength and a calming peace. Oh, she could lose her temper on occasion, and she was the first to admit it. She had her own ideas about things, but Mamma relied on her love of the Lord and the guidance of His Holy Spirit to get her through each and every day. She told Salina daily that God had never failed her and she was sure enough to know that He never would.

"My gift to you is upstairs." Mamma held out her hand, and the two of them went up to the sitting room on the second floor.

Salina carefully unwrapped the present. "A Bible, Mamma! Now I can read and study God's Word on my own—like when you have your quiet prayer time in the orchard."

"I hope it will be a source of strength and encouragement for you, darling. The Word of God is said to be a two-edged sword, and without it there isn't much hope of fighting our personal battles alone. Study His Word, Salina, and you will grow in knowledge of Jesus Christ and His great love for us. When we commit ourselves to Him, we can stand in His strength and He will lead us in His paths of righteousness," Mamma said softly.

Salina nodded in silent acknowledgment. She had been taught from an early age the difference between right and wrong, and while Mamma had always told her about God, Salina had finally come to believe in Him not just because Mamma said He existed, but because she had experienced His love and forgiveness for herself. She fingered the leather cover and again thanked Mamma for such a special gift.

Mamma smiled fondly at her daughter. "I want to give this to you as well." She slipped a gold filigree ring set with a square emerald gemstone from her finger and placed it in Salina's cupped hands. "My Grandma Nina—your great-grandma—gave this ring to my mamma on her sixteenth birthday. My mamma didn't live to see me turn sixteen, but she instructed my papa to give it to me on my sixteenth birthday," Mamma told Salina. "Now it's my turn to give it to you, sweetheart. Perhaps one day, if you should have a daughter of your own, you'll give it to her on her sixteenth birthday. A little family tradition passed down through the generations."

Salina hugged Mamma. "Thank you, Mamma, ever so much!"

Mamma stroked Salina's dark curls. This darling girl, who had inherited the Captain's coloring and deep green eyes but shared her own temperament and loving nature, was rapidly turning into a woman, and Mamma was powerless to slow the process even just for a little while longer. Mamma would have to learn to accept that but knew that it would not be an easy task. "I love you very much, Salina."

"I love you, too, Mamma," Salina smiled brightly.

"Well," Mamma hugged Salina, "we've got to get ready and get over to Ivywood. Mary Edith will have our heads if we're late for her wedding."

Jubilee was packing Salina's rose-pink watered-silk bridesmaid dress. "We'll git sum o' yer Aunt Priscilla's roses an' weave dem inta yer hair when we's git ta Ivywood. Bring along dat new brush. Jube'll put it ta good use."

Salina wondered if Ethan would make it back in time to leave with them. "Do you suppose he'll just meet us at Ivywood?"

"I'd suspect so," Mamma said as Peter Tom helped them into the carriage. "He knows the ceremony begins at eleven o'clock. That's why we've got to get going. It'll take us longer to get there than it will Ethan, I reckon."

Jubilee sat with Mamma and Salina, and the three of them talked of other weddings and parties they had attended in the years past. There hadn't been parties and barbecues as they were accustomed to attending since the war started, but Mamma smiled and shrugged. "You can always be sure of three events that change little over time: lovers marry, babies are born, and the aged pass on. People gather, regardless of circumstance, for events such as these."

Salina knew there was to be a ball after dinner, and she said to Mamma, "I can hardly wait to dance. It's been so long since there was an excuse for a house party!"

"It has been quite a long time," Mamma agreed, sadly acknowledging that it would probably be even longer until the next gathering.

In truth, it did seem like ages since a social event caused local people to congregate together. There would be music, lights, and laughter for a change, but deep down Salina knew it would only temporarily block out the war, if in fact it did at all.

☆☆☆☆☆☆☆

Ethan was already at Ivywood when Peter Tom drove the carriage up the long graveled lane to the Armstrongs' white-columned mansion. Lots of folks had arrived already, and the livery boys were busy hiding horses and buggies just as soon as their passengers disembarked at the bottom of the stairs leading up to a wide veranda.

Salina saw that her brother had already managed to locate Taylor Sue Carey. He towered over her. She tipped her russet-colored head back to look up into Ethan's face, revealing the love that shone plainly in her golden-brown eyes.

"Hello, Taylor Sue," Salina smiled knowingly, "Ethan."

The two girls hugged each other in greeting. "It's so good to see you, Salina! Mary Edith has been anxiously waiting for you to get here," Taylor Sue remarked. "She's had your Uncle Caleb hire a photographer to take everybody's picture, and Mary Edith wants you to change into your gown right away."

Salina started up the stairs, arm in arm with Taylor Sue, while Ethan escorted Mamma. Salina's steps faltered when, looking up to the veranda, she saw Cousin Lottie clothed in a rose-pink dress identical to the one Salina would be wearing for the ceremony. Lottie looked stunning in the gown, her golden tresses neatly plaited and curled. Salina could only hope that she'd look half as good in her own dress by the time Jubilee finished with her.

"Hello, Salina," Lottie called down to her. "My sister is panicked that you won't be ready in time, so do hurry upstairs. She's in the second room on the third floor."

Salina barely heard Lottie's sugary-sweet voice because her heartbeat was drumming rapidly in her ears. Jeremy stood on the veranda, legs braced apart, looking extremely handsome all dressed up in his Sunday meeting clothes. But what disturbed Salina even more than his attractive appearance was Lottie's possessive way of clinging to Jeremy's arm. He didn't seem to mind Lottie's nearness in the least.

"Miss Salina," Jeremy nodded courteously, touching the brim of his hat in deference when she at last reached the top step.

"Hello, Master Barnes," her voice came out in a throaty whisper. She dared not look into his eyes. She didn't want to see the mocking laughter she imagined would be shining in their blue depths.

Lottie took spiteful pleasure in Salina's discomfort. Lottie knew full well Jeremy had been over at Shadowcreek *again* this morning, and the idea of his paying attention to her Hastings cousin did not set well. Even though Salina's family was considered well-off, there was still question as to why her parents had not elected to send Salina to finishing school, as Lottie's had done with her.

Grudgingly, Lottie admitted that Salina was pretty, and with a little polishing she might prove to be a real threat when it came to collecting the adoration of the depleted male population. But on the other hand, Salina's hair was not the color of spun gold like Lottie's, nor did Salina know how to play the frail maiden when she was in the company of the opposite sex, as Lottie did. Salina was, as Mary Edith always said, "refreshingly honest." Lottie was of the opinion that Salina should have been told that it wasn't ladylike to speak her mind. The Southern boys who remained in the area spoke often and highly of Salina, much to Lottie's displeasure, and her cousin was usually far more interested in news of the battles than a girl ought to be, or so Lottie thought. If Jeremy Barnes was even the *slightest* bit interested in Salina Hastings, Lottie felt it was her duty and privilege to ensure that his attention was jarred from her cousin—and focused on herself instead.

Chapter Five

The Armstrong twins, Lottie and Mary Edith, though being identical in appearance, were of entirely different character. Mary Edith possessed grace, poise, and charm while Lottie was self-serving, spoiled, and believed in using any means necessary to gain whatever it was she wanted. Today Lottie wanted Jeremy Barnes, and Mary Edith knew her twin well enough to guess that there was already trouble brewing when Salina came up to the dressing room.

"Don't let my high-spirited sister get to you, Salina," Mary Edith pleaded. "I already told her I wouldn't stand for her underhanded maneuvering. I *refuse* to let her ruin my wedding day!"

Salina forced a smile. "I won't let Lottie bother me."

"I had hoped that by spending this past year at that boarding school in London she would have changed somewhat, but alas, that is not the case," Mary Edith rolled her eyes. "I do wonder if there's any hope for her at times. Lottie can be downright mean and not think twice about it. She is my twin sister, however, and I love her in spite of herself."

"We should all try to love one another," Salina managed.

Taylor Sue added, "Jesus taught His disciples to love their enemies..."

Salina shot a quick glance at Taylor Sue, realizing that the word *enemy* was certainly an apt description of Lottie. The quarrel between the two cousins had been going on for as long as Salina could remember, but she never did exactly understand why Lottie always initiated the trouble. Salina and Mary Edith got along well enough, but Lottie had a way of making Salina bear the brunt of unfounded lies, outrageous jealousies, and sly vindictiveness. Through their years of schooling at the co-op schoolhouse, the competition between the two cousins had been quite intense. Salina tried time and again to get along peaceably, but Lottie had rejected her friendly overtures. As Mary Edith mentioned, the year Lottie spent abroad had done nothing to alter her disposition, except perhaps to make her more cunning than ever. Mary Edith, Salina was thankful, possessed a much different temperament altogether. Neither Salina nor Mary Edith was aware that their closeness was one of the very things Lottie envied.

Enemy. The word struck Salina again, this time in a different sense. Since she and Lottie had never agreed on *any* subject, Salina was surprised that Lottie hadn't yet declared herself sympathetic to the Yankees just for the sake of argument. It would not be beyond Lottie to do that very thing.

Mary Edith, Salina, and Taylor Sue couldn't help giggling together. They each knew they should love Lottie, although admittedly it was not an easy task. Mary Edith said, "In truth, Salina, I think you should be commended for putting up with my sister the way you have. If I were you, and she was that horrid to me, I think I'd want to throttle her!"

Salina only smiled, but Taylor Sue knew that the very thought had crossed Salina's mind more than once. Taylor Sue had borne her own share of Lottie's meanness and personally thought a sound spanking years ago might have put her in her place. But then, knowing Lottie, it might not have.

Mamma and Aunt Priscilla were present when Jubilee helped Salina into the frock of rose-pink watered-silk. Jubilee had curled Salina's dark brown hair into ringlets and added pink satin ribbons and pink roses for effect. Salina pulled on the white fingerless gloves, which Taylor Sue had crocheted for her birthday gift, and Mary Edith pronounced her beautiful. Mary Edith had Jubilee go tell the photographer that Salina was ready to have her portrait taken.

The Irish photographer introduced himself with a thick brogue accent. "Me name's Sean Patrick O'Grady. 'Tis me pleasure ta be here takin' pictures of such beautiful subjects. Would ya mind sittin' right down in that there chair, lassie? I'll be with ya momentarily."

Salina sat very still, posed on the edge of the tapestry-backed chair. She glanced curiously at his camera atop a tripod. The mustached man pulled a black hood from the back of the camera over his head. She heard him say in a muffled voice, "If ya could smile fer me just a wee bit, Miss. A pretty young lassie such as yourself shouldn't hide such a charmin' smile from view. Sit very, very still. This won't take but half a minute to capture yer likeness."

After the first picture, Sean Patrick O'Grady had to replace the used iron plate with a fresh one. He put the new plate into the back of the multi-lens camera and covered his head with the black hood again to prevent any extra light from striking the plate and ruining the pictures. He removed a lens cap from the front of the camera for approximately thirty seconds, and then closed it back up. "How about one last time, lass?" the photographer asked permission to take a third picture. "Better safe than sorry, eh?"

Salina nodded. "If there is an extra, might I have it to send to my Daddy?"

"Ya shall have it," the photographer promised with a wink. "Fightin' in the war, is he?"

"Yes," Salina nodded. She looked at the photographer. "You aren't a soldier."

"No, lass, I'm not a soldier, but I follow the armies and take pictures of them who've pledged to fight so they can send photographs home to their loved ones. Lots of folk follow the armies—not only photographers, but tailors and bootmakers, and sutlers, and the like..."

"You must follow a Yankee army," Salina concluded. She knew from what Daddy had told her that the North had more of everything: men, guns and ammunition, railroads, ships, horses, and supplies. But the South had more to fight for—or so she'd been raised to believe.

"Aye, lassie, yer a smart one ta be figurin' that out," Sean Patrick O'Grady nodded. "But Miss Mary Edith, she insisted on picture-taking at this here wedding of hers, so her pa sent to Alexandria for a professional photographer, and that's how I come to be here. Meself, I got kin fightin' fer both sides against each other. I decided at the outbreak that I'd probably live a sight longer if'n I could work for the army rather than fight in it. 'Tis me job..." he let his explanation trail off. Then he said in a low voice, "I'd be obliged, lass, if we could keep this little exchange between us. I know there are some folk here today who'd not take kindly to my working for the Yanks at all."

"You're right about that," Salina nodded. "If I were you, I'd leave just as soon as I'd sold my last picture and be gone."

☆☆☆☆☆☆☆

Sean Patrick O'Grady wisely heeded the little lassie's advice. He'd heard some of the older gentlemen down in the drawing room ranting and raving about the Rebels and their Cause, and he didn't want to be party to it. He packed his equipment into his cart and weighed his money pouch in his hand. "Aye, O'Grady, tis a fine spot of work, all in all." He slapped the reins on the rump of his old mule and was on his way back toward Alexandria.

Not half a mile distant from Ivywood, Sean Patrick O'Grady was stopped by two mounted soldiers wearing gold-trimmed Union blue uniforms.

"Good day to ye," the photographer tipped his cap to the officers. "Sean Patrick O'Grady, at yer service."

"I am Captain Duncan Grant, United States Army," the higher ranking officer said. "This is Lieutenant Lance Colby. We'd like to ask you a few questions about that house where you've just come from and about the people inside."

O'Grady knew that although the officer was being polite, he wasn't really offering a choice in the matter. The captain would ask his questions, and O'Grady would be expected to answer, or be arrested. O'Grady smiled ruefully and replied, "Nice people, the Armstrongs. One of their daughters it is who's gettin' married. Just a small weddin' party with a few guests, nothin' to worry about, Capt'n."

"Any Reb soldiers there?" Lieutenant Colby asked directly.

"Them that I saw, maybe two, or three. Home on leave I heard one of 'em say. Few others were recoverin' wounded—one in a wheel-chair, another on crutches with part of a leg missin' from the knee down, another with just one arm left to him. Mostly the other men weren't army men, just young lads and gents too old to fight."

"Did you happen to see any young men who weren't soldiers, but might have been old enough to enlist?" Captain Grant asked. "One in particular—with dark hair, rather tall and rangy?"

The Irishman thought for a moment, then said, "I reckon there was a lad who'd match that description."

"The Hastings boy," Lieutenant Colby concluded. "Can you give us a more detailed description of him?"

"I can do better than that," the photographer said, "if you'll permit me." He rummaged through his traveling case and pulled out a small envelope that contained extra photographs which he hadn't sold off. He chose a leftover family portrait of the Hastings and handed it to Captain Grant. "That boy there," he pointed to Ethan, "was with a tall blond lad. One who looked like he could be a brother to your lieutenant here."

A grin split Captain Grant's face. He turned to Colby. "That's got to be Jeremy Barnes. And come to think of it," Duncan scratched his chin, noting Colby's blond hair, broad shoulders, and blue eyes, "he does bear a rather strong resemblance to you, Lieutenant. Although Barnes is quite a bit taller."

Lieutenant Colby bristled, sitting up even straighter in his saddle. He was not amused at being compared to the tall blond Rebel, but he clamped his jaw shut tightly to prevent a sharp retort aimed at his superior officer.

Duncan returned his attention to the portrait of Annelise, Salina, and Ethan Hastings. "Yes, that certainly is Garrett's son. How much do you want for this?"

O'Grady rubbed his stubbly chin. "Fifty dollars?"

"Fifty? No, Irish. I'll give you twenty." Duncan counted out Union greenbacks to pay for the purchase.

O'Grady recounted the bills carefully, then returned a smile to Duncan Grant. "Good enough, Capt'n. Thank ye."

Duncan tucked the tintype into his breast pocket. "Good day to you, Sean Patrick O'Grady. Best be on your way."

"Aye, sir!" the Irishman touched his cap.

"O'Grady?" Captain Grant turned halfway around in his saddle.

The photographer stopped his mule, "Aye, Capt'n?"

"Have you any other *spare* photographs?" Duncan wanted to know.

"Aye, one of the lassie, sittin' alone, if you're interested. Shall we call it another twenty dollars?" O'Grady queried.

"Let me see it first," Captain Grant ordered. He glanced at the tintype, noting that Garrett's little girl had grown into a striking young woman since the last time he'd seen her. He showed the photograph to Colby.

Lieutenant Colby nodded. "I've seen her. She is a pretty little thing, isn't she?"

Duncan didn't reply. Instead he complained to O'Grady, "You drive a hard bargain, Irish." He counted out twenty more dollars.

Sean Patrick O'Grady was satisfied and tipped his cap a third time. "Sure and it's been me pleasure doin' business with ye, Capt'n. Good day to ye!"

"And to you," Duncan Grant clenched his teeth. Now he'd have to wait until next month's payday to purchase a new pair of boots. *No matter,* he told himself, *for these tintypes, it was money well spent.*

✩✩✩✩✩✩✩

Reverend Yates performed the wedding ceremony of Mary Edith Armstrong and Randle Baxter at the foot of the marble staircase which dominated Ivywood's great hall. Salina stood, her back ramrod straight, in her place on the stairs. Absently, she wondered if one day she would ever love a man enough, or have a man love her enough, to become his lawfully wedded wife. Several times, she felt Jeremy's eyes on her from where he was seated in the audience. He winked at her when at last she acknowledged his glance with a very slight nod of her dark head. Jeremy looked bored just sitting there waiting for the wedding to be over with, and he covered his mouth with his hand when a large yawn overtook him.

It made Salina want to yawn as well, though she didn't dare while she was standing up in front of the entire assembly. She turned her attention back to what Reverend Yates was saying about loving, honoring, and cherishing, and then Randle and Mary Edith exchanged rings while repeating their sacred vows to one another.

As Randle kissed his new wife, the hall exploded with thunderous applause. No time was wasted between congratulating the newlyweds and being seated for the luncheon which was about to be served.

Taylor Sue found Salina among the mass of people. "You did a fine job up there," she complimented. "I hope you'll do as well when I need you to stand up in my wedding."

"You know I'd be honored, providing my brother ever gets around to asking you to marry him!" Salina laughed.

One of the Armstrongs' slaves sounded the bell when it was time to eat. Aunt Priscilla was in a fix. It took all the house servants she had to prepare the barbecued meal and serve it to the wedding guests. The youngest children, who were to sit together at a long table in the foyer, were without anyone to watch over them.

Taylor Sue had already gone into the main dining room, where she was quickly seated at Ethan's side, politely drawing his focus away from Lottie's exaggerated overtures toward him. Lottie had contrived to sit directly between Ethan and Jeremy, but since she'd lost Ethan to Taylor Sue, she instead turned her full attention on Jeremy, flirting with him unmercifully. Salina seethed on the inside. Suddenly her appetite vanished and she was lost in her own thoughts until she looked at the faces of the half dozen children seated on both sides of the long table.

"It will never do to leave those children unattended," Aunt Priscilla wrung her hands. "What shall I do?"

"I'll watch the children, Aunt Priscilla," Salina abruptly volunteered. "I don't mind being with them, really."

"Why, Salina, darling, how very thoughtful of you, but I'm sure Mary Edith will want to see you at her table," Aunt Priscilla argued, but she saw the sensibility, not to mention convenience, in the solution. Salina had a way with children and would keep a responsible watch over them. "Salina, dear, if you really wouldn't mind. If they give you any trouble, you just let me know and we'll make other arrangements."

"We'll be fine, Aunt Priscilla," Salina assured her aunt. She cast another wistful glance back at Lottie and Jeremy, then turned on her heel and entered the foyer.

The children ranged in age from three-to eleven-years-old. Billy Ray Lawrence was pulling the braid of one of the Kimball twins, possibly Mary—or was it Martha? Salina always had trouble telling them apart. Melanie Jane Porter ate her peach pie before her main dish, and little Jacob Langley knocked over his mug of milk. Augie Dalton, having cleaned his plate, was already asking for more food.

To keep a semblance of order at the table, Salina began to tell stories from the Bible, and the children listened with interest as she told of Joseph and his coat of many colors, of Noah and the Ark, and finally of David and Goliath.

"Do you think David was a Rebel and Goliath was a Yank?" Billy Ray asked.

"David was an Israelite and Goliath a Philistine," Salina answered. "There weren't any Rebels or Yankees back then."

"David prayed to God, and He answered with victory, if we pray, will our soldiers win?" Martha Kimball wanted to know.

"If it's God's will," Salina answered solemnly. "We should pray all that we can."

"Do you think those dirty Yankees pray to God, too?" Augie Dalton who was seven, asked.

"I imagine some of them might," Salina replied.

Billy Ray's eyebrows bunched together in confusion. "If we pray, and the Yankees pray, then how will God know who to answer?"

Salina pondered for a moment before answering. "I honestly don't know, Billy Ray. I would suppose it's a matter of which side is truly in God's will. I do know this much. It's a *terrible* thing for Americans to fight amongst themselves. My daddy had hoped it wouldn't come to such a conflict, but when Virginia seceded, his loyalties went with her. He refused to take up arms against his homeland, his family, and his friends, so he prayed for a long time, asking God what to do. He felt led to resign his command with the Union army and joined the Confederate forces instead, just like General Lee did. My daddy's a Virginian, and he'll fight to defend her. So far, I believe that God has answered my prayers in keeping him from harm."

"We pray for our daddy every night before we go to sleep," Mary Kimball nodded. "Our prayers have been answered, too. We got a letter from him just yesterday saying that he was doing just fine and was as well as could be expected. Mother's going to send him a package of food and clothing just as soon as she can."

"What does *secede* mean?" Melanie Jane Porter asked.

"It means to withdraw from the Union," Salina explained. "Eleven states broke away from the Federal government: South Carolina, Mississippi, Florida, Alabama, Georgia, Louisiana, Texas, Virginia, Arkansas, North Carolina, and Tennessee," she counted them off on her fingers in chronological order. "They formed a new government and called it the Confederacy. It's part of the reason for all the fighting. The North wants the Union to be whole again, but the South doesn't see eye to eye with her Northern sister states. The South wants to be left alone to govern herself, but the Northerners won't have any of that. They call it *States' Rights*." But there was more than that, Salina would learn in time. In addition to the Southerners' wish to establish their States' Rights philosophy, theirs was a cause to maintain their lifestyle—and that included the evil of slavery. Not only was the question of Union an issue, but also the right of freedom to all men, regardless of the color of their skin.

"My pa fights the Yanks from up North with General Lee," Billy Ray said proudly. "If the war lasts a long time, maybe I'll fight, too."

"Billy Ray, bite your tongue!" Salina scolded. "The battles have been going on for over a year now. Thousands of men have died. We should pray the fighting will end soon, not go on and on."

Billy Ray nodded, then a brief silence fell over the children. All of them were affected by the war; not one was immune. If it wasn't a father fighting, it was a brother, uncle, or cousin. The Southerners were usually, except in certain circumstances, too proud not to send their men to do what they believed was right.

Finally, three-year-old Jacob said, "Want another story."

"What would you like to hear?" Salina was open to suggestions and took Melanie Jane Porter's request for the story of Daniel in the lion's den.

By the time luncheon was over, Salina made up her mind not to care about the fact that Jeremy seemed contented enough in Lottie's company. She took the children with her on a walk down by the stream, hoping to clear her mind of her disappointment that Jeremy hadn't even said a word about her dress. Salina busied herself helping the girls braid wildflowers into little crowns for their heads, and she showed the boys how to make flat stones skip across the lazy, slow-moving water.

"Where'd you learn how to do that?" Augie Dalton asked. He tried numerous times to make his stones skip, but they just sank with a loud *ker-plop*.

Salina laughed. "Ethan taught me."

"Where'd you learn all those stories?" Mary and Martha Kimball asked in unison.

"Some my Mamma read to me when I was your age, and some I learned from Jubilee, my maid."

"Tell us another one," the children begged.

Chapter Six

*B*ecause her back was facing him, Jeremy Barnes knew Salina wasn't aware that he was there strolling along the bank of the stream. He purposely kept quiet so she wouldn't hear him just yet, for he found a certain sense of pleasure in simply listening to her carefree laughter. He smiled, amused, as she played clapping rhyme games with the girls. *Two years ago, she seemed little more than a child herself,* he thought. *In my absence she has become a fine young lady.* And then, with an insolent grin, he remembered the way she'd surprised him at this morning's shooting lesson by thanking him for his gift with a light kiss on his cheek. That bold action on her part served to remind him quite well that she wasn't just a girl after all. By this time, Salina had reached marriageable age—just as Mary Edith, Lottie, and Taylor Sue Carey had.

He leaned against a tree behind Salina and twirled the pink rose he'd plucked from Mrs. Armstrong's flower garden between his thumb and forefinger. It had taken some effort for Jeremy to escape

Lottie's watchful eye and to sneak out of the house after Salina left with the children. Lottie, Jeremy decided, was downright incorrigible. She'd spent her time equally divided up in flirting with Ethan, Charlie Graham—who was home from the front on a three-day pass—and himself. He didn't care for Lottie's tactics, and he just plain wasn't interested in a girl like her. He'd known one or two of her kind out in California, and he found he did well to avoid troubling himself with them. He watched Salina a little longer, then he touched her shoulder with the petals of the rosebud.

Salina had been oblivious to Jeremy's presence until his shadow crossed over her. She looked up at him with her thickly lashed green eyes, surprised to see him there.

"Hello," Jeremy said, flashing a disarming grin.

Salina was quick to remove the flowered crown from her dark head. "Why aren't you up at the main house?" she questioned.

"I got bored," Jeremy shrugged. "Besides, you all seemed to be having a good time, and I was hoping you'd not object to my joining you." Jeremy's bright smile was matched by the glittering sparkle in his deep blue eyes.

That was the mischievous sparkle Salina remembered all too well. She accepted his gift of the pink rosebud, sniffing its sweet fragrance. "Won't Lottie be missing you?" she asked, immediately wishing that she hadn't spoken what she was thinking aloud.

Salina's mild jealousy amused Jeremy. He thought she would have known him better than to think he had any designs on the likes of Lottie Armstrong. Still, he decided to let Salina find that out on her own. He sat down next to her and whispered near her ear, "Lottie may be the belle of the ball today, Salina, next to Mary Edith, of course. But one day you're going to outshine her. And I reckon that day is not long in coming. I'd be willing to bet money that's why she goes out of her way to slight you."

"I don't care what Cousin Lottie does, says, or thinks," Salina said adamantly. She felt her cheeks blush, and she was uncomfortable by his nearness and the intensity of his blue gaze. "I have an idea," she shifted away from him. "Why don't *you* tell the children a story? Surely they'd *love* to hear all about when you rode for the Pony Express."

"Yes! Yes! Please tell us!" The children eagerly circled around Jeremy, and they asked him at least a hundred questions about what it was like in the West. Had he ever seen any Indians? What was Sacramento like? Was there really gold there? Had he ever been to that faraway place called San Francisco? Did he ride the fastest horse ever? Had he ever been swimming in the Pacific Ocean?

Jeremy was an animated storyteller, and he readily answered their inquiries in great detail. Some of the stories Salina had already heard, but some she hadn't. She was just as interested in what Jeremy had to say as the rest of his captive audience, and this time she paid closer attention to the stories Jeremy told of the antics he had with another Express rider, a half-breed Indian named Drake.

After a while, the children went back to playing nearby, and that left Salina alone in Jeremy's company.

"Do you mind if I ask why you keep staring at me?" Salina finally gathered the nerve to ask.

Jeremy grinned. "I still can't get over how much you've changed, Salina. In two years' time, you've grown into a very pretty young lady, all nice and proper."

She met his dancing blue eyes. "You've changed, too, you know."

"How?" Jeremy wanted to know.

Salina shrugged. "You're just...different. The West has hardened you, I think."

"You may be right," Jeremy nodded. "Very perceptive—but then, you always were that." He chuckled softly, "When I think of the hours you and I spent talking and reading...it seems like an eternity ago."

She smiled as she, too, remembered the times they shared in what seemed to be ages gone by; so much had changed since those tranquil days. "I heard Cousin Lottie telling that you were talking about joining the cavalry. Is that true?" inquired Salina.

Jeremy kicked a stone with the toe of his boot. "Thinking, yes, but I haven't quite decided yet. Would you want me to?"

Salina shrugged. "Does what I think matter to you so much?"

"Yes," Jeremy replied honestly and without hesitation. "It does."

"My daddy's in the Confederate service, and I worry about him. If you were in the service, I suppose I should be anxious about you, as well," Salina hedged. "Would you want me to worry about you?"

"Only if you cared," Jeremy answered simply. "Do you?"

Before Salina could reply to Jeremy's question, Billy Ray came to show off his latest triumph. He'd captured a frog from the stream's edge—a big, fat, *ugly*, muddy one.

"Looky, Salina! See what I found?" Billy Ray held the frog up so Salina could inspect it.

Salina wrinkled her nose. Melanie Jane and the twins squealed. "That's just fine, Billy Ray," Salina said. "Now take him back over to the water, why don't you?"

As Billy Ray reluctantly turned to follow her instructions, the creature slipped free of his grasp and landed squarely in Salina's lap.

"Oh, no!" she gasped.

It took three attempts, but on the third try, Jeremy and Billy Ray managed to catch the slippery fellow. "We got him, Salina," Jeremy said.

Salina glanced down at her bridesmaid's dress, which was now splattered and smeared with reddish-brown mud. "Take that frog away from here now, Billy Ray!" she commanded.

"Ooohh!" Melanie Jane Porter cried shrilly. "Salina touched a *frog!*"

"Oh, Melanie Jane, it didn't hurt me any," Salina sighed. "They're just, well...they're a bit slimy, that's all. And dirty..." She looked up at Jeremy. "My gown..." she said, knowing she didn't have to explain to him her disappointment over the spoiling of her bridesmaid's dress.

Jeremy squatted down next to Salina. "I don't think there's any permanent damage done to the fabric, but there's not much we can do about getting you cleaned up unless we get back to the main house. We'll find Jubilee. She'll know what to do." Jeremy wiped a smudge of mud from Salina's cheek, and then offered her his hand. She placed her hand in his.

"Have you seen my brother at all?" Salina asked.

"He's paying court to Taylor Sue Carey," Jeremy answered. "Busy filling up her dance card for this evening, I reckon."

Up at the house, Jubilee clucked her disapproval. "An' what were ya doin' dere so close ta da watah?"

"But, Jubilee, I wasn't all that close to it. Billy Ray brought the frog to me," Salina explained.

Jeremy vouched for Salina. "Honest, Jubilee, it wasn't Miss Hastings's fault."

Jubilee crossed her arms over her chest. "Humph!" She examined Salina's skirt again. "Let's jist see what ah kin do—if somethin'. Y'all jist keep outta sight right here. Don't be goin' off until ah's come back, hear?"

"Yes, Jubilee," Salina nodded obediently.

"An' ya, Massah Jeremy, ya kin wait down in da parlour if ya've a notion ta."

Jeremy understood without a doubt that he'd been dismissed. "I'll take that as my cue to clear out of the dressing room before anyone else catches me in here." He bowed to Salina. "I will look for you later, Miss Hastings."

Salina was warmed by his disarming smile. "Very well, Master Barnes," she returned in kind. "Thank you for your assistance."

"I don't mind rescuing damsels in distress whenever I can," he said gallantly.

Salina watched Jeremy until Jubilee shut the door behind him. "Ah kin see fanciful thoughts runnin' through dat brain o' yores, chile. Ah knows ah tole ya ta give dat boy a chance, but ya listen ta Jube—ya be careful dat ya don' put too much meanin' on his words until ya finds out how often he says dem."

Salina nodded, and she couldn't help being curious to know who Jeremy was spending his time with while she was here upstairs. She had little doubt that if she were to return to the first floor now, she'd find him in Cousin Lottie's clutches again.

☆☆☆☆☆☆☆

"It's a good thing you had your picture taken when you did, darling," Mamma had come upstairs to freshen up when she found Salina and Jubilee trying to undo the mess the frog had done to Salina's rose-colored frock. "Mary Edith would have been fit to be tied if this had happened before the wedding ceremony."

"What can we do?" Salina asked.

"You wait here, and I'll take care of everything," Mamma assured her. She returned twenty minutes later with an old ball dress of Lottie's. "At least it's pink, although it might be a little short..."

"An' a liddle wide," Jubilee chuckled. "Miss Lottie don' eat like no bird, do she?"

"It will have to do." Salina knew she didn't have an alternative, though she felt self-conscious about the borrowed dress. "Do I look horrible?"

"You'll pass." Mamma turned Salina around to face the mirror. "It's not altogether horrible; it's just that it fits a little differently than a dress of your own might." She took the cameo brooch off her gown and used it to keep the front of Salina's borrowed dress from gaping at the bosom. "Much better."

Salina's head bobbed in agreement. "Do I have to go downstairs like this?"

Mamma nodded. "You do if you think you're going to be doing any dancing. Here's your dance card."

Salina was ready to forget about the dress. "Thank you, Mamma!"

"Don't thank me," Mamma said. "This is Mary Edith's doing, so you thank her when you get downstairs. She wasn't altogether pleased that you didn't take lunch in the main dining hall earlier, and until your Aunt Priscilla explained to her that you'd volunteered to sit with the children, she'd naturally just assumed that Lottie had somehow banished you to the foyer. Then Mary Edith found that your original dance card was missing and guessed that Lottie might have *mislaid* the card for you. This is a replacement."

Salina looked at her dance card. It already had three names penciled in: Ethan's, then Uncle Caleb's and Charlie Graham's, then Ethan's again.

"And Jeremy Barnes would like you to save the *Palmyra Schottische* for him," Mamma informed her. "He seems to recall that being your favorite dance."

"It is," Salina declared. "And I shall save it for him."

Mamma smiled down at her daughter. It wasn't difficult to see that Salina was becoming attached to the former Pony Express rider, and Mamma fervently hoped that Salina wouldn't be devastated if—or rather *when*—he left again.

"Look," Mamma showed Salina the tintypes she purchased from the Irish photographer. "The photographs turned out quite well. You can send them to Daddy in your next letter to him."

Salina had almost forgotten that they *had* to go home after the dance. "Yes, I'm certain he'll be happy to get them." She thought to herself, *But I won't have to send them, I'll just give it to him later tonight...*

☆☆☆☆☆☆☆

Red and orange light filtered through the windows of the ballroom as the sun set low in the western sky. The musicians tuned their instruments and it wasn't long before the first floor of Ivywood was filled with lively tunes and gaiety.

The newlyweds shared their first dance together. Randle led Mary Edith in a slow waltz, and then the other guests mingled and joined them.

Salina stood in the entryway watching the ladies swirling in the arms of their partners, their bell-like dresses whirling in colorful circular patterns across the ballroom floor.

"I believe it's my turn, little sister," Ethan tugged on her hand and led her in the steps of the cotillion. "What happened?"

Salina looked up innocently. "What ever do you mean?"

"Why are you wearing one of Lottie's old dresses?" Ethan asked.

She told him about the incident with Billy Ray's escaped frog, and Ethan laughed heartily. "I think I look horrible," Salina pouted.

"You could never look horrible," Ethan said firmly. "There are some here tonight who'd agree with me—wholeheartedly, I might add."

"If you're implying that Charlie Graham is one, I just finished dancing with him, and I didn't care for the way he insisted on holding me so close," Salina complained. "It isn't proper..."

"Jeremy didn't care for the way Charlie was holding you, either," Ethan whispered. His eyes sparkled teasingly.

"Oh, is that so?" Salina questioned. "Well, that's just too bad, isn't it?" On the opposite side of the room, Jeremy was currently twirling Lottie and looking as though he were enjoying himself immensely.

Ethan saw what Salina had seen. "He's only being polite to Lottie," Ethan assured Salina. "Merely returning the hospitality that her family has shown him since he's come back to Virginia."

Salina said nothing, and Ethan laughed. "You better watch out," he cautioned. "The color green you're turning is the same shade as the pea soup Jubilee makes."

"Oh, hush," Salina spoke firmly, but she dissolved into giggles. "For all her finishing school experience, Lottie can't even keep up with simple dance steps, can she?"

"One would wonder if poor Lottie didn't have two left feet." Ethan chuckled with her, then he whispered, "I've made up my mind, Salina."

"About what?" Salina asked, also whispering.

"About asking Mrs. Carey for her blessing. I'm going to ask Taylor Sue to marry me," Ethan confided.

"Here? Tonight?" Salina wanted to know.

"Well, maybe." Ethan's eyes scanned the dance floor. "If I can speak to Mrs. Carey, that is. I think she likes me well enough and wouldn't be opposed to the match."

"Ethan, you're trembling," Salina pointed out. "Are you nervous?"

He lifted his shoulders in a slight shrug. "A little, I suppose. I've never asked for anyone's hand in marriage before."

"Take a deep breath and relax. You'll be fine," Salina gave her brother her vote of confidence. "Why don't you go talk to her now?"

Ethan paled. "I...I can't. Not...not just right this minute," he stammered.

"You're right. You aren't *nervous;*, you're *scared*," Salina grinned. "But I believe you'll make a fine husband and father."

Ethan swallowed hard. "To be quite honest with you, I can't imagine myself as anybody's *father*."

Salina smiled and said, "You'll be fine if you learned anything at all from Daddy."

"I do want to be like him," Ethan said with fierce determination.

"You already are," Salina hugged him. "Mamma told me that you look just like he did when he was your age."

"Daddy..." Ethan sighed. "How I wish I could follow in his footsteps now."

"Don't talk of going off to war, Ethan. Mamma won't like it," Salina cautioned. "And I don't think Taylor Sue will either. Besides, think of the good you're able to do assisting Dr. Phillips."

"Don't you ever wish there was *something* you could do?" Ethan questioned. "I feel so helpless at Shadowcreek."

"We wouldn't make it without you," Salina said quickly. It was the truth. "If we didn't have you, Cromwell, and Peter Tom, how would we survive? We wouldn't, and you know it."

Ethan lowered his eyes, "That's why I keep the promise I made to Daddy about staying at home. I couldn't leave you or Mamma. It's my responsibility as man of the house to see that you're taken care of."

"I know," Salina squeezed his arm. "I also know what you mean about wanting to help out in some way or another. That's why Mamma and I work on sewing, mending, and making bandages for the Women's Assistance Guild. It's the *acceptable* way for a young lady to offer her services."

Ethan chuckled again, "I suppose you're right, but I know you like a little more *adventure* and a little less *propriety*. You've Daddy's sense of daring, just as I have."

"Maybe I do, maybe I don't," was Salina's reply. She bowed to him when the music stopped, and the band was allowed to take a break. "Why, there's Mrs. Carey, right over there." She pointed Ethan in the direction of the hall and gave him a gentle shove. "I dare you to go talk to her about Taylor Sue."

Ethan squared his shoulders. "Here goes," he muttered under his breath and swallowed loud enough for Salina to hear.

She giggled. "I can hardly wait for my new sister-in-law," she goaded.

Ethan glared at Salina. "You hush, now, and keep your mouth shut until I have a chance to talk to Taylor Sue myself."

"I won't say another word," Salina promised with a wink.

During the band's intermission, Mary Edith spoke with some of the other ladies who were members of the Women's Assistance Guild. They concocted an idea to help raise some money right here at the dance for much-needed medicines and shoes that would be sent to soldiers at the front lines.

Uncle Caleb climbed up on the platform in front of the musicians and explained: "For the next hour or so, a half-dollar will be charged for each set. Gentlemen, you must pay for the privilege of dancing with your favorite lady. The money earned will be collected by Reverend Yates, and he'll see to it that the medicines and things are purchased and distributed to our brave boys in gray."

Shouts of revelry greeted the fund-raising proposition. Men scurried to find the lady of their choice, although some ladies made certain that they were *found* by the gentleman of *their* choice.

Salina danced, set after set. Finally, one of her partners kindly took her to the punch bowl so she could have a bit of refreshment before continuing on. Her handbag was filling up with money, and she was pleased that this particular "adventure" would be contributed to the war effort. *Only here at the Armstrongs' could something like this be dreamed up,* she thought, shaking her dark head in amusement, *especially when one considers that they are one of the wealthiest families in the area, and they have the most wealthy friends who can afford to spend money on frivolous things such as dances.*

Taylor Sue and Ethan came to get a drink at the punch bowl. They looked as though they shared a secret between them. They were both smiling broadly, and Taylor Sue's dimples were clearly visible.

"I'm down to my last fifty cents, Salina," Ethan remarked with a wide grin. "I thought I'd spend it on you."

"You've already danced with me twice," Salina returned a smile, reading the look in her brother's gray-green eyes. *He must have asked, and she must have accepted!* she thought happily. "Why not take Taylor Sue for another quadrille?"

Taylor Sue smiled prettily up at Ethan. "Your sister has made a brilliant suggestion, don't you agree?"

"We'll dance the very next one," Ethan promised Taylor Sue, then winked at Salina. "How are you faring?"

Salina checked the contents of her handbag. "Rather well, I believe."

Taylor Sue sipped her punch. "You must be. Lottie keeps glaring at you every time you take the floor."

Salina sighed, "I wish she didn't dislike me so much."

Ethan chuckled. "Perhaps the reason she's jealous this time is because you're raising more money than she is. This is the first set you haven't participated in since Uncle Caleb made the announcement. Lottie's only danced half that number, and I think I'm being generous."

"Then go spend your last fifty cents on Lottie," Taylor Sue encouraged. She looked into her own handbag. "I'm doing quite well for myself."

"I suppose you leave me little choice than to perform my duty." Ethan bowed at the waist. "Don't go away, I'll be back," he squeezed Taylor Sue's hand behind the folds of her hooped skirt.

Taylor Sue watched Ethan saunter away to find Cousin Lottie. "He is such a fine gentleman," she sighed.

Salina couldn't pass up the opportunity to tease. "Well spoken, by one who loves him so much."

The freckles which dotted the bridge of Taylor Sue's nose faded into the same lovely shade of pink her cheeks were turning, but she didn't deny what Salina had said. She did love him, with all her heart. "Salina?"

"Yes?" Salina smiled and hugged her dearest friend.

"You already know Ethan's asked me to become his wife, don't you?" Taylor Sue accused.

Salina nodded. "And, are you going to?"

Taylor Sue giggled. "Yes! Did you honestly think I'd tell him no?"

"Maybe some dreams do come true." Salina hooked her arm through Taylor Sue's. "Now tell me, did he get down on his knee and ask you?"

"As a matter of fact he did," Taylor Sue laughed. "He took me out to the rose garden..."

"Excuse me," Charlie Graham interrupted. "Miss Salina, I'd be most honored if I could buy another dance with you."

Salina made herself smile pleasantly, and as she left Taylor Sue at the punch bowl she said over her shoulder, "Only for the Cause."

Taylor Sue hid her sympathetic grin behind her fan.

Chapter Seven

Charlie Graham wasn't a bad dancer; it was more the fact that he'd consumed a little too much of Uncle Caleb's private stock of whiskey in celebration, and he was certainly having a good time at Salina's expense. Over and over he kept stepping on her toes, excusing himself for it, and pulling her closer and closer to his body.

Jeremy stood alone near the punch bowl, sipping the cool, fruity juice. He mentally upbraided himself, silently admitting that it bothered him to see Salina never lacking in dance partners. Each time the band played a new tune, she was whisked into the arms of another man. Now, swirling in the arms of Charlie Graham, she was giggling at something he'd said to her. Jeremy swallowed the taste of his own jealousy and decided to put a stop to it. He cut in on their waltz. "If you'll pardon us, Charlie." Jeremy offered his arm to Salina, and she hesitantly placed her lace-gloved hand in his.

"What's this now?" Charlie asked indignantly. "I paid my share."

Jeremy's sapphire blue eyes were focused on Salina's pretty face. He handed her a five-dollar note to add to her collection for the Cause.

"What kind of money is *that*?" Charlie wanted to know.

"Union greenbacks," Jeremy stated evenly. "Worth more than Confederate scrip, I'm sorry to say."

"*Yankee* money!" Charlie roared. "Who the...Just who do you think you are trying to buy a dance from a proud Southern belle with dirty *Yankee* money? I challenge you, Barnes!" Charlie had his fingers on the handle of the pistol in the holster circling his waist.

Uncle Caleb instantly appeared in the midst of the trouble before it spread any further. "Barnes is right, Charlie. Union money will fetch us a good deal more than Confederate currency. That's just the way it is. You know it, and I know it. No need to fight about that. Barnes wasn't intending to slight Miss Hastings's honor—no, no, on the contrary. In fact, it's more of a compliment that he regard her highly enough to contribute ten times above and beyond the half-dollar asked for."

Charlie was unwillingly led away by Uncle Caleb, and Salina was left in the circle of Jeremy's strong arms. The band struck up the opening strains of the *Palmyra Schottische*, Salina's favorite, and she allowed Jeremy to lead her through the steps with graceful ease.

A gleam danced in Jeremy's eyes as he met Salina's look of disapproval. "I believe I mentioned to your mamma that I had claimed this dance with you."

"She relayed your message," Salina acknowledged, "but that doesn't give you license to create such a scene with Charlie."

Jeremy chuckled knowingly. "You're the center of attention. Doesn't that please you?"

"No," Salina replied in haste. "That's more Lottie's style, not mine. I prefer not having everyone stare at me."

"You like staying in the background, out of sight?" Jeremy asked.

"I didn't say that." Salina said. "I'm just not the kind who's fond of all the attention—as you so obviously are."

"Let's just say I'm the kind that once having seen something I want, I pursue it," Jeremy said ominously.

Salina's lashes swept to conceal her eyes, and she kept quiet.

"Cat got your tongue?" Jeremy needled.

"You're a very good dancer," Salina said conversationally. "Did you brush up on your skill in San Francisco?"

"Not so much there as in St. Joseph," Jeremy replied. "You move as though you dance among the clouds."

"Thank you for saying so." Salina smiled slightly. "And did you pick up your talent for provoking trouble while you were in St. Joseph as well?"

"You've known me for years, Salina, and you know that I've been in and out of trouble all my life. I'd have accepted Charlie's challenge," Jeremy murmured near her ear. "I didn't like the way he was holding you."

"You would have beaten him in a duel," Salina said with certainty, not mentioning that the way Charlie had held her was none of Jeremy's affair.

"I might have hurt him, but I wouldn't have killed him," Jeremy said honestly.

Salina knew that he meant it. His statement unwillingly turned her thoughts to the very real probability that he would indeed kill people if he joined up to fight with the cavalry, and she shuddered in the circle of his arms.

Jeremy glanced around at the other dancers on the floor with them. Like Salina, he noticed that of the guests in attendance, more of them were women than men. The lack of men was attributed to the war. Nearly all of the men of military age were off trying to lick the Yankees. The men who were present this evening at Ivywood for the wedding were either soldiers on leave or recuperating from injury, or men too old or young to fight. Proud Southern men left their women-folk behind to keep the farms and plantations running as best as they could. A few of the gray- or butternut-clad soldiers had empty sleeves or pant-legs to serve as a silent reminder of the horrors of amputations conducted in the field hospitals.

Salina observed and saw these things as well. "Those poor, brave men..."

"War isn't pretty, Salina. It's the most hateful thing there ever was," Jeremy said lowly. "What started out as a glorious, romantic notion has turned savage. A costly debt to be exacted in blood."

"I'm not blind, Jeremy Barnes. I have seen some of the consequences. There has been skirmishing quite close to here—at Manassas and at Fairfax Court House," she reminded him.

"But have you seen it firsthand, Salina? Right up close?" he inquired.

"Well, no," she answered. "And I can't say that I'm sorry about that. I just continue to hope and pray that those I know out in the field will be protected from any harm."

"Pray hard," Jeremy muttered. Before the dance was complete, he suggested, "Let's take a stroll in the garden for a breath of fresh air, shall we?"

"Master Barnes," Salina said lightly, "how forward of you."

A smile teased the corners of Jeremy's mouth. "Salina, you're certainly old enough to make that remark mean something, but not tonight. I simply need to talk to you—alone."

Salina swallowed, her pride a tad bit stung by the merriment in Jeremy's blue eyes. She didn't like being the object of his amusement. "My mamma has been watching me like a hawk. She'd surely see us and come after us in order to keep appearances proper."

"No, I don't think so. Your mamma's out in the foyer talking to Mrs. Carey—either about the Women's Assistance Guild, or about the fact that they're bound to end up as in-laws. Come on," Jeremy took her small hand in his larger one, and together they slipped out the glass-paned door and into the cool of the dark garden.

☆☆☆☆☆☆☆

Inside a gazebo covered with climbing roses, Salina stood and looked out over the shadowy, fragrant garden. Jeremy stood behind her. Neither said anything as they merely watched the lights flickering from the main house and listened to the strains of music floating on the evening breeze. Finally, she asked, "Well? I thought you were going to bring me out here to talk."

"Yes," Jeremy nodded. He handed her a folded note.

"What's this?" she asked.

"Nothing for you to be concerned about. Just take it to your father. He'll explain," Jeremy said cryptically.

Salina tucked the note into her handbag, but her curiosity made her ask, "Explain what?"

Jeremy grasped Salina's shoulders, turning her to face him. His eyes lingered over each detail of her face.

Salina was uncomfortable beneath his intense stare. "Why are you looking at me like that again?"

"I need to know—beyond the shadow of a doubt—that you are still the trustworthy type, Salina." Jeremy lightly touched her cheek. "I have to be absolutely certain of it."

Meeting his eyes with her inquisitive green ones, she said, "You're deliberately keeping something from me. Won't you tell me what it is?"

Jeremy nodded once. In a low voice he murmured, "What you and

I discuss here mustn't ever be discussed with anyone else, anywhere else. You can't tell Ethan, Taylor Sue, your mamma—or Jubilee. *No one must know*. It must remain in the strictest confidence between you and me."

Salina was unsure of this mysterious side of Jeremy that she'd never seen before. It reminded her of the way Daddy acted sometimes. She looked at Jeremy and quickly promised, "All right, you have my word. I'll not tell a soul."

"Good, that's what I wanted to hear," Jeremy's sigh illustrated his relief.

"What's this all about?" she asked. Salina would not volunteer anything she had learned from her daddy. She wanted to hear what Jeremy had to say for himself

"I told you that I've been in contact with your father, and that I know that he's coming to visit you tonight, after you get home," Jeremy said.

Salina nodded, waiting for him to go on.

"The last time I saw him was a week ago. He told me then that he'd be back from Richmond in time for your birthday."

Salina concluded that Jeremy must have been the *someone* Daddy was waiting to meet in the schoolhouse. "And today is my birthday," she confirmed. "How is it that you've managed to be in touch with my daddy when the rest of us don't hear from him for months at a time?"

Jeremy smiled. "I ran into him while I was in California, down in San Diego, and we decided to go into—business—together."

"What kind of business?" Salina wanted to know. "Daddy's working for the army, sort of."

"I'll *sort of* be working for the army, too, in a manner of speaking," Jeremy replied. "Although I haven't technically enlisted, and my name's not on any regimental muster sheet, I suppose I could be considered a *volunteer* for the present time. There are many details..." he sighed.

"Tell me about this business you and Daddy are conducting," Salina prompted. "What do you do?"

"We work on reconnaissance missions," Jeremy explained, "gathering information about the enemy: positions of troops, sizes, strengths, weaknesses, and even their next movement if you're fortunate to stumble across orders..."

"You mean *spying*," Salina said plainly. "Daddy did tell me he works for the Secret Service and that would lead me to believe that he's a spy."

"Yes," Jeremy answered bluntly.

"And you're one as well?" she asked.

Jeremy nodded. "I helped your father collect a good deal of information in preparation for the next Confederate campaign he's planning for the War Department. I brought some of the information with me, and he's already taken it to President Davis."

"The plans are to capture California," Salina murmured. She caught his look of surprise, "Daddy mentioned it to me, when I saw him last week. Do you know the plans?"

"No," Jeremy shook his blond head. "I'm only told what I need to know when I need to know it. You could ask your father. I'll wager he might let you in on some secrets."

Salina smiled. Evidently Jeremy didn't know that Daddy had already promised to do just that. "Why are you telling me this?" she queried.

"As a precaution, I guess. I've been thinking lately that the Network could put someone like you to good use and the Yankees would never suspect..."

"Network?" Salina was growing more intrigued. "What is that?"

"Captain Hastings has established a Network of people in various locations who gather information and pass it along to him. Sometimes it's related to the western campaign, sometimes it has to do with whatever might be happening in our own backyard, so to speak. The Network runs from Richmond, Virginia, right up to the Union capital at Washington. But it also extends as far north as Canada, south to Mexico, and west to San Francisco and San Diego. The Network is like a chain, and messages are relayed from one link to another. Those messages are, more often than not, in secret code, so that if anyone on the outside were to find something, it wouldn't make sense to them. There are translators, people who code messages or decode them, and there are couriers who transport the messages. Your father has enlisted me as a courier."

"Who else knows you're involved in this?" Salina queried.

"You, Captain Hastings, and a handful of key local people," Jeremy replied.

Salina nodded. "So Ethan doesn't know."

Jeremy shook his head, "No. Captain Hastings thought it was best not to get Ethan involved. He reasons that if he were ever captured by the Yankees, they might suspect that Ethan was working with him. He wants to avoid casting any unnecessary suspicions. Your father thinks that the Yankees are already watching out for him, and he knows that his work may draw suspicion to not only Ethan who is his son, but to your mamma as well, simply because she is the Captain's wife. Within the week that he's been back in Virginia, Captain Hastings feels that Yankees have assigned someone to follow him, and that's why he's being extremely cautious. Since his return, he's bound to wait for the decision from the War Department, and in the meantime he's drawn a local assignment for further covert operations."

"Meaning?" Salina raised an eyebrow in question.

Jeremy smiled. "Covert operations are hidden, disguised actions. Understand?" He saw Salina nod affirmatively. "Captain Hastings has orders that have him working in this vicinity for the time being. If the War Department approves of the western campaign, there has to be some time to plan things out. Captain Hastings will keep himself busy until the time comes to put his plans into action."

"He'll be nearby!" Salina was pleased.

"Yes, but it might be more dangerous for him here—especially if he's truly being followed," Jeremy told her.

Salina's mind was racing, thinking, comprehending the importance of the things Jeremy was sharing with her. It gave her a chance to use her intelligence, and she liked that very much.

She thought of how Mamma had been raised under the teaching that the Southern lady's only station in life was in servitude to her husband coupled with the responsibilities of bearing him many children and successfully managing their household. Southern women were demanded to be of fine moral character, virtuous and pious, tender, kind, strong, hospitable, and caring—yet they weren't often encouraged to *think* for themselves. This War Between the States was forcing women to be more independent than they'd ever been allowed. They had to work and think and do things the men had previously taken care of, all in order to survive. No one knew how long the fighting would rage between the North and the South, but the South had been relatively unprepared, and now the womenfolk were stepping in to help wherever they were needed.

And Salina wanted to help wherever she could—not just passively through the Women's Assistance Guild. "I can help," she whispered aloud.

Jeremy chuckled, "Of course, Salina. You could be a secret weapon against the Yankees—a sixteen-year-old girl spy for the Confederacy..." His eyes opened wide, and he stopped his teasing. The significance of what he'd just said jolted him. "My word, Salina, you *could* help us."

"How?" she challenged.

"You're young, and you're a girl..." Ideas were rapidly forming in Jeremy's mind.

"And you've just this instant discovered the fact?" Salina questioned, pouting.

"I didn't mean it like that. I meant that you would arouse very little suspicion. I'm going to talk to the Captain about it and see what he thinks..." Jeremy was still holding Salina's hand. Her skin was soft and the smallness of her hand was enveloped by the largeness of Jeremy's covering hers. "I'll talk to him tonight, Salina. I promise you that."

☆☆☆☆☆☆☆

"I've been looking for you everywhere, Salina," Ethan complained. He was quick to note Jeremy was right behind his sister. "And Lottie's been looking for you," he said to his friend.

Jeremy shrugged. "What for?"

"I didn't ask her," Ethan said. "But I am asking you where you've been, since you've obviously been together."

"We were in the gazebo talking, Ethan," Salina said. "I don't see any reason to be so upset about that."

He shot a warning glance at Jeremy, but said to Salina, "I'm not upset about that. I'm upset because I didn't know where to find you when Mamma called for you. She's fainted again, Salina. Jubilee's with her now, but she's insisting she can care for Mamma better at home than here."

"Mamma would be more comfortable at home anyway," Salina supposed. "How soon before we can leave?"

"Just as soon as I give Peter Tom the word to bring her down to the carriage," Ethan said. "Say goodbye to Mary Edith and Randle, and then meet us on the veranda."

Salina also said goodbye to Taylor Sue. "We didn't get much of a chance to talk."

"You seemed to be spending all your time in the company of Jeremy Barnes," Taylor Sue pointed out, "and at the next Guild meeting, I expect to learn why. Just by looking at him a person can see he's taken with you. I suppose you've stirred up enough attention what with that near-duel situation between him and Charlie Graham. You're going to get yourself talked about, Salina."

"I don't care," Salina told Taylor Sue. "Is the Guild meeting at Shadowcreek or at Carillon?"

"It was at Carillon last time. I believe my mother has already spoken to yours about hosting the meeting at Shadowcreek this time."

"When?" Salina asked.

"The first of September." Taylor Sue hugged her quickly. "I'll see you then. Goodbye."

The journey home in the dark was slow going, but at last they reached the lane leading to Shadowcreek. Peter Tom carried Mamma upstairs to her bedchamber, and Jubilee fussed over her. Ethan looked concerned after conducting a brief examination. "I could send for Dr. Phillips," Ethan said.

"There's no need for all that," Mamma said weakly. "I'm just tuckered out, that's all."

"You've been working too hard," Ethan reprimanded. "It's draining the life from you, and you need to be healthy if you're going to make it through this pregnancy."

Mamma nodded. "I promise I'll try to slow down a bit, but you know as well as I do what needs to be done around here."

"Jubilee and I can handle it," Salina squeezed Mamma's hand. "You need your rest."

"I want you to stop worrying that this baby is going to be another mouth to feed," Ethan said, almost reading Mamma's very thoughts. "And I think you should write Daddy and tell him."

"He's in enough danger without being distracted by us here at home," Mamma argued.

"It's his right to know, and as I told you before, he'll know the next time he comes home anyway because you can't hide it for much longer," Ethan said firmly.

"I know," Mamma nodded. Tears came to her eyes. "I wish your Daddy was here now..."

Salina said comfortingly, "It's going to be all right, Mamma. We're going to make it through."

Ethan kissed Mamma's forehead. "Remember what Reverend Yates preached in his sermon from the psalms last Sunday: Truly my soul silently waits for God; from Him cometh my salvation. He alone is my rock and my salvation; He is my defense; I shall not be greatly moved. We must stand and let God be our defense against what goes on around us beyond our control. He is our rock."

"Amen," Mamma nodded.

Ethan sat down on the edge of the bed. He took one of Mamma's hands and one of Salina's. "Heavenly Father," he prayed, "we thank You for this baby that you've given Mamma and Daddy. We pray that You will bless Mamma and strengthen her. Cause the baby to grow strong inside of her and be a healthy little one when the time comes for it to be born. Keep Your shield around Daddy, wherever he might be, and keep the Yankees away from Shadowcreek. We ask this in Jesus' precious name, Amen."

Chapter Eight

*A*in't no saprize ta fin' ya still awake an' wid dat candle burnin'," Jubilee came to check on Salina before going to bed herself.

"I couldn't sleep, Jubilee. So much has happened today," Salina said, excitement glowing in her eyes. "I should write it all down so that I can remember it—if I had a journal, like the one Mamma keeps..."

Jubilee pulled a small package wrapped in brown paper from the pocket of her apron. "Dere jist ain't been time ta letcha have dis, seein' as da day was so filled wid all kines o' activities."

Salina unwrapped the square and smiled up at the maidservant. "Jubilee, a journal of my very own! Now I can write everything down." She pulled the coverlet back and sat up.

Jubilee confiscated the leather-bound book. "Dere's allays tomorrow fer dat. Now it's best dat ya git sum sleep afore da sun comes up already."

It was after midnight, and Salina obediently settled comfortably back into the four poster bed. "Will you sing to me for a while?"

"Ah s'pose ah could," Jubilee agreed. The black woman sang in her deep, rich voice:

> *The riverbed will make a very good road*
> *Follow the drinking gourd*
> *The dead trees show you the way*
> *Follow the drinking gourd*
> *Left foot, peg foot, traveling on*
> *Follow the drinking gourd*
>
> *Follow the drinking gourd*
> *Follow the drinking gourd*
> *For the old man is a-waitin' for to carry you to freedom*
> *If you follow the drinking gourd.*

Salina was familiar with the song, and the riddle contained in its lines. Jubilee had told her the tale of the drinking gourd, said to be the Big Dipper constellation, which pointed the way North. This verse, along with those which followed, included directions to guide runaway slaves from the South.

"Jubilee?" Salina whispered the Negro servant's name. "Have you ever wanted to run away from Shadowcreek and go up North?"

"Naw, Missy. Ah didn'. But, if'n ah belonged ta sum other folk besides Miz Annelise an' Massah Garrett, da circumstance mighta been dif'rent. Ah knows plenty dat do wish ta go up North, an' even sum dat did. My own brother, he done took my youngest gal wid him when he done gone an' escape nigh unto ten year ago. Ah pray ta Sweet Jesus dat deys safe an' healthy, but Jube's neber have dat dream. No, Missy, not Jube."

"You don't ever dream about not being a slave?" Salina was curious.

"Missy, ah been a slave all my life. Ah's born one, an' tis likely ah'll die one. Ah wouldna know what ah should do if'n ah wasn't. Ah don' think dere's too many folk like ya an' Miz Annelise up North, and ah wouldna wanna be anywhere ah couldna be wid y'all," Jubilee told Salina.

"I can't imagine life without you, Jubilee. You've always been here for Mamma and me," Salina said affectionately. "But this war is turning into more than just an issue over States' Rights, Ethan says. The North has already suggested that not only will they fight to restore the Union, but they'll fight to free all the slaves in the South. Would you stay with us then, Jubilee, even if you were free?"

"Yas, Missy, jist as long as da Good Lord allows. Jube ain't goin' nowhere nohow." Jubilee stroked Salina's curls and accidentally caught a tangle. "Would ya be wantin' Jube ta brush out yer hair, Missy?"

Salina nodded, and Jubilee used the new silver-handled brush. Jubilee tugged the bristles through Salina's long dark brown curls, and Salina winced several times, holding her tongue from protest.

"Dese here hurls o'yers shore is tangled up, Missy," Jubilee chided.

"I can feel that," Salina said between clenched teeth.

Jubilee smiled broadly. "Ah reckon twas all dat dancin' ah seen ya doin' wid dat young Massah Barnes."

Salina's cheeks flushed, "I only danced with Jeremy twice."

"Yas, Missy," Jubilee nodded knowingly. "An' Miss Lottie were in a stew da whole entire time ya was swirlin' and twirlin' in dat young man's arms. Imagine nearly creatin' cause fer a duel, an' den ya went sneakin' off ta dat rose garden wid dat boy..."

"Really, Jubilee—how you do go on," Salina rolled her eyes.

Jubilee chuckled, "If'n dere's a way ta find trouble, ya seem ta got dat knack, Missy."

"But I was good today," Salina protested. "I behaved."

"Humph." Jubilee set the brush aside. "Good enough ta still outshine dat high and mighty Lottie—even in a borrowed dress."

"Imagine that," Salina began to laugh with her maidservant.

Jubilee hugged Salina, "Chile, sometimes ya is wicked."

"Mischievous—that's what Daddy calls me." Suddenly Salina remembered that she was supposed to be waiting for his arrival. In fact, he might even be here already, but wondered if the light in her room was keeping him away from the house. She put her hand to her mouth to cover a large, contrived yawn. "Mmmm," she sighed, "maybe I'm more sleepy than I thought."

"Tired, ere ya?" Jubilee looked at Salina suspiciously, but held her tongue. She squeezed Salina's shoulder and whispered, "Sweet dreams, chile."

"Good night, Jubilee," Salina snuggled down into her pillow. "And thank you."

"Fer what is ya thankin' me fer?" asked Jubilee.

"For being here," Salina said. She rolled over, still thinking about her adventures of the day, and she didn't remember drifting off to sleep.

☆☆☆☆☆☆☆

Salina was awake again the instant she felt a wide-palmed hand clamp down tightly over her mouth.

"Hush, now, Sally-girl," the Southern baritone drawled. "It's just your daddy, and I can't have you screamin' to wake the household."

Enough moonlight flooded the upstairs bedroom so that Salina could see and recognize her daddy's rugged features. "Hello, Daddy!" she whispered in his ear when he'd taken his hand from her mouth and gathered her securely in his embrace.

"I'm here, sweet Sally," the Captain crooned, rocking her to and fro in the cradle of his arms.

"You've grown whiskers," Salina rubbed her cheek lovingly against the Captain's. She sat up quickly, "Is it safe for you to be here?"

He flashed a warming smile. "I took all the necessary precautions, so don't you worry your pretty little head. I promised you I'd be back with your birthday present, and so here I am. Though by now, I reckon yesterday was actually your birthday if you judge by the time told by the chimes downstairs."

"I'm just glad you're here," Salina hugged him.

The Captain lit the small candlestick on Salina's nightstand then went to the window seat to retrieve his haversack. From the worn leather pouch he withdrew a china-headed doll dressed in emerald-green taffeta.

"A doll? Daddy, I'm sixteen years old," Salina pouted, but tried not to look as terribly disappointed as she felt. "I'm too grown up to play with dolls now."

The Captain had partially expected such a reaction from his daughter. "Ah, but not too old to *collect* them. Even your Mamma has some of her old dolls on a shelf in our room, right?"

"Well, yes, I see your point," Salina nodded.

"This is a very special doll, Sally. She came from Richmond, smuggled right through the Yankee blockade, all the way from Paris, France. President Davis thought she was a *remarkable* doll, Sally, and I was sure you'd treasure her."

Salina regretted having slighted her daddy's gift. "She is pretty." Salina gently touched the hand-painted face. "Her dress is the same color as my eyes."

"I know," the Captain nodded with a wink. "Mine, too."

Fingering the crisp, smooth material, Salina watched the sheen of candlelight dance on the folds of the skirt. "I will treasure her because you brought her to me."

"That's my girl, and Sally..."

"Yes, Daddy?"

"I want you to take *especially* good care of that doll. I truly want you to think of her as a very dear, very precious treasure. *Never* leave her just any old where, keep her here, in your room, and that way she's not likely to attract any undue attention. And if you leave Shadowcreek for any reason, you must hide her away in a very safe, secret place."

"Like under the window seat?" Salina queried.

The Captain nodded. He put his finger to his lips. "Our secret?"

"Of course," Salina agreed solemnly. "I'm glad you were able to come for my birthday, Daddy."

"I did promise, and you know I'll always keep my word of honor." The Captain kissed the top of her head. "Oh, I almost forgot. This is for you, too." He handed her a note.

On the piece of paper were written rows of nonsensical words. She looked up at him and asked excitedly, "Daddy, is this a coded message from the Network?"

"Network? Now where'd you hear about that?" the Captain asked, but had a notion about who had told her.

"A courier told me," Salina answered, "by the name of Jeremy Barnes."

The Captain rubbed his whiskered jaw. "And what else did Barnes have to say?"

Salina retrieved Jeremy's note and handed it to the Captain. "He gave me this to give to you. He said he was going to talk to you about my working with you because the Yankees wouldn't suspect me."

"Jeremy's a smart lad—and he's exactly right, Sally. I told you last week that you and I had some grown-up things to discuss. I was hoping that you might want to learn how to use the codes and serve as a translator."

"Me? You think I could?" Salina's eyes widened.

"Have you learned how to shoot?" the Captain asked.

Salina nodded, "I've been practicing with Ethan every morning. It wasn't so difficult, once I got the hang of it."

"Coding and decoding is much the same principle, once you get the hang of it, it's easy," the Captain said. "Are you interested, Sally? It's a very daring job, and one that could put you in danger. Do you understand the risk involved?"

She nodded. "If a spy is caught by the enemy, they're hanged."

The Captain nodded somberly. "I debated with myself for a long time, not wanting to expose you to it, but I came to the realization that we need you, Sally. For the good of the Confederacy. It's important, and you know full well I wouldn't ask it of you otherwise."

"I know that, Daddy, and I'm proud to be of service," Salina said confidently. "What do I do?"

"*Here* is why your new doll is so special..." The Captain lifted the doll's lacy pinafore to reveal a small square of letters perfectly embroidered in neat, even rows on the taffeta beneath the lace. He explained how to use the sequenced letters to translate the lines on the piece of paper. He smiled outright at how easily she caught on. The message read: *To my darling Sally-girl, Happy Sixteenth Birthday, with all my love, Daddy.*

"Very good," the Captain was proud of her rapid progress. He handed her another piece of paper. "Try this one."

Salina used the clue he'd given to her, and within several minutes of dedicated concentration, she had unscrambled the message from Jeremy. It said: *I trust her. If you're still debating about bringing her in, I'm for it. Signed, J.B.*

Salina looked up at her daddy in question.

The Captain grinned. "Seems you've won Barnes over. That's a start. You two will work together."

"Do you send coded messages like this, Daddy?" Salina asked.

"Every day, darlin'," the Captain sighed his admission. "Every day." His expression became distant, closed.

For a swift moment Salina thought that this operation might be more dangerous than he was letting on, probably because he didn't want her to worry, or to be frightened. He told her he needed her help, and she wouldn't let him down. "What is it, Daddy?"

He touched her cheek and smiled slightly. "Jeremy is certainly right. *You* can help us where no one else can." His green gaze bored into Salina's curious eyes for a full minute. He didn't speak, and his eyes filled with deliberate contemplation.

Salina whispered, "Do you have any more secrets you want me to keep?"

"As a matter of fact, I do. Quick," the Captain commanded. "Get your wrapper, and I'll show you some more secrets."

Salina obediently donned her robe and a pair of slippers. Firmly squeezing her Daddy's hand, she willingly followed him down through the concealed, mazed passageway that came out of the house near the creek. "You haven't told anyone about that passageway, have you?"

"No, Daddy. But I think Jubilee knows about it already. She always seems to know everything," Salina said with wonder.

"But Jubilee will keep quiet," the Captain said with certainty.

"She's loyal to us, especially to your mamma. Sally, if Mamma were to find out about any of this, she'd be extremely upset."

"I know, Daddy, but she won't find out," Salina promised. "She worries about you, you know, where you are and what you're doing. She says its enough to turn her hair gray."

The Captain's smile was tinged with mischief. "Mamma hasn't always approved of what I do, but she's always stood beside me. We had a terrible argument when I told her I was resigning my commission in the United States army only to be commissioned as a Secret Service agent for the Confederacy. She didn't like it one bit, and I can't say as I blame her. I had a hard time convincing her that a man's got to do what a man's got to do. She knows I'm fighting for a cause, though at times it seems a little unclear as to the precise reasons *why*. All I know anymore is that it is my honor and duty as a Virginian to defend what belongs to me, and although I love Mamma dearly, she hasn't always understood a soldier's way of thinking."

"She's concerned because she loves you so very much, Daddy," Salina said. "You will be able to see her tonight, won't you?"

"Yes, right after we finish with the business at hand," the Captain nodded.

Stealthily, the Captain and Salina crept along the fence, past the spring house and the chicken coop, over to the smokehouse.

The Captain said in a low whisper, "You mustn't tell a soul—not Mamma, not Ethan, and not Taylor Sue Carey."

"I promise," Salina nodded gravely. Daddy echoed Jeremy's demand of her silence. "Does Jeremy know?"

"No, only you and I know." The Captain's keen eyes scanned the landscape around them, looking for any signs of life among the woods on the banks of the creek. He ushered Salina into the smokehouse. He uncovered his secret hiding place, under the third flagstone just to the right of the fire pit.

He lifted a small leather wallet from the hidden recess beneath the stone, added some gold coins and some of that Yankee paper money called greenbacks. He opened one of the maps of New Mexico Territory and showed Salina different places: Santa Fe, Las Cruces, Fort Craig and Fort Union, Albuquerque, Valverde, and Glorieta Pass. He traced the route the Confederates had marched out from El Paso, Texas, and then he showed her how the Union volunteers from Colorado had cut off access to the supply wagons. Then he showed her the route of retreat, back to Texas.

"This time, the campaign will be more thoroughly researched and better prepared. I've got contacts in San Diego, San Francisco, and Virginia City in Nevada. I reported to President Davis and have submitted a possible plan of attack. I'm waiting now for the War Department to approve the plans and then issue my orders." Carefully, the Captain replaced the flagstone. "These other items will be used by the Network as necessary and you, Sally, will be the translator. By using the code from your doll's dress to interpret or send messages, you'll be able to help me with local assignments while I'm waiting to gain approval for the western campaign. That doll of yours is very important, for not only does she hold the secret code, she contains..." He stopped abruptly.

"She contains what, Daddy?" Salina prodded.

The Captain shook his head, putting his finger to his lips, wordlessly commanding her to keep still and quiet.

Salina listened, but she heard only the breeze in the trees—until a horse sighed in the night.

Cautiously, the Captain peeked out the smokehouse door, but he saw nothing, no one. He let out the breath he'd been holding.

"That might have been Starfire or Baron," Salina whispered, indicating her horse and Ethan's. "We have a hidden corral in the woods."

The Captain shook his head. "No, I think someone's following me."

"Who?" Salina wanted to know. "Yankees?"

"Someone who was once a friend of mine—who is now supposed to be my enemy," the Captain replied with a trace of sadness in his voice. He cleared his throat, the explanation of the contents of the doll forgotten, and said, "This is all you need to know for the moment: You can use the code to translate messages or send messages. Jeremy will be the courier. He knows of others connected with the Network. You will learn when it is appropriate for you to know, but not until then."

"Are these people spies, too?" she asked.

"In a manner of speaking, but unofficially, of course. They are local people—some might even be our neighbors, Sally, so don't be surprised. But each has volunteered to help with the task of collecting valuable information about the enemy in any way they can. The information is passed through the chain until it reaches its destination—sometimes that might be to the War Department at Richmond, or it may be information to be relayed to a commanding officer in field headquarters. It varies, as you'll come to see."

The more Salina listened, the more interested she became.

"And you'll talk to Jeremy about our working together—secretly, of course."

"Yes," the Captain nodded. He noticed that Salina was shivering in the night air. "Come on, let's get you back up to the house."

Retracing their steps, the Captain looked over his shoulder twice, again feeling as though something or someone was out there watching them from the trees. He shook the feeling off and got Salina quickly back inside.

"You go on back to bed, Sally-girl. I'm going to see Mamma before I leave, and I want to talk to Ethan," the Captain said.

"Before you leave? You're not staying then?" Salina asked.

"Only for a few hours, I'm afraid. I bear dispatches from Richmond to be delivered to General Lee. I have a good idea where to look for him." The Captain gently swatted Salina's behind, "Go on, now."

"Will you come and kiss me goodbye?" Salina squeezed her Daddy's middle tightly.

"Yes, darlin'." He gave her a crushing hug.

Salina climbed into the four poster bed, clutching her new doll to her side. She had too many thoughts running through her mind to think of sleep. Daddy had kept his promise. He'd given her a birthday present, and he'd brought her into the Network. It made her feel proud to know that he trusted her with so much. She snuggled with the china-headed doll. It was a very special present, indeed, and she realized that if the doll ever fell into the wrong hands, there could certainly be trouble.

She had heard stories last year about a lady named Rose Greenhow, who was a spy for the Confederacy. Mrs. Greenhow had been arrested in Washington because of her Southern sympathies and imprisoned for her role in forwarding information to the proper channels warning the Southern armies that Union troops were marching toward Centreville. The Southerners were prepared, and so defeated the Yankees at Manassas, near Bull Run.

I will guard this doll safely, Salina silently vowed. She decided to name her doll Celeste because Daddy said she had come all the way from France.

Chapter Nine

Mamma cried tears of joy to find her husband unhurt, and in her arms. "You're safe!" she breathed into the stillness. "Thank You, Heavenly Father, for answering my prayers!"

"Amen," Captain Hastings agreed. He kissed his wife tenderly. "How I have missed you!"

"How long can you stay?" Mamma was immediately concerned for his well-being. "Are you sure it's safe for you to be here at all?"

"It's getting more difficult," the Captain answered honestly. "But tonight there was nothing that could keep me from seeing Salina, Ethan, and you."

"Where have you been?" Mamma asked, gently touching his whiskered face.

"New Mexico Territory," the Captain replied. "The Confederacy is planning another attack in the far west, but please, don't ask me anymore than that, Annelise. The less you know, the better."

"I worry about you so," Mamma needlessly reminded him.

"Yes, I know," he nodded. "I worry about you all back here, too." He crossed to the window, scanning the front lawn below. "Have there been many patrols?"

"Lots of Yankees travel by the Little River Turnpike," Mamma confirmed. "But so do a fair amount of our soldiers what with the Warrenton Turnpike so near. There's always someone on the cross-roads these days, or so it seems."

The Captain held Mamma close to him. He wondered if it was his imagination, or was his wife indeed a little plumper since the last time he'd been home three months ago? He said fiercely, "I don't know what I'd do if something ever happened to you—or the children— while I was away."

Mamma smiled up at him. "If you spend your time worrying about us, you'll not have your full concentration on your work. I want you to mind your business, however much I dislike it, and come home to me whenever you possibly can."

"Yes, ma'am." The Captain returned her smile and snapped a mock salute. "I'll take that as a direct order."

"Good." Mamma put her head on his shoulder. "You see, you can't get captured or shot at or do anything that will keep you from coming back here because..."

"Because?" The Captain lifted her chin in order to see her sparkling eyes.

"Because I'd like you to see your new child when it's born," Mamma said softly. "I wouldn't want the baby to grow up without knowing you were its father."

"A baby?" The Captain was startled. "We're going to have a baby?"

Mamma nodded, pleased by the happiness welling in the Captain's eyes. "So far so good," she said.

"Oh, Annelise! This is wonderful news!" He hugged her tightly. "What do Ethan and Salina think? Do they know?"

"Yes—Ethan had it figured first. You know how he's been working with Dr. Phillips and learning all about medicine. He's read every book Dr. Phillips owns, and he goes with him on calls regularly now."

"Phillips is a fine doctor," the Captain nodded. "If he wasn't so old, the army might have drafted him."

"He's been called on to look after wounded from time to time. He does what he can to help heal those on either side," Mamma said.

"Ethan's become a knowledgeable assistant, and I think Dr. Phillips likes knowing that Ethan is skilled enough to carry on the practice when the time comes."

"Good for Ethan," the Captain said proudly. "At least he's found a productive way to spend his time. He was so angry with me for not allowing him to enlist in the army."

Mamma nodded. "His anger is fading. He's much more concerned with fulfilling his word—looking after the estate and after Salina and me. Now the baby will be another addition."

The Captain sensed her apprehension. "Aren't you happy about being pregnant, Annelise?"

Mamma lowered her eyes. The Captain always had a way of reading her mind. "I would be happier if I wasn't scared," she admitted. "We have enough resources for now, and we've planted some things that will be ready to harvest that should last us through the winter. We'll make do."

The Captain muttered, "You wouldn't have to be working at all if the war hadn't come."

"We've had this discussion before. Lots of things would be different *if the war hadn't come*, but it has, and it doesn't show any signs of a peaceful conclusion in the very near future," Mamma stated. "Things are changing, and we change with them. The children are resilient, they adjust better than I. I'm used to the old ways, the old conventions, the old South. I have the feeling nothing will be the way it was when this is all over."

"I have to agree with you," the Captain said sadly. "Nothing will be the same."

For a few moments, they were silent, holding each other, enjoying each other's nearness.

"I'm thankful this place is set so far back from the lane," the Captain said, stroking Mamma's auburn hair. "Hopefully the surrounding trees will keep you safely hidden away. At least the horses haven't been taken yet."

"Thank the Lord for that. We keep them in a little corral in the woods. Recently Peter Tom put the cow out as well, and we only have a couple of pigs that we got in trade for some of our corn in the back of the barn," Mamma said. "Jubilee, Salina, and I have been canning and preparing for the colder months. I've spread out the supplies, storing some things in the cellar, others in the attic, the spring house, and the kitchen pantry. There's a stash in the barn loft, too. If soldiers do come, they won't find everything we have in one place."

"Smart thinking," the Captain smiled. "It seems you're managing well enough without me."

"Hardly." Mamma kissed him. "I'd rather you were here with me and not off traipsing across the west or sneaking around the country-side, and you know it."

The Captain chuckled. "Yes, I do know it. And I wish the same thing—that I was here with my loved ones and sharing your lives. I feel like I'm missing out on so much when I'm out in the field."

"You did miss the wedding over at Ivywood. Salina was a bridesmaid for Mary Edith, and she wore her hair pinned up, her hoops wide, and she danced and danced. And of course, she couldn't get through the evening without sparking just a hint of trouble..." Mamma laughed. "Charlie Graham practically challenged Jeremy Barnes to a duel right in the middle of the dance floor."

"What happened?" the Captain wanted to know. Once, some twenty years ago, he himself had been involved in a duel, and he'd won. His marriage to Mamma was testimony to that incident.

Mamma was remembering as well. She had been the cause for the duel just as Salina nearly had been at the wedding. Mamma told the Captain about the fundraising dance and the Yankee greenbacks.

"Charlie's always had a loose hold on his temper," the Captain nodded.

"And knowing the way Jeremy's capable of shooting... Speaking of shooting, he and Ethan are teaching Salina how to protect herself," Mamma said. "What do you think of that?"

"It was my idea," the Captain had to admit. "I sent word to Ethan that Salina should be taught. Remember when I taught you how to handle a revolver?"

"That's not the point," Mamma argued. "Teaching Salina to shoot is quite another matter."

"You were her age when I taught you how to shoot," the Captain countered. "I believe Salina's old enough to handle it. She's blossom-ing into a very fine young lady right before our very eyes," he murmured. "And she's just as smart and pretty as you are." He kissed Mamma soundly so she couldn't argue with him anymore.

Mamma laughed, and then she sighed, leaning her head against his shoulder. "It was so good to see the children happy tonight. For a brief instant it seemed the war was non-existent, yet there are so many constant reminders. And then Jeremy could hardly keep his eyes off Salina. Ethan proposed to Taylor Sue Carey, and she's accepted him."

This news of Ethan's engagement did not surprise the Captain as much as the news of the baby had. He figured that eventually Ethan would get around to asking for Taylor Sue's hand. They'd grown up together, and he believed they would be a most suitable match. "Here I go away for three months and all kinds of events happen," the Captain complained. "What else is going on around here that I should know about?"

Mamma told him the news of the local neighbors, and whatever word she had of their other friends who were caught up in the horrendous fighting. She sadly reported that two of their neighbors' sons had been killed during the Seven Days' Battle outside of Richmond at the end of June. "And I've heard conditions in Centreville are ghastly and many of the houses have been taken over and used as Union headquarters. The town has been occupied by both armies, and they leave little but destruction in their wake."

"So many men have died already, Annelise," the Captain choked on the words. "And so many more will lose their lives before this fight is settled."

Mamma put her finger to his lips. "Sssshhh," she crooned. "Close your eyes and rest. Forget about the dreaded war..."

"If only it were that easy," the Captain muttered, but he did as his wife suggested, closing his eyes and relaxing for the time being. In a few minutes, he'd have to tell her to be on her guard, to keep watch for a Yankee he felt sure would be following him soon, if not already...

☆☆☆☆☆☆☆

Through her open bedroom window, Salina heard the sound of horses again, this time much more distinct than before. Then she heard the muffled sound of boots on the veranda below and the sound of a gun hammer cocking. She bolted out of bed, not bothering with her robe or slippers, to hurry along the hall to Ethan's room. Daddy wasn't there.

"He was here about half hour ago." Ethan rubbed the sleep from his eyes. "No doubt he's with Mamma now."

"I think there's somebody out there, Ethan. We have to warn him. If he's found here, won't they capture him?" Salina asked, her voice holding a trace of panic.

"Simmer down, Salina. Depends on which side is out there. I'll go get him. You stay here." Ethan went in the direction of Mamma's room, but Salina was unable to make herself sit still, so she followed him.

Apparently, the Captain had already been alert to the noises outside. "Looks like I'll be leavin' quicker than I thought," he said as he slipped into a gray short jacket with yellow piping trim which signified the cavalry branch of service. He tried to force a smile for the sake of his children.

Mamma had tears in her large brown eyes. "God be with you, Garrett," she clung to his hand.

A banging at the front door startled them all, but forced them into quick action. "Sally, come with me," the Captain commanded. "Ethan, go back to your room—let your Mamma handle this. Cromwell will answer the door, and I'll simply disappear..." He kissed his wife, silently begging her to take care of herself and their unborn child. He hugged Ethan and told him he was proud of having such a fine son.

The Captain and Salina hurried back to her room. "Remember," the Captain said, holding Salina by the shoulders, "keep everything we've talked about between you and me. Someone from the Network will be in touch with you soon. You're a big girl now, Sally. I wouldn't ask any of this of you if I didn't think you could be trusted to do the job."

"I'll do my very best, Daddy. You have my word of honor, and I won't let you down," Salina vowed.

The Captain nodded, and he touched Salina's cheek. "I believe you will, and I'm proud of you for it. I love you, Sally-girl. I'll come back just as soon as I can. Remind Mamma and your brother of how much I love them as well."

"I will," Salina assured him.

The Captain slipped into the opening of the secret passageway, and Salina replaced the wall panel and the tapestry hanging that covered it, once he was safely on the other side. "Lord Jesus, please watch over him!" she prayed fervently.

Downstairs, Cromwell, one of three of the Hastings' remaining servants, had unwillingly allowed a blue-coated visitor entrance into Shadowcreek's main hall.

"Good evening, or perhaps I should say good morning. My apologies for disturbing you at this late hour," the blond-haired Yankee said to Cromwell. "My name is Lieutenant Lance Colby. My men and I have run out of water, and we wondered if we might fill our canteens from your well."

"You may, Lieutenant," Mamma answered from the landing of the stairs, and then she added sweetly, "And then you, and your men, may get off this land."

"Thank you kindly for your hospitality, ma'am," Lieutenant Colby said with a slight edge of sarcasm in his voice. He tipped his hat to Mamma, and without causing too much suspicion, Colby glanced around, taking mental inventory of what he saw, which he would report back to Captain Grant. "We'll be on our way directly."

"Then I shan't detain you from taking your leave," Mamma said graciously. "Good morning, Lieutenant." She regally walked back up the top most steps and returned to her room. She sat down in the nearest chair, practically out of breath. How on earth had she dared talk to a Yankee as she had? The minute she was sure that the small detachment of Yankees had indeed moved on, she flew to Salina's room. Ethan was right on her heels.

"What about Daddy, Salina? Did he get away all right?" Ethan questioned.

"Yes," Salina nodded. "He said that he loves us all and that he'll be back when he can."

Mamma embraced her son and daughter. She offered up a sincere prayer for their own safety and especially the Captain's. "Lord, please, keep Your hand on him and bring him back to us!"

☆☆☆☆☆☆☆

"No sign of him, sir." Lieutenant Colby had ridden off after he and his comrades filled their canteens at the Hastings' well, and then doubled back to Shadowcreek, where Captain Grant was waiting for a report. "If Captain Hastings truly was here, he got away clean."

"Hmmm..." Captain Grant was deep in thought. "We may have to go about this in a different way..." He reined his impatient horse, then headed once more for the shelter of the trees and beckoned for his lieutenant to follow without question.

☆☆☆☆☆☆☆

Hot orange fire glowed in the huge stone fireplace. Jubilee stirred the makings of supper in a cauldron with a long-handled ladle. Salina sat on a wooden stool nearby, snapping string beans into a bowl. She looked up when Jeremy Barnes entered the kitchen.

"Good afternoon, Master Barnes," Salina said with a bright smile.

"Hello, Miss Hastings," Jeremy replied formally. He nodded to Jubilee. "Might I have a word with you, Miss Hastings? Outside?"

Jubilee continued to stir. Salina set the bowl of beans on the table. "Jubilee, I'll be back shortly to finish this up."

"Humph," Jubilee nodded. She liked Jeremy Barnes well enough, but she didn't quite trust him. Not after that little stunt of taking Salina into the Armstrongs' garden unchaperoned. "Dis war done got rid o' what's allays been fittin' and proper," she muttered under her breath. She was as disapproving as Miz Annelise was at the way convention and tradition were changing the ways all around them.

Salina walked with Jeremy as far as the rail fence that surrounded the vegetable garden. "Did you have something you wanted to tell me?" she asked.

"Last night I did some thinking. There are some things that I have need to take care of now that I'm back in Virginia. I packed up what things I have and thanked the Armstrongs profusely for feeding and sheltering me since my return. This morning I intended to go to Middleburg, where I must face my aunt and settle my business with her. Since Uncle John is off fighting for the Union, he won't be there, thank God. I know that my Aunt Isabelle treated me as kindly as she could, under the circumstances, while I lived there. I owe her a debt and I'm going to pay it in full. But now Middleburg will have to be postponed because on my way over here to tell you goodbye, I found this." He withdrew a small, folded scrap of paper from the cuff of his frock coat. "Have you learned to decode messages yet?"

Salina briefly glanced at the note. It looked much like the one Daddy had shown her the night before. "Yes, I have learned," she answered. "Where did you happen upon that?"

"It was left for me in a hiding place that only your father and I share. He must still be in the area, because this can't be from anyone else," Jeremy said.

Salina smiled tentatively and nodded. She took the note from his hand. "I am that translator that you spoke of, Jeremy."

"So he's gone ahead and brought you in," Jeremy nodded. "I'm not surprised." He decided to test her. "Can you make out the message?"

"I've got to go to the main house. Stay here." Salina took the note and went to her room where she could use Celeste's secret code to decipher the message.

Jeremy was waiting impatiently when she returned to him. "Well?" he asked, even though he instinctively knew she had correctly translate the coded words.

Salina read the translation which gave him detailed instructions where to find vials of morphine and quinine. The medicines, constantly in short supply, were to be delivered to a temporary hospital where wounded from the battle at Cedar Mountain were being cared for. The Confederates had clashed with the Yankees at Cedar Mountain on the ninth of August, nearly two weeks ago.

"That certainly alters my trip to Middleburg," Jeremy reconfirmed. "I'll just have to go visit Aunt Isabelle some other time." He smiled down at Salina. "I'll be saying farewell and be on my way. You are a very clever young lady, Miss Hastings." He lifted her hand to his lips and kissed it.

"Thank you for saying so." Salina was warmed by Jeremy's praise, yet saddened by his leaving.

"I'll come back here before I leave for Middleburg," Jeremy told her. "I'll want to see you before I go away again." He untied the yellow ribbon that confined Salina's dark curls and pulled it free from her hair. "I'll be taking this with me," he said lowly, "so I have something to remind me of you."

"I'll miss you," Salina looked into Jeremy's blue eyes.

Though he hadn't been back in Virginia for very long, and they hadn't spent as much time together as he would have liked, Jeremy knew he was going to miss her, too. "Goodbye, Salina." He kissed her on the cheek and hurriedly stalked off to where he'd tethered Comet. He tipped his hat when he had settled in his saddle, and then he rode away.

Salina hummed to herself all the way back to the kitchen, her loose curls fluttering down her back and around her face.

Chapter Ten

*P*leased with Salina's improve-
ment at target practice, Ethan applauded her efforts. "Well done! Very
good. Now," he set up another target for Salina to hit, "back up another
ten paces."

"Ethan I can't hit that. It's too far," Salina complained.

"Aw, come on, little sister. Just aim and shoot. Surprise me,"
Ethan cajoled.

Salina raised her pistol, pointed, and pulled the trigger. Her shot
zoomed left of the mark. "I told you so," Salina pouted.

Ethan chuckled. "Salina, you've hit everything else this morning.
One missed shot is not bad."

"Humph," Salina bit her bottom lip, arms folded across her chest.

Ethan stared past Salina, over her head and through a gap in the
trees, to focus on the rider heading toward the Little River Turnpike at
breakneck speed. Salina recognized the Union blue uniform, and she
scowled silently.

"That's the third scout in two days' time," Ethan muttered. "I don't like it. Something's brewing."

Salina nodded in wordless agreement. She could feel the tension in the air. News from the battle front had been sketchy at best, but they knew some details of the skirmishes that took place along the Rappahannock River. It was reported that Jeb Stuart's cavalry had raided the headquarters of Union General John Pope at Catlett's Station on the twenty-third of August. There were stories of how the bold Southern cavalry leader had captured not only copies of pertinent letters, a valuable dispatch book, and prisoners from Pope's staff during the raid, but he had also came to be in possession of the Union general's dress coat in retaliation for his taking Stuart's favorite plumed hat a few days before at Verdiersville.

Rumors on Stonewall Jackson's whereabouts were rampant, but no one seemed to know for sure. Some claimed he was heading toward Manassas. Skirmishes between Confederate soldiers and Union soldiers had already happened at Bristoe and Manassas Junction.

Ethan's voice brought Salina back to the present. "You've done so well these past few days, I think that deserves a reward. Would you like to ride over to Fairfax Court House with me? I need to pick up a few things for Dr. Phillips at the Emporium and take them over to his office."

Salina forgot all about the Union scout. "I'll run up to the house and ask Mamma if it's all right."

Upon their arrival at Fairfax Court House, Ethan assisted Salina out of her sidesaddle, then secured both of their horses at a hitching post near the hotel. The main street of the town bustled with activity. The townsfolk seemed to be buzzing over something. Together, Ethan and Salina walked down the wooden plank sidewalk from the hotel to the Emporium, across from a white-frame church.

Inside the Emporium, Ethan and Salina overheard the shopkeeper discussing Stonewall Jackson's latest triumph over General Pope.

"I heard tell that when that Yankee Pope got to Manassas Junction right about noontime, Stonewall was already gone—just up and disappeared. Jeb Stuart's cavalry was right behind Stonewall's men wreaking havoc in their wake," the shopkeeper said proudly.

The customer to whom the shopkeeper was speaking was a tall, gray-haired man dressed in a black broadcloth suit. In a gravely voice he said, "Latest word seems to be about the gathering over yonder at Centreville."

"That sure would explain why the cannons sound so close," the shopkeeper added. "Centreville's not ten miles from here."

The gray-haired man said, "Pope is hoping to corner Stonewall this time. He'll need all the luck he can get to accomplish such a feat."

The shopkeeper chuckled, "He sure will. Stonewall Jackson's a sly one, that's for certain."

Salina wanted to stay and listen to them talk some more, but Ethan dragged her away, reminding her that they were there to do a job for Dr. Phillips, not eavesdrop on other people's conversations. When they'd collected everything on Dr. Phillips's list, Ethan paid for the goods and on a whim bought a length of green satin ribbon for his sister. "It matches your eyes," Ethan said by way of explanation, handing it to Salina. "Licorice?" he asked, appealing to his sister's sweet tooth.

"Thank you, Ethan," Salina smiled, pleased. "You are so thoughtful sometimes."

"I do try," he shrugged off her compliment. He placed a firm hold on her elbow, guiding her in the direction of the door. "Come on, let's go."

The black-suited stranger made it a point to tip his hat in their direction as Salina followed Ethan outside.

☆☆☆☆☆☆

Disguised as an old, gray-haired man, Duncan Grant watched the dark-haired lad lead his younger sister from the Emporium. He couldn't believe his good fortune to have run into the two of them here in Fairfax. There was positively no mistaking their resemblance to their father, Garrett Hastings. Duncan was certain that neither of the young Hastings had recognized him at all. And why should they, since it had been years since their last meeting?

Captain Grant left the Emporium in a hurry. He wanted to find Lieutenant Colby and make sure he was following their movements. He wondered if Garrett Hastings might risk enlisting his own son's aid in scouting for the Confederacy. Not only would Duncan need to keep an eye on the Rebel Captain, but he decided it might be wise to keep watch on the lad as well. Colby had been right to suggest that Barnes be followed, but Barnes had disappeared—just as Garrett Hastings had the familiar habit of doing.

☆☆☆☆☆☆

An old woman approached Ethan before he reached the horses tethered in front of the Emporium. "Excuse me, son. Could you please tell me if you are indeed one Master Ethan Hastings?"

"Yes, I am he," Ethan said, cocking his head to one side. "Who is it that I have the pleasure of addressing?"

"I'm Tabitha Wheeler," the spritely old woman said. "I run the boarding house down a little ways past the wagon shop. A friend of yours is staying with me, and he begs that you might call on him."

"A friend?" Salina inquired.

"Does this friend have a name?" asked Ethan.

Tabitha glanced around, then answered in hushed tones, "Master Jeremy Barnes is the name of your friend. Please come to the boarding house, Master Hastings, and bring your sister with you."

"Would you tell Master Barnes that we'll be along directly?" Ethan nodded.

"Be happy to," Tabitha grinned, revealing a smile which was minus a few teeth.

"I wonder why Jeremy's staying at the boarding house." Salina was puzzled.

"I don't know, but I'm going to find out," Ethan said with determination. "It's been days since he's been out to Shadowcreek for a visit, and that's not like him. I've been curious as to what he's been up to."

Salina presumed that Jeremy had been at Cedar Mountain, delivering the medicines, but she thought he would have returned before now. "Let's go find out."

Tabitha Wheeler led Ethan and Salina to a room on the second floor of the boarding house. Ethan cautiously opened the door. Inside, Jeremy lay motionless in the big brass bed. He was pale, and his dark eyelashes fluttered restlessly against his wan cheeks. A patchwork quilt covered him from the waist down. His bare shoulder was bandaged with a bloody dressing. Another bandage encircled his brow.

"Dear Lord!" Salina gasped, immediately whispering a prayer. "Thank You for keeping him alive, but please, let him heal quickly!"

Ethan, too, was shaken at seeing his friend so unmoving, so still. Jeremy's chest rose and fell with each shallow breath, but that was the only sign of life visible. "What happened to him?" Ethan asked hoarsely.

Tabitha crossed the floor and leaned over the bed. She felt Jeremy's fevered forehead then wiped her hands on her starched apron. "To me, it looked like it might have been a minié-ball from a Union rifle that grazed his temple, and a sabre slash tore open his shoulder." The old woman squeezed both Ethan and Salina's hands. "He's a strong lad. He'll live to fight another day. I had him propped up, almost sitting, to feed him some broth a little earlier. That's when he saw the two of you out the window. He insisted that I bring you to him."

"How long has he been here?" Salina asked. She glanced out the window, having a bird's-eye view of the main street through the town. The old man in the black suit from the Emporium was leaning against the hitching post out in front of the store. Salina shivered in the August heat.

"He's been here since late yesterday," Tabitha answered Salina's question. "Rode over from Groveton way—at least that's where I reckon he was wounded. There's been rather heavy fighting going on in these parts in the last few days. The Yanks are after Jackson and Stuart."

"Yes, we've heard," Ethan nodded.

"We could hear the cannon fire as far as Chantilly," Salina added. "How long will Jeremy have to stay here?"

"Well, now, that's why he wanted y'all to come calling. You see, I believe the lad is being hunted down. Somebody's following him, and although he really shouldn't be moved, I'm afraid for his life if he isn't taken to safety," Tabitha confided.

Salina's mind was racing. "Ethan, we've only got the horses. If we had the carriage or wagon, we could transport him."

"He's lost a lot of blood," Ethan said, examining Jeremy's wounds. He cleaned them and redressed them with clean white bandages. "He's burning with fever. He shouldn't be moved, but we don't have any choice. I'll ride back for the wagon. Salina, you'll have to stay here with Jeremy. If he wakes up, assure him that things are all right."

Salina nodded and whispered, "Of course I'll stay with him."

Ethan hooked his forefinger beneath Salina's chin and lifted her face so her eyes met his. "Don't be afraid. Tabitha says he'll be fine, and with the proper care, he'll be healing in no time. Won't hurt to pray—a lot. I'll be back just as soon as I can."

"All right," Salina replied in a whisper. "For you and for Jeremy, I'll be brave."

"Good girl." Ethan quickly hugged her, then he was gone.

☆☆☆☆☆☆☆

Salina sat in the back of the wagon with Jeremy's head resting in her lap. She tried to keep him as comfortable as possible against the jarring motion of the wagon. She was thankful that Jeremy had passed out shortly after leaving Fairfax; otherwise, he might have screamed in agony because of the constant jostling.

"We're almost home, Salina," Ethan called over his shoulder. "Looks like it might rain soon." He glanced up at the dark clouds gathering in the skies.

Dusk was falling, and Mamma was on the veranda waiting anxiously for her children to come home. She hurried down the stairs as they approached.

"Peter Tom!" Mamma called when she saw Jeremy's still form. "Peter Tom!"

"Yas, Miz Annelise?" The strong black man came from the barn.

"Peter Tom, carry Master Barnes up to the blue room at once. Carefully..." Mamma instructed. "Salina, find Jubilee, quickly. Bring her to tend Jeremy."

"I've already treated the wounds, Mamma. I did that at the boarding house. I'll change the dressings again when we get him upstairs—he's bleeding again. In the meantime, we have to try to get his fever down. He's awfully hot," Ethan said. "I'll be up as soon as I've seen to the horses.

Mamma had been worried about the prolonged absence of Salina and Ethan, but when Ethan had come for the wagon, explaining that Jeremy had been hurt, she'd immediately sent him back with instructions to hurry and bring him to Shadowcreek. "I was so worried about you two," Mamma told Salina. "I imagined all kinds of terrible things happening: I thought Ethan might have been captured, or that you had been taken by the Yankees."

"Mamma, why would the Yankees bother me?" Salina asked.

"Oh, I don't know!" Mamma wrung her hands together. She realized too clearly that if the Yankees knew about the Captain's whereabouts, as he had warned her that they might, what would prevent the Yankees from suspecting any of them? "I just want you to stay close to me," Mamma said. "I don't want anything to happen."

Keeping out from underfoot, Salina watched Jubilee and Ethan tend to Jeremy's wounds. Jubilee had gathered clean muslin dressings and some ointment to promote healing and keep infection from spreading. Ethan gave him some medicine to kill the pain.

Mamma put her hand to Jeremy's cheek to feel how hot he was. "Salina, would you mind fetching two pitchers full of cold water from the spring house? Ask Peter Tom to bring a sizable chunk of ice as well, please."

Mamma used the ice to form a cold compress for his forehead. She dipped a cloth into the cold water and bathed Jeremy's arms and chest. "We'll let him rest for a time, and then we'll check on him again."

For two hours after supper, Salina sat alone at Jeremy's bedside, applying more cold cloths to his sweaty brow. She jumped when his eyes slowly opened. "You startled me," she admitted in a low whisper.

For a minute or two, Jeremy tried to get his bearings. When he looked into Salina's concerned eyes, his eyebrows drew close together, depicting his disorientation.

"You're at Shadowcreek." Salina smiled gently, rinsing a cloth in the porcelain basin and wringing it out again. She dabbed his brow with the cool rag. "You were hurt—at Groveton, I think. Ethan and I found you at Tabitha Wheeler's boarding house in Fairfax."

"Hmmmm," Jeremy groaned. He licked his dry lips. His eyes went to the water pitcher on the nightstand and to the cup nearby.

"You want something to drink," Salina guessed correctly. She held the cup to his lips, but the liquid dribbled down the side of his neck. "Here," she said, helping him ever so gently to raise his head a bit. "Try again."

He nodded, wordlessly thanking her. His eyes closed wearily, and Salina thought he was asleep. She stood, looking down on him, knowing she should tell Mamma that he'd regained consciousness.

Jeremy caught her hand, his eyes imploring her to stay near him. "I..." his voice was harsh and scratchy, "I h-ave a mes-sage."

Salina didn't have to ask what kind of message he meant. "Where?"

"Jack-et...pock-et," he whispered. "From...Ce-dar...Moun...tain..."

Salina searched the pockets of his gray wool jacket trimmed with butternut collar and cuffs. It was a Confederate soldier's uniform. "Jeremy, this is a cavalry jacket—have you truly joined up?"

Jeremy slowly shook his head. "Dis-guise..."

She let out a sigh of relief. "You've been thinking about it, and I know Ethan is just itching to..."

Jeremy nodded. "You...know...too...m-uch...for...your...own...g-ood," he said with strained words. "Clev-er lit-tle Sa-lina."

She smiled at him. Her fingers closed around the folded piece of paper in the pocket, and then they felt a thin ribbon of satin. It was her hair ribbon. It pleased her immensely to know that Jeremy kept it with him, as he said he would. "I'll be back in just a minute," she told him, going down the hall to her own room to use the secret decoding square embroidered under Celeste's pinafore.

Ethan was with Jeremy when she returned. Ethan was examining Jeremy and all the while telling him of the battles that had been taking place so near to Chantilly.

"Lee's got forces gathering at Manassas," Ethan said.

"I...know," Jeremy breathed.

"If only..." Ethan left his sentence hanging when he heard Salina's light footsteps on the wooden floor.

"Ethan, could you please fetch me another chunk of ice from the spring house? The one Peter Tom brought has melted clean away. You yourself said we've got to keep Jeremy cool."

Ethan's expression questioned both his sister and his friend. When neither spoke, he shrugged. "I'll get it right away."

Jeremy managed a half-smile. "Clev-er lit-tle Sa-lina..."

Salina sat on the edge of the bed. She whispered, "The message sends eternal thanks for the medicines that you brought. There is some concern over Pope's maneuvers. He hasn't given up pursuing Stonewall Jackson. The supplies Jackson took at Manassas Junction have run out. There is a stolen shipment of ammunition hidden, just waiting to be delivered to Lee's men. And there is food and clothing."

"Y-es," Jeremy nodded. "I ha-ve...the map...I know where...the hi-ding place is..."

"But you can't ride," Salina said matter of factly. "You're not well, Jeremy. Someone else in the Network will have to make the delivery."

"No-one...else...has...been...noti-fied," he said.

"I can notify someone," Salina suggested. "I can decode messages—to put something into code would be a simple matter of reversing the procedure, right?"

"I should... th-ink so," Jeremy agreed. "I'll... t-ell you wh-ere to t-ake... the mes-sage..."

☆☆☆☆☆☆☆

Through the night and the next day, Mamma and Salina took turns sitting with Jeremy during the long hours. Cannons rumbled loudly in the distance, but Salina kept still and read aloud to him from *DeBow's Review*, a literary journal, not knowing if he could hear her or not. The fever raged within him, but by the second morning, the fever had broken.

The rain was threatening again. Sunday morning, the last day of August, was hot and humid. Ethan had been over to Carillon, the Carey estate, to treat a slave who had sustained a minor injury. Salina guessed that Ethan might have taken the opportunity to see Taylor Sue while he was there as well.

Jubilee set a breakfast plate in front of Ethan, when he finally arrived. He guzzled a glass of milk, and then he told Mamma and Salina what he'd learned on his trip to Centreville.

"There's been fighting at Manassas for the past two days—near Bull Run in just about the same place as they fought there last year," Ethan said. "The battle began on Friday afternoon and continued until dark. Jubal Early's regiment arrived late, but his men were fresh, and they charged gallantly with lowered bayonets into Major-General Kearny's division of Union troops. Reports say that the Yankees scattered in confusion, retreating in all directions."

"That explains why the artillery fire sounded so close again. Were many men hurt?" Mamma asked.

Ethan nodded. "I'm afraid the casualty lists were long, but Daddy's name was not among them."

"Thank God," Mamma sighed, her hand over her heart. "Who knows if he's even near Manassas? Your Daddy's orders take him all over the South, and sometimes east to Washington. But at least we can still consider him safe."

"How did the battle end?" Salina wanted to know. "Did we win?"

Ethan nodded and stated proudly, "The Union couldn't break Stonewall Jackson's line. Friday evening, the Union and Confederate soldiers occupied positions between Bull Run and the turnpike—the camps were within shooting distance of each other. Saturday afternoon, just yesterday, the Yankees attacked on a three-mile front from the Warrenton Turnpike all the way to Sudley Church."

"And speaking of church, if we don't depart now, we'll be late to Sunday service," Mamma scolded. "I'll check in on Jeremy right quick and we'll leave. Jubilee will watch over him while we're away."

"And on the way to church, you can tell us the rest of what happened," Salina insisted, hurrying off to find her bonnet.

On the road to the church, Ethan told how the Union troops had unknowingly marched to the place where General Lee had gathered the bulk of his artillery and how, when Stonewall Jackson's men had run out of ammunition, they hurled rocks from the railroad embankment at the enemy. They refused to give up.

"The Stone Bridge over Bull Run caused a bottleneck for Pope's retreating forces," Ethan added. "Hundreds of Union prisoners of war are now in Confederate hands. The fighting ceased when darkness fell and the rain came down."

"Sounds as though Pope's Army of the Potomac took quite a beating," Mamma murmured softly, shaking her head.

"They did," Ethan confirmed. "And so Pope ordered his regiments back to Centreville. Unfortunately, General Lee was unable to pursue the Yankee retreat."

"What are they trying to do?" Salina asked.

"Well," Ethan scratched his dark head, "as far as I can figure it, General Lee must want to cut off the Union retreat so that they can't return to the safety of the forts around Washington. Perhaps General Lee might make a strike into Northern territory. At present, Pope and the Army of the Potomac will have to make it his duty to prevent our Army of Northern Virginia from doing that."

"An invasion of the North would bring the war to *them*—see how *they* like fighting in their own land," Mamma said bitterly.

Ethan nodded. "If General Lee could cut off Pope's retreat to Washington, perhaps Abraham Lincoln would sue for peace."

"Do you really think that's possible?" asked Mamma.

Ethan shrugged. "I suppose it would depend on if surrounding Pope's Union army was successful."

"Then we'll pray that it is," Salina said simply.

Through the long church service, sitting on the hard wooden pews, Salina tried desperately to concentrate on what Reverend Yates was saying. Her mind, however, repeatedly wandered back to Shadowcreek, worrying about Jeremy and dwelling on the fighting. She prayed earnestly for both her Daddy and for Jeremy's speedy recovery.

The Reverend was reading from the book of Joshua, and Salina's attention focused abruptly when she heard him say: "The Lord spoke to Joshua saying, *'Have I not commanded thee? Be strong and of a good courage; do not be afraid, neither be thou dismayed: for the Lord thy God is with thee whithersoever thou goest.'*"

Salina looked down at her Bible and whispered to herself, "The Lord *my* God is with *me* wherever *I* go." She suddenly felt a profound sense of comfort from those words, and she committed them to memory to draw from at a later time of need.

Salina's favorite part of Sunday church meetings was the time of singing and worship. The congregation usually sang the hymns a cappella and slightly off-key. Salina lifted her sweet, melodic voice in praise and hope of her Heavenly Father. Mamma sang the harmony:

> *There's a land that is fairer than the day*
> *And by faith we shall see it afar*

While the Father waits over the way
To prepare us a dwelling place there.

In the sweet by and by
We shall meet on that beautiful shore.
In the sweet by and by
We shall meet on that beautiful shore.

We shall sing on that beautiful shore
The melodious songs of the blest
And our spirits shall sorrow no more
Nor sigh for the blessing of rest.

In the sweet by and by
We shall meet on that beautiful shore.
In the sweet by and by
We shall meet on that beautiful shore.

To our bountiful Father above
We will offer a tribute of praise
For the glorious gift of His love
And the blessings that hallow our days.

In the sweet by and by
We shall meet on that beautiful shore.
In the sweet by and by
We shall meet on that beautiful shore.

Ethan, sitting on the other side of Mamma, didn't sing at all. Even though he knew the psalms encouraged the saints to make a joyful *noise* unto the Lord, he was still self-conscious when his voice sometimes cracked without any warning.

Reverend Yates shook each person's hand after the service as they exited the stone church. When Salina's turn came to shake the Reverend's hand, she secretly passed the coded message she'd written into Reverend Yates' palm, just as Jeremy had instructed her to do.

Revered Yates quickly concealed his surprised expression and casually slipped the note into the pocket of his coat, to be read afterwards, in private. He nodded and smiled at Salina. "May the good Lord bless thee and keep thee, Miss."

"Thank you, Reverend Yates." Salina returned his smile. She continued down the stairs after Ethan and Mamma, doing her best to hide the excitement she felt at having made another contact with someone in the Network.

Cousin Lottie was standing nearby, glaring at Salina, but Salina didn't notice. All she could see was the gray-haired man in the black broadcloth suit—the same one she had seen at the Emporium in Fairfax. He was perched on a great black horse, only partially hidden in a grove of trees across from the church.

The black horse reared, breaking the brief eye contact that Salina momentarily shared with the old man. Salina watched him ride away, unnerved by the feeling that the old man might have recognized her. Had he been watching for her specifically?

Chapter Eleven

I'm telling you, Ethan, it was the *same* man." Salina was sitting at the foot of Jeremy's bed, Ethan was in the rocking chair. She turned to Jeremy. "When we were in Fairfax the other day to pick up some things for Dr. Phillips, we heard him discussing the fighting with the shopkeeper in the Emporium."

"I do remember now," Ethan nodded in recollection. "Tall, perhaps he stands at six feet, but there's a sense of command about him. He had gray hair, but to me he moved like a man much younger than he appeared to be, and he seemed almost familiar somehow..."

"But what was he doing at church?" Salina wanted to know. "We've known most of the people in Reverend Yates's congregation all our lives. We would have noticed a newcomer in the service. Why do you think he just rode off after he saw me standing there?"

Jeremy didn't like it a bit. If someone on the outside of the Network knew that Salina was a link, there could be good reason to worry about her. Without saying so, he silently wondered if it was the same man who was trailing him since Cedar Mountain. Captain Hastings had warned him that he might be followed. *Or could it be that he was watching Ethan and not Salina?*

"I want you to be especially careful, both of you," Jeremy finally said. "Ethan, you ride out quite frequently with all the medical emergencies that demand your attention. Watch yourself, and watch your back." He looked directly at Salina when he said, "Never can tell where the old man may show up next."

She nodded, understanding his implied warning to her as well.

Jeremy turned back to Ethan. "You said that Pope's Yankees were regrouping at Centreville. General Lee will come after him."

"I reckon so," Ethan agreed. "In fact, on the way home we saw several Confederate cavalry units near Chantilly."

"That's why we took the back roads home," Salina nodded.

Jeremy attempted to sit up in bed. Salina was immediately at his side. "It's too soon, Jeremy. You aren't healed properly yet," she protested, settling him once more beneath the patchwork quilt.

Ethan's voice was firm, "You're not going anywhere until you're healed up, Barnes. Get that through your thick skull right now." In truth, Jeremy was doing better than Ethan expected in such a short amount of time. Salina's prayers were being answered for that speedy recovery, but Jeremy wasn't fully well as of yet. He still needed more time and more rest.

Jeremy groaned. "You don't understand, Ethan."

"Oh, I understand, but I don't think you do. Each time you start thinking that you're going to be the brave warrior, you start moving and you risk reopening that wound. Keep still and give it a chance to mend," Ethan ordered. "The sooner you mend, the sooner you can leave. It's as simple as that."

"If only that were true," Jeremy muttered as Ethan rechecked the injury to his shoulder.

Jubilee appeared at the guest room door. "Massah Ethan, Missy Salina, y'all better cum downstairs a-right now. Miz Annelise got some company dat ain't entirely welcome here. Massah Barnes, ah knows ya be hurt'n all, but Miz Annelise, she thinks it'd be best if we hid ya fer a little time." She helped Jeremy from the bed, carefully putting a robe he'd borrowed from Ethan around his shoulders. "Ya jist lean on Jube if'n ya feel weak. Massah Ethan, Missy Salina, y'all best be hurryin' ta Miz Annelise—she needs ya. Git goin', da both o' ya."

Ethan went on ahead, but Salina hesitated. "Take Jeremy to my room, Jubilee. There's a place where he'll be well hidden..."

"Chile, ah been workin' in dis house a-fore ya was ever born. Ah knows every nook'n'cranny an ah knows what's ta be done. Git on now," Jubilee shooed Salina away.

The look of pain on Jeremy's face made Salina wince. "Jeremy..."

"Go on, Salina. Jubilee will take care of me just fine. You'll see." It took great effort on his part to smile his reassurance to her.

When he was sure Salina had gone downstairs, Jeremy asked Jubilee, "What's the trouble down there?"

"No trouble exceptin' dat yer uncle is downstairs," Jubilee muttered. "We cain't let him find ya here, and dat's fer certain."

"He wants to kill me," Jeremy stated simply.

Jubilee nodded. "Ah reckon dere ain't no plainer truth den dat, Massah Jeremy. No plainer truth."

Salina arrived on the veranda in time to stand with Mamma against the dismounting detachment of Yankee soldiers.

"Good afternoon, Mrs. Hastings," one of the blue-coated Yankees said as he boldly climbed the stairs and crossed the veranda. "Howdy, Ethan, Miss Salina."

Salina replied evenly, "Hello, Major Barnes." Inside, her stomach roiled and lurched as she faced Jeremy's Uncle John. His repulsive appearance combined with instances she knew from Jeremy's past colored her view of the Major. She remembered too clearly the time prior to Jeremy's departure for the West when she'd witnessed this man's vengeance in purpled bruises on Jeremy's arms and face.

Major Barnes tipped his cap, revealing his thinning, unkempt hair. "I understand my nephew has returned from California. He used to spend a fair amount of time here before he went away, and I was wondering if you might have seen him around in the last few days."

Ethan answered the Major's question, "He did come by, about a week ago. He seems to have done quite well for himself out West. When I see him again, shall I pass along your best regards, Major?"

Major Barnes thin lips pressed into a hard line, his dark eyes burned with hatred. "I'm determined to find that boy long before you have a chance to pass on my regards."

Salina stood next to Mamma and said nothing. She knew full well Ethan wouldn't volunteer any information that would endanger Jeremy.

Major Barnes spoke harshly, "Well, then I guess we'll get down to business. I'm here with my men," the Major motioned to the soldiers behind him, "to requisition supplies."

"What kind of supplies?" Mamma asked.

"Food mostly. My troops are hungry. We have orders to take whatever we need," Major Barnes told them in a menacing tone. "We were told to make this house our headquarters, but I managed to convince the Brigadier-General to change his mind. I suggested that either the Reid House—or even Carillon—might be in a more suitable location for our operations. I assured him that you'd be more than willing to supply food in return for being allowed to keep your house. And I'm sure there are other neighbors in the area who'll feel the same way." His heartless smile chilled Salina, cutting coldly to the bone in spite of the August heat.

Ethan visibly stiffened when Major Barnes made mention of Carillon, Taylor Sue's home. Salina knew he was doing everything in his power to restrain himself, and she knew how concerned he was over Taylor Sue's well-being.

"If you'll tell us what you'll be needing, I'll have the servants fetch whatever it is—providing we have what you're after," Mamma replied, raising her chin with Southern pride.

"We'll have no need of your slaves, Mrs. Hastings." John Barnes' eyes narrowed with controlled anger. "My men are very capable of carrying their own supplies. And you might as well know, ma'am, that President Lincoln intends to free your slaves. All of the Negroes in Southern bondage will be granted their freedom in due time."

"We'll see about that, now, won't we, Major Barnes?" Mamma replied gently, not responding to the underlying threat in the major's tone. "If your men will follow me, I'll see that they get whatever they need."

"Good. I'd hate to have to use force to obtain compliance with a military order." Major Barnes grinned wickedly, a trickle of tobacco juice in one corner of his mouth. "Say, Miss Salina," the Yankee Major turned to Hastings's daughter, "you haven't seen your pa riding around these parts lately, have you?"

"Major Barnes, I have not seen my Daddy in some time, but I'm not sure I would tell you, even if I had," Salina remarked softly.

"Honest little thing, ain't ya?" John Barnes chortled. "That's all right, you don't have to tell me anything. One day we'll find Captain Hastings, and then..."

"He's fighting for Virginia's honor," Ethan interrupted. "Perhaps with Lee's troops even now."

A cold gleam hardened Major Barnes's eyes. "Don't matter where he is, boy. I'm just waiting until that traitor spy makes one mistake. Then he's ours, and you can rest assured that we'll track him down."

Mamma went pale. Salina swallowed hard. She was sure he was bluffing, baiting them to get a reaction, and she prayed Ethan would keep still.

But Ethan's eyes shone with indignant fire, and between clenched teeth he said, "At least he's honorably fulfilling his duty to the South, which is more than I can say for you, Major."

Salina yelped when Ethan's head snapped back from the force of the Major's heavy blow. The Major poked his gloved finger into Ethan's chest. "You'd do well, *boy*, to keep a civil tongue in your head. I could have you arrested, you know, because we figure none of you here would be above sheltering Rebel scum. However, I'm in a generous mood, so my men are here only to take what we need and be quick about it," Major Barnes ground out between his tobacco-stained teeth.

Ethan rubbed his jaw, biting back any additional comments, but that didn't prevent him from leveling an icy glare back at the Major.

Mamma stepped in front of Ethan and looked up at John Barnes. "Please, take whatever you need."

In thirty minutes' time, the Union soldiers confiscated nearly two-thirds of the Hastings' carefully guarded food supply, including flour, molasses, dried fruits, and canned meats. But they didn't stop at food. They also took pillows, blankets, and over half of their store of kerosene oil and candles.

Salina saw one Yankee carrying the quilt from her bed that she'd made with Mamma's and Jubilee's help. As the soldier tied the patchwork spread to the back of his saddle, she thought, *Celeste!...and Jeremy...*

Tears stung Salina's eyes, and Mamma whispered, "We'll make another to replace it."

Salina shook her head, shaking Mamma's hand from her arm. She ran up the stairs to her room and didn't stop to breathe until she lifted the top of the window seat and found the French china doll in the chest precisely where she'd left it. She sighed with great relief, sitting down heavily on the window seat, but she was shaking uncontrollably.

She glanced quickly at the tapestry hanging on the wall. The panel to the secret passageway was well concealed, so she had little doubt that Jeremy was still safely hidden on the other side. She looked around the room and saw that everything else was undisturbed, just the way she'd left it. The only thing that Yankee had taken was the quilt, and she fervently thanked God for that.

Outside on the veranda, Major Barnes told Mamma, "You've been the picture of Southern hospitality, Mrs. Hastings. We'll be back if we need horses."

"If you can find any," Mamma muttered under her breath. She gripped Ethan's hand so tightly, her knuckles turned white, but she willed him not to say anything else to the enemy officer.

"You behave yourself, *boy*, and I won't have to take you away from your sweet mamma and your precious little sister," Major Barnes said sarcastically. He patted Ethan's throbbing cheek none too gently. The gesture was intended to inflict more hurt, but Ethan's bruised pride stung far worse than the welt on his face did.

Ethan was so angry he could have spit in the Major's pock-marked face, but instead he clenched his jaw tightly and remained furiously silent.

In the distance, the sounds of skirmish echoed in the air. Major Barnes quickly mounted and ordered his men to ride in the direction the shots came from.

"The armies must be close by," Mamma shuddered. "I hope and pray they aren't heading this way..." She hugged Ethan, forcing back tears. "Let's find your sister and get busy. There's work to be done."

☆☆☆☆☆☆☆

When she was certain that the Yankees had gone, Mamma had Ethan, Peter Tom, and Cromwell begin taking inventory of the remaining food and supplies. Then she went upstairs to find Salina and to see if Jeremy was settled back in the guest room.

Mamma heard Salina's muffled sobs before she reached the room where Jeremy Barnes lay propped up against the headboard with pillows. "I w-was afraid, J-Jeremy. R-really and t-truly sc-scared..." she cried softly. "I g-guess I'm n-not v-very st-strong, and-and I d-don't know if I c-can b-be..."

"Sssshhh." Jeremy wiped her tears with his thumb. He glanced up and saw Mamma in the doorway. "Everything's going to be fine, Salina. Uncle John didn't find me, so there's no need to fret so." He squeezed her hand reassuringly.

"Salina, sweetheart, are you all right?" Mamma touched her shoulder.

Salina straightened up, wondering how much of the discussion with Jeremy Mamma might have heard. She wiped her eyes with the back of her hand. "Is there s-something that y-you w-want m-me t-to d-do, M-Mamma?" she sniffled.

"Ethan is working with Peter Tom and Cromwell. Jubilee has been helping me in the pantry," Mamma said. "You ran off, and I was worried about you."

"Uncle John frightened her," Jeremy said to Mamma. "He's mean enough to frighten just about anyone."

"Yes, well, we are certainly thankful that he didn't take Ethan away. For a minute there, I thought he was really going to," Mamma admitted. "But he didn't, and we have to go on from here. We'll definitely have to be more careful while you're with us, Jeremy. I suppose Salina told you that he was looking for you."

"Yes, Salina told me about it. Here's hoping Captain Hastings is well away from here. Uncle John believes in the philosophy of 'shoot now, ask questions later.' As soon as I am able, I'll be moving on. I refuse to stay any longer than I must if I am endangering you for helping me," Jeremy stated.

"You're not leaving until those wounds are healed, Jeremy Barnes, and I'll not have it otherwise," Mamma countered.

Ethan came up to Jeremy's room. He handed Mamma a list of what was left after the Yankee raid. "Well," Mamma said, trying her best to sound encouraging, "it's not much, but I'm certain we'll make due. The Lord is faithful, and He will provide." She hoped that outwardly she appeared strong. It would never do to have them know that on the inside she was shaking like a leaf yet seething with anger at the same time. "Let's thank the Lord that they took only what they did and didn't take over our home."

Salina admired Mamma's continued faith. She desired that one day her own faith would be as deep and as strong. In the past few weeks she'd prayed more than she ever had before, but she was certain that everyone prayed more than they usually might due to the war. Salina wanted to rely on God to lead and protect her at all times, the good and the bad. In her own strength, she was utterly weak and defenseless, but in Christ Jesus was salvation and strength, and she had nothing to fear.

More and more, Salina drew comfort and reassurance in some of the psalms she read. That Sunday evening, after their small supper, Salina sat with Jeremy and read aloud to him:

> *The Lord also will be a refuge*
> *for the oppressed,*
> *A refuge in times of trouble.*
> *And those who know Your name*
> *will put their trust in You;*
> *For You, Lord, have not*
> *forsaken those who seek you.*

"Have you ever felt forsaken, Salina?" Jeremy asked quietly.

"No," Salina answered. "I reckon I never have."

Jeremy sighed heavily. "I forget that you're not much more than a child. How could you?"

Salina's green-eyed glance met Jeremy's blue one. She felt her temper flaring at the way he was taunting her. "Have you ever felt forsaken?" she asked in return.

"Yes," Jeremy replied somberly, the teasing gone. "When my father died and my mother left me here in Virginia while she returned to England, I felt forsaken. And when the court granted Uncle John my guardianship until my eighteenth year, I felt like I'd been forsaken. And when I was lying on the roadside after the skirmishing at Groveton, I felt forsaken then, too. I've survived, though, to live and learn my lessons through these trials. Looking back, I can see that God has been faithful in keeping His promise that He would never leave me or forsake me. And He keeps reminding me that He loves me, even through these dark times."

"Everyone has dark times," Salina said. "Trials and tribulations supposedly build character in each of us."

Jeremy nodded. "When I feel lost and there are no immediate answers to any of my prayers, sometimes I think that maybe God can't hear me. But then something usually happens to reassure me that He is always listening, and He knows my mind, my heart, and my needs even before I pray to Him. He hears my cries, and He comforts me in my weaknesses. I am weak, but He is strong. I lean on Him, and you can, too. Earlier you were saying that you didn't think you could be strong. You will be, because I believe God supplies us with the strength we need to fulfill the tasks He sets before us. If we let Him lead us, He will. It's just when we think we can do it on our own that we fail. Keep your eyes on Jesus, Salina, and He'll give you the strength to carry on."

"The Lord is our strength and our salvation," Salina quoted. *"Whom then shall we fear?"*

"I can't imagine *not* trusting God to work through me. When I think that working for the Network could mean signing my own death warrant, I certainly feel better knowing where I'll wind up if I should be killed on an assignment or in a battle."

"Don't talk of battles and dying. I don't want to think of it," Salina said.

"But Salina, it's reality. It's part of our lives in this day and age. It might not be easy, but it's something we must learn to deal with," Jeremy said brusquely. "If there's a lesson I've learned from these wounds of mine, it's that I'm very human, and that war is not a grand adventure—it's ugly, and it kills."

"I never said it was pretty." Salina's feathers were a little ruffled. She didn't care for the way Jeremy implied that she didn't understand the consequences of the fighting. "I'm a little bit more aware of life and how things are than you might think, Jeremy Barnes. I know full well that battles are dangerous and they result in thousands of wounded and dead. I know, too, that if I am discovered as a link to the Network, my own life could be at risk. My daddy thinks I'm capable enough to keep some very big secrets, and you have said you trust me, so there's no call for you to talk to me as though I can't comprehend the situation at hand!"

She abruptly turned and left the room, failing to catch a glimpse of the grin that parted Jeremy's lips or hearing the low chuckle that rumbled in his throat. He had the distinct impression that if he weren't a recovering invalid, she just might have been tempted to throw a pillow at him!

Chapter Twelve

$\mathcal{M}$amma tossed and turned, unable to sleep. The thunder and lightning of a summer storm kept pace with her restless emotions. She thought about Major Barnes and his threats to find the Captain, but even more than that, she thought of Salina and the way she'd gone to Jeremy Barnes for comfort. That part bothered her, making her feel a little uneasy and perhaps a bit jealous.

Ever since the day she was born, Salina had been the proverbial apple of her daddy's eye. While the Captain was off fighting, it had afforded mother and daughter the opportunity to grow closer. Mamma had been pleased at the prospect. While Salina without a doubt took after her father, she had things deep inside that favored her Mamma's nature as well, and Mamma wanted to nurture those traits. The idea that Jeremy might come between the two of them troubled Mamma. She was reminded that one day Salina would be all grown up and would rely on a husband rather than her family. Salina was certainly considered old enough to be married, and it was plain as day that

110

Jeremy Barnes was the one she had her eye on. Mamma prayed fervently that Salina might not have dreamed that far into the future as yet.

The grandfather clock downstairs chimed eleven times. Mamma went to Salina's room. She held her candle up, checking to see if by chance Salina was still awake. The four poster bed was empty. "Sweetheart?"

"I'm over here, Mamma," Salina whispered. She sat perched on the edge of the window seat, staring off into the shadowy orchard. "Blow out the candle, Mamma. I don't want them to see us."

"Them? Who?" Mamma hurriedly extinguished the flickering orange flame. "Salina, who is out there?"

"They must be some scouts—three or four Yankees—camped right over there, in the orchard," Salina replied. "See their fire?"

Mamma could indeed see the leaping flames and the gray smoke rising against the otherwise black night sky. "What do you suppose they're doing there?"

Salina shrugged her shoulders. "I reckon they're trying to find a good, safe retreat back to Washington. I wonder if they are Major Barnes's men—or some of the soldiers involved in the skirmishing we heard a few hours ago. They don't seem to be overly concerned about keeping their whereabouts a secret."

"I should say not if they're burning such a conspicuous camp-fire," Mamma agreed.

Salina nodded. "And, if you listen closely, you can hear them singing. I think one of them has a Jew's harp."

Mamma was still, and then she could hear the Yankees singing and the twanging notes of a Jew's harp accompanying them:

> *Oh, we'll rally 'round the flag, boys,*
> *we'll rally once again,*
> *Shouting the battle cry of freedom;*
> *We will rally from the hillside,*
> *we'll gather from the plain,*
> *Shouting the battle cry of freedom.*
>
> *The Union forever, Hurrah, boys, hurrah!*
> *Down with the Traitor, Up with the Star;*
> *While we rally 'round the flag, boys, rally once again,*
> *Shouting the battle cry of freedom.*

"Jaunty little tune for soldiers so recently defeated near Manassas, don't you think?" Mamma whispered the question.

Salina only nodded, her eyes focused on a movement she detected in the shadows near the barn.

A white flash of lightning illuminated the yard for a split second, and Salina drew in a quick breath. Near the corner of the barn stood the old man from Fairfax. He wasn't dressed in the black suit she'd seen him in before. This time he wore a blue cape, to protect him from the sudden downpour of rain, and a blue hat with a curled plume sagging on its brim. The old man was a *Yankee!*

Salina sat back from the window. "He's been watching the house," she murmured. "I wonder what he could want with us."

"Darling, close that window before you catch your death of cold," Mamma ordered softly as the rain continued to come cascading down.

Salina obeyed, lowering the window sash with one hand. Mamma was mildly shocked to see a pistol in Salina's other hand.

"So, the boys truly have been teaching you how to shoot," Mamma surmised, still not pleased by the knowledge that her daughter was becoming proficient in the use of firearms.

"Yes," Salina nodded. "I told you that they were. They tell me I'm getting on quite nicely with my target practice."

"Do you honestly think you could have hit the barn from *here*?" asked Mamma.

"I *could* have hit him," Salina nodded, "even if he'd been another twenty paces further away."

"Salina! Proper young ladies *do not* go around sniping at Yankee soldiers!" Mamma objected.

"But, Mamma, if he had made even the slightest move on this house, I might have been obliged to fire a warning shot at him," Salina said. "He's the enemy."

Mamma reached for Salina's pistol. "Salina, sweetheart, guns are not playthings. They're dangerous."

"It's a method of protection," Salina said, quietly, "to be used *only* in self-defense. I'm not a child, Mamma!"

Tears collected in Mamma's eyes. "Oh, darling, this is not what I came in here to talk to you about. I came in here because..."

"Because why?" Salina asked.

"Because you're growing away from me, and I don't want us to drift apart," Mamma said sadly. "I enjoy sharing things with you and talking to you, and since Jeremy Barnes has returned, you've spent more time with him than you have me. I want us to always be close,

Salina. I love you very much and I'm not ready to share you with anyone else."

"I love you, too, Mamma," Salina laid her head on Mamma's shoulder. "What do you mean when you say you're not ready to share me with anyone?"

"Sweetheart, I've seen you and Jeremy together. It's very obvious that you care for him, and that he in turn cares for you—but you're both young. I wouldn't want anything to happen that would cause you to be unhappy or feel hurt."

"Are you implying that I care for him too much?" Salina asked.

"I'm just saying be careful. Emotions and feelings are tender things. Sometimes they can get trampled on by someone without their meaning to or even knowing about it," Mamma cautioned. "Loving a man can make you strong, or it can make you weak. It all depends on the man, I would suppose..."

"Jeremy Barnes is a good man," Salina said quickly.

"Yes, I agree," Mamma nodded, though reluctantly. "Please, Salina, all I ask is that you think about what I've said. I only want the best for you, my darling, in its proper time and season."

Another flash of lightning showed Salina that the old man had vacated his post near the barn. "He's gone now," she whispered and turned to Mamma again.

"Salina..." Mamma whispered as her eyelashes swept down over her pale cheeks, and she fainted again.

"Mamma!" Salina cradled her in her arms. "Jubilee! Jubilee, come quick!"

Jubilee arrived at the same time Ethan burst into her room. He carried Mamma to her room, and as Jubilee was settling her into bed, she came to.

"I'm all right now," Mamma insisted, her hand shielding her eyes from the kerosene lamp light.

Ethan was relieved to see there was some color back in her cheeks. "This is not going to be an easy pregnancy for you, is it?"

"Jubilee can take care of me, Ethan. She always has. I suppose I fainted because so much has happened today—Major Barnes coming here this afternoon, seeing Yankees camped so close by, knowing that you're still teaching your sister how to be a sharpshooter. Well, I declare it makes me dizzy just thinking about it all. I'll be fine, really."

"I want you to stay in bed and rest, Mamma. Tomorrow, I want you to just take it easy," Ethan said in his most doctor-sounding voice. "Salina and I can run the estate for a day without you."

"I can't stay in bed, Ethan. There's going to be a Women's Assistance Guild meeting here in the morning," Mamma reminded him. "I won't do anything but sit and sew, I promise."

"You did tell Daddy about the baby when he was here, didn't you?" Salina asked.

Mamma smiled weakly. "Yes. He was very happy, and he said he'd try not to worry too much, but he probably wouldn't be able to help himself." She reached for Salina's hand. "Darling, that man you saw from your bedroom window—have you seen him before?"

Salina nodded affirmatively.

"When Daddy was here," Mamma sighed, "he warned me that there would be people who might be trying to track him down."

"Like Major Barnes," Salina said.

"Perhaps," Mamma agreed. "But he mentioned another name to me—a certain Yankee Captain by the name of Duncan Grant. You might remember him. He was Daddy's good friend—a classmate from West Point. They even fought together in Mexico."

"I remember him," Ethan recalled. "He'd come visit from time to time. But the last time he came to Shadowcreek must be at least five years ago."

Salina nodded. She, too, remembered Daddy's friend Duncan. He was from Pennsylvania. His family had a farm and business there in a town called Gettysburg. He was a kind man, Salina recalled, and she smiled thinking of him giving piggyback rides and playing games with her and Ethan. Duncan could play a harmonica sweetly and dance all night. He'd always been a welcomed, if rare, guest at Shadowcreek, and his visits passed by all too quickly.

"The first time I ever laid eyes on him, Duncan Grant was asking me to dance at the Officer's Ball following the West Point graduation ceremonies," Mamma said. "And I still believe to this day that he was out to deliberately provoke your daddy. Odd, but I seem to recollect your daddy proposing to me that very night—not long after I'd been dancing with Duncan, as a matter of fact..."

"Do you think it was him by the barn?" Salina interrupted.

"Well, actually, I'm not quite sure," Mamma said with uncertainty in her voice. "I didn't get a clear look at his face. But that man looked... well, I know that Duncan's not nearly *that* old."

"What if he wore a disguise," Salina wondered aloud. "Ethan, the other day you said he didn't appear to be as old as he looked."

Mamma rubbed her arms to ward away a sudden chill. She whispered, "Salina, as much as I hate that Daddy has to be away, I wish there was a way to tell him *not* to come home just now."

"I think I might know of a way to get a message to him," Salina said cautiously. "I've *heard* that messages can get passed through the lines of communication... providing one knows where to deliver the message."

"I reckon Jeremy Barnes might have such contacts," Mamma slowly said. "Please, would you ask him?"

Salina smiled. "I'll see to it that a message gets conveyed to Daddy. Trust me, Mamma."

☆☆☆☆☆☆☆☆

"Missy Salina, Missy Salina, open dose tired old eyes, chile. Come on, now. Ya gots ta wake on up. Da Rev'ren, he be needin' ta speak wid ya. Come on, Missy Salina." Jubilee shook Salina's shoulder until Salina opened and rubbed her tired eyes. She reluctantly followed Jubilee to the cellar, where Reverend Yates was waiting for her.

The Reverend begged her pardon. "My apologies for disturbing you at this time of night, Miss Salina. However, I have just received a response to your message."

"Jeremy is somewhat better, but he's still not fully healed," Salina yawned. "I'm not convinced he should ride."

"I think I have found an alternative route for delivery," Reverend Yates assured her. I'll need you to let me handle it because we don't want the courier to know of your involvement."

"What do you have in mind?" Salina asked.

"I want to send your manservant, Peter Tom, to Stonewall Jackson with this." The Reverend pulled a packet from the inner breast pocket of his coat. "Your father forwarded this to us from his current location. Inside are details of Yankee troop positions, routes of repaired railroads, and some intercepted telegraph communications between Washington and General Pope. These documents, in addition to the food, clothing, and ammunition your message indicated, all must be delivered to Stonewall Jackson—tonight. Peter Tom will know where to find him once I read the enclosed note to him."

"But Peter Tom already knows how to read. Mamma taught all our servants to read and write," Salina confided.

"It would be wise if you didn't let that become common knowledge, Miss Salina. Lots of Southerners would be mighty displeased because they believe it's a waste of time trying to educate the Negroes.

It's also against the law," the Reverend reminded her.

"What do you think, Reverend Yates?" asked Salina. "Do you think it's a waste of time to educate the slaves?"

"No, I don't think it's a waste of time. I believe that they are human beings of God's creation, just as we are, and should be treated as such. I am opposed to slavery. However, I'm not about to stand by idle, watching as the Yankees insist on turning Virginia into a battleground. No, I don't like this war one bit." The Reverend shook his balding head.

"Is that why you joined the Network?" Salina asked.

"Yes." Reverend Yates pushed his wire-rimmed glasses up to prevent their sliding down his nose. "Two wrongs don't make a right, and I will not bear arms, but I'd be disloyal if I did nothing to defend my homeland, Virginia. Aside from my personal feeling, however, your father happens to be a *very* convincing gentleman. He didn't *exactly* twist my arm, but he's a very persuasive fellow, Captain Hastings is."

Salina smiled. She knew quite well that her daddy had a certain knack about getting people to do precisely what he wanted them to do. "When he asked me if I knew how to keep a secret, I had no idea that he would trust me with so much."

"Ah, but you're the trustworthy sort, Miss Salina, if you'll permit me to say so. As it says in the gospels: to those who are faithful over the little things, they will also be given responsibility over much bigger things—that's a Yates paraphrase," the Reverend winked. "But the principle is the same."

Again Salina smiled. "Daddy says I'm good cover. You must be, too."

"The Yankees don't often suspect folk like us," Reverend Yates grinned. "I'll admit I was indeed surprised to receive a message from you. I'd never have imagined...but let's get back to the business at hand. With Jeremy unable to participate at present, we have little choice but to rely on Peter Tom to make the delivery. He's carried messages for your father before; besides, we can't risk getting Ethan tangled up in this—or expose you. And in the meantime, pass a word of caution along to Jeremy. Tell him that the Union's scout, Captain Duncan Grant, has been reassigned duty in Washington, but he has left his lieutenant to keep an eye on the area. The fellow's name is Lance Colby, I'm told."

"Why would Duncan Grant be following Jeremy? I thought he was after my daddy." Salina's eyebrows bunched together.

Reverend Yates nodded. "Oh, he is. And for a time, he had Ethan under surveillance, but that proved fruitless. By deduction, he's focused now on Jeremy, and I suspect Duncan Grant is just hoping that Jeremy might lead him to Captain Hastings. Captain Grant trailed Jeremy from Groveton to Fairfax to here at Shadowcreek. Network sources say that he's been disguised as an old man, but that one is as full of juice as they come. He has a familiarity with this area."

Salina blinked, letting his words sink in. "Yes, he would since he's been here before. I have seen Duncan Grant disguised as an old man, Reverend. First at the Emporium in Fairfax, then at church, and earlier tonight he was spying on our main house from the barnyard."

Reverend Yates squeezed Salina's shoulder. "You must be very, *very* careful. Captain Grant is one of the best agents the Union has. Very much your father's equal, if the truth be known."

"They were friends once, my daddy and Captain Grant," Salina said, finding it difficult to accept that the war had severed the relationship between the men.

"Yes, I've heard that. This war has torn families as well as friendships apart at the seams," Reverend Yates said, shaking his head sadly. "All I can say to you, Miss Salina, is that Jeremy should be away as soon as he's able. That should draw Lieutenant Colby away from Shadowcreek. Tell Jeremy to go back to Tabitha Wheeler's boarding house. She'll see that he's taken care of. And you watch your step, Miss Salina. We can't allow Duncan Grant to become suspicious of your part in the Network. Now that you've become involved, you're a valuable link to us."

"I'll be careful," Salina promised. "I'll be sure to tell Jeremy what you've said, and we'll go on from there."

"Good girl," the Reverend nodded. "I want you to know that you may call on me for any reason if you should have a need to."

"Thank you, Reverend," Salina replied.

"Next time I speak to your father, I'll be sure to commend him on the bravery of his daughter. Have you a message you would like sent to him?" Reverend Yates asked.

"Please," Salina nodded. "Just tell him to stay put and not come to Shadowcreek until things settle down here. If Jeremy leaves, and it is safe, then Daddy could come home—but only if he should absolutely need to."

"I'll tell him," Reverend Yates assured her. "I'll be in touch with you very soon."

"I'll be waiting," Salina replied. "And you'll go ahead with the mission to Stonewall Jackson?"

The Reverend nodded, "Peter Tom will find this packet in a hollow oak near Carillon's Mill. Inside are the documents and the instructions as to where to find General Jackson. It's imperative that he reach the General's headquarters before dawn. Don't you worry about a thing, Salina. I'll take care of it from my end and send word to you of the outcome." Reverend Yates slipped out into the darkness and the rain.

Salina had to be satisfied with that and returned to her room. A sense of pride filled her again just knowing that she was getting away with things no one would ever dream of. A smile lit her face but faded when Jeremy appeared at her doorway. "You and I have got to have a little talk."

☆☆☆☆☆☆☆

Captain Duncan Grant secured his gray-haired wig and adjusted the fake whiskers that concealed his handsome face. He was angry. How was it that Garrett Hastings kept getting his hands on vital information? The man seemed to be *everywhere* these days—everywhere, yet nowhere to be found. Captain Grant debated whether to confiscate the documents or to let them pass to the Confederates at Pleasant Valley. Finally, he made up his mind.

"We can't afford to let the Rebs have the upper hand here," Captain Grant exchanged falsified documents for the real ones and kept the official papers instead. "I want you to take the packet to Stonewall Jackson, just like you're being asked to do," he said quietly to the freeman at his side. "However, I'll keep the real information. The Rebs won't know the documents are fakes until it's too late to do anything about it. And what they don't know right now can't hurt them."

"No, suh, t'won't hurt a bit," the black man nodded.

"And you'll report back to me with Confederate troop positions," Captain Grant commanded.

Peter Tom nodded. "Yas, suh. Caps?"

"Yes?" Duncan queried.

"Well, suh, ah been watchin' dat Hastings boy. Seems he ain't got no part o' it. He jist works fer da doc, dat's all. It's dat Barnes boy who be in it up ta his neck. What 'bout him, Caps?"

"He's out of commission with his injuries for awhile, I think, but you're right. I have reason to believe it's Barnes who's working with Captain Hastings, not Ethan after all. I want you to keep an eye on Barnes if you can." Duncan Grant studied his reflection in a small looking glass. Satisfied that his disguise was securely in place, he said, "Let's get going. I'll ride with you as far as the turnpike. I've received new orders to report back to my office at the War Department in Washington. Somehow, while I'm there, I've got to convince my commanding officer that even though Hastings isn't here, there is certainly more than meets the eye. I intend to be the one to find out—before Major John Barnes can carry out his demented threats of revenge against his nephew. Jeremy could be valuable to us, especially if we can get him to lead us to Hastings. Tell Colby that, would you?"

"Yas, suh, Caps. Will do." Peter Tom tipped his cap. He mounted an old mare and trotted off in the direction of Pleasant Valley and Stonewall Jackson's encampment.

☆☆☆☆☆☆☆

"By staying here, I'm only putting you and your family in danger. If that old man—Captain Grant—is really after me, his search will ultimately lead him to you, Salina. You've got to understand that is why I have to go." Jeremy's blue eyes were filled with concern for her. "You said Stonewall Jackson is at Pleasant Valley?"

"That's what Reverend Yates told me, but you're not completely well," Salina protested. "You haven't given yourself enough time to rest or get your strength back. What if you start bleeding again?"

"I'll survive. I'll go stay with Tabitha. She'll hide me and let me rest there at the boarding house," Jeremy said, "just as soon as I finish with the business at hand. Did you read those documents?"

Salina nodded silently. She had read the documents before Reverend Yates took them away to be hidden in the hollow oak tree. Salina bit her tongue to keep from telling Jeremy how much she wanted him to stay, or how frightened she was that he'd be captured and sent to a Yankee prison.

"Look at me," Jeremy ordered softly.

Her eyes held fast to his intense gaze.

"It's not forever," he whispered. "I'll be back."

"My daddy always says the same thing," she said stoically. "He's never lied to me yet."

"Have I lied to you since we started working together?" he asked her.

"No," Salina replied.

"If everything works out, I'll be back in a few days," Jeremy told her. "If not..."

"It will work out. You'll be safe at Tabitha's boarding house,"

Salina said determinedly. "You just have to be careful."

Jeremy smiled. "I will. I'll be in touch very soon. I'll send you a message through the Network. You'll see." He carefully gathered her into his strong arms and hugged her, then he roughly set her away from him. "You watch yourself, little lady. I expect you to be here when I get back."

"I'm not the one who's going anywhere," she murmured.

Jeremy lowered his head and lightly kissed Salina's cheek just next to her mouth. "Wait for me, Salina. I will be back."

Jubilee caught Jeremy leaving Salina's room. "It jist ain't fittin' all dis sneakin' around in da halls. Whatya be doin' tippy-toein' outta Miss Salina's room fer?" she voiced her displeasure. "Ya gots a room o'yer own, an' ya should be dere sleepin' dis time o' night!"

Jeremy merely chuckled and kept walking down the hall.

"Where do ya think yer goin' anyhow?" Jubilee wanted to know.

"I'm leaving, Jubilee. You won't have to worry about me tippy-toein' out of Miss Salina's room anymore. Just do me a favor and keep it between us. Ethan'll light into me something fierce if he finds out."

"Humph!" Jubilee concealed her smile. "Yas, Massah Ethan'd take it up wid ya, an' Miz Annelise probably cum afta ya wid a switch!" Jubilee went into Salina's room mumbling, "It jist ain' fittin'—nope, it jist ain't."

"He just came to tell me goodbye, Jubilee," Salina tried to explain.

"An' yer goin' ta miss him," Jubilee stated. She saw Salina nod, and then Jubilee put her arms around Salina in an effort to comfort her. "Chile, ya gots ta listen ta Jube. Dat boy'll be back here jist as soon as he kin be."

"What makes you so sure of that?" Salina's voice wavered slightly.

Jubilee smiled and stroked Salina's dark hair. "Land sakes, Missy, ah knows he be a-cumin' back cuz dis be where ya ere. He'll be back."

"Oh, I do hope you're right," Jubilee," Salina admitted. "I shouldn't care about him the way I do, but I can't help it."

Jubilee said with mock sternness, "Ya git on back ta sleep now. Jist a few hours an' company'll be arrivin'. Ah won't say nothin' ta Miz Annelise 'bout dis, but ah wants ya sleepin' jist like dat!" Jubilee snapped her fingers.

"Thank you, Jubilee. I'll be ready by the time the ladies arrive for the Women's Assistance Guild meeting, never fear."

"Humph!" Jubilee tucked Salina in, and then she sat on the edge of the bed, softly singing Salina to sleep.

Chapter Thirteen

*D*awn on the first morning of the month of September was a beautiful one. Rain had come down most of the previous night, but the morning sun shone brightly over the area surrounding Chantilly. By nine-thirty, however, the clouds once more gathered menacingly, and the sky was turned from bright, pale blue to heavy, leaden gray.

The ladies were due to arrive within the next quarter of an hour. Salina was up early in order to help Jubilee prepare for their guests while Mamma slept late. Neither mentioned Salina's nocturnal adventures of the night before.

Ethan was freshly bathed and had on clean trousers and a starched white shirt under his vest. His dark hair was damp and curling in ringlets at the base of his neck and around his ears.

"Expecting someone?" Salina couldn't pass up the opportunity to tease Ethan. "Did I forget to mention that Taylor Sue isn't coming today?"

"Hush up, Salina," Ethan ordered gruffly. "Just help me tie this cravat."

"Please?" Salina asked saucily.

"Please." Ethan rolled his eyes. "Would you mind hurrying a bit? Their carriage should be here any minute."

Salina slowly and deliberately knotted Ethan's tie. "Are you going to give her the ring today?"

"None of your business, Miss Nosy," Ethan snapped.

"Why are you getting so nervous? The Careys will all be here, all afternoon. They're bringing bandages to be rolled and uniforms to be mended with them. You know how Mrs. Carey is always recruiting volunteers to help the Women's Assistance Guild for the war effort. If you hang around the parlour long enough, maybe she'll have you darning and knitting socks with the rest of us."

"Salina, I need your help," Ethan admitted. "Just help me get a few minutes alone with Taylor Sue. Please, I'm begging you. I know you can find some excuse, some way to get her out from under the watchful eyes of Mrs. Carey and Mamma. Will you do that for me?"

Salina grinned. "For you, Ethan, I'll see what I can do."

Ethan hugged his little sister. "You're an angel, Salina."

That made her laugh. "No, I don't think so. It's just that I know the two of you haven't had much time alone together since you asked Taylor Sue to be your wife. I want the two of you to have a chance to talk, so you can decide *when* this joyous event will be taking place. I truly like the happily-ever-after stories, Ethan."

"So you'll work on it?" Ethan wanted to be sure.

"You'll have to trust me on this one, Ethan," Salina giggled. "I'll do my very best."

Ethan tugged playfully at one of her curls, but his voice was somber. "You know, Salina, I'd trust you with my life."

"I think it's supposed to be the other way around, isn't it? The little sister looking up to the older brother?" Salina countered.

Ethan's expression was grave. "You seem to be the strong one, Salina."

"I don't think so," Salina argued. "There are times when I fall apart at the silliest little things."

"And then there are times when you won't shed a tear," Ethan commented. "Like this morning, for instance. You can't honestly tell me that you weren't disappointed to learn that Jeremy left sometime last night leaving only a note in farewell."

Salina shrugged instead of answering.

Ethan watched her eyes, but he couldn't read anything in her expression. "The strength I see in you encourages me and other people around you, too. It's a rare trait, Salina. Mamma is strong, too. I believe it's a gift—one good to have in times like these."

"I think you may be right about that," Salina nodded in agreement.

Taylor Sue, her younger sister Jennilee, and Mrs. Carey arrived at Shadowcreek nearly an hour late. Mrs. Carey appeared distraught while Peter Tom, recently returned from General Jackson's encampment, helped her from the fancy black buggy.

"Oh, Annelise, I do apologize, but the troops! They were everywhere, marching right along," Mrs. Carey told Mamma. "The Yankee soldiers who have commandeered our house seem to be pleasant enough. They even posted a guard for us so that nothing would be unnecessarily damaged."

"Are you sure it's wise to leave Carillon for the entire afternoon, with just the Yankees there?" Mamma was concerned.

"We three were getting cabin fever," Mrs. Carey declared. "The Colonel assured me that nothing would happen in our absence today."

"Whose troops were on the turnpike?" asked Salina.

"They were Stonewall Jackson's troops," Jennilee, who was fourteen and shared her sister's freckles, answered. "I asked one of them where they were going, but he said he didn't rightly know. He was just a-marchin' along and following the cadence, like the rest of the column. I asked him if he'd ever met Papa, but he said he hadn't, and he kept going."

"Those poor men," Taylor Sue added. "They looked so hungry and weary, yet they marched without complaint. I wish there was more that we could do for those brave soldiers in gray."

"Well," Mamma took a peek inside one of the boxes, "it looks as though you've brought enough bandages and sewing for the entire Army of Northern Virginia. Certainly there's enough to keep us busy for quite some time."

"And we shouldn't lose a minute," Mrs. Carey nodded decisively. "I believe we should commence work immediately. The other ladies will join us when they arrive. Although, I do wonder if all this military activity has made them decide to stay at home. Reverend Yates told me that he will take whatever we have accomplished to Willow Springs tomorrow for the wounded who are still being cared for there since the battle at Manassas."

Aunt Priscilla and Cousin Lottie Armstrong arrived, followed by Mrs. Joetta Warner. Mary Edith, who was now Mrs. Baxter, came over with Mrs. Yates, but that was all. Evidently the others had remained at their homes, just as Mrs. Carey suspected they might.

Salina refrained from bursting out in giggles each time Ethan invented an excuse to enter the parlour with hopes of speaking to Taylor Sue. Mamma and Salina exchanged knowing glances as Taylor Sue flushed scarlet each time Ethan cast a sheepish grin her way.

During the noontime meal, Salina sat between Mamma and Joetta Warner. Joetta told them that her husband, Hank, had finally sent for her and their four-year-old son, Austin. "Hank has worked in a prosperous silver mine for nearly a year, and now he's got a foreman's job there. The pay is good, and he's having a house built for us in Virginia City. It looks like Austin and I will be making the trip to Nevada within the next few weeks," Joetta explained. "I can hardly wait to see Hank again."

"You must miss him terribly," Mamma said, understanding first-hand the feeling of missing one's husband.

"I do," Joetta confirmed.

The other ladies learned of Joetta's plans to join her husband out west, they were delighted at her seemingly bright future and wished her all the best.

"But we shall miss you sorely, Joetta," Mrs. Carey said. "You're one of the fastest knitters we have in the Guild. I declare you can knit two pairs of socks in the same amount of time it takes for any of the rest to make one!"

☆☆☆☆☆☆☆

If there was one thing Cousin Lottie was capable of, it was chattering away incessantly. Salina and Taylor Sue were fairly convinced that Lottie rambled on and on simply because she enjoyed the sound of her own voice. And today, Lottie's favorite topic was Jeremy Barnes.

Taylor Sue leaned over and whispered, "She's looking for a reaction from you, Salina. Don't give her the satisfaction."

"Jeremy says *this* and Jeremy says *that*," Salina whispered and forced a smile. "I didn't realize he'd stayed at Ivywood long enough to say so much."

Taylor Sue giggled. "He probably didn't say half of what she's claiming. You know as well as I do Lottie has a talent for fixing the truth to suit her needs." She set the garment she'd been working on in her lap and arched her back to stretch. "I do declare I've been hunched over this sewing ever since we finished eating. Mother, do you mind if we take a little break?"

Mrs. Carey nodded, declaring that a short recess of fifteen minutes was in order.

That was all the time Salina needed to coax Taylor Sue upstairs. "I want to show you the new pattern Mamma and I are going to use on my next quilt."

Taylor Sue glanced gratefully at Salina. She knew Ethan was upstairs, but how to get to see him alone for a few minutes was more than she thought she could manage. Salina seemed to have this all worked out.

Mamma must have sensed the reason for the girls wanting to take a break. Jennilee looked as though she were going to ask if she could follow, but Mamma distracted her. Unfortunately, there wasn't much Mamma could do when Mary Edith asked, "May I join you?"

"Certainly," Salina extended her invitation. "Lottie?"

Lottie lifted her nose and sniffed. "I'm quite all right, thank you just the same. I'd rather keep on working here with the rest of the ladies while you take a rest." She took a large piece of muslin and tore it up into various sized bandages.

Mary Edith smiled. "You do that, Lottie. Don't miss us while we're gone. We'll be back in a few minutes."

Ethan was reading in the library when he saw his sister, his cousin, and Taylor Sue pass through the upstairs hallway. He set the medical book he'd been studying down and followed them to Salina's room.

"Why, hello, Ethan," Salina greeted him with a mischievous smile. "I was just going to show Mary Edith and Taylor Sue the pattern for the new quilt Mamma and I are going to make to replace the one those raiding Yankees took from me."

Ethan's eyes were glued to Taylor Sue's beaming face. "I see," he nodded.

Taylor Sue stared up into Ethan's handsome face. She whispered, "My favorite pattern is the double wedding ring design."

Salina and Mary Edith swallowed their mirth over Taylor Sue's rather broad hint to Ethan. Salina said conversationally, "Mamma said she's going to teach me how to make the flower garden pattern this time, or perhaps a log cabin design."

"I have a flower garden quilt," Mary Edith added. "The one I have is mostly of blue and white material, and it's rather striking."

Ethan had no desire to stand there discussing quilt patterns or the fabric they were made of. Boldly, he took Taylor Sue's hand. "May I see you—alone—in the library, please?"

Salina and Mary Edith shooed Taylor Sue to go along with Ethan. "Go! You've only got fifteen minutes," Salina whispered. "Don't forget that you two aren't supposed to be left unchaperoned for long! Mrs. Carey will be furious if she finds out."

"She won't," Ethan called over his shoulder. He winked at his sister. "We'll be back in a few minutes."

Mary Edith sat on the window seat. She studied the quilted pillow Salina made out of mismatched scraps of material Jubilee saved for her. "This one is quite colorful, isn't it?"

"You'll not tell?" Salina asked.

"No, of course not," Mary Edith shook her head and smiled. "Randle and I used to have to sneak off together—far away from Lottie—just to have a few minutes alone to try and get to know each other. I'm sure Ethan and Taylor Sue simply want to talk to each other. Although, I know Ethan and he's bound to try to steal a kiss or maybe two."

Salina grinned. "I'm sure you're right about my brother." Then she added, "I meant to tell you thank you, Mary Edith, for having me stand up with you when you got married. And I wanted to apologize for that little rift between Charlie Graham and Jeremy Barnes. I hope I didn't embarrass you."

"Not at all. It was an honor, Salina," Mary Edith giggled. "And as usual, as far as you're concerned, a real adventure!"

"How is it—being married?" Salina asked curiously.

Mary Edith lifted her shoulders in a dainty shrug. "I don't know if I rightly know. Randle and I spent only two days together after our wedding before he was called back to the ship. I've been living in the cottage alone for the past few weeks, but I think Lottie might come to visit for a spell. Maybe the place won't seem so empty with her there, too."

Mary Edith was sixteen, the same age as Salina. Uncle Caleb had arranged the match between her and Randle Baxter over a year ago. It was a prosperous match, one involving sizable amounts of rich, valuable acreage. Randle was eleven years older than Mary Edith, but they liked each other well enough, and she claimed she was already growing fond of him. Salina shuddered at the thought of an arranged match. Personally, she wanted to be able to choose her own husband, when the time came, and she would want to love him—as Taylor Sue loved Ethan and as Mamma loved Daddy. *I wish Jeremy would love me*, she thought wistfully.

Minutes passed and Salina wondered if she shouldn't go get Taylor Sue.

"Let them have a little more time. In fact, you wait here, and I'll go back downstairs to keep anyone from coming up to check on things," Mary Edith suggested. "Just don't be too long, or the mammas will get suspicious."

"I'm sure Ethan and Taylor Sue will be most appreciative—Ethan especially," Salina grinned.

"I envy Taylor Sue," Mary Edith confided. "One day, I hope Randle will smile at me the way Ethan smiles at her—with all of his love showing in his eyes."

Mary Edith quickly went downstairs, and a moment later Taylor Sue stood in Salina's room with Ethan holding her hand.

"Look," Taylor Sue beamed. She held out her hand so that Salina could see the engagement ring that Ethan had given her.

"This does make it official then, doesn't it?" Salina hugged Taylor Sue affectionately. "I've always dreamed of you and I being sisters. Now we will be."

Ethan put an arm around Taylor Sue's shoulders. "We're going to go down and make the announcement right now. What do you think of a Christmas wedding?"

"I like it!" Salina laughed. "Ethan, what's wrong?"

Ethan was staring out the window. "I could have sworn that was Jeremy riding Comet up the lane. He left early this morning, before sunup, saying he couldn't stay here—yet he's back. Something must be wrong."

"Are you sure it's Jeremy?" Salina asked, concerned.

"You go on and find out," Taylor Sue nodded. "Salina and I will be along directly."

They sat on the edge of Salina's bed, whispering and giggling together. "I'm really and truly going to be his wife. Oh, Salina, I'm scared, though."

"Of becoming the next Mrs. Hastings?" Salina asked.

"No," Taylor Sue shook her head. "I'm so afraid that Ethan's going to break his promise to your father and join up with the army regardless. I know how much he longs to fight for the South."

"He won't leave," Salina said. "Ethan would never break his word. Honor means too much to him. And now that you're going to be married, well, that's all the more reason for him to stay here."

"You know what he asked me? He asked if I'd have him even if he wasn't a soldier. Of course, I told him. Don't you think that's odd that he'd ask such a thing?" Taylor Sue inquired. She absently touched the doll leaning against Salina's pillows.

"I've heard there are lots of girls who won't have a boy as her sweetheart unless he's wearing the gray or butternut of the Southern military uniform," Salina replied. "Men are considered braver and more courageous if they're fighting."

"Well I think Ethan is as courageous as any one of them, and at least he's not getting shot at!" Taylor Sue exclaimed. "Both of our fathers are fighting the Yankees—isn't that enough to give?" Not expecting Salina to answer, Taylor Sue took a closer look at the doll propped up with pillows at the head of the bed. "Salina, this is beautiful embroidery on this little pinafore—such fine, detailed stitches. Did you work this?"

"No," Salina shook her head, instantly taking Celeste from Taylor Sue's hands. "This looks more like your work than it ever will mine," she said as she smoothed down the ruffled lace pinafore. "I can't seem to get my stitches to ever come out that straight."

"Did you get her for your birthday?" Taylor Sue asked. "She looks so pretty and new."

"Daddy brought her to me," Salina confided, squeezing Celeste tightly. "I told him I was too old to play with dolls now, but he suggested that I could collect dolls instead." She set Celeste aside.

"I just couldn't bear to part with some of my old dolls when I thought I was too grown up for them. They grew up with me, and they're like old friends. Now I just say they are part of my collection, like you do, and they sit prettily on a shelf," Taylor Sue smiled. "Should we go down now?"

Salina nodded. She slid off the bed, accidentally knocking Celeste to the floor with a crash. "Oh, no!" Salina cried out.

"Oh, Salina, how dreadful," Taylor Sue said sympathetically. She bent down to examine the damage. "Look here, her face isn't broken, but I'm afraid the back of her head is." Even as Taylor Sue spoke, another piece of the broken china head fell into her hand. "Oh, Salina, look! What is that?"

Salina's eyes grew round with surprise. "Oh my goodness!" The two girls' eyes locked together. Salina said quickly, "I won't tell anyone that you and Ethan were kissing in the library as long as you *promise* me that you won't tell another living soul about this doll."

Taylor Sue quickly nodded her agreement. "I promise, Salina. Not a word. What's inside of her?"

From within the broken doll, several secretly hidden items now emerged: a tiny leather-bound book filled with writing, several vials of medicine, some documents that looked official enough to have been stolen from the Union War Department, and five hundred dollars worth of Union greenbacks. The last item was a key, but there were no instructions for any of the items.

"Not a word," Salina insisted again.

Taylor Sue shook her head. "Not a word. But Salina, *why* is all that in your doll? It looks—well, it looks *dangerous*."

"If anyone catches me with these things, they could very well be dangerous," Salina whispered. "These are some very valuable items. Someone has been trusting me with some very serious secrets. Only, I didn't know about this." Salina picked up the broken pieces of Celeste's china head and said to Taylor Sue, "On the night Daddy brought her to me, he mentioned something about the contents, but I didn't know what he meant. Now I do."

"If you give the pieces to Jubilee, I'm sure she could mend it for you," Taylor Sue said. "We really better get downstairs."

Salina hid Celeste in the storage area under the window seat. "I'll ask Jubilee to see to it. Maybe one day I can explain to you what this is about, when I know more for myself."

Taylor Sue quickly shook her head. "I don't want to know what you're up to, Salina. Don't tell me anything—leastways not right now. I promise you I'll never say a word."

"Thank you for your silence." Salina hugged her.

They went downstairs to find that Jeremy Barnes had indeed been the one Ethan had seen from the window. He watched Salina come down and then walk across the entryway to stand directly in front of him. The look in her eyes was one of question, but he seemed to look right past her. Without preamble he said to Ethan, "I've been with Stuart's cavalry. They're spoiling for a fight."

☆☆☆☆☆☆☆

"Why, Jeremy Barnes, we thought you'd gone away," Mamma chided. "Why didn't you come up to the house for the noon meal if you were here? We had plenty, since the other ladies each brought along a dish. Are you hungry now?"

"No, Mrs. Hastings, but thank you," Jeremy bowed slightly at the waist.

"You look a little pale," Mamma noted. "Are you sure you're fully healed?"

"I'll do well enough, ma'am," Jeremy nodded respectfully. "I'm feeling better than I have in days." He could see Salina's mamma didn't quite believe him, but he flashed a smile anyway.

"Come into the parlour, and tell us where you've been," Mamma led him in to where the ladies were gathered.

"Jeremy!" Lottie breathed his name in a worshipful sigh.

"Lottie," Jeremy nodded politely. "Good afternoon, ladies."

"Is something wrong, Jeremy?" Aunt Priscilla asked. "You look as though you have something disagreeable to share with us."

"Well, Jeremy, do tell us where you've been," Lottie coaxed with a sweet smile. "Start at the beginning and tell us."

"Yes, tell us," the other ladies echoed.

"I've been with Jeb Stuart's cavalry. We joined Stonewall Jackson's troops long about nine-thirty this morning near Chantilly. Some of the scouts skirmished with the 20th Massachusetts regiment on the turnpike near Germantown. Now Stuart is looking for guides who know this area well in order to skirt the Yankees and find a way to get in behind them. I've come to ask Ethan if he'd care to take a ride with me."

Ethan's eyes snapped with the challenge. "I'm at your service!"

Both Mamma and Taylor Sue paled. "You mean you want to take him into combat," Mamma guessed.

"No, not to fight, Mrs. Hastings, just to scout the enemy positions. Stonewall Jackson's troops are marching down the Little River Turnpike, heading for Ox Hill. The Yankees have made a headquarters for themselves over at the Millan House," Jeremy said. "We just need to find out what it is they have on their minds."

"So close?" Mrs. Yates asked. "Yankees and Rebels in such close proximity?"

"That's a potentially dangerous situation, wouldn't you agree, Jeremy?" Mary Edith asked.

Jeremy nodded. "I know I haven't the right to ask it, Mrs. Hastings, but will you allow Ethan to ride with me and work for General Stuart—just temporarily? We'll be back before sundown."

Mamma clutched the arms of the tapestry-backed rocking chair until her knuckles had gone white. "You're certain it's not a permanent position?"

Jeremy nodded his assurance. "Just a single mission to reconnoiter around Germantown and back, that's all."

"This is war, Jeremy Barnes, how can one be assured of anything?" Mamma asked stiffly. "You're young, and you think you are invincible, but you should be reminded that you are not immortal." She refrained from mentioning in front of her guests the wounds he'd received in the fighting at Groveton.

"Yes, ma'am," Jeremy bowed his sandy-blond head. "What you are saying is true, but it would help us a great deal if Ethan could come along." He could see Mrs. Hastings was afraid, as was Taylor Sue. He was himself, a little, but he wasn't about to admit that to anyone.

Salina saw Mamma nod her silent approval. Taking a deep breath, Mamma said, "Be back here before dark, Master Barnes."

"Yes, ma'am," he swallowed. Jeremy glanced not at Salina but at Taylor Sue, who was firmly gripping Ethan's hand. "I'll meet you outside, Ethan." Jeremy stalked off, down the veranda steps to where Peter Tom held Comet's reins.

Ethan nodded to Mamma. "I'll be back." He kissed the top of Salina's head and whispered, "It's going to work out just fine, don't you worry."

"Ethan, what about the announcement?" Taylor Sue sounded terribly forlorn. She didn't want him to ride away with Jeremy. She wanted him to stay.

"We'll tell them just as soon as I come home," Ethan promised. He kissed her, right there in front of all the ladies, and then he left.

Salina sat on the settee with Taylor Sue, hugging her and telling her it was all right to cry.

Lottie scrambled out of her chair.

"Where are you going, young lady?" Aunt Priscilla queried.

"I'd like to wish them Godspeed," Lottie said.

Taylor Sue looked up at Salina. "You'd better go tell Jeremy goodbye for yourself."

Salina went outside to bid Jeremy farewell, but she stopped abruptly at the edge of the veranda. A hard knot twisted in her stomach as she witnessed Jeremy kissing Lottie.

"You be careful," Lottie sweetly admonished, her arms draped around his neck.

Jeremy looked up to see Salina standing there, rooted in one spot near the door. He plainly saw the hurt expression on her face, and he tried to escape from Lottie's clinging arms. "Salina," he called after her.

She didn't answer him. She turned back to the house, not wanting Jeremy to see the stark envy or the tears in her eyes.

Lottie smiled smugly. *It worked!* she gloated silently. She had wanted to make Salina jealous and had decided that kissing Jeremy was a sure way to irritate her cousin. "Perhaps Salina just couldn't bear to say goodbye again," she cooed at him.

Jeremy didn't have time to go back up to the house to explain the situation to Salina. He'd simply have to talk to her later. He glared at Lottie, seeing through her ploy. "Stay away from her," he ordered. "And stay away from *me!*"

Lottie recoiled as if Jeremy had slapped her. "Go on, then! See if you can't get yourself killed, why don't you?" she hissed angrily.

"Why, Lottie, thank you ever so much for such heartfelt concern over my well-being," his words mocked her. Then he restated, "Stay away from Salina."

As he rode down the lane to catch up with Ethan, Jeremy let out a blood-curdling holler—the Rebel yell. It sounded like half-Indian war whoop and half-wolf howl with a touch of wildcat thrown in for good measure.

It was a fierce wail. It made Salina's skin crawl and her spine tingle. Then she heard it again, *"Woh-who-ey!"* She rubbed her arms in order to ward off the chills. It was not the kind of parting she had imagined.

Lottie returned to the parlour looking extremely pleased with herself. Her intention had been to make Salina angry, and it had worked even better than she'd expected. Lottie caught Salina's eye, and she grinned maliciously.

Chapter Fourteen

Not long after Ethan and Jeremy departed, additional gunshots and small arms fire were clearly heard by the women sewing in the parlour.

"Listen!" Salina looked up from her mending, her eyes wide.

"But those shots could be miles away," Jennilee Carey said matter-of-factly. "A few days ago, we could hear the artillery from the battle at Manassas clear to Carillon."

"Those shots are coming from the direction of Germantown," Taylor Sue realized aloud. She glanced at Salina and then at the grandfather clock. She murmured, "Jeremy said that he and Ethan would be back before dark, but those storm clouds are making it seem dark *now*."

"And that wind is downright fierce," Mary Edith commented, looking out at the wildly dancing trees in the yard. "It appears quite a storm is brewing out there."

Mamma diligently kept on sewing, trying in vain not to think about the danger her son—as well as her husband—might be in. "You're all more than welcome to stay here at Shadowcreek to wait out the storm—and the skirmishing."

Repeated volleys of gunfire sounded from unseen rifles. The ladies attempted, ineffectively, to keep themselves busy. A brooding silence fell among them. Four chimes rang from the grandfather clock. More shots were heard—this time from the direction of Ox Hill. That could only mean more soldiers were engaging in the fight. The floor boards vibrated and the windows rattled each time the opposing artillery fired their cannons. Hearts pounded with the strength of each blast. Everyone was on edge.

The Reverend Yates was an unexpected guest at Shadowcreek that September afternoon. Jubilee quickly ushered him into the parlour. "I've come to fetch Ethan. There are too many wounded and not enough capable hands." Reverend Yates' distress was evident.

"Ethan isn't here, Reverend," Mamma said. "He's gone off with Jeremy Barnes. I don't know when they'll return. Have you tried to find Dr. Phillips?"

"I'm told he's still at Sudley Church treating the wounded from the recent engagement at Manassas," Reverend Yates replied. "I'm sure all of you have heard the artillery fire this afternoon. The fighting is very heavy at Ox Hill, near the Reid farm, even as we speak. There's a makeshift field hospital behind our lines over at Chantilly mansion. Some of the wounded have been taken there already and there are bound to be more—many, many more."

"I'm no doctor, Reverend Yates, but I know enough about nursing that I can help if need be," Mamma stood, untying her apron. "I will go with you."

"I'll go, too," Joetta Warner readily volunteered.

Salina stood up bravely. "Taylor Sue and I can help, too, Reverend Yates."

"Salina, you precious thing," Aunt Priscilla smiled condescendingly. "A hospital is not a suitable place for an impressionable girl such as yourself."

"I must agree with Mrs. Armstrong," Mrs. Carey said firmly. "While it's gallant of you to offer, Salina, this isn't anything like making bandages or needlework mending." She turned to Joetta. "If we ladies all go, who will mind the girls? Would you mind staying with them while Mrs. Armstrong, Mrs. Yates, Mrs. Hastings, and I go with Reverend Yates in order to tend to those poor wounded soldiers?"

Joetta Warner lifted her shoulders in a resigned shrug and nodded her compliance. "If you really think it necessary, I'll stay."

Mary Edith was just as glad that her married status did not require her to go with the other matrons. She had a tendency to grow faint at the sight of blood. Lottie shared Mary Edith's squeamishness, but she was indignant. Having to be watched over by Joetta did not set well with her. A glance across the parlour caught Salina's eye. The two cousins stared icily at each other, neither blinking or breaking eye contact.

Mamma touched Salina's shoulder. "Sweetheart, you'll behave while I'm gone?" The question held a trace of warning.

"Of course, Mamma," Salina nodded demurely. "Don't worry about anything here. We'll keep watch for the boys. I suppose you'll be gone for hours and hours?"

"I don't rightly know. I'm sure we'll stay as long as we're needed," Mamma kissed Salina's cheek. She whispered, "Pray, Salina."

"I have been," Salina nodded, and she hugged Mamma goodbye.

The front door closed with a heavy, solid thud. Taylor Sue wrung her hands. "Oh, Salina, I'm trying desperately not to think the worst—that Ethan might be hurt or captured."

"Sssshhhhh." Salina put an arm around Taylor Sue's shoulders and gave a comforting squeeze. "I'm sure they'll be back very soon." She hoped she sounded convincing.

The other girls returned to their stitching, giving their unsteady hands something constructive to do. Salina sat down on the sofa, mending untouched in her lap, and looked out the front parlour window. In the back of her mind, she could still see Jeremy kissing Lottie, and it troubled her more deeply than she cared to admit. *It shouldn't matter this much,* she scolded herself mentally. *But it hurts.* The revelation echoed through her brain. She shook her head, refusing to dwell another minute on the incident. Instead, she watched as Reverend Yates tried to maneuver his carriage down the slippery gravel drive. The conveyance neared the narrow bridge which spanned the gurgling creek, and the horses grew skittish. A tremendous crack rent the air at the exact same moment a jagged bolt of white lightning struck a tree on the opposite side of the bridge. The horses, afraid and uncontrollable, reared on their hind legs, overturning the carriage and its occupants.

"Mamma!" Salina screamed, witnessing the carriage slide sideways down the embankment and into the creek. She ran from the house without bothering to stop for a shawl. She only knew that Mamma was in that carriage, and she sprinted across the yard screaming, "Mamma! Mamma!"

Outside it was difficult to distinguish between the rumbles of thunder and the mixture of roaring cannons and barking rifles. Salina ceased to be concerned about the battle which seemed to be edging closer and closer. She didn't see the flashes of fire from the sharpshooters in a nearby cornfield or in the shadows of the woods of the next ridge. She didn't feel the rain which was pouring down in torrents. Her goal was fixed—to simply reach the overturned carriage.

Mrs. Carey had been thrown clear of the carriage, and she looked stunned, in shock. Reverend Yates was limping and Mrs. Yates bleeding from a cut above her left eye. Aunt Priscilla climbed out of the toppled vehicle unassisted, but Salina could see that Mamma was still inside.

Salina acted quickly, knowing that she had to calm the wild-eyed horses. If the animals bolted again, they would drag the carriage along behind them. She crooned in a gentle but audible tone, "Be still, now, Jacob. Just settle right down, now." Miraculously, Salina managed to get the huge horse to obey her, and she got Reverend Yates to help her tie the lap robe over the horse's head so that his eyes would be temporarily blinded. Once the frightful lightning and driving rain were out of sight, Jacob calmed considerably, as did Esau, the second horse of the matched pair, when Reverend Yates tied his jacket over the horse's eyes.

"Good thinking, Salina!" Reverend Yates hugged her to him. "Quick as a whip, little lady!"

"Mamma!" Salina cried, pushing his arms away. "What's happened to Mamma?" Her question was nearly drowned out by the volume of thunder and the noise of artillery fire from Ox Hill.

Jubilee came flying down to the creek from the main house, yelling for Peter Tom and Cromwell at the top of her lungs. Even as the two black men began to rescue their mistress from the fallen carriage, the conveyance inched steadily downward toward the creek. No sooner had they pulled Mamma free, the carriage crashed down the embankment.

Jubilee bent protectively over Mamma's still body. The heavy raindrops plastered Mamma's auburn ringlets to her head. Blood oozed from one corner of her mouth.

"Git on back in dat house, chile!" Jubilee shouted at Salina.

"Is she dead?" cried Salina, squeezing one of Mamma's cold, unresponsive hands.

"No, she ain't dead, but ya's gonna be if'n ya don' do as ah says! Now git!" Jubilee roared.

Salina had never seen Jubilee so distraught before, and it frightened her. Reluctantly she retreated to the shelter of the veranda, and she hugged the corner pillar as though she were holding on for dear life. Across the ridges, in the woods, she now saw the sparks of fire from the guns being fired by the opposing armies. She prayed fervently that the fighting would end before it endangered the house. "Please, don't let them get so close, Heavenly Father. We've got more than enough trouble as it is!"

It seemed that time stood still after Cromwell and Peter Tom carried Mamma to her bedchamber. Salina paced restlessly in the parlour, waiting, and waiting, and waiting. Jubilee was upstairs with Mamma, tending to her injuries. She had refused Salina's help and all but banished her from Mamma's room. The grandfather clock chimed five times. The knot of terror in Salina's stomach tightened.

Mary Edith found a blanket for Salina to wrap up in, and she insisted Salina sit down and drink some of the hot, spiced cider Joetta had prepared. Then Joetta went up to sit with Mrs. Yates, who was resting in one of the guest bedrooms on the second floor. Jennilee sat near Taylor Sue, silent and scared. Lottie jumped at each flash of lightning, then again at each clap of thunder.

The Reverend did not want to leave Shadowcreek, especially considering what had just happened, but with Dr. Phillips away at Sudley Church and Ethan nowhere to be found, he felt it imperative to get to Chantilly. He knew that the injured ladies were resting as comfortably as possible. Jubilee was capable of seeing to their needs, but the Reverend silently feared that Annelise Hastings was in a bad way. He tried not to let Salina know how concerned he was, but he supposed she, too, knew something was terribly wrong. Reverend Yates departed in the midst of storm and battle, praying that Ethan would return quickly.

Thick darkness descended. The rolling thunder and crashing explosions melded together into a great, endless, nerve-wracking rumble. The fighting sounded so fierce and the storm so severe that no one heard Ethan and Jeremy return until they thudded their muddy boots right into the parlour.

Salina dropped her blanket and hurled herself into Ethan's arms. "Thank God you're here!" she sobbed into the crook of his neck.

"Salina, what is it?" Ethan immediately sensed his little sister's despair.

Tears streaked Salina's pale face. "There's been an accident. Mamma's been hurt."

Ethan roughly put Salina into Jeremy's arms. "Hold her here," he ordered gruffly, taking the stairs two at time to find out exactly what was wrong.

Jeremy was soaked to the skin from the downpour, but Salina's body heat warmed them both. He wrapped her securely in the blanket and sat down with her on his lap. Absently he stroked her tangled damp curls and held her hand firmly. "Sssshhhhh." He rocked back and forth, holding her gently in his strong arms.

Mary Edith and Jennilee continued with their stitching, trying to draw Lottie into their conversation, but Lottie silently seethed inside at the sight of Jeremy and Salina together. Her earlier feeling of triumph over kissing Jeremy in the yard vanished. She wished Mrs. Carey would be shocked by the way Salina clung to Jeremy and object loudly to it.

Mrs. Carey did object. "Why, it just isn't proper! He seems a bit *familiar*, wouldn't you say?"

Taylor Sue tried to calm her mother before she really did create a scene. "Honestly, Mother, Jeremy is merely comforting Salina in her time of need. I would hope that Ethan would do the same for me, if I were in her position. What harm is there in that?"

Mrs. Carey did not answer, but Salina had clearly heard the stern disapproval in her tone. Unbidden, the memory of how Jeremy had been holding Lottie in his arms only a few short hours before returned vividly. Salina stiffened and sat up straight, putting distance between herself and Jeremy. She whispered hoarsely, "I'm quite all right now, Master Barnes. I thank you for your show of concern for my well-being."

Jeremy frowned, confused. "You're sure you're all right?"

"Much better," Salina said coolly. In the depths of his blue eyes she thought she saw a great deal of care, but she was unsure if it was *truly* there or if she *imagined* what she wanted to see. "What time is it, please?"

"Just a little past five o'clock. Outside it's as dark as midnight and the storm is raging on," answered Jeremy. "I don't rightly know how our soldiers can even see where the Yankees they're supposed to be shooting at are."

"You're going to be chilled to the bone," Taylor Sue coaxed Salina into drinking more hot cider. Jeremy downed a pewter mugful himself.

Ethan came downstairs. He looked to have aged somewhat, or perhaps it was the odd way the lamplight flickered over his angular features that caused his expression to look so hard.

"What is it?" Salina jumped up. "Is Mamma all right? Ethan, please tell me. Is she all right?"

"Mamma'll be fine, given time," Ethan squeezed his sister's shoulders as she faced him. "Salina, she lost the baby."

☆☆☆☆☆☆☆

The storm let up somewhat. The cannons had ceased to roar. All the spare bedrooms were full of guests, and Jeremy returned to the room he had occupied after Salina and Ethan brought him to Shadowcreek from Tabitha Wheeler's boarding house. Ethan had thanked Jeremy for his offer of assistance at Chantilly but assured him that it would be better if he stayed put and kept an eye on all the ladies. Salina seemed to be avoiding his company.

Ethan took care in packing his precious few medical instruments and a small quantity of supplies into a leather saddlebag. He was nearly ready to go. He went down the hall to Salina's bedroom.

"Y-you're l-leaving for Chan-tilly." She accepted the inevitable.

Ethan nodded. She'd been crying again, and he knew she was still very upset. He hoped talking would perhaps calm her and motioned for her to sit down beside him on the window seat. He described to Salina the ride to and from Germantown. "We got shot at by Union pickets," he said, "but they didn't pay us too much attention. Soon they were too busy joining in the fighting and they didn't give us a second thought. As far as we could tell, most of the fighting was on Ox Hill, near Ox Road—in Reid's cornfield, the grassy field next to that, and the woods beyond. The roads are little more than slow rivers of quagmire and the thick, red mud sucks at every step of man or beast. Either the darkness and rain stopped the fighting or the gun powder got too wet to work effectively."

"Wh-what th-en?" Salina hiccuped softly. Her tears had ceased to flow.

Ethan answered, "Hand to hand combat with fists, knives, bayonets, sabres, or rifle butts used as clubs. Many men have been killed or wounded. That's why I must go. I can be of use there. I've done all I can for Mamma. Jubilee will watch over her now, as she always has done."

Salina sighed. "I w-wonder where D-daddy is on a n-night l-like th-this." She peeked out the window. She whispered raggedly, "Ethan, h-he's th-there—*again*."

Ethan blew out the kerosene lamp. "Where? Show me!"

At first, the darkness cloaked the shadowy form, but Salina explained where to look for the old man, and there, sure enough, Ethan recognized him. "Jeremy is convinced that old man's been assigned to follow him. Salina, if I tell you something, will you promise you won't tell another living soul?"

"What?" she raised her eyebrows in question.

Ethan whispered, "Jeremy is a sort of spy. He works with people who keep Daddy supplied with information. Sometimes he's a courier and he delivers items that have been smuggled through the lines—documents, medicine, even food or horses where they're needed."

Salina lowered her eyes. "I know, Ethan."

"You *know*? But how?" Ethan asked. "Did Jeremy tell you this?"

Salina nodded. "Yes." She hesitated for a moment, biting her lip, but then she decided to confess, "We work together, he and I do."

"You?!" Ethan exclaimed in surprise. "Salina, you're just... well... you're just a *girl*!"

"Yes—a girl whom no one would suspect," Salina replied, lifting her chin to a defiant angle. "If I hadn't told you, you wouldn't have suspected me of such a thing. My own family treats me as though I am nothing more a child—and so does Jeremy, at times. So, why should the Yankees see me any differently than you do? They'd never guess in a million years. But Ethan, you mustn't say a word to *anyone*. It might endanger the lives of the others involved in the Network."

Ethan's laugh was harsh and disbelieving. "Daddy brought *you* into the Network, but he didn't even trust *me*?"

"It wasn't a matter of trust, son," Captain Hastings's voice startled both Salina and Ethan. The Captain slipped though the secret door in the wall panel of Salina's bedroom. "It was a matter of safety."

"Daddy!" Salina went to him, hugging him regardless of his wet oilcloth coat. "Oh, you're back! And safe!"

"For the most part," the Captain smiled ruefully. "Yankee bullet grazed my arm, but it's just a nick, really."

Salina helped the Captain out of his wet jacket and immediately found the blood-stains on his shirt.

"You need a clean dressing for this." Ethan examined the Captain's arm, then proceeded to use a clean wrap to replace the bloody one. The Captain winced but chose to ignore his pain.

"Having you and Jeremy working together might have been too great a risk," the Captain explained as Ethan worked. "It could have presented a situation too easily discovered by Union agents. At the time, when I needed more help, I believed Salina would bring far less suspicion, if any, and therefore, she was a safer link than you would be. You're my son, Ethan, and that naturally casts suspicion upon you. Now, however, since Jeremy's taken you out scouting, I can see that you've tasted the adventure—and you're going to hanker after more."

Ethan denied the truth of the Captain's words, shaking his head firmly, "I gave you my word that I would stay here and look after Mamma and Salina. I *will* do my duty, to you and this family."

"I'm comforted to hear it," the Captain sighed gratefully. "I still don't think you fully understand just how much I rely on you to do precisely that. It makes me feel better knowing that I can count on you not to run off and get yourself killed."

Ethan sighed, half understanding, yet still half yearning to be part of the endeavor. "You're in command, sir, and you know what's best."

"Thank you for trusting me, Ethan. It means the world to me," the Captain told him.

Salina was watching for the old man, but there were no movements in the shadows. A flash of lightning revealed that he had deserted his post. "He's gone," Salina murmured.

"The old man?" the Captain questioned. "Yes. I waited until he seemed convinced that nothing was going on here. Has he been around much?"

"Some," Salina nodded. "Reverend Yates thinks he's following Jeremy."

"That he is," the Captain affirmed. "Never let it be said that Duncan Grant does not follow orders."

"So it really *is* Duncan!" Salina blinked in wonder. "We suspected, but we weren't completely sure..."

The Captain laughed. "I wonder if Duncan truly thinks I can't see through that disguise of his." Captain Hastings stared out the window. "He's one of my oldest and dearest friends, and if it weren't for the fact that he is a Union secret agent, I might have invited him in to escape the storm. But he is my enemy. So far, we have managed to avoid each other since the war started, but the longer the conflict wears on, it seems that we are drawn closer to each other. We haven't crossed paths as of yet, and I'd just as soon keep it that way. The trouble is, I have a bad feeling that a confrontation is inevitable."

"Would Duncan Grant turn you in to the Yankees?" Ethan asked.

"I wouldn't expect him to do anything else. Friendship or no, Captain Grant would merely be following orders, as I would be, if the tables were turned," the Captain answered gruffly. "How I miss the old days," he lamented wistfully, "when we used to hunt and fish and talk together. The capers we pulled off at West Point! Although, if I remember correctly, Duncan never earned a single demerit. I had enough for both of us. A right proper soldier, our Duncan Grant. He lives by the book, and he would die for the Union. No, it's best we keep out of each other's way. My head tells me he is the enemy, but my heart still reminds me of the friendship we used to share." The Captain paused, reflecting back on some of the adventures with Duncan Grant as his companion. He shook his dark head, setting his mind on the issues at hand. "Now, tell me. What's been going on here that I should know about?"

Sudden tears brimmed Salina's eyes and a lump formed in Ethan's throat. Neither was capable of speaking an answer.

"Something's very wrong. Come on, tell me," the Captain insisted.

"Mamma was in an accident this afternoon," Salina said with a trembling voice. "She was hurt, and..."

"And?" the Captain prodded. "Ethan?"

"And she lost the baby," Ethan completed Salina's unfinished sentence. "Jubilee is with her now, and so is Mrs. Carey."

Salina added, "We have a houseful of people because of the storm and the battle."

"I see." The Captain ran his fingers through his wet black hair. "She lost the baby..." He felt as though he'd been kicked in his gut, and breathing became difficult to him. He scowled, "If I'd have been here, this might not have happened this way."

"It was an accident," Ethan declared. "She's miscarried before. Who's to say the very same thing couldn't have happened even if you had been here?"

The Captain swallowed hard. "I appreciate what you're trying to say, Ethan, really I do. And you're right, my being here or not being here doesn't change the situation." He sighed raggedly. "There are times when I don't understand exactly how God works, but He does, in His own time. His ways are not our ways, and I must trust that in His infinite wisdom He is working to bring all things unto His glory..." The Captain's voice broke into a stifled sob. He quickly straightened his shoulders and angrily wiped tears from his high cheekbones. "Ethan, somehow get Mrs. Carey away from Mamma. Jubilee can be trusted not to say anything to anyone."

Without knocking, Jubilee suddenly burst into Salina's darkened room. "Massah Ethan—ah knows ya's here. Ya's gots ta cum quick. Miz Annelise, she bein' so hot wid da fever, she be a-callin' an' a-callin' out for Massah Garrett. Ahs hopin' ya kin git her ta quiet down sum, Massah Ethan."

"Jubilee," the Captain spoke the loyal maidservant's name softly.

"Massah Garrett? Lord Almighty be praised!" Jubilee cried. "Thank ya, Sweet Jesus, fer sendin' ya home, Massah Garrett. Miz Annelise, she be needin' ya real bad."

"Where is Mrs. Carey now?" the Captain asked.

"Ah sent her on ta bed sum time ago wid sum nice hot tea—Jube's own special brew. Miz Carey won' be wakin' up til noon tamorrow," Jubilee said with certainty and a conspiratorial wink. "Ya kin count on dat fer sure."

The Captain did not reply. He was already out the door and down the hall.

☆☆☆☆☆☆☆

"Daddy looks as though his heart is about to break," Salina whispered to Ethan when the Captain returned from Mamma's room.

"It just might be. He loves her so very much," Ethan nodded. "This baby meant a lot to both of them."

"I thought the two of you would be asleep by now. Have you any idea how late it is?" the Captain asked more harshly than he intended. He had cried in front of them once tonight. It would never do to let them catch him with tears in his eyes a second time.

"Jeremy wants to talk to you," Ethan said.

"And so do I," Salina nodded.

"I want to help somehow," Ethan stated evenly.

The Captain had anticipated Ethan's remark. "I suppose it can't hurt to have two couriers. Besides, there's going to be a new focus in information the Network will be sending this way from now on."

"Is the campaign on, then, Daddy?" Salina asked.

He nodded. "We'll talk about it a little bit later. For now let's go see what Barnes has to say for himself."

Jeremy gave the Captain his report and then asked, "What news do you have of the battle? Ethan and I made the ride to Germantown, as General Stuart ordered, but we've stayed close to the house the rest of the time. Even though we're so near the action, we haven't heard much about the outcome."

"I'm not sure which side won this battle," the Captain admitted. "Our army is in possession of the field, but we didn't crush the Yankees like we should have. The way I figure it, that must mean a stalemate. I am under the impression that this has made General Lee more determined than ever to invade Maryland. His desire is to take the war North. A victory for us there may prove to England and France that the Confederacy is an independent country. If they will acknowledge that, there's a good chance they would send us aid. They could even help us destroy the blockade. The Southern army is in need of everything: food, clothing, arms and ammunition, horses, men, funding. We lost many men on that field today—so did the Yankees. Word has it that two of the Union's commanders were killed: Brigadier-General Isaac Stevens and Major-General Philip Kearny. I'm told it wasn't long after their deaths that the battle came to an end—that, along with the thick darkness and the driving rain."

"When do you think Lee will invade Maryland?" Jeremy asked.

"I don't know yet. I was with General Jackson not two hours ago, and his troops were already packing up and getting ready to move. It's long past midnight," the Captain checked his pocket watch, then glanced back at Jeremy.

Jeremy was looking at Salina, who pointedly refused to acknowledge him. The Captain smiled to himself and thought, *So, Salina's made a conquest of my right-hand man...*

Salina showed Captain Hastings what had happened to Celeste. "The night you gave her to me, you were going to tell me about the contents, but we never got to it. When she broke open, I found all those things inside. I have the key right here." She drew a thin scarlet ribbon from around her neck on which the key secretly hung beneath her nightgown.

"You keep that safely hidden until I send word to Reverend Yates to go get the trunk which that key will open. It's at the Tanners' now, over in Alexandria. But presently it's far too dangerous," the Captain warned. "Don't you worry about Celeste, Salina. She served her purpose well." He took the embroidered dress from the doll and tossed it into the fire burning in the grate. "I have a copy of a new code for you. Come, you and I have some work to do."

Salina followed the Captain back to her room. Ethan glanced back at Jeremy and shook his head in amazement. "My own sister has been keeping secrets from me."

Jeremy's voice held a certain degree of admiration. "She is a brave young lady."

"Why didn't you tell her that?" Ethan questioned. "She usually blushes so when you say nice things to her."

"I know," Jeremy nodded. "But I don't think flowery phrases would have met with her approval tonight."

"Is it my imagination, or is she deliberately pretending that you're invisible?" Ethan prodded.

"Quite deliberate," Jeremy affirmed. "Your sister caught me kissing Lottie before you and I rode away this afternoon. Salina isn't in the frame of mind to let me explain that Lottie threw herself at me while Salina was inside. Lottie was kissing me before I knew to expect it—although I reckon she timed it just so Salina *would* see us. How does one go about explaining that?"

Ethan shrugged, containing his amusement. "I know my sister well. Salina won't listen to reason until she's good and ready to do so."

"I was afraid of that," Jeremy muttered. "I guess I'll just have to bide my time, then."

"I guess so," Ethan chuckled heartily. Within the quarter hour he was riding Baron on his way to Chantilly.

☆☆☆☆☆☆☆

Using the secret passageway down to the smokehouse, Salina and the Captain got only slightly wet rather than completely drenched by the rain.

The Captain had important details to discuss with his daughter. "Sally, those documents that were delivered to Stonewall Jackson when he was at Pleasant Valley were not the same ones I forwarded to Reverend Yates. You're sure Peter Tom made the delivery?"

"Reverend Yates had it all arranged," Salina nodded. "What do you suppose happened?"

"I don't know," the Captain said, uncertain. "If he said Peter Tom would make the delivery, I have no reason to doubt his word. But the fact remains that somewhere those documents were switched—either before Peter Tom picked them up at Carillon or after. The question is *when*? And by *whom*? And where are those original documents now? The Captain privately seethed. He had a strong feeling that Duncan Grant had a part in this. "Sally-girl, you must be *ever so* careful."

"I'll be on my guard more than ever, Daddy," Salina promised.

The Captain squeezed Salina's hand. "It won't do us any more good to dwell on this as it would to cry over spilt milk. We have other things yet to accomplish. The messages that will come from now on will be items such as lists of names, maps of the western territories, and probably any other confiscated Union documents we can get our hands on."

"Like those things that I found inside of Celeste?" Salina queried. "They were all about places and Union-held forts in New Mexico Territory."

"Yes. And what about the book?" the Captain asked.

"Right here." Salina handed it to the Captain. "It's full of scrawled words, and I'm sure they're in code, but not ours."

"You're right, Sally-girl." The Captain was not only pleased but impressed with her deduction. "That book belongs to Duncan, only I haven't been able to make heads or tails of it as of yet. The next time I'm in Washington, I intend to see if I can't find the code so we can decipher this and learn if it's of any relevance. You just hang on to that for now."

"What about the rest of these things?" Salina asked. "Shall I hang on to them, too?"

"Next time Ethan makes his rounds with Dr. Phillips, have him drop them off with Tabitha. She'll safeguard them for us. She's a very important link for us, too," the Captain nodded. "She is in a very advantageous position, and she collects all sorts of information from unsuspecting patrons. She knows now that you're involved, so the two of you can use each other as a point of contact, if need be."

Realization registered in Salina's memory. "You know, I didn't think much about it at the time, but it was *she* who cared for Jeremy after he was wounded at Groveton. We brought him here to Shadowcreek because Tabitha knew somebody was following him."

"Duncan," the Captain muttered. "It all comes back to Duncan Grant. He's trying to get to me through Jeremy." He took a deep breath, cleared his throat, and swiftly changed the topic. "Forward any documents pertaining to the western campaign on to Tabitha. She'll keep them until it is safe for me to retrieve them. While General Lee is planning to invade the North, we are still formulating the plans to capture the west. The Confederacy needs money badly, Sally. Gold and silver abound in California, Nevada, Arizona, and New Mexico. We could surely use the funds to support our army."

"You mentioned that you've a trunk stored at the Tanners'. What's in there?" Salina wanted to know.

The Captain was a little evasive, "Oh, just some of my things. Nothing that concerns you—yet. I simply don't want to leave that spare key laying around, so I want you to keep it for me. I'll bring the trunk here when the time is right. Are you sure you're up to all this secret service hush-hush, Sally-girl?"

"I'll do my best for you," Salina vowed. "I told you that I would."

"That's my little darlin'." The Captain's green eyes were filled with love and pride. "Well," he said abruptly, "I should be going. I have a long ride to the Tanners' in this weather."

"Isn't it dangerous for you to be in Alexandria, Daddy? Especially since the town is occupied by Union troops?" Salina was afraid for him.

"I go to Washington only when it's absolutely necessary, Sally. Staying in Alexandria with the Tanners is my cover. On occasion I've posed as a reporter for Will's little newspaper. He's got a column in which 'Gary Hayes' writes editorials. In truth, it's all Will's writing, but by my slipping into the role, I've been able to get into some places and gather information that I would never have been able to without acting the part."

"No one in Washington has recognized you?" Salina was incredulous.

The Captain grinned. "I'm a very good actor, Sally—with a good disguise. You should see me. If I wasn't such a good farmer and didn't love Virginia soil and my family so much, I might have made a passable living on the stage. Who knows?"

"It scares me," Salina said. A chill crept the length of her spine.

The Captain kissed the top of her head. "Don't you worry about me, Sally. I can take care of myself. You must take care of things here while I'm away."

Salina nodded.

"Send word to me of your Mamma's condition in care of the Tanners. But use the code name of 'Gary Hayes', and don't mention any specific names. I'll only be there a few days. The business in Washington won't take me long, and then I'm almost certain that I'll be ordered back to San Francisco to lay the groundwork for the western campaign. I want to know how she is doing before I go."

"I'll be sure to let you know, Daddy." Salina hugged him tightly.

The Captain whispered, "God be with you, Sally."

"And with you, Daddy," she returned. "Please be careful."

"I will. Be strong and courageous." The Captain hugged her tightly. "I won't come back up to the house now, so you go on. You're doing a fine job, Sally—a fine job! I love you dearly."

"I love you, too, Daddy. Goodbye!" She scurried back to the secret passageway and returned to the warmth of her bedroom.

Chapter Fifteen

Salina, perched at Mamma's bedside, held Mamma's lifeless hand to her cheek. Silent tears streamed down her cheeks, mourning for the little baby that was lost and praying over and over that Mamma would be all right. Jubilee came and found her, and immediately shooed Salina back to her own room. "Ah'll cum git ya if'n she calls," Jubilee said crossly. "Dere's no sense in ya worryin' yersef sick."

"But why can't I stay by her?" " Salina asked. "Why don't you want me around, Jubilee?"

" Yer jist underfoot, Missy. Ah gots work ta do in takin' care o' Miz Annelise. Ah done tole ya, if ah need ya, ah'll cum afta ya," Jubilee said sternly.

Salina's eyes filled with tears again, but she went away, as Jubilee ordered. She passed Ethan's open bedroom door. He was awake, having only two hours of sleep after spending the wee morning hours at Chantilly, and he asked her how Mamma was doing.

"I don't know. Jubilee keeps telling me to go away. She says I'm underfoot all the time," Salina sniffed, hurt by knowing she wasn't wanted.

"Jubilee's hurting because Mamma's hurting," Ethan told her. "She just doesn't want you to see that, and so she sends you away. Maybe tomorrow Jubilee will let you help care for Mamma."

"Do you think Mamma's going to be all right?'" Salina asked.

"Oh, eventually, I'm sure she'll be fine again," Ethan nodded. "She's going to be terribly disappointed when she wakes up and finds out what happened."

Salina only nodded.

Ethan touched her cheek. "Don't fret so, Salina. Jubilee and Mrs. Carey have both dealt with situations like this before. They'll give Mamma the best care they know how."

"You're going back to the field hospital so soon?'" Salina asked, noting that he was packing a haversack with fresh clothes and a little food, extra candles, and the last of his carefully hoarded medicines.

"Yes, I'm going back to Chantilly," Ethan confirmed. "There is so much to do.'" He failed to mention that he thought Salina could be of use in the post-operative wards, in fear she would demand to go with him. "By the way, Jeremy would like to see you."

"Tell him I'm exhausted, and I'm not up to it just now." Salina tossed her head. "If he must have a companion to talk to, tell him to find Lottie. I'm sure she'd give him her *undivided* attention."

"Salina..." Ethan began, but he let her go. It wasn't his place to explain. Jeremy would have to fix this little misunderstanding himself. Ethan wasn't about to come between them. It was their business, not his.

☆☆☆☆☆☆☆

The afternoon didn't bring any change to Mamma's condition, and Jubilee still hovered over her protectively. Salina couldn't stand to be in the house anymore, and she went to sulk in the orchard alone.

Reverend Yates found her there. "Good day, Miss Salina."

"Hello, Reverend Yates," Salina answered his greeting. "Mrs. Yates is up at the main house. Joetta Warner and the Armstrongs left about an hour ago."

"Well, I haven't come to see any of them anyway. I've come to talk to you." The Reverend dismounted from Esau's back. "I came to ask a favor of you."

Salina nodded, wordlessly telling him that she would help if it was in her power to do so.

"You're quite aware that the battle at Ox Hill left us with many wounded, and we're sorely shorthanded. Yesterday, when you offered to help, the ladies deemed a field hospital no place for you. The fact remains that since the accident here yesterday, we've lost some of our capable hands. We need you, Salina, and Taylor Sue, if she's willing. Ethan thinks the two of you would be a great help. I intend to speak to Mrs. Carey myself about it," the Reverend said.

"Well, Jubilee certainly won't let me be with Mamma," Salina pouted. "So why should they miss me if I go with you to tend the wounded soldiers?"

Mrs. Carey still wasn't overly fond of the idea, but she relented. "I understand that there is a dire need of able-bodied to aid the broken bodies. I'll give my permission, although it is with reservations," she said to Taylor Sue and Salina. "I hope that I can explain to Annelise that I thought I was doing the right thing by allowing the girls to go with you, Reverend."

"I'm sure Mrs. Hastings will understand that they can do a world of good there," the Reverend nodded. "Come along, girls. Ethan has been working for hours on end. Dr. Phillips arrived early this morning. The number of wounded seems endless."

On the drive to the Chantilly mansion, Reverend Yates told them a little bit about what to expect. "I am truly sorry to have to bring the two of you into this, but there is no alternative at this point. I knew I could rely on the two of you—the other girls aren't cut from the same cloth as you are. Both of you are strong, and I pray this doesn't shock you too badly."

The girls nodded and listened intently to what the Reverend said, but his words did not completely prepare them for what they found when they arrived at Chantilly.

Before she could think twice about what she was doing, Salina was put to work. She was taken to a room where soldiers were recovering from surgeries. Salina read to, wiped fevered brows of, fed, and sang softly to the wounded Rebel soldiers. Taylor Sue did the same in another room of the house. There were bodies everywhere, or so it seemed, all craving attention. Some rested quietly, patiently, while others moaned loudly in unrelieved pain. The stench of blood and dirtiness was almost more than the girls could stand, but they made it through because they saw first-hand how badly these men needed their ministrations.

On a guarded table lay the corpse of a Union officer. He was dressed in a fine blue uniform with shiny gold buttons. Several Confederate soldiers crowded around the body, just looking and whispering together. Salina asked one of the orderlies who the dead man was.

"That there is Major-General Phil Kearny," the orderly replied. "He was killed last night when he rode into our lines by mistake. He tried to escape, and they shot him down, only they did not know at the time who he was until after he'd fallen. Stonewall Jackson came to identify Kearny's body. I gather they used to know each other well before the war. General Lee, he ordered the body to be guarded so that no one could do any harm to him. Kearny might've lost his arm in the Mexican War, but in this war he lost his life..." the orderly trailed off as he went back to his assigned duties.

Salina wrung her hands, somewhat taken back at the sight of Kearny laying in state. With thoughts of the dead man filling her head, she unexpectedly backed directly into a gray-clad man with white hair and a white beard. "Oh, excuse me, sir," she murmured a hasty apology.

The man's dark eyes were kind, but they held a haunting sadness tinged with pain in their depths. "No harm done," he said softly with a small trace of a smile, patting Salina gently on the shoulder. He continued on past her, toward the body of the Union general. The men who had gathered around the table saluted the bearded Confederate General, and he nodded his acknowledgment. "Where is my aide?" he asked.

The aide stepped forward, "Yes, General Lee?"

"Take this," he held a letter, "to General Hooker at the Union headquarters. See that Kearny's body is taken under escort and a flag of truce through the lines."

"Yes, sir," the aide saluted.

"Poor Kearny," General Lee said, shaking his head.

Salina blinked and looked up again at the sad face of General Robert E. Lee, the beloved Confederate leader of the Army of Northern Virginia, and Salina—having heard Daddy, Ethan, and Jeremy speak of him often—was in awe at having seen him so close. General Lee nodded once more to Salina as she stood watching the scene, and then he turned and walked through to another area of the house.

Salina hurried to the ward where Taylor Sue was working. "I saw him with my own two eyes, Taylor Sue. I can't believe I bumped right into him—our own *General Lee!*"

Through snatches of conversations, Salina and Taylor Sue learned that some of the wounded were taken from the battlefield by wagons and ambulances to St. Mary's Catholic Church where a lady named Clara Barton tended to even more of the injured and dying. The Union was calling the fight the Battle of Chantilly, but the Confederates referred to it as the Battle of Ox Hill.

Salina and Taylor Sue did all they could to make the soldiers comfortable and, if possible, forget their pain for a time. There was the usual shortage of medicine, and food was not exactly plentiful. Salina found that the soldiers who could talk were very willing to do so. They told her details that she filed away for later reference. perhaps something that might be useful to Daddy or to Jeremy.

Ethan stayed on to assist the surgeons. Reverend Yates took the girls back to Shadowcreek after a meager lunch had been fed to the wounded. They were tired, but they knew they had done much good in their day of work.

☆☆☆☆☆☆☆

Captain Hastings, unknown to anyone in the house, had spent most of the day holed up in the secret passageway. Too many guests at Shadowcreek and too many troops on the turnpike prevented a clean escape, and so he was forced to bide his time.

In the mid-afternoon Jubilee had helped him sneak into Mamma's room so he could spend just a few more minutes with her before he'd move on again. Mamma was burning with fever, but the delirium from the night before was waning.

"Just know that I love you, Annelise, with all my heart," the Captain whispered raggedly. "Forgive me when I say that sometimes we do what we think we must, what we think is right, and what we are called to do." He gingerly kissed her brow.

"I know," she whispered in a shaky voice. "I just wish..."

"Sssshhh," the Captain put his finger to her lips. "You rest, and get well. Jubilee's concocting something to help you sleep through the night. You'll need to regain your strength, and you won't unless you do what she tells you."

Mamma nodded tiredly. Her eyes were shiny and her color high due to the heat of the fever, and the Captain's tears came freely as he prayed over his beloved Annelise.

Salina found the Captain in her room when she returned from working at Chantilly. "You're here?" she asked in disbelief.

"I couldn't get away, so I stayed. But I'm leaving now," the Captain said. "I'm taking Jeremy with me. Duncan Grant is an extremely clever fellow, and I don't want him putting any pieces of our little puzzle together. We'll just have to wait and see what General Lee's next course of action will be, and then we'll make our move."

Salina told him about the body of the Yankee's General Kearny and about mistakenly bumping into General Lee.

The Captain smiled at the tale. "I reckon General Lee is the best general there ever was, or ever will be. He's a very respected man. Lee is devoted to his command, and he has brought victory to the Army of Northern Virginia. He can make something happen in the field of battle where it seems nothing could exist. The Union wanted him on their side, you know, and they offered him a choice command. Yet Lee declined for the love of Virginia. I think that is part of why his men will follow him wherever he leads. He is true to his convictions. I know I would follow him, if I were in the regular army. The Confederate Secret Service, however, is an entirely different matter." He hugged Salina, "I'm sorry about having to burn Celeste's dress."

"No matter," Salina shrugged it off. "I'll make her another, and a bonnet to match so it will hide the repaired crack in her china head."

"That's my Sally-girl." The Captain kissed her. "Tell Ethan that when the time comes, he'll ride as a courier in Jeremy's place. And please, when you aren't putting so much effort into nursing those wounded soldiers, make sure you look after Mamma for me."

"If Jubilee would allow it," Salina mused.

The Captain bowed his head. "I do wonder if the baby would have been another strong son, like Ethan, or another brave little Rebel girl like you."

Salina whispered, "I know how you mourn, Daddy, but please don't let thoughts of us here at home muddle those of your work. Together we will survive. We are strong. We pray every day that the Lord will guide us and keep us—and He already has. I've seen answers to some of my prayers. In the book of Ecclesiastes it says there is a time for *every* purpose under heaven—a time to weep, and a time to laugh; a time to mourn, and a time to dance...a time of war, and a time of peace. I am confident the Lord has us in His hand, and we must take His will, as it comes, one day at a time."

"When did you get to be so wise, Sally-girl?" the Captain shook his head, thinking that she seemed very grown up at this moment.

Salina smiled. "I don't know. I just say whatever comes to mind—what I've been taught by you, or by Mamma. I've been reading my new Bible a good deal, too. God *is* faithful, Daddy. I have faith that He'll continue to keep us in His care."

"Good for you," the Captain tapped the end of her nose with his finger. "Reading God's Word will help you learn how much He loves all His children. You already know how much I love you, Sally-girl."

"I love you so, Daddy. Come back to us soon." She kissed his whiskered cheek.

"Just as soon as I possibly can, darlin'. Salina," he called her by her full name, rather than her nickname. "be very careful." He closed the secret panel behind him and was gone.

☆☆☆☆☆☆☆

In the days which followed the brutal fighting, damages from the battle were accounted and the slow process of mending the brokeness began. The soldiers were taken care of—wounded men with treatment, dead ones with burial. Mrs. Yates and Mrs. Carey joined Taylor Sue and Salina in their nursing duties at the Chantilly mansion. The strangeness of it all quickly became common daily routine. Salina wrote letters home for some of the soldiers, to wives, mothers, and sweethearts. There were times when she was asked to sing. One of the wounded, Lieutenant Mason, played an accordion while Salina sang *Dixie, The Bonnie Blue Flag*, and a melancholy tune called *Lorena*.

The men cheered and clapped, urging her to sing some more.

"Tomorrow," Salina promised. "I must go home now, and see how my Mamma is doing."

Mamma was recovering slowly. She slept most of the time, and she wasn't always aware of the brief visits when Jubilee reluctantly allowed Salina to see her. The chill Mamma had taken on the night of the accident had been followed by a raging fever. The fever, in turn, had been replaced by a growing depression which descended on her normally cheery spirit.

Salina fell into the habit of retiring to her room early and writing in the diary Jubilee gave her. She wrote about the long days she worked and the loneliness she felt, especially since no one seemed to be around to listen to her.

September 4, 1862

> *I went to Chantilly again today. Some of the soldiers*
> *who are able will be sent back to their regiments soon.*
> *Others will be sent home when the doctors say that they*
> *can be moved, and then there are those who are trans-*
> *ported to bigger hospital facilities. Some are very bad off.*
> *Three of the men Taylor Sue was taking care of died—two*
> *yesterday, and one this morning. I know Mamma didn't*
> *want me to go there at first, she didn't like the idea of my*
> *dealing with the nightmarish scenes I have witnessed. But*
> *my being there is a good thing, I can feel it—I believe that*
> *tending to them might indeed be a blessing to them. They*
> *look forward to Taylor Sue's and my arrival. I'm glad we*
> *are able to help in any way we can. This is a wretched*
> *war—I've heard Mamma say so at least a hundred times.*
> *But it can't last forever—one day, someone is going to*
> *win. I wonder when that day will be. There are some who*
> *never thought this war would last as long as it has. They*
> *thought it would be over in a matter of months—it's going*
> *on the second year. I believe things have to get better.*

Salina read the last sentence again and wondered if she'd written it because she was trying to convince herself to believe that things *would* get better.

But things didn't get better. Four days after the battle at Ox Hill, the Network brought Salina the news that her Daddy had been arrested and was being held prisoner at the Old Capitol Prison in Washington.

☆☆☆☆☆☆☆

Taylor Sue watched with a sense of odd fascination as Salina decoded a message from a man named Will Tanner who lived in Alexandria. "Who is this Will Tanner?" she inquired.

Salina replied, "Will is the husband of my Aunt Ruby. Aunt Ruby became a widow when my Uncle Holden—one of my daddy's brothers—was killed in the war with Mexico. A few years ago, she remarried, and now she and Will live in Alexandria. Will is the editor of a newspaper there."

"Are Ruby and Will a part of this Network of your father's?" Taylor Sue wanted to know.

Salina nodded. She reread the message. According to the translation, it was time to get the trunk. Daddy had ordered as much just before he was arrested. Salina bit her lower lip. "I've got to go to Washington."

"That's ridiculous," Taylor Sue said. "How do you propose getting there?"

"I'll ride Starfire," Salina said simply. "Tabitha will know the way. She'll tell me how to get there."

"And what if you're stopped by a patrol?" Taylor Sue asked. "It's much too dangerous, Salina. Alexandria is a Union-occupied town."

"I know that. But my daddy's in prison. He'll need me to continue with the Network until his release." To Salina's way of thinking, it seemed logical enough. "God only knows where Jeremy is, and Reverend Yates relies on the communications from Daddy. Ethan will soon run out of medicine, and who knows what the status of the western campaign is if Daddy's behind bars? Can't you see I've got to go?"

"You're mother will never allow it, Salina," Taylor Sue said with certainty. "Neither will Ethan."

"Ethan is too busy with Dr. Phillips at Chantilly. He won't notice I'm missing until after I'm gone. Mamma—well, Jubilee hardly lets me see her anyway, so she won't know to miss me. I'm not going to ask for permission. I'm just going to go. Daddy wouldn't send word to have the trunk moved unless he thought it was important enough to do so," Salina pointed out.

"It's a half-day's ride from here," Taylor Sue reminded her. "I can't let you go alone, Salina. I'll just have to go with you."

"And what will you tell *your* mother?" questioned Salina. "She'll forbid you, and if you breathe a word of this to Ethan, he'll..."

"He'll pitch a fit," Taylor Sue nodded. "I know Ethan—very well. That's why we should leave right after we finish up at the hospital today. Be ready to go. I don't know if I can help you with any of this Network business, but at least I can give you moral support."

Salina smiled. "You'd do this for me?"

Taylor Sue nodded. "I can see by that stubborn set of your jaw that you're going regardless. Jeremy and Ethan have their roles in contributing to the Cause. This will be our contribution."

Salina warned, "As you said, it's dangerous, and risky, and..."

Taylor Sue put her hand over Salina's mouth. "Don't talk so much, or I just might change my mind. It requires daring, and we've at least got that."

After their long hours at the field hospital, the girls rode to the parsonage to wait until darkness fell. Reverend Yates was beside himself when they explained what they intended to do. "Have the two of you gone daft? I can't allow this."

"Reverend Yates, not long ago, you told me I could count on you for help, should I need it. I need it now," Salina implored with her expressive eyes. "You're the one who brought the message to me from the Tanners."

Reverend Yates paced the floor. Captain Hastings had told him to trust Salina. He paced some more. He didn't want Salina to become involved any deeper than she was, but it appeared there was no way around it. And what of Taylor Sue Carey? She was old enough to make her own choices. Finally he nodded. "You can go to the Tanners, pick up the trunk, and come directly home."

Salina shook her head, "No. I'm going to see my daddy as well."

"Somehow, I figured you'd say that," the Reverend sighed. "You'll have to stay with the Tanners until it's safe for you to visit the prison. Captain Hastings uses an alias name in Washington..."

"Gary Hayes," Salina supplied the fake name of the "reporter" whom Captain Hastings pretended to be.

Reverend Yates nodded. When would he cease to be surprised by this little lady who was so obviously her father's daughter? "Gary Hayes is the man the Union *thinks* they've arrested. If they were to learn that he is in truth Garrett Hastings, he could face the gallows."

"We'll have to come up with a plan on our way to Alexandria, then," Salina decided, but she thought it might be easier said than done. "We'll think of something, Reverend."

"How will you get the trunk back here? Without a wagon, you have no way to transport it," the Reverend argued.

Salina smiled. "You wouldn't mind meeting us in Alexandria, would you, Reverend?"

"Meet you in Alexandria? Why, that's preposterous!" The Reverend shook his head, but then the notion settled in. "Well, I suppose I could tell your mothers that I was going to bring you back. Ethan will be furious when he finds out."

"Then we won't tell him until it's absolutely necessary to do so," Salina grinned.

Reverend Yates nodded. "All right, I'll meet you there. I'll leave at first light tomorrow morning. See if there's a chance that you might visit the Captain—Mr. Hayes, I mean—before I get there. He'll tell you what he wants accomplished."

"Thank you, Reverend." Salina's gratitude showed in her green eyes. "We'll stop by way of Tabitha's boarding house."

"Yes, do that. She'll have directions, and perhaps even a change of clothes." Reverend Yates looked down at the girls' blood-spattered work dresses. "God go with you."

"Would you pray for us?" Taylor Sue requested.

"By all means." The Reverend joined hands with the girls, and the three agreed together as he asked for protection and favorable circumstances throughout their mission.

At the boarding house in Fairfax, Tabitha had Salina and Taylor Sue change into trousers and flannel shirts. She gave them each a long coat to keep them warm. "This way you'll not be bogged down with petticoats and the like. You'll need passes to get through the Yankee lines," Tabitha said with certainty.

Tabitha sat down and created two sets of traveling papers. "These military passes will get you through the picket lines. If you stick to the route I've indicated, you probably won't need these at all—but better to be prepared than not." Tabitha wrote fake names on each of the traveling passes. "Salina, you will use the name Sarah. Taylor Sue will pose as Teresa. You're sisters going to visit your Uncle Gary Hayes. Here is the Tanners' address. By the time you come back from your journey, I'll have those dresses washed up for you, and I'll get the bloodstains out."

"Thank you," Taylor Sue said gratefully.

"You've been a tremendous help," Salina also thanked her. "Tabitha?"

"Yes, my dear?" The old woman tipped her head to one side.

"You've not heard any word about Jeremy Barnes, have you?" Salina shyly asked.

"No, Salina, I'm afraid he's not made contact in days. That might mean it's just not safe for him to try," Tabitha said encouragingly. "No news is good news. If they're dead, their names usually show up on casualty lists. If they're not dead, they're usually hiding." She winked. "Off with you both. You've a hard night's ride ahead of you."

Chapter Sixteen

*W*ill and Ruby Tanner worked long into the night in order to get the latest edition of their newspaper printed in time for circulation first thing in the morning. The front page had its standard articles pertaining to the most recent battles, but the editorial section would again feature a thought-provoking piece authored by 'Gary Hayes' in its column.

Gary Hayes, through the mighty power of the pen, was attacking the abolitionists again—this time denouncing them for wanting to free the Southern slaves without giving thought to the results their freedom would bring. While an opponent of the distasteful tradition of slavery in the South, Gary Hayes sought to analyze the situation in a practical manner. He posed difficult questions about employment, housing, and education for the black-skinned people that the North was not rushing to answer. There were factions in the North that didn't want the slaves freed any more than the Southerners did. Some Northern men were willing to fight to preserve the Union, but were adamant when it came to slavery—and they would quit rather than be party to its dissolution. Yet at the rate things were headed, slavery was quickly becoming the main focus of the war, and States' Rights and secession were paling by comparison. Gary Hayes wrote with the purpose of challenging readers, to make them contemplate these uncomfortable questions, if not act upon them.

The light rapping on the back door almost went unheard. Ruby answered, peeking out into the darkness. "My goodness—what's this now?"

"May we come in, Mrs. Tanner?" Salina asked in a low voice.

"And why should I be letting two street urchins such as yourselves in here at this time of night?" Ruby questioned.

Salina took off her wide-brimmed hat and let her hair fall. "Because the Network instructed me to come to you."

"My word!" Ruby, astonished to find her niece on the back stoop, swept Salina and Taylor Sue quickly inside. "Come—hurry!"

"We're here because I was sent word about a certain traveling trunk which is said to be in your possession," Salina clarified. Then she smiled. "Hello, Aunt Ruby. How are you?"

Ruby shook her head in amazement. Just by looking at Salina, Ruby could see the strong resemblance this girl bore to her father. "Garrett said she'd come, Will, and sure enough he was right! You're either mighty brave, Salina—or plumb crazy, child. Who might this be?"

"This is Taylor Sue Carey. She's going to be my sister-in-law someday soon. She wouldn't allow me to come alone, so I had to bring her with me. She's promised to never say a word about anything concerning the Network. Daddy will vouch for her."

"Well, now," Ruby stood with her hands on her wide hips, studying the pair before her, "who exactly sent you to us?"

"Tabitha Wheeler," Salina answered. "She gave us aliases and suggested that we appear as sisters, the nieces of Gary Hayes."

"Tabitha Wheeler is a clever one," Will nodded. "Come on in and set yourselves down. Ruby'll fix you something to eat, and we'll talk about this."

"Tabitha said you'd have details for me," Salina said after taking a sip of cold milk. Taylor Sue sat quietly, listening, while she ate her stew.

"Aye," Will chuckled, "she sure is Garrett's. Doesn't waste any time in getting down to the business at hand."

Salina smiled, pleased at Mr. Tanner's compliment. "I want to know everything you think it's safe to tell me. And I want to know what happened to land Daddy in prison."

"How much do you know about your father's Washington cover?" Ruby asked.

"Enough," Salina answered with a light shrug. "I know more about his work in the western territories."

Ruby and Will exchanged a speaking glance. They, too, knew of the Confederacy's plans of capturing the West. Will didn't want to discuss the western campaign, though. He answered Salina, saying, "It started when I began to write editorials under the pen name of Gary Hayes. I did a few series, and our subscribers must have liked what they were reading because the circulation of our little paper doubled and then tripled in no time. So, I kept writing. When your father came to town, he needed cover to be able to go in and talk to some people in high places. We concocted the notion of him being Gary Hayes. He hasn't actually written any of the articles himself, but he brings me information so that I can."

"The thing you must understand about the Federal Government is that Abraham Lincoln will go to extremes to get done what he wants accomplished," Ruby added. "He ordered the U.S. Secret Service to stop the flow of information to the South at all costs. In the meantime, he has authorized the arrest and imprisonment of anyone even remotely suspected to have Southern sympathies."

"This time, Garrett happened to be here in town just after we published a particularly searing piece about the ineptness of the Northern Generals," Will told the girls. "Just after Pope's failure at the second battle at Bull Run—or Manassas you probably call it—and the battle at Chantilly..."

"Ox Hill," Salina smiled. "Funny how the North and South can't even agree on what to call their battles."

"The Southerners name them after the nearest town, like Manassas, but the Northerners name them after the nearest body of water, like Bull Run," Ruby said. "The same is true of Shiloh or Pittsburg Landing in Tennessee."

"In any case," Will got them back on track, "Lincoln replaced General John Pope with General George B. McClellan four days ago. The next day, Garrett was at Willard's Hotel in Washington, talking with someone from the White House, when somebody must have recognized him as Gary Hayes, and turned him in. I feel just awful about his being in prison on my account. The article was rather controversial, but they've never given Garrett—I mean Gary Hayes—any trouble before this. Somebody evidently had a bee in their bonnet, and I feel I'm to blame for his arrest." Will lowered his head, his shoulders slumped, and he stared down at his folded hands with a heavy sigh.

Salina touched Will's shoulder. "It's not your fault, Mr. Tanner. Daddy could have been arrested anywhere. He's wanted by the Yankees, and he knows it. He takes the risks knowing full well there's a chance involved. We have to thank God that he's been taken in with the Yankees thinking he's Gary Hayes. If they knew he was Garrett Hastings, well, I really don't like to think of what might happen then." A chill ran through Salina as she remembered talking with Daddy and Reverend Yates about spies being hanged if they were caught. "If they think he's a journalist with Southern sympathies, won't they have to file charges and prove his guilt?" she asked.

Will shook his head. "Lincoln's taken it upon himself to suspend the writ of *habeus corpus*."

Taylor Sue asked, "What does that mean?"

"*Habeus corpus* requires that a prisoner be brought before a court in order to decide the legality of his being kept in custody," Will explained. "Lincoln, for as long as the war lasts, has suspended this right. There's no telling how long Garrett will be in prison."

"Will they let me see him?" Salina wanted to know. "I'm his daughter!"

"Gary Hayes hasn't got a daughter," Ruby reminded her. She tipped her head to one side, "But I reckon he's got a *niece*," she glanced at Taylor Sue with a grin, "or two."

"He does at that," Will chuckled. "Ruby, why don't you get these little ladies settled in for the night, and we'll come up with a plan of action for them by morning."

Ruby knew how her husband's mind worked. "Come along, then. We've got a nice little hideaway up in the attic. It's where your father stays whenever he has business in Washington."

Taylor Sue was asleep in no time, but Salina sat on the floor next to the trunk. She took the key from around her neck, about to open the trunk, when another series of yawns overtook her. The trunk could wait, she decided. Tomorrow would be soon enough to explore its contents. She climbed into the trundle bed next to Taylor Sue's bed, pulling the quilts up to her chin. Downstairs she could hear Ruby and Will as they resumed their work on the newspaper. Salina yawned tiredly. In the morning, Ruby and Will would have a plan, and Reverend Yates should be here soon. *But I want to see my daddy...*

☆☆☆☆☆☆☆

"Your mothers were fit to be tied," Reverend Yates told Salina and Taylor Sue at breakfast.

Salina toyed with the biscuits and gravy on her plate. "Mamma's really upset, isn't she?"

The Reverend nodded. "I've instructions to bring the two of you home just as quickly as possible."

"Well," Ruby interrupted, "they've come all this way—they're not leaving just yet. Will and I have a plan to get Salina, excuse me, *Sarah* here in to see her *uncle*."

The Reverend nodded. "I was hoping that would be the case."

Taylor Sue helped Ruby get Salina ready for her visit to Washington. They put her hair up and pinned a fashionable hat with a feather on top. She wore one of Ruby's best gowns and borrowed a pair of shoes in place of the boots she brought with her.

"I have the pleasure of introducing to you Miss *Sarah Hayes*." Ruby paraded Salina before Will and the Reverend. "How does she look?"

"Every inch a lady." Will winked at her.

Taylor Sue handed her a pair of beige fingerless gloves and a lacy parasol. "You'd be a fine actress, Salina, if you ever wanted to perform on stage."

Salina laughed, but her stomach quivered. She thought it peculiar that Taylor Sue's words should echo Daddy's about acting. Salina was nervous and excited, but she didn't dare admit, even to herself, that she was even the tiniest bit scared.

Will drove Salina to the Old Capitol Prison on the corner of First Street and Maryland Avenue. He told Salina of the imprisonment of Mrs. Rose Greenhow and Miss Belle Boyd—both of whom were Southern spies. The ladies, following their incarceration at the Old Capitol, were deported back to Richmond.

"I've heard of them both," Salina nodded. "Mrs. Greenhow was able to get information to General P.T. Beauregard that helped us win the first battle at Manassas, and Belle Boyd supplied information to General Stonewall Jackson during the Valley campaign."

Will nodded. "Don't you worry your pretty little head, *Sarah*. Just act with confidence, and there's little doubt they'll question anything you say or do."

Salina nodded. "You'll wait out here for me?"

"Yes," Will said. "I suspect this whole thing will be over soon. Go on now. I'll be praying."

"Thank you," Salina whispered.

Her wide hoop swung gracefully as she walked across the street to the entrance of the Old Capitol Prison. Salina spoke briefly with one of the sentries, and within minutes she was seated in the superintendent's office, given permission to see her "uncle," and then escorted through dark corridors and up rickety stairs to the cell where "Gary Hayes" was confined.

Captain Hastings schooled his features to show no surprise at the appearance of his daughter in his prison cell. "Hello there," he said with a spreading grin, his heart nearly bursting with pride at her pluck for coming to him.

"Hello, *Uncle Gary*," Salina said with a wavering smile. She held her arms out. "Come and give your favorite niece *Sarah* a hug as reward for coming to visit with you in this dreadful place!"

He did as she commanded, noting how she managed to convey the jist of the charade and her fake name to him. "You're wonderful," he murmured in her ear. He was constantly aware of the sentry outside who paced the hallway, back and forth, back and forth.

Salina had expected to be locked in with Daddy, but he explained that open doors were rewards for good behavior.

"Have they told you why you're here?" Salina asked.

The Captain answered, "It's my understanding that by exercising freedom of speech and press—as indicated in the Constitution—I have stretched the nerves of some prominent people here in Washington. An article was labeled treasonous, so here I am."

Sarah glanced over her shoulder and out the door. The rooms across the hall were filled with an assortment of captives.

"Most of us jailed here are political prisoners, *Sarah*," the Captain said by way of explanation. "Although, I gather there is quite a selection of smugglers, blockade runners, and spies here as well. It's good of you to visit."

Between the lines of his casual phrases, Salina sensed the underlying warning in Daddy's words. He was somehow telling her that if she weren't cautious, she, too, could be imprisoned if it were discovered that she was a link to the Network.

"Will you sing, Sarah? The boys across the hall were telling me how Miss Belle Boyd was here, just last month, and she used to sing for them. Would you sing for us now?" the Captain entreated her.

Salina knew better than to sing any of the songs from home, and she couldn't bring herself to sing any of the Northern songs, like *Battle Hymn of the Republic* or *Battle Cry of Freedom*, so she decided upon three hymns from church: *All Hail the Power of Jesus' Name, Amazing Grace,* and *Rock of Ages.*

She received a rousing thunder of applause and requests for more. She was just about to begin *Sweet By and By* when the superintendent appeared at the door of the cell. He clapped, slowly and loudly. "Well done, little lady. Quite a voice."

Sarah swallowed and curtsied. "Thank you, sir."

"Where did you come from?" the superintendent asked. "I detect a hint of Southern drawl in your words."

"Perhaps because I came from Alexandria," Salina answered evenly. "Just across the Potomac River."

"You don't say." The superintendent glanced over her slight form. "How'd you like to take your uncle right back over the Potomac with you when you leave? You tell him to behave and perhaps he won't have to be our guest again."

"I'm being released?" the Captain was quick to inquire.

"Got your release papers right here." The superintendent fanned himself with the documents. "Seems that little investigation the detective was conducting turned out to be a wild goose chase."

Captain Hastings nodded. "I see."

Salina stood close to Daddy, holding his hand firmly. "May I really take him out of here?"

"Aye, Miss, just as soon as we clear him through the front office. Follow me," the superintendent ordered gruffly.

The Captain dared to look down at Salina, whose eyes were dancing with joy. His glance warned her than they were not yet out the door. But twenty minutes later, they were.

Will Tanner had a look of astonishment on his face. "Good day to you, *Mr. Hayes.*"

The Captain grinned. "And to you, Mr. Tanner. It seems the Yanks had quite a time making charges stick."

"It does seem that way," Will nodded. "Shall we go home now? I'm quite certain Ruby will have a big dinner planned."

"Shall we go, *Sarah*?" Daddy asked. He turned to see what it was that captured her attention. The old man from Fairfax leaned against a lamppost half a block away. He touched the brim of his hat in acknowledgment.

Captain Hastings nodded, then helped Salina into Will's carriage. "Don't hurry, Will. Just drive at a regular pace."

Salina leaned over and whispered, "That's him, the old man from Fairfax—or Duncan Grant, I suppose I should say."

"Yes," Captain Hastings muttered. "And no doubt he can see through my charade just as easily as I can see though his."

"Do you really think so?" Salina asked. "Then he'll know about me."

"Nothing more than being my daughter, Sally," the Captain assured her. "The old man has been here in Washington for the past few days—ever since my arrest, in fact—and that's not like him. He usually roams the countryside. I believe he was the one who tipped off the detective who worked on my case."

"But the charges didn't stick," Salina said.

"I know, and I don't think that he meant for them to. I think this little prison interlude was meant as a warning. I got too close," Captain Hastings said. "Duncan didn't like it."

"How do you know that?" Salina asked.

"Let's just say I *borrowed* some documents I found in Duncan's office after hours one night when I paid a friendly visit in his absence. That upset him, and so he simply returned the favor. Did you hear the superintendent mention an investigation?"

"Yes," Salina nodded.

"Well, I'd venture to guess that Duncan set the whole thing up, then threw the roadblocks in so they'd have no proof," the Captain said. "Right kind of him, don't you think?"

Salina glanced back, not seeing the old man due to the distance they had traveled. "Yes, right kind of him." She looked up at her daddy. "Why do you think he let you get away?"

The Captain shrugged. "Duncan's up to something. He's looking for me, yes, but I think, too, he's trying to figure out what I'm doing. He can't do that if I'm locked up, now can he?"

"I suppose you're right. If you're in prison, you're not operating the Network, and then there's nothing for him to track. That's why you've got to be more careful than ever!" Salina warned, then she asked, "Where are the documents now?"

"In my trunk," the Captain said.

"Which is safely stowed in the attic, Captain, never fear," Will said.

"I need you to take that home with you, Sally. It's not safe to leave it here. I don't want Duncan to stumble upon it so close to Washington, and I don't want the Tanners implicated."

"Taylor Sue and I came on horseback, but Reverend Yates brought his wagon," Salina informed him. "We'll take it back to Chantilly."

"Taylor Sue Carey is with you?" the Captain asked. "Why on earth?"

Salina smiled. "She wouldn't let me come by myself. She insisted."

"What did your Mamma say about that?" Captain Hastings wanted to know.

Salina fidgeted. "Well, Mamma doesn't exactly know where I am at the moment."

"Sally," the Captain raised an eyebrow in question. "What have you done now?"

☆☆☆☆☆☆☆

"I do declare, Ruby," Captain Hastings sat back in his chair and rubbed his full stomach, "your chicken and dumplings are almost as good as my wife's."

"They ought to be, Captain," Ruby smiled. "It's your wife's recipe."

The Captain grinned. "No wonder I recognized them." He checked his pocket watch and said to Reverend Yates, "I suppose we should settle the business of the trunk."

"Whenever you're ready," the Reverend nodded.

Ruby asked tactfully, "Taylor Sue, might I enlist your help with the dishes now that dinner is over?"

"Of course," Taylor Sue smiled, thankful for a legitimate task to keep her busy while Salina went upstairs to the attic with the men. Once the door at the top of the stairs was shut firmly, Taylor Sue confided to Ruby, "All that secret stuff doesn't interest me much, but Salina thrives on it."

Ruby nodded. "I understand she's getting quite good at it."

Taylor Sue agreed, "Better her than me."

Upstairs, the Captain used his own key to the trunk to unlock it. Inside were Yankee uniforms, Rebel uniforms, and a few articles of civilian clothing. There were books and Northern newspapers, and even a few photographs. "I'll be much more comfortable when I'm back in my own uniform," Captain Hastings declared.

"Isn't that dangerous for you to wear gray behind Union lines, Daddy?" Salina asked.

Captain Hastings held Salina's shoulders in a firm grasp. "Yes, it's dangerous, but if I'm caught in my own uniform, they will treat me as a prisoner of war. If I'm caught in civilian clothes, and they know I've been spying..."

"They will hang him for certain," the Reverend concluded.

"Yes," the Captain nodded. "The Yankees would arrest Will and Ruby if they find Confederate uniforms here. They'd call it treason and take them away. That's why we've got to get the trunk back to Shadowcreek. The Gary Hayes articles have made the Yankees suspicious. There's no telling if or when they might decide to come here and conduct an unwarranted search."

Captain Hastings emptied the contents onto the trundle bed. He showed Salina how to get into the false bottom of the trunk. "If someone didn't know where to look closely, they'd miss the fact that there's a secret cache here."

Under the bottom panel of the trunk the documents from Duncan Grant's office were hidden. Captain Hastings pulled them out of the leather envelope and spread them out on the desk. He recited a check list of the items the pages contained: maps, instructions, gold and silver shipment schedules, mail schedules, steamer schedules, and a list of the names of stagecoach station masters who were loyal to the Confederacy.

"Once our armies invade Arizona and New Mexico, Nevada will be the next objective. The gold and silver mined there is shipped east at regular intervals. These schedules will help determine when our men should make a strike on the railroads. The mail schedules are important because some of the precious metals are carried by the U.S. Mail—same for the steamer ships. These maps need to be put into the hands of Hank Warner in Virginia City, Nevada. He'll need them to plan a raid there."

"Hank Warner?" Salina was surprised. "Joetta's husband?"

"Correct." The Captain tapped Salina's nose with his finger. "I told you that there are people you wouldn't suspect involved in this, didn't I?"

"Yes, you did," Salina nodded. "Is it safe to mail the maps to Hank Warner?"

The Captain smiled. "You see Joetta from time to time, Sally. I was hoping you might volunteer to post her next letter to her husband. We'd enclose these maps, and then it wouldn't look so suspicious. Hank says Joetta writes to him on a regular basis, so no one should suspect anything out of the ordinary."

"I see her at the Chantilly post office quite a bit," Salina said. "When I'm there checking for letters from you."

"Good. Then you'll see to it?" he asked.

"Of course," Salina said simply.

"I have mailed some other documents that I found. I sent them by express to Mamma's sister, Genevieve, in San Francisco," the Captain said.

Salina looked startled. "But I know for a fact Aunt Genevieve's husband is a staunch supporter of the Union, Daddy. Mamma says so."

"The package will be safe enough with Genevieve. She'll hold it until..." the Captain glanced at Reverend Yates, who shook his head. Silently, the Captain agreed that this probably wasn't the best time to disclose to Salina that he had plans to send her, Ethan, and Annelise west to escape the war-torn east. "She'll keep it until she's contacted by the Network," the Captain said instead. He piled the items he'd taken from the trunk back on top of the false bottom.

"What about the maps and these other documents? Don't you want them hidden?" Salina asked.

Captain Hastings shook his head. "You and Taylor Sue are going to smuggle them through the lines, beneath your hoops."

"But, Daddy, Tabitha gave us boys' clothes to wear on the trip here," Salina explained.

"Never fear, Miss Salina," Reverend Yates said. "I've brought a trunk of my own. This one has your own clothes in it, yours and Taylor Sue's."

Salina looked from Reverend Yates, to Daddy, to Will, who simply winked at her. She shook her dark head. "You think of everything, don't you?"

Will Tanner returned her smile. "We do try, Salina. We have to."

The Captain held Salina firmly by the shoulders. "Sally..."

She looked up into his troubled eyes. "What, Daddy?"

"Sally-girl, if something were to happen to me, so that I was unable to go on working on the western campaign..."

Salina started to argue that nothing was going to happen, but the Captain put his finger to her lips to silence her and he continued, "Anything could happen and you've got to accept that right here and now. You know the dangers and the risks and the purpose. We've discussed this all before. This time, I need to know without any doubt that you'd keep working with the Network if I weren't here, and carry on. Would you do that, Sally? Would you do whatever might be asked of you, in my place, to keep things on schedule? It's a big responsibility, more than a father should ask of his daughter, but these are desperate times, and I must know if I can count on you."

Salina remembered Jeremy saying once that working for the Network was like signing his own death warrant, and Daddy was willing to risk his life for it as well. She nodded. "You can rely on me, Daddy. But nothing's going to happen to you."

The Captain hugged her closely, not wanting to let her go. "I pray you're right!"

☆☆☆☆☆☆☆

Lance Colby seethed privately. He paced the floor in Duncan's office in an agitated gait.

"Something on your mind, Lieutenant?" Duncan Grant asked.

Colby opened his mouth to speak, but then snapped it shut again. He shook his dark blond head in a negative motion.

Duncan didn't believe him. He glanced at his lieutenant. "Speak your mind, Colby."

The pacing came to an abrupt halt. Lieutenant Colby braced his arms, elbows locked, and stared at Captain Grant across the desk between them. "I can't believe you let him get away."

"Garrett Hastings, you mean?" Duncan sat back in his chair, folding his hands across his chest.

"Yes," Colby nodded briefly. "I know that man was a friend of yours, but we had him locked up, and you let him walk. Our orders are to stop information from reaching Southern points. With him in jail, his network of spies and couriers would have been at a loss without him."

"If you think that, you've got a lot to learn about Garrett Hastings," Duncan said between clenched teeth. "He'd have a contingency plan, you can be sure of that. And keeping him behind bars would have only delayed an attempted escape. You remember when he broke in here and took those maps and things?"

Lance Colby nodded.

"Well, you know Hastings was searched when he was taken to the Old Capitol and *nothing was found*," Captain Grant said. "I'm inclined to believe someone's holding the documents elsewhere for him. I need Hastings out of prison so that he will lead me to the documents. Do you understand now?"

"I see your point," Colby lowered his light blue gaze. "You're hoping that we can catch him when he goes after the documents, that way we can steal them back."

"I'm hoping it will be that simple," Duncan admitted, but in the back of his mind he knew nothing was simple when it concerned Captain Hastings. "You saw him leave the Tanners' print shop?"

"Yes, two hours ago," Colby confirmed. "He was not headed in the direction of Chantilly. He was heading toward Frederick, Maryland. According to some early reconnaissance reports, General Lee is marching troops in a northerly direction."

"Hmmm," Captain Grant pursed his lips together, his brow furrowed with deep thought.

Colby started to pace again. "Are you thinking that he might make contact with Barnes?"

"Well, we know Barnes enlisted and is riding with Jeb Stuart," Duncan nodded. "There's another good reason for letting his release be processed. If he doesn't lead us to those documents, perhaps we can capture Barnes."

"Before Major John Barnes does," Colby added. "If the Major gets to Jeremy before we do, he'll have the boy killed before we can question him."

Duncan nodded grimly. "I tend to agree with you. Major Barnes would not hesitate to create an *accident*. I need Jeremy alive if he's to be of any use to us." He reached for a quill to dip into the inkwell and scrawled an order on a piece of parchment paper. "Take this to Colonel Miller at the War Department."

Colby read the lines, which composed Captain Grant's formal request for a transfer of duty from Washington to General McClellan's headquarters. A smile formed on Lieutenant Colby's lips. "Very good, sir. Consider it done." Colby started for the door, then stopped. "Sir?"

"Yes, Lieutenant?" Captain Grant inquired.

"I meant no disrespect, questioning your judgment," Colby explained.

Duncan Grant waved the apology aside. "Don't think about it. Just think about how hard we'll have to ride to catch up with McClellan and the rest of the Army of the Potomac."

Chapter Seventeen

*T*hank ya, Miss," a recovering in-
fantry soldier said. "Thank ya kindly." The private leaned back into
his pillow, tired and still hungry. Salina fed him a whole bowl of grits,
but it didn't quite fill his stomach. It tasted good, though, and he truly
couldn't complain after going for weeks without much food at all, or
any shoes. To lie in bed, without having to march, was almost a treat.

"Dr. Phillips will be here to check on you shortly, Private Samuels.
Is the pain very bad today?" asked Salina.

"I'm getting used to it, Miss. Thank you for asking. I'm lucky,"
Private Samuels said. "Yesterday the Doc told me if my wound had
been an inch deeper or wider, I'd have lost the leg for all the damage
that shell-fire did to me."

"Yes, you are blessed," Salina nodded. "I'll be back in a little
while. I've promised Colonel Crawford that I would read another
chapter of his Sir Walter Scott novel this afternoon."

"I'll be seeing you later then, Miss." Private Samuels reached up to tip his cap to her but then remembered he didn't have a cap on.

Salina returned the private's smile. He was only seventeen, a year younger than Ethan. "You just call me if you need anything."

"Yes, Miss," Private Samuels replied.

Salina moved through the ward. She shivered as she passed the room which had been used as the operating room following the battle. It was from there that she had heard the haunting sounds of moaning and shrieking caused by operations and amputations after the fighting. Salina had controlled her curiosity and stayed where she should, not venturing where she shouldn't.

Salina passed Taylor Sue, who was writing a letter home for a blinded soldier. "How are you holding up?"

"Fine," Taylor Sue answered. "I'm glad that Joetta Warner and Mrs. Armstrong will be here soon to relieve us."

Salina yawned, "I am rather tired today."

"You haven't had a decent night's sleep since we came back from Alexandria a week ago," Taylor Sue pointed out. "You should go home and rest. Sleepwalking isn't going to benefit anyone here. In fact, I would wager that you don't even know what day it is."

"Yes, I do. It's Monday, the fifteenth day of September of the year 1862." Salina stuck her tongue out at Taylor Sue.

Taylor Sue laughed. "Go home, Salina."

"I'll sleep tonight, that's for sure," Salina said. She left Taylor Sue and went to read to Colonel Crawford.

Pulling up a ladder-backed chair next to the Colonel's cot, Salina thumbed through the yellowed pages of *Ivanhoe* to locate the book-mark. "What chapter did we leave off with yesterday?" She continued to search. "Ah, here it is." She glanced out the window. "The sun is shining, Colonel. It's a beautiful day. How are you feeling? Do you still have a fever?" Salina put her hand to the Colonel's brow and found it chilled, rather than hot. She snatched her hand away quickly, wiping it on her blood-speckled apron. "Colonel Crawford?"

No response. The Colonel's chest did not rise and fall with breath, nor did he open his eyes at all. A most serene expression had settled over the officer's face, and Salina realized he was not in pain anymore. She pulled the sheet over his head.

"Orderly!" Salina called, huge tears in her emerald eyes. Her voice was choked up. "Orderly!" she called again, this time louder.

The first orderly whistled for a second orderly, and together they took away the Colonel's stiff body on a stretcher. Salina's shoulders shook with sobs. Dr. Phillips put an arm around her shoulders, drawing her away, outside for a breath of fresh air.

"Why don't you run along home to Shadowcreek, Miss Salina. There's nothing happening that can't wait for Mrs. Warner or Mrs. Armstrong to get here," the doctor said.

Salina nodded, wiping the tears away with the back of her hand. "I've never t-touched a d-dead man b-before."

"It pains me to have to see you here at all. You and Miss Taylor Sue shouldn't have to view the casualties of war firsthand," Dr. Phillips shook his graying head and took his wire-rimmed spectacles from his eyes. "The two of you are brave and have worked like tireless troopers. I'm proud to have your much-needed assistance and service. You do cheer up the recovery rooms considerably."

"I want to do what I can, Dr. Phillips." Salina's sobs were lessening.

"Death is never an easy thing," Dr. Phillips said somberly. "But for some, it is a release, God rest their souls."

Salina walked slowly across the ravaged fields and through the scarred orchard on her way home to Shadowcreek. Bullets had mown down cornstalks once taller than she was, and many of the trees had minié balls imbedded in their trunks. The past week had taken its toll on her, and she was more weary than she thought.

Upon the return from Alexandria, Reverend Yates had been kind enough to smooth the way. Mamma was more relieved that Salina was home safely than she was angry about her leaving. Salina had explained how she didn't feel wanted or needed during the time when Mamma was so sick, so she didn't think Mamma would notice or care that she had gone.

Mamma immediately informed Jubilee that Salina was not to be banished from her room anymore. Mamma encouraged Salina to come visit whenever she was not working at Chantilly. She said she was partly to blame for Salina's disappearance because she'd been too depressed to think of anything but losing the baby, and she admitted to shutting Salina and Ethan out. For the past three days, Mamma had made great strides in her recovery, and she had even come to supper in the dining room last night.

Ethan, on the other hand, had been downright furious. In fact, he still hadn't spoken to Salina since her return, and she didn't know if he'd talked to Taylor Sue or not. The two of them had yet to announce their engagement. Salina knew that Ethan avoided the rooms where she and Taylor Sue tended to the wounded. She had tried to ask him if he'd heard from Jeremy, but Ethan's reply was a curt "No."

Jeremy. Salina hugged her elbows close to her body and kept plodding through the field. *I shouldn't have been so cross at Jeremy for kissing Lottie that day,* she told herself. She had been so hurt that he'd taken the time to bid her cousin goodbye yet couldn't spare a moment to say farewell to her before he rode off howling that terrifying wail. She had no idea when she'd see him again or when she'd have the chance to apologize for acting so cool toward him.

"Missy Salina," Peter Tom met her at the edge of the vegetable garden, "Ah's got a d'livery fer ya, Missy." He pulled a sealed envelope from the back pocket of his coveralls. "Tabitha Wheeler from Fairfax done brung it over. She tole me it was mightily important dat ah was ta give it ta ya jist as soon as ya arrived home. She said ya might be expectin' it."

"Thank you, Peter Tom." Salina accepted the envelope from his hand. "You've done what you were instructed to do."

"Ah didn' open it, Missy. It gots yer name on it," the black man said.

Salina cast a sharp glance at Peter Tom, who lowered his eyes immediately to avoid her curious stare. What had he meant by a remark such as that, she wondered. But she was too weary to contemplate the idea just now. "Yes, I can see that it's got my name on it." Salina read the familiar script—it was Jeremy's handwriting—and a serene warmth circled her heart. She climbed the stairs of the veranda two at a time and plopped down in one of the wicker rocking chairs. She drew a tiny leather pouch from her pocket which contained the latest deciphering code Daddy had given her. She used it to translate Jeremy's letter:

My Darling Salina—September 9, 1862

> *I've never called you that before—darling—but that is how I've come to think of you over the last few weeks. Since my return from California, I've grown to care for you a great deal, Salina, more than I was willing to admit while I was with you. That's one of the reasons I left with your father without saying goodbye. I didn't know what I could say to you without receiving anything but a cool, distant response. You acted so reserved when Ethan and I came back from Germantown, but I know the reason why. Lottie was out of line, doing what she did, and I hope*

you'll forgive me for not taking the time to explain that I did not initiate that kiss you witnessed. I hope you understand that I would have rather been kissing you, if you'll permit me to say so. I also hope that you'll not be too angry with me for joining up with General Stuart's cavalry. You know, as I did, that it was inevitable that I would officially join the Confederate forces. I couldn't sit around any longer and not enlist to fight. I pray that your displeasure will spend itself during my absence and that you will welcome me fondly if and when I have leave to come see you.

I'm guessing that since my departure with your father, Duncan Grant has given up his watch of Shadowcreek. With us gone, he has no valid reason for spying on you and your family.

I am in Maryland. General Lee hopes to gain a victory here in enemy territory to influence England and France to support the Confederacy. Last night we had a minor skirmish in Urbana, right in the middle of General Stuart's ball.

We were acquiring supplies in Urbana when General Stuart decided that we needed a little revelry to boost morale. He gave orders to turn the hall at a deserted girls' school into a ballroom. I heard tell that the cavaliers danced with all the pretty girls who were invited to the festivities. I didn't do any dancing as I was assigned to guard the horses. Our pickets were fired on by a detachment of Union cavalry and I alerted the rest of our company to the skirmish. I saw that the hall indeed looked festive, and the soldiers, grabbing their sabres and carbines from where they hung on the walls, left the girls where they stood—promising to come back and finish the dancing.

The Yankees' attack was broken by the 1st North Carolina Cavalry, and then the men resumed their party. I returned to my post for the remainder of the night, thinking of when we danced together at Ivywood. I miss you, Salina.

I know that we are riding further north, but that's all I can tell you. I will write again, I promise, when I can. In the meantime, pray that the Lord will keep us and guide us in our quest. I met up with your father this morning. He told me of your daring trip to Washington to visit him in

prison. *I've mentioned this to you before, but you still
amaze me for being so brave, Salina. Your father sends
his love—and I send mine.*

*Pvt. Jeremy Barnes
1st Virginia Cavalry
Confederate States of America*

The pages dropped to Salina's lap. So, Jeremy *had* joined Jeb
Stuart's cavalry. A delighted smile creased the corners of her mouth.
She was glad to know where he was, and that he was fine, but to learn
that he loved her was indeed welcome news. Extremely pleased,
Salina tucked the letter into her pocket and then went upstairs to check
on Mamma. Within the hour, Salina lay sprawled across her bed, fast
asleep, with the faint notes of a war-time tune weaving its way through
her dreams of a sandy-haired horse soldier.

☆☆☆☆☆☆☆

"Ethan, please!" Dust particles and bits of hay fluttered as Salina
angrily stomped her foot on the barn floor. "You can't ignore me
forever! You've got to talk to me! I need you to talk to me."

"You haven't *needed* me since you joined the Network, Salina!"
Ethan exploded angrily. "You used to confide in me, and I felt I could
confide in you, too. But now I don't even feel like I know you at all!"

"Why not?" Salina asked. "I'm still me. I'm your sister."

"My sister who sends and receives coded messages? My sister
who tends to wounded soldiers? My sister who runs away to Alexandria and Washington without telling anyone and takes my intended
with her? My sister who fancies herself in love with my best friend?
The Salina I knew had a keen sense of adventure, but she wasn't as wild
as all this," Ethan said stubbornly. "I miss the old Salina."

Salina raised her chin, meeting Ethan's gray-green eyes squarely.
"I'm not wild. I'm just growing up. Maybe the old Salina is gone,
Ethan. I don't play with dolls, sit and embroider, or have quiet little tea
parties on the lawn anymore. This is the new Salina, and like her or not,
I'm still your sister. I have my reasons for doing what I do, or feeling
how I feel, or believing what I believe. You cannot dictate to me what
I should think or how I should act!" She fled the barn and found herself
headed for the kitchen where Jubilee was busy canning fruit for the
coming winter.

Jubilee had already apologized for keeping Salina away from Mamma's bedside. She was properly contrite for not having paid any mind to Salina's emotional hurts as well as her own. They had made their peace, and Jubilee was back to her usual ways since Mamma's condition was improving for the better.

"Massah Ethan, he'll cum 'round, Missy. Don' ya fret," Jubilee nodded knowingly, squeezing Salina gently in a one-armed hug.

"Were we yelling so loud that you could hear us from the barn?" Salina asked. She took the iron ladle from Jubilee and kept stirring in an evenly paced, circular motion.

"Loud an' clear," Missy," Jubilee said simply. "Dat boy, he don' like da way tings are changin' all 'round while he be helpless ta do anythin'. He gots ta learn dat life goes on. Change happen, no stoppin' it. A body gots ta adjust ta new changes an' den go on from dere."

Salina whispered sadly, "He says he misses me, but I miss him, too!"

"He'll cum 'round," Jubilee said prophetically. "Wait an' see, Missy."

A few hours later, Ethan found Salina in the library, studying an atlas. From over her shoulder he pointed to where the Maryland and Virginia borders touched on the map. "Here's Harper's Ferry. This is Sharpsburg," he said.

"What about them?" Salina asked. She was so pleased to have him talking to her to that she was willing to forget that he owed her an apology.

"Reverend Yates got a message through the Network. According to the sources, Stonewall Jackson has captured Harper's Ferry and General Lee has set up his headquarters near Sharpsburg, close to Antietam Creek there in Maryland. The Union's General McClellan is leading the Army of the Potomac to confront General Lee."

Sometime later, Salina and Ethan learned that the Yankee McClellan had discovered a lost copy of General Lee's Special Order No. 191, and therefore knew that Lee had divided his Army of Northern Virginia into two smaller forces. McClellan had made plans to march against the separate Confederate units, who were outnumbered by the masses of Union troops closing in. Once again, however, McClellan failed to follow through with his plans, much to the dismay of President Abraham Lincoln.

Reports of the battle that transpired at Sharpsburg were horrible. The newspapers claimed it to be the "Bloodiest Day" of the entire war to date. General Lee's ragtag army had been forced to retreat back to Virginia while the Yankees claimed the fight as a Northern victory.

Southern hopes of European intervention disintegrated while Lincoln took the opportunity to issue what he called a preliminary proclamation of emancipation. Freedom was to be granted to all slaves held in each of the states that were in rebellion. Time would tell what kind of ramifications such an edict would bring.

Chapter Eighteen

Mornings quickly resumed their now-dull routine once the last of the wounded soldiers had been taken away by ambulance wagons to Fairfax Station. There was no more need for Salina and Taylor Sue to serve as nurses.

A new restlessness nearly drove Salina mad. There was nothing to do but wait. With no word from Reverend Yates, Jeremy, or her daddy, Salina had little to combat the boredom that swept over her. She tried to fill her time helping Jubilee with the daily chores, but that, too, was merely busy work.

One afternoon, three days after the fighting at Sharpsburg, Salina jumped at the chance to go to the Chantilly post office. Mamma wanted to send a letter to her sister, Genevieve Dumont, who lived in San Francisco.

Salina secretly put Mamma's letter with the documents she and Taylor Sue smuggled out of Alexandria. Then she talked Jubilee into walking to Chantilly with her. They would pass Joetta Warner's house on the way, and Salina would volunteer to post a letter for her in which she could slip the maps to Hank Warner.

"I received a letter from Jeremy," Salina confided to Jubilee, just as she always had.

"An' what has Massah Barnes gots ta say fer hissef?" Jubilee asked.

Salina told her about his joining the cavalry, and Jeb Stuart's ball in Urbana, and then she hesitated. "And he said..."

"An' he says what?" Jubilee prodded.

"He says that he's come to care for me a great deal," Salina answered, a blush stealing over her cheeks.

Jubilee grinned. "Jist lookin' at yer face is enough ta tell Jube ya's in love wid him. It's dat same look he gits on his face, too. Miz Annelise, she figured dis would happen, but ah reckon she didn' figure so soon."

Salina merely smiled, her color high, emerald eyes dancing.

Cousin Lottie and Uncle Caleb were at the post office when Salina and Jubilee arrived. "Why Salina," Lottie purred like a spoiled kitten, "how ever have you been?"

"As well as can be expected," Salina replied politely. "And you, Lottie?"

"Oh, just fine," Lottie gushed. "I hear you've been tending to those poor, wretched, wounded soldiers since the Battle of Ox Hill."

"Yes, I have been," Salina answered. "Some of us are willing to do all that we can to help wherever we're needed most."

Lottie tossed her blonde curls. "Well, I'm sure you're made of much tougher stuff than I, Salina. I'm just so delicate, I'd surely faint at the sight of blood. It was ghastly, wasn't it?"

"I did what I could," Salina stated coolly.

"Oh, yes, I've heard *all* about it from Mary Edith. Practically everyone is talking about what brave girls you and Taylor Sue Carey are," Lottie grudgingly admired. Then she put on her most sober expression. "But please, let me extend my sympathies, I am deeply sorry."

"Sorry for what, Lottie?" Salina refrained from asking *What have you done this time?*

"Oh, dear..." Lottie put a hand to her cheek. "Haven't you seen the casualty lists? Your father is listed as missing at Sharpsburg—and so is Jeremy Barnes."

Jubilee felt Salina's grip tighten around her hand, and she saw all the color drain away from Salina's cheeks. "Cum on, Missy, we's gots ta post dose dere letters o' Miz Annelise's and Miz Joetta's."

"Lottie," Salina touched her cousin's arm. "Are you quite sure?"

Cousin Lottie's pathetic smile held a trace of wickedness. "Salina Hastings, would I lie to you? I saw their names with my own two eyes. Go see for yourself." She pointed to the bulletin board where the casualty lists were posted.

Salina waited in line with Jubilee to read through the list tacked up on the wall for public display. Under the "B's" was Private Jeremy Barnes, 1st Virginia Cavalry, *Missing*; Under the "H's" *Missing* was also printed next to Captain Garrett Hastings's name.

"Lord, hab mercy!" Jubilee cried.

Salina bit back the sobs that nearly threatened to choke her. She spied Taylor Sue, Jennilee, and Mrs. Carey across the room. Their lace handkerchiefs were wet with tears.

"Have you had bad news, too?" Salina asked.

Taylor Sue sadly replied in a hoarse whisper, "Papa was wounded at Sharpsburg."

"Oh, Taylor Sue, I'm sorry!" Salina hugged her friend, her heart hurting for her. She squeezed both Jennilee and Taylor Sue's hands. "Our prayers will be with you."

"What about your father?" Taylor Sue struggled to ask. "Is he all right?"

Salina shook her head. "He's listed as missing, and so is Jeremy." In her mind she tried to cling to the hope that they were both alive and well, out there somewhere...missing, rather than dead.

"Salina, I thank God Ethan is not out there fighting," Taylor Sue said emphatically.

Salina nodded. "But Ethan's not going to sit for this. I don't suspect he'll take it well."

Jubilee and Salina hurried back to Shadowcreek. Judging from the expression on Ethan's face when they returned, he'd already learned the bad news.

"Mamma is going to be devastated," Ethan hugged Salina tightly, "as if she hasn't had to suffer enough as it is."

"She's going to be heartbroken," Salina agreed, and the tears she'd been holding escaped down her cheeks. "What are we going to do?"

"We'll have to tell her," Ethan decided.

"Do you want to tell her, or shall I?" Salina asked.

Ethan squared his shoulders. "Let's both go to her. She'll need us now more than ever."

☆☆☆☆☆☆☆

"Look, I can't help you if you won't talk to me!" Duncan Grant pounded his fist on the table. The candlestick swayed, threatening to fall over from the force of the blow. "Garrett, are you hearing me at all?"

Captain Hastings lifted his head from where it had been resting in his hands, his elbows on the table. His eyes sparkled with green fire. "You're asking me to denounce my own kind — to turn my back on what I believe in."

"I'm asking you to sign the Oath of Allegiance," Duncan said, gritting his teeth. "All that means is that you won't take up arms against the United States."

"I can't do it," Garrett shook his dark head. "Would you, Duncan? If the Rebs had captured you, and I came to visit you in prison, would you give up so easily?"

"No," Duncan admitted. "I've put my life on the line for my country, as you have yours. A piece of paper wouldn't change my convictions one bit."

Garrett Hastings leaned back in the chair. "I won't sign that piece of paper," he murmured. "I guess that means you'll have to hang me."

"You aren't making this easy on me," Duncan Grant said angrily. "Although, you haven't made any of this easy for the past two years."

A wry smile touched Garrett's lips. "Had a hard time tracking me down, did you?"

"Until recently," Duncan conceded. "What did you do with the documents you took from my office?"

"What would you have done with them?" Garrett countered.

"Forwarded them to the War Department at my earliest convenience," Duncan sighed. "Which means the Confederacy is probably already in possession of them. We're too much alike, you and I. It's a pity we don't see eye to eye anymore."

"Yes, a pity," Garrett agreed. "You arranged for my release last time I was arrested, why not now?"

"That was the Old Capitol. I had to jerk a few strings to make that turn out all right. This—this is much different. If you'd been taken in uniform, it might not have come to this. But instead of rotting in a prisoner of war camp, you will be executed for the crimes of spying and treason. You are a traitor in the eyes of the Federal Government. Executed, Garrett—never to see Salina, Ethan, or your wife again. Doesn't that frighten you?"

Garrett shook his dark head, his deep green eyes holding Duncan's level glare. "No. I knew the risks, and I took them anyway. I have made my peace with God. You're the only one I've disappointed, I think. I wish it could have been otherwise."

Duncan Grant sighed heavily. "You're forcing my hand."

Garrett crossed his arms over his broad chest. "Do what you must, Duncan. I'm not afraid to die."

Pulling a chair closer to the table, Duncan finally sat down. "If you're truly not afraid, then I might have a plan to get you out. The way I see it, you have but two choices: to die by hanging or die trying to escape. If you succeed in the escape, you won't be dead, and I'm sure we would meet again, if that be the case."

Garrett spoke quietly, "You'd risk it for me?"

"You are my dearest friend—you have been for years. I would die in your place if I could," Duncan vowed. "You...you have a family who loves you and would mourn you. I am alone, so no one would miss me as much as they would miss you, Garrett. Are you game?"

It did not take long for Garrett to decide. He had nothing to lose save the life which they planned to take from him. "Tell me what you want me to do."

Duncan produced a map of Washington and outlined the roads that would take Garrett first to be questioned extensively by the military commission at the War Department, then to the place of his execution. "This road here," Duncan pointed, "this would offer you your best chance."

Garrett nodded. He knew of the place. "Will you be there?"

"No," Duncan shook his head. "It seems I've been conveniently ordered on an assignment out of town tomorrow. My superiors—some of whom you once served with—suspect our friendship, and they want to be sure I'm well out of the way. You'll be on your own."

"Do I have time to write home?" Garrett asked.

Duncan agreed to spare him the time. "Do it quickly. I will see it is posted. I give you my word of honor."

When Garrett had finished the letter, Duncan tucked it into his pocket. "Very well." He turned away from his friend, crossing the room to the door.

"Duncan, wait!" Garrett called. Duncan paused. Garrett embraced the Yankee Captain tightly. "Thank you for this."

"Don't thank me," Duncan muttered bitterly. "I'm sending you to your death."

"Thank you for the chance, then," Garrett said, a huge lump formed in his throat. "Think of me when I'm gone—of the good times we shared long before the war drove us apart. Tell my wife I'll always love her. Give the letter to my children. Duncan?"

"Yes?" Duncan Grant was hard-pressed to meet his dear friend's questioning glance.

"Duncan, would it be too much to hope that you could find it in your heart to look after them should I be unable to do so myself?" inquired Garrett, a catch in his voice.

"Consider it done," Duncan nodded. "Goodbye, Garrett."

"Goodbye, Duncan," Garrett's words were clear and calm, his stance was defiant.

The barred door closed between them with a heavy, resounding slam.

☆☆☆☆☆☆☆

"Whoa there, Esau. Whoa, Jacob," Reverend Yates ordered his team, halting the wagon. He wasn't looking forward to his visit to Shadowcreek today. He rolled his eyes heavenward, imploring the Heavenly Father, "Please, gracious God, go before me, and give me the strength for what I am about to tell the Hastings."

Mamma, at last up from her sickbed, ushered the Reverend into the parlour. Salina, curious to see if there was news from the Network, hid on the stairs to listen. Peter Tom brought in the locked traveling trunk that had been stored at the parsonage ever since being brought back from Alexandria. Reverend Yates handed a small package to Mamma.

"Thank you, Peter Tom," Reverend Yates nodded to the black man. "Mrs. Hastings, I wish I could say I came to bring you glad tidings. Here, why don't you have a seat?"

Mamma followed Reverend Yates' instructions obediently. Nervously she twisted her wedding band around her finger. In a soft voice that wavered, she said, "Something dreadful has happened to Garrett. That's why you've come, isn't it?"

Reverend Yates cleared his throat, "Mrs. Hastings, your husband was a very brave man, and a valiant soldier. His services to the Confederacy are invaluable..."

Mamma interrupted, "They found out Garrett was a spy, didn't they?"

The Reverend swallowed. He opened his mouth, yet no words came.

"Didn't they?" Mamma demanded. "Oh, dear Lord, he's *dead*." Mamma shut her eyes, and put a fist to her mouth to stifle the scream welling in her throat. "No," she shook her head in denial. Her eyes begged Reverend Yates to contradict what she supposed. "Reverend?"

Reverend Yates relayed the details briefly. "A few days ago, Captain Hastings was captured by the Yankees not far from Sharpsburg. He was waiting to be tried for treason against the United States. Yesterday he made an attempt to escape, but it was foiled, and as a result, he was shot down. I am truly sorry."

Mamma's voice was an anguished whisper, "No more than I, Reverend. No more than I." She refused to let the burning teardrops fall as she sank down into the rocking chair.

"If there is anything at all that I can do for you, please feel free to ask. My wife and I will help you get in touch with anyone you like, anything," the Reverend offered.

"I'll remember that," Mamma replied in monotone. "Thank you for your kindness, Reverend Yates. I realize your visit here to tell me cannot be an enjoyable task. You have always been a good friend to Garrett. I'm sure he would appreciate your coming to inform me," she escorted him through the entryway to the massive oak front door.

From her vantage point on the stairs, Salina watched Mamma lean heavily against the door when Reverend Yates was gone. Mamma's shoulders began to shake with violent, noiseless sobs. "Oh, Garrett!" she cried while tears streamed down her pale face. "Gar-rett..." She fell to her knees and whimpered while shudders wracked her body. "D-dear God, I c-can't take any m-more..."

Salina, too, was crying. She couldn't move from the hiding place on the stairs. She felt as though the life had been sapped from her entire being. *My daddy...*

Long minutes passed. Mamma heaved a great sigh, and she shouted Jubilee's name. Salina scrambled up the stairs, out of sight.

With eerie calm Mamma said to Jubilee, "Captain Hastings has been killed. Please find Salina and Ethan—send them to me in the library. Have Peter Tom put this trunk in there as well." Then her voice faltered, "Jubilee, I don't know how to tell them."

"Dose poor chillen," Jubilee took Mamma into her arms. "An' pore Miz Annelise."

Mamma raised her chin and straightened her back. "After I talk to Ethan and Salina, I would like to have a word with you, Peter

Tom, and Cromwell. Please meet me in the gazebo near the orchard in fifteen minutes."

"Yassum, will do," Jubilee nodded. "Ah's gonna find dem chillen. Pore Missy Salina, pore Massah Ethan."

☆☆☆☆☆☆☆

Salina sat rigidly still on the edge of a big leather reading chair in the cozy library. She held Celeste close, but not so tightly as to wrinkle her new dress or to dislodge the bonnet that concealed the mended cracks in the back of the French doll's china head. Salina felt the need to be close to something that reminded her of Daddy. She felt numb. Mentally, she counted all the red books on the shelves directly to the left of her, then all the blue ones, then finally the green ones.

Ethan paced the floor anxiously, a grim expression drawing his bushy eyebrows close together. He stopped abruptly when Mamma joined them in the library.

Mamma swallowed hard, glancing from her son to her daughter. "I have some bad news." She sat down in a wing-back chair next to the one Salina occupied. She did not trust her knees to keep from buckling again.

"We know about Daddy," Salina whispered hoarsely. "I was on the stairs," she confessed.

"Eavesdropping again?" Mamma raised an eyebrow in accusation.

Salina nodded. "I thought perhaps Reverend Yates was going to tell us that Daddy would be here soon. Instead he said Daddy's not coming back at all." Her chin quivered with this last statement.

Mamma looked to Ethan. "Were you listening as well?"

"Yes," Ethan admitted. "I was in the hallway. I didn't know Salina was on the stairs."

"The pair of you certainly inherited your daddy's spying talents, haven't you?" Mamma snapped. "He'd be alive if it wasn't for *spying*!" Her heart was breaking, and though she didn't mean to, she took her fears and frustrations out on Salina and Ethan.

Ethan took Mamma's hand in his own. "What do we do now?"

"We must be strong for each other," Salina instantly replied. "Daddy would want us to be."

"We're all we've got," Ethan added.

"Yes," Mamma nodded, hot tears blurred her vision. "Reverend Yates brought that trunk and this package." She sorted though a number of handwritten pages. "These are Daddy's effects—but, I can't make anything of it. It's all gibberish..."

"May I see it, Mamma?" Salina asked quietly.

"Darling, it's simply line after line of scrambled words," Mamma explained.

"Yes, I know." Salina held out her hand, and Mamma hesitantly relinquished the letter to her daughter.

The letter contained Daddy's goodbyes to each of them. He explained that Duncan Grant had a plan to help him escape, but if these letters reached Shadowcreek, it meant that the attempted escape had failed. *"Don't take time to weep for me,"* part of Captain Hastings's letter said. *"There is too much to be done. If I am killed, suspicion will be thrown upon you, my loved ones. The Yankees will not give up. I know without a doubt they will pursue the search."*

Salina untied the scarlet ribbon from around her neck. She turned the key in the lock and opened the lid with ease.

"Goodness!" Mamma exclaimed. "Where on earth did you get that, Salina?"

Salina looked to Ethan, and he nodded. She smiled tenderly. "I found it inside of Celeste when she broke open after falling off my bed. There was Union money inside—which is in a safe place; medicine—which Ethan and Dr. Phillips used up at the field hospital after the fighting; and then there were some other papers and a small book, like a diary."

Mamma's eyes widened in shocked surprise as suddenly it dawned on her. "Garrett has been using you as a screen for his covert operations." Her disbelief was unmistakable.

"Yes, Mamma, he has," Salina conceded. "But that's all I can tell you. It will be easier for you to say that you know nothing if I don't tell you anymore than that."

Mamma turned to Ethan. "And you? Are you in on this spy business as well?"

Ethan answered, "Somewhat, but not as deeply as Salina is involved, nor Jer..."

Salina cast a warning glance that silenced Ethan at once.

Mamma concluded, "Nor Jeremy Barnes. I had already guessed that much. That young man reminds me of your daddy in far too many ways." She wrung her hands staring at Salina with a wounded look in her eyes. "When I think of the shooting lessons, and the secrets, and your gallivanting off to Washington...it all fits now—and I don't like it one bit!"

Salina shifted in her chair, uncomfortable at having caused Mamma such displeasure. She asked, "What else is in the package, Mamma?"

Mamma held up a gray cavalry jacket that she had once made for the Captain. She quickly set aside the jacket as an overwhelming rush of tears washed down her face. Salina started to cry again, and even Ethan got misty-eyed.

Lovingly, Mamma's fingers gently caressed the other items that had belonged to the Captain: reading glasses, riding gloves, an empty wallet, a hat with a broken ostrich plume on the brim, some traveling papers, and the copy of his last orders.

Mamma suddenly stated, "I have to speak with the servants." She dropped the items into the chair as she stood. "Ethan, I'm going to free them. If they want to leave, I'll give them what money we can spare. Otherwise, they are welcome to stay with us."

"Free the slaves?" Ethan almost laughed at the incongruity of the situation. "Why, that's what this whole war is all about Mamma—States' Rights and keeping our property. That's what we're fighting for, isn't it?"

Mamma didn't have a clear-cut answer to Ethan's question. Instead she replied, "Keeping slaves is how the Hastings built a living out of Shadowcreek. Your Daddy wasn't a great believer in slavery, but he was raised with it, as I was, as you both were. It's just our Southern way. Before this land would pass to you, Ethan, Daddy vowed that what slaves were here at the time would be freed. Times were changing, and your daddy tried to keep abreast of the times. He allowed his slaves to work toward their freedom, and when they were gone, he did not replace them by buying new stock. Then war came, and the Yankees invaded the South, so he went to fight to defend what belonged to him. Now he's dead. He gave his life for honor, and duty, and pride in his land and in his family..." Mamma took a deep breath. "We're running out of resources, Ethan. If another raiding party comes though here—Yankee or Rebel—we won't have enough to support ourselves, let alone the servants. I'm going to give them their papers, that way they can leave freely if they should so desire."

"I'll come with you." Ethan put his arm around Mamma's shoulders, offering his strength for her to lean upon.

Salina remained in the library after Ethan and Mamma went down to the gazebo. She took out the blue Yankee uniforms, each of a different rank, with caps and boots. Two coats, several books, a Bible, and a tintype portrait of Mamma on her wedding day were among the other articles in the trunk. Salina removed field glasses and a leather pouch from the traveling trunk. The pouch contained passports with fictitious names, forged papers to cross enemy lines, a pair of train tickets for the Baltimore and Ohio Railroad, train schedules and stagecoach schedules running from St. Joseph, Missouri to San Francisco, California. A handful of medicine bottles were wrapped with Union greenbacks. When the trunk was empty, Salina lifted the false bottom. It was here that she found a small piece of paper bearing a cryptic message meant specifically for her:

> *Now it's up to you, darlin'. Be strong and coura-*
> *geous. Your aunt will be in possession of the package I*
> *sent west by the end of the month. I have faith that you*
> *will diligently carry on. The documents in the trunk are*
> *linked to the documents in the package. You will have to*
> *put the pieces together. Only then can the steps be taken*
> *which will set the campaign in motion. Timing is very im-*
> *portant. You will learn what you need to know when you*
> *need to know it. Start with the reverend—he'll know what*
> *needs to be done. You can do this. I fully believe that.*

Salina tucked the note into her pocket and continued sorting. Here she found not only the documents Daddy had shown her in Alexandria pertaining to the western campaign, but in addition she discovered a bundle of letters with return addresses bearing the names of General Robert E. Lee and General Jeb Stuart.

"If Jeremy were here, he'd know what to do with all this," she whispered aloud. She penned a message to Reverend Yates, requesting that he visit at his earliest convenience. Salina would ask him to take the trunk and its contents to Tabitha in Fairfax. She had an uneasy feeling that it was not safe to keep the trunk here at Shadowcreek. Looking through the items again, Salina studied each one carefully. Daddy had entrusted all of this to her. Each was indeed important, yet she sensed there was something *more*. Something she couldn't quite put her finger on.

Chapter Nineteen

*O*ver the next two days, ladies from the neighboring farms and plantations came to Shadowcreek to offer their condolences. They brought with them whatever food they could spare. Reverend Yates conducted a memorial service in the Shadowcreek parlour, giving tribute to the late Captain Garrett Hastings. His body, they were told, had been buried in a graveyard in Pennsylvania, but no one knew the reason why.

Salina disliked the way she looked so pale in her black mourning dress. She detested dark clothes, but the black was to represent the sorrow and the grief. She felt a good deal of both, yet she managed to keep most of it concealed inside, like Mamma and Ethan did.

The Hastings had done their crying privately, so when they were called upon by their neighbors, they expressed nothing more than gratitude and a sense of strength gained from one another to endure these trying times.

When Reverend Yates left Shadowcreek, he took with him the

trunk and all the papers. He told Salina he would drive into Fairfax first thing in the morning and deliver it to Tabitha for safekeeping. "Duncan Grant might not be around anymore, but still we must be on guard," the Reverend told Salina. "He may have eyes that we don't know about, so you beware, Miss Salina."

Through the long night, Salina kept tossing and turning, while memories of Daddy flashed continuously behind her closed eyelids. Dreams disturbed her sleep, and Salina found staring at the darkness in her room preferable to the images that haunted her.

A loud crash, the sound of breaking glass, and a scream from the servants' quarters made Salina leap from her bed. She drew aside the lace curtain and looked out the window. Peter Tom and Jubilee—Cromwell was no longer with them, for he'd taken Mamma's offer of freedom—were running toward the barnyard. Mamma was standing there in her nightgown, shouting directions. Salina's gaze followed to where Mamma was frantically pointing. The barn was on fire!

Great billows of gray smoke appeared against the ebony sky while dangerous, glowing orange flames licked furiously at the wooden structure. The servants were quick to bring buckets of water from the well, but the fire was already hot and vicious, and there was little they could do to keep it from spreading.

"Thank You, God, that the horses are still corralled in the woods!" Salina prayed thankfully. But she knew the cow and the pigs were in the barn. Peter Tom ran into the burning structure in an attempt to save the livestock, and Jubilee was holding Mamma back from running into the flames herself.

Salina grabbed her robe, left her slippers, and scurried to the top of the staircase—where she stopped dead in her tracks. At long last she stood face-to-face with the old man from Fairfax—Captain Duncan Grant himself. *"You?"* she cried out.

He wore a Union blue uniform, and he stood as still as a statue with one hand curling around the banister, the other aiming a Colt revolver directly at Salina. "Whoa, there, little lady," the old man said. The voice was not old as its owner appeared to be, and it held no trace of a Southern accent.

Salina lifted her chin defiantly. "I know who you are! You have no right to come into our house uninvited!"

"As true as that may be, honey, this isn't the time for formalities. I need to get you, your brother, and your mamma out of here just as quickly as possible. Go get dressed as fast as you can," he ordered.

"Why should I?" Salina demanded.

He took two steps towards her, his steely eyes showing strong determination. "Because I said so, that's why. Now scoot."

Salina fled to her room, but she stopped in front of the armoire where most of her dresses were stored.

"I thought I told you to get dressed," the old man said roughly upon entering her room.

"Jubilee usually dresses me," Salina said simply.

"You can't dress yourself?" the Yankee Captain asked incredulously.

"Well, I can't reach the buttons down the back," Salina retorted. "Nor lace my stays."

"Lord, grant me patience," the old man rolled his eyes heavenward. He yanked open the doors of the armoire, sorting through the frilled and ruffled dresses. "These won't do at all. I've seen you out riding in more practical clothes. Where are those?"

Salina did not reply.

"Never mind, I've got something for you to wear." The old man sighed impatiently. He pulled off his gray wig and the set of false whiskers he wore. "No need for the disguise anymore, seeing as you know already who I am," he said to himself more than to Salina. He took off his backpack and pulled out a small blue jacket, a woolen shirt, and a pair of pants with a yellow stripe down each leg. "Forget the corset stays for the time being. Can you put these pants on all by yourself?"

"Of course," Salina informed him.

"Good, then get to it," he ordered brusquely.

"Am I to understand that you want me to pretend I'm a Yankee soldier in this uniform?" Salina asked.

"I'm hoping you'll appear to be one, if only from a distance," Captain Grant answered. "You can roll up the legs if they are too long. I've got a pair of boots for you to wear, and a cap. You'll have to hide those masses of curls."

Salina stood perfectly still. She was amazed at the transformation of the man's face, from older to younger. Up until now, the old man had seemed unreal, like a shadow—there, but not really. Now he stood before her, living flesh and blood, and there was no denying that he was indeed a real being.

The Yankee Captain returned his gun to its holster on his hip. His large hands gripped Salina's shoulders tightly. His arresting eyes matched the severity of his tone. "I need you to do exactly what I tell you to do, and be quick about it. We don't have much time. Where is your mamma?"

When Salina didn't answer, Duncan muttered, "You're just about as stubborn as your father." He repeated his question a little bit louder, but between clenched teeth, "Where is your mamma?"

A mop handle came down hard on the back of his head. He yelped in pain, then twisted the make-shift weapon out of Mamma's small hands. *"Yeee-owww!"* He pushed her away, toward the bed in the center of Salina's room. "That hurts!" he ground out angrily, rubbing the back of his head, feeling no blood. "Regular little spitfire, Annelise. You certainly haven't changed!"

"Duncan?" Mamma asked, disbelieving that she'd just whacked her husband's best friend in the head. "Duncan Grant. Garrett was right—you *were* following him."

Captain Grant gingerly touched the swelling lump on his skull. "Yes, ma'am. Just following my orders."

"Garrett's dead, in case you haven't heard," Mamma said bitterly. "So why are you here now?"

Duncan Grant lowered his eyes. "I know about Garrett's death, Annelise. I am very sorry about that."

"Sorry? You're probably the one who pulled the trigger!" Mamma accused.

Duncan shook his chestnut-colored head. "No, Annelise, you know me better than that. I don't care if you believe me or not, but I was trying to help him escape from the prison. I was with Garrett the night before he died, and I gave him my word of honor that I would see that you were looked after. That's why I'm here—to fulfill my vow." He turned to Salina, "You know that I'm a Union scout."

Salina nodded.

Duncan continued, "There is a company of men behind me led by Major John Barnes. He has in his possession orders to arrest you two and Ethan. Major Barnes would be only too happy to take you prisoner, and I think you know that well enough. Once they have you in custody, they will burn this place to the ground. No questions asked."

"Why? What have we done?" Salina demanded. "Why do his orders allow him to do this?"

"This is war, not peacetime. I can't prove that the three of you have done anything but be related to Garrett Hastings," Duncan admitted, gently resting his hand on Mamma's arm. "But Major Barnes doesn't see it that way. He's convinced you're all spying, and he won't let it rest now that Garrett is dead. Major Barnes found out that Garrett stole some documents from my office in Washington, and his command has been sent here to search the premises for those same documents. I'd prefer to be the one to find them first, for they are rather crucial from the Union standpoint. You wouldn't happen to know anything about these papers, would you, Annelise?"

Mamma replied, "And if I did, would you truly expect me to tell you?"

"No, I suppose it wouldn't be honorable." He shook his head. "Honor, duty, loyalty—sometimes I get confused at the definitions behind those words."

Salina watched Captain Grant intently. It was quite evident he had no inclination that *she* might know about the documents, not that her answer to his question would have differed any from Mamma's. The point was that he didn't even question her. *Daddy was right,* she thought. *The Yankees wouldn't suspect someone like me...*

"We haven't much time," Duncan Grant repeated. "I'm risking my neck to help you save yours. I'm doing this because Garrett was my friend, and I know he'd do for me what I'm attempting to do for you had the situation been reversed. If war had not come, things might well be different tonight. But at this point, I'm asking you, please, to obey me without further resistance. If you don't, we may all die because of it."

Salina clearly saw the glimmer of sincerity in his pewter-gray eyes. "Mamma?" she waited for Mamma to decide whether or not to do as the Yankee Captain instructed.

"It seems we have little choice but to follow your orders, Duncan," Mamma nodded.

"Thank you," he bowed at the waist. "Where is your son?"

"I sent Ethan to Ivywood to get help from the Armstrongs to extinguish the fire in our barn," Mamma answered. "You wouldn't happen to know anything about that fire, would you?"

"I'm afraid I do," Duncan replied with a hard swallow. "I didn't start it, but I know who did. It is meant to be a signal to Major Barnes' men that I have arrived and met no opposition. He'll be here shortly. Get changed, both of you. Time is of the essence. Pack whatever you can into one satchel apiece. Take any money or small valuables, but that's probably all you'll have room for."

"This whole house is valuable to me, Duncan," Mamma's chin quivered.

"I realize that, Annelise, but it isn't of value to the Union army. They will thoroughly search this house, and then they will destroy it. Trust me—I've seen it happen more times than I like to admit.

Sometimes we officers are assigned orders that we may not agree with, but we are bound to carry them out. If anyone should discover that I've warned you or helped you escape, they'll stretch my neck without thinking twice about it. I've got a job to do, and your job is to mind me," Duncan said sternly, handing Mamma a uniform much like the one he'd given Salina to wear.

"Come, Salina, let's not keep the good Captain waiting." Mamma didn't hide the sarcasm in her voice. This man was Garrett's friend and had been a friend to her as well. She knew that he was trustworthy, but he was fighting on the side of the Union, which made them enemies. If Duncan was willing to risk helping them for Garrett's sake, then there wasn't much she could do aside from what he asked.

Jubilee came rushing in from the burning barn. "Ahs sorry, Miz Annelise, but Peter Tom, he don' think he kin save it."

"Don't worry, Jubilee, the barn is the least of our troubles at the moment," Mamma said. "Please, go with Salina and gather the contents of the safe in the library. Make sure you get all of Garrett's letters and things from my room..."

Jubilee heard Duncan's boots thud on the floor. "A Yankee soldier, Miz Annelise!"

"Yes, Jubilee, I know." Mamma turned to look over her shoulder at the handsome, gray-eyed captain. Duncan's eyes were compelling her to hurry. "Surely you remember Captain Duncan Grant, Jubilee. He's been a guest here many times in the past. Now he's helping us get out of here."

"An' yas gonna go wid him?" Jubilee asked, incredulous.

"It appears Major Barnes is after us," Mamma nodded. "I already told you that you're free to leave. You have your release papers. You could go North, Jubilee."

"An ahs tole ya ah ain't leavin' ya," Jubilee insisted. "Ah'll jist have ta be followin' dis Yankee too, ah see."

Mamma hugged Jubilee. "Come on, we've got to get a move on. We've tried the Captain's patience just about as much as we dare. Run along and help Salina pack her things."

Salina grabbed Celeste and tucked her into the carpetbag. Jubilee nodded sagely as Salina explained, "She's the last thing Daddy ever gave me. Oh, Jubilee—what do you suppose will become of us?"

"Only da good Lord, He knows," Jubilee replied gravely. "Come on, chile, keep movin'."

They brought their bags down to the entryway where Duncan Grant was waiting for them. Mamma said softly, "I think we're ready. Ethan hasn't returned yet?"

"No," Duncan replied. "Ivywood isn't that far from here. Do you suppose he went somewhere else?"

Salina spoke up, "Maybe to Carillon or to Dr. Phillips."

"Ah, yes, the doctoring. Your brother's rather gifted at that sort of thing, isn't he?" Duncan asked. "That could be useful, when the time comes."

"When the time comes for what?" asked Salina.

"Never you mind," Duncan patted her cheek. He glanced up at Annelise.

"May I ask a favor of you, Captain Grant?" Mamma inquired.

"If it's within my power, you shall have it," the Captain said.

"There is a small crate with some old family heirlooms in the library, albums and Hastings family records. Might I persuade you to hide the crate somewhere safe so that we may come back for it when the Yankees have gone?" Mamma spoke her petition.

"I'll see what I can do," the Captain assured her.

"Thank you." Mamma gathered her satchel and squared her shoulders. "Lead on, Duncan."

Outside, Peter Tom was holding the horses ready. Duncan secured the satchels behind the saddles. Mamma touched Salina's cheek. She had pinned Salina's thick, curling hair up under the Union cap and poked extra holes in the belt to make it cinch small enough around Salina's tiny waist. The belt was a must, or Salina's borrowed pants might drop to her ankles. "I hope you'll pass, sweetheart. You're much too pretty to be mistaken for a boy."

"You don't have far to ride," the Yankee Captain assured her. "This is just a temporary disguise. Are you two ready to go?"

Salina watched Duncan stalk past them. She turned to Mamma, "This is a time of testing."

"I have no doubt of that," Mamma said with certainty. She quoted a psalm, *"The Lord is my strength and my salvation, whom then shall I fear?"* She took one last look at the house that had been her home since the day Garrett Hastings had first brought her here as a young bride.

"Come on!" Duncan Grant shouted.

"What about my brother?" Salina wanted to know.

"My lieutenant will find him," Duncan informed her. "I'll ride with you to the edge of Shadowcreek, but Peter Tom will take you the rest of the way."

At the boundary of the Hastings property, Captain Grant muttered something to Peter Tom, and the black man put an envelope into his pocket. The Captain reined his horse next to Salina's. "I've one thing to ask you."

"Yes?" Salina queried. Her heart slammed in her chest. Did he know of the secrets she kept?

"Where is Jeremy Barnes?" Duncan questioned.

Salina looked surprised. "Why, I thought you'd know where he was. The casualty lists at the post office showed him as missing after the battle near Antietam Creek. I honestly don't know where he is."

"If you did, would you have told me?" Duncan tested her trust.

Salina shrugged. "Maybe, maybe not. It would have depended on the circumstances."

"Well, if nothing else, at least you're honest," the Captain cracked a smile. "Peter Tom has my instructions. Follow him, and do what he says until I get back."

"Goodbye, Captain Grant," Salina said.

"Yes," Mamma echoed. "Goodbye, Duncan. And thank you."

Duncan Grant bent forward at the waist in a bow of sorts. "I wish I could say it had been a pleasure." He rode away, praying their disguises would let them slip unseen past Major Barnes' men.

"Cum on, den, let's be off," Peter Tom prodded. "Y'all know da way ta Ivywood. Don' be laggin' ba-hind, Jubilee. Giddup!"

"Why are you taking us to Ivywood?" Mamma asked.

"Cuz dose be da Caps orders," Peter Tom replied. "It might look natural-like, ifn y'all was stayin' wid relatives on da night yer house gots burned, leastways dats da way Caps done figured it. Carillon's too dangerous wid da headquarters dere. It'll be safe fer ya dere at Ivywood, don' ya fret."

Salina looked closely at the strong, broad-shouldered black man who'd served her father for as long as she could remember. "Peter Tom, you work for Captain Grant, don't you?"

Peter Tom smiled widely. "Yas, Missy. Hab done fer nigh unto a year now. Surprised, ere ya?"

"Yes, I am." Salina looked into the black man's shadowy face, thinking back on the times he'd carried messages between the lines for Daddy. She knew Peter Tom could read and write. He'd prove a valuable asset to Duncan Grant, she was sure. Then the fear edged into her mind. Peter Tom would have *known* the contents of the materials he carried directly into General Jackson's camp when Jeremy was unable to be the courier. *He* had to be the one who switched the documents. How much more did Peter Tom truly know? She recalled the letter from Jeremy that he'd brought to her, and Peter Tom had admitted that he *hadn't opened* the envelope because it had her name on it. Salina shuddered. "Have you been working for *both* sides, Peter Tom?"

"Yas, Missy, liddle bit. I done sum work fer Massah Garrett, but mostly, ah works for Caps now. Ah was ta be a gift from Massah Garrett ta Caps once upon a time, but Caps he said no thank ya, suh. An' so ah stayed here an' worked fer Massah Garrett. Caps axed me ta help wid watchin' tings from time ta time. So ah's did, as ah was oblige ta. Ya understand, Missy Salina?"

"I think so," Salina nodded. "You trust Captain Grant?"

"Wid my life, Missy. An' wid yers, too," Peter Tom said confidently.

The four riders hadn't gone far when they heard Major Barnes arrive with his men at Shadowcreek. Shouts, crashes, horses, soldiers, destruction, and havoc—all of these things brought fresh tears to Salina's eyes. *We can't look back,* she thought to herself. *It's all in the past. Our hope is in Jesus Christ and the future before us...* The smell of the fire made it hard to breathe. She saw that Jubilee and Mamma were crying. Tears of combined sorrow and anger spilled silently down their cheeks.

Ethan, held at gun point by a Union lieutenant, was already at Ivywood when Mamma, Salina, and Jubilee rode up the drive. "I demand to know what's going on here! Peter Tom, what are you doing here? What is happening?"

Salina had to look twice at Duncan's lieutenant, for at a first glance he had almost looked like Jeremy to her. She tore her eyes away from the blond Yankee lieutenant and told her brother what had happened at Shadowcreek. Ethan was livid. Peter Tom promised an explanation once they got settled inside. "We'll discuss Caps plan fer y'all. Ya might not like it much, but dat ain't none o' my neber-mind. Ahs jist followin' da orders."

☆☆☆☆☆☆☆

Peter Tom read Captain Grant's orders aloud. They were to stay put at Ivywood and wait.

"That's it?" Ethan asked. "Just sit here and wait?"

"Dat be it," Peter Tom nodded.

"And what if Major Barnes finds out we're here?" Salina asked.

Uncle Caleb joined them. "Have no fear. The Major can't take any action against you. Captain Grant has supplied an order from the War Department that allows for your protection. Technically, you're in

Captain Grant's custody, so he's responsible for you. He won't let anything happen to you."

"You sound so sure," Ethan noted.

Uncle Caleb didn't reveal to them that Captain Grant had paid him, handsomely, to see that the Hastings were not subjected to any unnecessary danger. "I am. You're to remain here with us, as our guests, until Captain Grant returns."

"And when will that be?" Mamma wanted to know.

"I don't rightly know," Uncle Caleb admitted.

"Caps'll let us know, when da time is right," Peter Tom said confidently. "Jist follow dem simple orders ta wait, and everythin' gonna be jist fine."

Ethan cast a cutting glance at the tall black man. He bit his tongue to avoid a sharp retort. He didn't think things were going to be just fine, but he would bide his time until something could be done to better the situation they found themselves thrust into.

Salina didn't want to wait either. The wheels of her mind turned fast and furious in an effort to figure out what their next move should be. At the moment, she knew only that Duncan Grant *must not* be permitted to discover that Daddy's trunk was with Reverend Yates, and that somehow, she'd have to get to Fairfax to have Tabitha send a telegram to Aunt Genevieve in San Francisco.

Jubilee bustled around the guest bedroom allotted to Mamma and Salina. "Is dere anythin' ah kin do fer ya, Miz Annelise?"

"I don't think so, Jubilee," Mamma sighed, "but thank you." She was lost in her own turbulent thoughts. "Salina, darling, would you like Jubilee to brush out your hair?"

Salina nodded. "Maybe it will help me relax some." She sat on the edge of the bed while Jubilee fussed with her curls, pulling the silver-plated brush in a downward motion.

Mamma took Salina's hand in her own and squeezed it. "We've been through quite a bit in the last few weeks, haven't we?"

Salina agreed. "Jeremy's return, my birthday and Mary Edith's wedding, the battles, your accident, tending the wounded, visiting Daddy in Washington, his death, and now the destruction of Shadowcreek..."

"Salina, I don't ever want you to run off again, like you did to Washington," Mamma said with a shudder. "If I had been alert enough to understand that no one was paying any attention to you, well, I would have done things differently. I can't tell you how terrified I was when Reverend Yates came and told Mrs. Carey and I that you and

Taylor Sue had gone off alone. Promise me you'll never do anything so foolish again."

"I promise, Mamma. I'll talk to you first before I go anywhere," Salina assured her.

"You sound as though plans to go somewhere are in the works," Mamma said.

Salina shrugged. "We'll have to wait and see, but I'll let you know." She allowed Jubilee's soothing brush strokes relax her.

"You're missing Daddy, aren't you?" Mamma presumed.

Salina whispered, "I thought I missed him a lot whenever he went away, but I miss him more than ever now that I know he's not coming back."

Mamma wiped a tear from Salina's cheek. "I miss him, too, darling. Ever so much."

"When did Daddy first tell you he loved you?" Salina asked curiously.

Mamma answered without hesitation, "Just a few days before he left for West Point."

Salina smiled. "And did you love him then?"

"More than life itself," Mamma replied wistfully. Oliver Spencer had strongly objected to Garrett Hastings as a suitable match for her, but she had become Garrett's wife in spite of her father's wishes. Though it took a considerable amount of time, Oliver had grown accustomed to their marriage and belatedly gave the young couple his blessing. "Is there a point to this conversation, young lady?"

"I was just curious," Salina evaded.

"Where does Jeremy Barnes figure into this?" Mamma asked suspiciously.

Salina lifted her shoulder in another shrugging motion. "I just worry about him."

"Well," Mamma concluded, "you wouldn't worry about him unless you care for him, and that's a fact. You do care for Jeremy, don't you, Salina?"

"Yes." Salina didn't see any reason to hide it. "And he cares for me, Mamma. He told me so."

"Hmmm," Mamma pressed her lips firmly together. "Of course, that's really not news. All one had to do was take a look at that boy's face and see that he's smitten with you. Just give it time, Salina. Don't rush into anything just because there's a war on."

"I do wonder if Ethan and Taylor Sue will ever really get married amidst all this turmoil," Salina laughed softly. "It took him long enough to ask her, and now all this!"

Mamma smiled. "It is good to hear you laugh, darling. I wish you could laugh much more often, the way you ought to. You've had a share of heartaches for one your age."

"You've endured much more than I have, Mamma. I don't know how you can be so strong all of the time," Salina shook her head.

"Strength comes over time, sweetheart. One learns to cope with situations. Experiences help us grow, and prayer keeps us in touch with God's will. The Lord cautioned His disciples that they would encounter trials and tribulations in their lives — and they did, but He was with them. Once we decide to commit our lives completely to Christ, we can claim His promises as His children. One of those promises is that He will be there with us in the dark times. His love will see us though," Mamma said encouragingly.

"Daddy used to say that things often seem the darkest just before the dawn," Salina remembered his words vividly.

"Yes." Mamma, too, had heard him say that. "And our Heavenly Father won't give us more than we can bear. You get some sleep, now. We'll talk some more in the morning."

"Mamma, I love you." Salina hugged her. She sensed that something was going to come between them, and it made her uneasy.

"I love you, too, sweetheart." Mamma kissed the top of her head. "What on earth would I do without you by me?"

Chapter Twenty

*S*unday morning's service was the most concise sermon Reverend Yates had ever preached. The small congregation sung the last hymn and exited the church building long before noon. He praised the Lord when he saw Ethan, Salina, and their mother sitting in their usual pew. It would save him a drive out to Ivywood to see them and allow him more time to plan.

Joetta Warner was the last straggler down the church steps today. The Reverend listened politely, if impatiently, his thoughts far away, as Joetta told him and Mrs. Yates all about the latest letter from her husband. "I just can't believe he's sending for us. It seems he's been gone for such a long time. Hank sent money for train tickets and stagecoach passage for Austin and me. We leave tomorrow morning," Joetta said excitedly. "I've got so much packing to do between now and then. I do wonder what life will be like for us in the West. Do you suppose Virginia City, Nevada will be anything like life here in the state of Virginia?"

"I don't rightly know, Mrs. Warner... You're leaving *tomorrow*?" The Reverend was suddenly paying *very* close attention to what Joetta was saying. "Why, that *is* soon. What time must you leave?"

"On the early train out of Fairfax Station," Joetta nodded anxiously. "We'll have to spend the night in Washington. Reverend, is it too much to hope that you might know someone there who would allow me to hire a spare bedroom for the evening? Then Austin and I will be on our way on the first train, day after tomorrow, departing for St. Joseph, Missouri. That's where we'll board the stagecoach. I guess I'm a little nervous about traveling on our own. It's an awful long way to Nevada."

Reverend Yates smiled, a plan unfolding before his very eyes. "You don't worry about that. You'll be just fine. And as a matter of fact, I do have some friends who would be more than happy to let you stay in one of their spare bedrooms. They don't live in Washington itself. They live just this side of the Potomac, in Alexandria. Will and Ruby Tanner are their names. In fact, I'll go straight home and write the necessary letters of introduction and bring them over to your place later on this afternoon."

"That's very kind of you, Reverend Yates," Joetta said gratefully. "I'd be much obliged."

When Joetta went in search of Austin, her four-year-old son, Reverend Yates whispered to his wife, "Tell Ethan Hastings to bring his sister and Taylor Sue Carey to the schoolhouse on Shadowcreek land within the hour."

Mrs. Yates nodded obediently. "And I'll distract Annelise somehow."

The Reverend smiled tenderly at his wife. "Thank you, dear."

☆☆☆☆☆☆☆

Taylor Sue rode to the schoolhouse as quickly as her horse would carry her. She expected she would be late to the gathering because she had promised Salina that after church she would ask the postmaster if there was any mail for the Hastings. The postmaster gave Taylor Sue a letter addressed to Salina from Jeremy Barnes.

September 20, 1862

My darling Salina:
When I close my eyes, I long to see your pretty face—
but instead all I see are the ravages of battles that raged

*at South Mountain and Antietam Creek. I can still hear
the pounding artillery and taste the powder smoke and
sulfur that thickened the air above the battlefields. My
heart skitters and thuds with the frightful memory of it all.
I watched in a daze as my comrades around me got blown
up or shot down. The wounds I came away with are very
minor, mere scratches, really. God miraculously had His
hand on me, for I am not dead, but I have been captured. I
bribed one of the guards to send this to you, and I pray
that it truly does arrive.*

*Salina, your father has also been caught. He is in this
prison, somewhere, though I am not sure exactly which
cell. They have refused to let us see each other. Captain
Grant visited earlier today in order to begin his inquisi-
tion. He not only had questions, but he had my wounds examined by a reluctant surgeon. I believe Ethan is more
medically qualified than this fellow seemed to be. They
only want to keep me alive until they can hang me themselves, of that I am sure. In light of that, I am writing to let
you know how much I love you. I don't want you to have
any doubt of that. Salina, I beg of you, pray for a miracle,
for that's what it's going to take to get me out of here—
and away from my uncle. I will try to be strong and courageous in the face of my enemies and I will think of you
always, for thoughts of you are the only things that give
me any comfort. Pray without ceasing...*

*Your devoted horse soldier,
Jeremy Barnes
1st Virginia Cavalry-CSA*

"Is everything all right?" Taylor Sue asked, concerned at the hurt
so visible in Salina's eyes.

"He's alive," Salina replied with a sigh of relief. "For the time
being anyway. When Jeremy wrote this, he knew Daddy had been
captured by the Yankees. Daddy ended up dead when he tried to
escape, and knowing Jeremy, he would do the same thing. Jeremy
would much rather die trying to live than dangle at the end of a
hangman's noose."

Taylor Sue shuddered. "That's morbid, Salina. Do stop thinking
of it."

"That's the truth," Salina countered, but she did as Taylor Sue requested and changed the subject. "What's in the basket?"

"Food," Taylor Sue answered. "Since the Yankees have taken over our house as their headquarters, we lack in little—except firewood. The officers seem to be able to procure most anything they so desire. It's amazing how well their supply lines operate."

Ethan accepted the sandwich Taylor Sue offered him, but he stayed by the window as the lookout. He wondered what was keeping Reverend Yates. Mamma had ridden back to Ivywood with Aunt Priscilla, Uncle Caleb, Lottie, and Mary Edith. Ethan convinced her that they wouldn't be gone for very long. He didn't want to worry her anymore than necessary.

"How are you getting along over at Ivywood?" Taylor Sue asked Salina.

Salina rolled her eyes. "I keep to myself and stay in my room most of the time. Mary Edith is visiting, so at least her being there has helped these last few days pass by quickly enough. Lottie is as unbearable as ever, and Peter Tom is always hovering. He'll be fit to be tied when he sees that we're not with Mamma when she gets back. He didn't want to let us out of his sight, you know, but Mamma insisted that we be allowed to attend church service, and she won the argument."

Reverend Yates arrived, a little out of breath. "Forgive me. I should have been here sooner, but I received another message from Tabitha by way of the Tanners."

"Something's wrong." Salina immediately assumed the worst. "What's happened to Jeremy?"

"Nothing more that I'm aware of since his transfer from the prison to the hospital. I'm told that he lapsed into another fever, and evidently Captain Grant ordered that he be taken under a doctor's care. Captain Grant needs Jeremy alive, not dead."

"So, Jeremy now owes his life to the good Yankee Captain just as we do," Ethan said between clenched teeth.

"That appears to be so," Reverend Yates grinned and shrugged. "It almost makes one wonder if this Captain Grant isn't an angel in disguise."

Ethan did not share the Reverend's humor. "He's a Yank, with or without a disguise," he spat.

"What news do the Tanners send if it doesn't pertain to Jeremy?" Salina asked.

Reverend Yates looked at the girls and said bluntly, "The news pertains to the two of you."

"Us?" Taylor Sue's golden-brown eyes grew round with surprise. "What have we got to do with anything?"

"The Yankees have at last reached the conclusion that it was Garrett Hastings, and not Gary Hayes, who was incarcerated at the Old Capitol Prison. With that in mind, they're trying to locate you in hopes of recovering the documents Salina's father obtained from Captain Grant's office at the War Department," Reverend Yates said. "Someone was spying on you while you both stayed with the Tanners — my guess being Lieutenant Colby. Warrants have been issued for your arrests. The Yankees want to bring you in for questioning, which could potentially mean imprisonment, and since they would not be required to press any charges, God alone knows how long they might keep you."

"But *I'm* the one they're wanting to question," Salina said softly. "Why do they want Taylor Sue?"

"Guilt by association. By the way, Will Tanner is still writing articles," Reverend Yates mentioned. "Gary Hayes will live on as long as they don't connect him to Will."

Ethan didn't like it. "Captain Grant must know that warrants have been issued for the girls' arrests. He will come back to Ivywood, and then he'll take Salina and Taylor Sue to Washington, won't he?"

"I reckon that's what will happen," the Reverend nodded. "That's why I've come. I was going through the things in the traveling trunk again, and suddenly it dawned on me. Those railroad and stagecoach schedules may have been *intentionally* left for the two of you. There are *two* train tickets, and more than enough money for *two* passengers aboard a stage. Captain Hastings must have been anticipating something like this could happen. He made allowances for your route of escape."

"Reverend Yates," Salina began, "running away to Alexandria and Washington was less than twenty-five miles and two days' adventure. You're talking about Taylor Sue and I traveling all the way to San Francisco, aren't you?"

"No!" Ethan said emphatically. "Mamma will never allow it."

"My mother would pitch an absolute fit if I were to even *mention* it to her. She's still angry with me for going with Salina to Alexandria," Taylor Sue said.

The Reverend shook his balding head. "I didn't think it would go this far, but as it stands those Yankees aren't leaving us much of an alternative. And they will find you if we don't get you out of here. Salina, think. The western campaign must still go on. You are the connection to make that a possibility. The Captain told you as much the last time you saw him. He sent a package to San Francisco, and I know he intended to go there himself to retrieve the contents, but since his death, you are the only one who can take his place. He talked to you of the plans and he showed you the maps. You have the knowledge of how to use the codes. Tabitha is hiding the rest of the information you need. *Someone* has to put it all together. Salina, you are certainly capable of that."

Salina nodded slowly. Reverend Yates was right. There was no one else to send to San Francisco, and now would be the time to leave, especially when she considered that the Yankees were on to the charade she and Taylor Sue carried out. "Well, we can't just stay and wonder *when* the Yankees will come, for they certainly will," Salina said aloud. "I imagine they would deal severely with us not only because I'm Garrett Hastings' daughter, but because they believe I'm in possession of those documents as well." She walked over to Taylor Sue and hugged her. "I'm so sorry for implicating you in all of this."

"Don't apologize, Salina. You've nothing to be sorry for. You didn't know it would turn out like this," Taylor Sue pointed out.

"They can't travel across the country by themselves," Ethan declared. "I'll have to go with them."

"That's certainly an idea, but not the one I have in mind." Reverend Yates shook his head. "The Lord Himself provided a plan this very morning after the service." He explained how Joetta Warner was at this minute home packing to leave in the morning on her journey west to join her husband. "Hank Warner wants his family with him," Reverend Yates said simply. He watched as the wheels turned in Salina's head.

"Hank Warner! Of course—in Virginia City!" Salina actually smiled. "We could travel with Joetta, and then we wouldn't be alone." She turned to her brother. "Ethan, this could work. Hank Warner is one of Daddy's western contacts. He could help us when we reach Nevada."

"Joetta told my wife that she didn't like the idea of traveling alone with Austin. With you and Taylor Sue to accompany her, you all can look after each other." Reverend Yates nodded, pleased with the solution. "All things work together for good."

"How are you going to explain this to Mamma?" Ethan wanted to know.

"I don't know yet. She's not going to like it," Salina predicted. "Reverend Yates, I need to send a telegraph to Aunt Genevieve in San Francisco."

"Tabitha already took care of the sending of it and the receiving of a reply. Your Aunt Genevieve has received the package, and she'll look forward to your arrival in about six weeks' time. You can wire her from the express office in Virginia City to let her know which day you will arrive in San Francisco so that she can meet you there."

Ethan stepped closer to Taylor Sue and took her hand in his. "I guess it's settled, then. You'll be going away for a while. I can't say that I like it, but I don't want you to stay here if it means you could be captured. The Reverend has a sound plan, and no matter how big a fit your mother pitches, she'll have to see the reasoning behind it, just as Mamma will."

Taylor Sue bit her lip. "I'll go, but promise me something. Promise me we'll be married just as soon as I get back."

"The very same day if we can manage," Ethan vowed.

"What do we do now, Reverend?" Salina asked. "Where should we go? What time do you want us ready?"

"I will ride with Taylor Sue to Carillon. I'll have to explain it to her mother," the Reverend said. "Are you sure you can explain it to yours?"

Ethan nodded. "She'll come around. She won't like it, but she'll see the necessity. The trick will be avoiding Peter Tom at Ivywood and the Yankee officers at Carillon."

"Amen," Reverend Yates sighed. "I think everyone should stay where they are tonight, so as not to arouse any unnecessary suspicions, and then we'll meet at first light at Joetta Warner's. She lives the closest to Fairfax Station. My advice would be to pack as little as possible to travel lightly."

Salina's laugh was edged with a certain hardness. "Most everything I owned was destroyed in the fire. It certainly won't take me long to pack."

The Reverend nodded in understanding. "I'll bring the trunk. That will have to go with you. I'll pack it securely, and then we'll put some of Taylor Sue's frilly dresses and girlie things right up on top. That should give the impression that the two of you are sharing the traveling trunk between you," the Reverend suggested.

"I wish we knew when Duncan Grant was coming back." Salina rubbed her arms. She had a strange feeling that he might be nearer than they expected.

"We'd better get going. Mamma's sure to be worried, and Peter Tom will be livid," Ethan said.

"Taylor Sue, are you ready?" asked Reverend Yates.

Taylor Sue cast a panicked look up at Ethan. "Will I see you before we leave?"

Ethan smiled down at his love. "I insist on riding with all of you to the train station. We'll have time to talk." He tapped the end of her nose with his fingertip. "Until tomorrow," he whispered, and he kissed her soundly, right in front of his sister and Reverend Yates.

"I'll look forward to marrying the two of you just as soon as the girls come home," Reverend Yates chuckled.

☆☆☆☆☆☆

Quiet and still—Shadowcreek was little more than burnt ashes and rubble. The brick chimneys remained, standing like mute sentinels over what used to be home to Ethan and Salina.

"Captain Grant was right," Salina whispered, wiping a single tear that rolled down her cheek. "Major Barnes carried out his orders of destruction to the letter."

"I shouldn't have agreed to let you come here." Ethan pulled Baron's reins, halting him next to Salina's horse. "It would have been better if you'd have remembered the house the way it used to be in happier times than these."

Salina shrugged. "Mamma says that the Lord gives, and the Lord takes away. But when He takes away, He gives something else instead."

"Come on, let's get out of here." Ethan had checked over his shoulder twice. He didn't like the feeling he had that they were being watched.

"Wait," Salina said. She went to where the smokehouse used to be and picked through the debris until she found what she was looking for. "This is why we had to come here." She unearthed the flagstone under which were the maps, the bag of gold and silver coins, and the supply of Union greenbacks. "Now, we can leave." She hid them in the pockets of the short jacket she wore, and she asked, "Do you remember the tutor we had telling us a story of pirates and maps and buried treasure?"

"Yes, vaguely. Why?" Ethan asked.

"In this case the treasure *is* the map," she grinned at her brother, but then the smile faded as she met his serious eyes. "You're angry with me again, aren't you?"

"Angry with the situation, not with you specifically," Ethan clarified. "Aren't you the least bit frightened about what's happening?

You take it all in stride, Salina. It makes me wonder if you grasp the gravity of what's truly going on here."

She threw her dark head back and laughed harshly. "Frightened? Scared? Afraid? You don't think I'm any of those things? Ethan, I'm so scared I think I've gone past the point of feeling anymore. I've become numb," Salina told him. "I thought I was being so brave wanting to help Daddy here and there—and at the beginning that's what I did. I saw no harm in wanting to serve the Cause. But then things beyond my control started to happen, and I'm not just helping anymore. I'm running for my life all because I wanted to help Daddy fight for our country, to defend Virginia! It does no good to wish things were the way they used to be, because they never will be. We have to move forward from here. There's no turning back."

"So true," Ethan nodded. He wasn't sure why, but it made him feel better to know that Salina was afraid. Perhaps he liked knowing she was just as human as he was. He desperately wished he could protect both Salina and Taylor Sue without them having to go west, yet he knew they were in danger if they stayed, and they would inevitably be on a train before noontime tomorrow.

Salina heard a crunching of leaves to the right of them. "Show yourself!" she ordered, reaching for her pearl-handled pistol. "Here's where the shooting lessons will come in handy," she muttered under her breath.

There was no reply to Salina's command except for the whispering branches in the trees above. She quickly climbed a tree stump to mount Starfire, but another movement in the woods spooked the horse and he reared. Salina was knocked to the ground.

"Salina!" Ethan tried to catch her, but she fell just out of his reach.

"Uhhh," Salina bit back a cry even though the pain stabbed through her left arm. Someone was out there, watching. Cradling her arm, she let Ethan assist her. "Don't touch it, Ethan, it hurts," she whispered.

"Salina, let me take a look at it. If it's broken, I'll put a splint on it, and then I'll treat you when we get back to Ivywood. I've got my medical kit at the Armstrongs."

Salina sat as still as she possibly could while Ethan hastily splinted her arm. "That'll do temporarily. We'll have to ride hard, but only as much as you can stand."

"I'll keep the pace," Salina nodded, but she could feel her fingers throbbing and they looked to be swelling already. "Take the shortcut across the creek. It'll get us back faster."

☆☆☆☆☆☆☆

"Please say something, Mamma," Salina implored.

Mamma sat very still, the only movement was that of her hands twisting the lace handkerchief she held into a tight knot. "What would you have me say, darling? I am completely at a loss."

"Tell me what you're thinking, then." Salina tried not to flinch as Ethan silently began his examination of her broken arm and preparations for a plaster cast.

Mamma continued to stare at the pattern of the carpeting on the floor. "I think of Job, in the Bible, who had everything taken from him in one day. He lost his family, all his worldly possessions and was struck ill, yet he did not curse God. I think I feel a little like Job must have felt, and I will not curse Him, either."

Salina swallowed. Mamma had lost almost everything—a baby, her husband, her home, and now her daughter. After tomorrow, Ethan would be the only thing remaining, though Salina expected that he would not stay long. With his medical knowledge, he could perform a great service to the Confederacy. Somehow, Salina knew that Mamma would not raise any objections when that time came. She would accept it gracefully, as she was now accepting Salina's imminent departure. Mamma used to have a fiery spirit, but sadly Salina thought that she had lost her will to fight. It was hers to accept, not to challenge.

In no time at all, Ethan was checking his handiwork. It was a good cast, thick to last over the course of a long journey. "When you get to San Francisco, you'll have to find a doctor there to have it off. You should be healed right as rain by then."

Salina nodded.

During supper, Aunt Priscilla and Mary Edith fussed over Salina, cutting her food into small pieces for her and presenting her with any little thing she asked for.

Lottie pouted, as usual, whenever she was not the center of attention. Following the meal, she promptly retreated to the drawing room and played a piece by Beethoven—a feat which required a pair of healthy hands. Privately, she seethed at having the Hastings stay at Ivywood.

Uncle Caleb followed Lottie into the drawing room and suggested that she perform a mini-concert for the evening's entertainment, and she was more than happy to do just that. "You play beautifully, daughter," Uncle Caleb complimented in attempt to ease hurt feelings.

Over the years he'd often played peacemaker, humoring Lottie out of her frequent black moods.

While Lottie's music filled the air, Jubilee whispered to Mamma, "Peter Tom, he needs ta speak wid da three o' ya. Says he gots word from dat Yankee Capt'n."

"I'll be along directly." Mamma motioned for Ethan and Salina to stay put then quickly followed Jubilee out the side door. Peter Tom had been extremely upset when the children had come back so late from church, and now Mamma was trying to avoid a scene.

"Miz Annelise, where're Missy Salina and Massah Ethan?" the black man looked past her.

"They're in the drawing room, listening quietly to Miss Lottie playing the pianoforte," Mamma said. "Was there something you wanted, Peter Tom?"

"Missy Salina, her arm—it was broke den?" Peter Tom inquired.

"How did you know it was broken?" Mamma asked quizzically.

"'Twas me in da woods watchin'. When dey didn' cum back an' didn' cum back from da church, ah figured ah gots ta go lookin' fer 'em. Ah found 'em, but I didn' mean fer Missy Salina ta git herself hurt."

"Funny thing about the spy business," Mamma said curtly. "In the end someone always seems to get hurt."

Peter Tom cleared his throat, uncomfortable. "Miz Annelise, Caps be on his way back here ta collect y'all. He wants me ta tell da three o' ya ta have yersefs ready ta go by noontime tamorrow."

"Go where, Peter Tom?" Mamma asked.

Peter Tom shrugged. "Don' know. Caps jist tell me ta have ya ready. He didn' tell me where he'll be takin' ya."

"I see. Noon tomorrow then," Mamma nodded demurely. "Thank you, Peter Tom."

He tipped his hat. "Yas, Miz Annelise."

Early the next morning, Ethan and Salina were ready to sneak out of the house. Jubilee had fixed some very potent tea for Peter Tom, and she reckoned he'd sleep the entire day away. Of course, Jubilee also put some of the same sedative in Miss Lottie's teacup, just to make certain that nosy young lady didn't spoil anybody's plans.

In the pink and gray dawn, Salina hugged Mamma fiercely. "Are you sure you'll be all right here?"

"I can handle Duncan Grant, if that's what you mean," Mamma assured her. "Genevieve will take care of you while I can't. Just be safe on the trip, and mind what Joetta says to do."

Salina nodded and managed a weak smile. "I love you, Mamma. I'll send word when I can and let you know when we arrive in San Francisco."

"God go with you, my darling." Mamma squeezed her tightly, and then she watched Salina ride away. Mamma managed to get back to her room and under the covers before the convulsive sobs washed through her. Only the Lord knew when—or if—she'd ever see her daughter again. "Father God, she is in Your hands. Protect her and fill her with Your love. Let her rely on You, and seek after You. This I pray in Jesus' holy name..."

Chapter Twenty-One

Oh my goodness! What have you done to yourself, Salina?" Ruby Tanner asked.

"I fell off my horse," Salina answered. "It doesn't hurt so much today as it did yesterday, that's for sure. Ruby, this is Joetta Warner and her son, Austin. They're friends of ours who are traveling as far as Virginia City, Nevada."

"Pleasure to meet you, Joetta. Please come in and feel right at home." She shook Austin's chubby little hand. "I understand your train doesn't leave until tomorrow morning," Ruby said. She went to the door leading to the print shop. "Will, they're here."

Introductions were made again. "Hope you'll be comfortable, ma'am." Will volunteered to take Austin and show him how the printing of a newspaper was done. Joetta was grateful.

"I could show Joetta to her room," Taylor Sue offered.

"That would be fine," Joetta nodded. "I didn't realize I was so exhausted, but I truly am."

"Why don't you lie down for a bit?" Ruby suggested. "I'll wake you when it's time to eat."

"I'll keep an eye on Austin," Taylor Sue assured Joetta. "It's no bother, really."

Ruby and Salina were left alone in the front parlour. "You've got yourself in a fine scrape. Are you up to it?"

Salina's eyes flashed with challenge. "I can do it."

"There's a brave girl," Ruby smiled. "I like your confidence—reminds me of your father. I felt so bad when I heard about that..."

"I'd rather not talk about that, Aunt Ruby, if you don't mind," Salina said softly.

"I know what it's like to lose someone you love, Salina. I lost your Uncle Holden to war. You never quite get over it, but you learn that life goes on regardless. Things go on changing even while we are helpless to stop them. But as you said, you'd rather not talk about it. Would you rather talk about Jeremy Barnes instead?" A smile dimpled Ruby's cheeks.

"He's still safe?" Salina questioned, unaware that her hand flew to rest against her hammering heart.

"Safe and recovering. I went to visit him just yesterday. I thought you might like me to drive you to where they've got him so you can see him before you leave," Ruby winked.

"They'll let me see him?" Salina asked breathlessly. "Really?"

"I'm sure of it," Ruby said with a nod. "A dear friend of mine is a nurse there, and she never turns away a soldier's sweetheart, especially if she's traveled a great distance to see him."

Salina asked, "Where is Jeremy?"

"In Washington, at Harewood Hospital," Ruby replied. "Get your wrap. I'll tell Will and Taylor Sue where we're going."

Ruby drove the carriage to the hospital, which was not far from the Soldiers' Home. "That's where the Lincolns spend time in the summer months," Ruby told Salina. "It's cooler sometimes here than over at the White House."

Salina swallowed. She had little chance and little to fear even if she *were* to run across the Union's President. He certainly couldn't know who she was, yet she felt an uneasiness just being in the Union capital at all. She must be careful, and she prayed that the Yankees wouldn't dream to look for her or Taylor Sue right here in Washington itself.

"I've got some shopping to do," Ruby said. "I'll make sure Grace can sneak you in, and then I'll come back to fetch you in, say, an hour?"

"Sounds fine by me," Salina nodded.

Ruby's friend, Grace, was seated at a desk, shuffling through some paperwork. Ruby quickly explained to her that Salina would only be in Washington today and asked if there was a way that she could get inside to visit her sweetheart before she left. Grace found a nurse's smock apron and snood for Salina to wear so she would blend inconspicuously, and then Grace led her to the ward where Jeremy Barnes lay mending from his wounds and recuperating from his bout with the fever.

As she crossed the wooden floor, seeing that the walls were lined with cots, Salina searched the faces of the wounded men, looking for one in particular. Some of the faces were pale, others sweating, some were in need of a shave, still others had dull, expressionless eyes.

"Here you are, Miss." Grace stopped at the foot of a bed containing one sandy-haired Confederate.

He rested on his side, his back to Salina, reading a New Testament.

"Hello, Jeremy," her voice was scarcely more than a whisper.

Jeremy Barnes rolled over to find that the sweet, familiar voice was not just a figment of his overactive imagination. He'd been daydreaming about her less than five minutes ago, and here she was by his side. *"Salina!"*

A trembling smile touched her lips, and a cry of joy escaped her throat. "Oh, Jeremy!" He was bruised and cut, but otherwise, he looked as though he'd live to ride another day. Instinctively, Salina counted his limbs, just to make sure he was still in full possession of his arms and legs. There was a white bandage circling his middle, confining his rib cage, signifying the bones were either cracked or broken. "Are you all right? You look awful!"

"Thank you ever so much for such kind words," he grinned. "You, on the other hand, look absolutely wonderful. Pull up that chair and sit down here by me," Jeremy gently commanded. "What's happened to you?" he wanted to know when his eyes finally left her face and landed on the plaster cast she wore.

She explained that her injured arm was the result of her fall from Starfire. Then she said, "I got both your letters."

"I wrote that last one before I found out Captain Hastings had been shot. Salina, I'm so sorry." Jeremy's thumb caressed the back of her hand. "I know how much you loved him. I imagine you must miss him greatly."

Salina nodded. "It was a hard blow. Knowing he was always in the thick of danger doesn't make it any easier. I didn't expect him to be able to be killed. Other men died—not my daddy."

Jeremy squeezed her hand comfortingly.

Salina turned the subject away from Daddy's death. "Tell me what's happened to you since you've become a horse soldier."

Jeremy told her of the fighting at Sharpsburg: the severity of the battle all around the Dunkard Church, the masses of dead bodies in Bloody Lane, the action on Burnside Bridge. "I was captured during the retreat. I strayed just a little too far from the rest of my unit while I was trying to pick apples. I'd lost quite a bit of blood, and I was so hungry. I thought something to eat would give me the strength to go on. That's when the bluebellies came out of nowhere. I ended up in prison until Duncan Grant had me moved here. The fever was so hot I thought I wanted to die." Suddenly he asked, "Salina, what are you doing *here*?"

"I'm here to visit you," she said simply. "I heard of your condition, but I wanted to be sure for myself." She glanced at the men lying in the cots on either side of Jeremy. The man on the left was a Yankee; the man on the right was a Southerner captured at the same time Jeremy had been. Both were in a morphine-induced stupor, but in Jeremy's blue eyes Salina found a warning to be cautious about what was spoken aloud. Salina kept her voice low, to keep from being overheard. "I missed you, and I worried about you, and I pray for you every night," she said. "I've read your letters a hundred times..."

Jeremy was pleased by her admission. "Good. I want you to know I speak the truth. I do love you."

"I'm glad," Salina said happily.

Jeremy raised an eyebrow, inquiring, "Won't you say it?"

"Say that I love you?" Salina asked coyly.

"Do you?" he prodded.

"Yes. I love you, Jeremy. I'm surprised you didn't already have that part figured out," Salina whispered. "I guess that's why I was so jealous when I saw Lottie kissing you. You didn't even make time to tell me goodbye, yet you were there with her. That hurt, and I was angry when you and Ethan got back from Germantown."

"So you avoided me," Jeremy concluded.

"Yes," Salina nodded. "It was stupid and childish of me. My cousin would do anything in her power to keep us apart."

"I thought I told you before, Salina. Lottie isn't the one I'm interested in. When I first came back to Chantilly, I watched you, and I was delighted to discover the lady in you reveal herself. I've grown rather fond of the lady. You're very special to me, Salina," Jeremy told her. He propped himself up on one elbow, and his eyes willed her to lean closer to the cot.

Salina sat forward on the edge of the chair, and Jeremy put his palm lightly to her cheek. He saw no resistance in her emerald eyes, and he took the liberty of pressing his lips against hers. Her lashes fell to conceal her eyes, and she kissed him back. That made Jeremy smile broadly.

Opening her eyes slowly, Salina encountered Jeremy's deep blue glance. She was embarrassed that he had the nerve to kiss her in front of all these other wounded men and a handful of nurses. Though the pressure of his mouth on hers had not been unpleasant, she was sure Mamma would say that it wasn't proper for a young lady to be kissed in public. Salina felt herself blush.

"That's a lovely shade of pink your cheeks are turning," Jeremy chuckled, his brow gently resting against her forehead. "The color becomes you. It's so good to see you, Salina."

Salina quickly sat up straight. Again she turned the topic of conversation to something else. "The Network is still in operation, even though Daddy's dead."

"How?" Jeremy was curious.

"Me," Salina answered. "He's entrusted me with the plans he was working on. That's the real reason I'm here in Washington. The Yankees have put out warrants for our arrest. Taylor Sue and I are going to California, Jeremy."

"California!" Jeremy blurted. "Salina, are you out of your mind?! You can't possibly travel all the way across the country to California..."

Salina interrupted in a low tone, "Daddy set it all up, Jeremy. Everything. Train tickets, stagecoach schedules, greenbacks, maps, traveling papers, and a list of contacts. He sent a package to my Aunt Genevieve in San Francisco, and that package is intended for my use to put together the final bits and pieces of the plans for the western campaign."

"Captain Hastings left an awful lot riding on your shoulders," Jeremy disapproved. It wasn't that he didn't think Salina capable of carrying it out; he just didn't like the danger she would be exposed to along the way. "What does your mamma think of all this?"

"She had little choice but to agree. She knows Taylor Sue and I are under suspicion. We had to leave. Captain Grant was on his way back to question us," Salina said. "Taylor Sue left Carillon and I left Ivywood."

"Ivywood? Why were you there instead of at Shadowcreek?" Jeremy questioned.

"Shadowcreek is gone, Jeremy, burned to the ground. Captain

Grant came and got us out before your uncle came with his command to search and destroy. He has a skill for destruction, Major Barnes does."

"Yes, I know," Jeremy remembered all too well. His fingers curled tightly into white-knuckled fists.

Salina took his hands in her own. "And we've found out that Peter Tom has been working for both sides—North and South. Ethan suspects that Captain Grant plans to take Mamma north with him for questioning. After Ethan rode with us to Fairfax Station, he wasn't planning to return to Ivywood. He says he's going to enlist as a surgeon's assistant. Dr. Phillips certified his exam, and Ethan can be of much-needed service with the medical corps. I'm sure he went to join up with Stonewall Jackson's corps."

"He has a knack for healing," Jeremy nodded. He leaned back and sighed, trying to digest all of what Salina had just told him. "Nothing stays the same."

"You're right," Salina agreed.

Jeremy studied her. "Clever little Salina."

She smiled, but sadly. "This visit is in part to say goodbye, Jeremy. I don't know when I'll return."

Again Jeremy let her know he wasn't entirely pleased with this westward adventure she was bent on seeing though, yet he was not in a position to counteract her determination. "At least let me give you the names of some people who can be of help to you along the way. I want you to be *very* cautious. If the Yankees are indeed after you, you make it just as difficult as you possibly can for them to find you. Your lives may depend on your ability to not draw attention to yourselves. Be very, very careful, Salina. I don't want anything to happen to you."

"We'll be very careful," Salina nodded her assurance.

Jeremy increased his grip on her hand. "All right, listen to me. When you get to St. Joseph you're bound to need a place to stay. Go see Mrs. Collins at the Riverbend Hotel. Tell her I asked her to give you my old room where I used to stay, and she'll see that you're well taken care of. Then you go to the freight office and ask for a stagecoach driver named Drake. He and I rode the express together; we know each other well. You tell him that I've sent you, and he'll take care of the rest. He'll know what to do."

"Can I trust him?" asked Salina.

"Yes," Jeremy said. "Though Drake and I never actually discussed our political views, I'm certain his sympathies are not with the Union."

"How will I know this Drake?" she inquired.

"He's kind of hard to miss," Jeremy chuckled. "Drake is a half-breed Kiowa-Apache Indian. He's tall, like me, has long black hair down to his waist, coppery-colored skin, and turquoise blue eyes. He has a pierced ear with a gold hoop and a long, jagged, white scar that runs across his forehead," Jeremy traced his finger along his own forehead above his eyebrows. "Drake is fairly notorious in St. Joe. It shouldn't be difficult for you to locate him. Don't go with any other driver, Salina. Make sure you wait for Drake's outfit—no matter how long it takes. It can't be more than a few days. When I get out of here, I'll try to wire him and tell him you'll be coming."

"You're a prisoner here," she unnecessarily reminded him. "When—how—did you think you were getting out of here?" Salina asked, glancing again at the room full of other wounded soldiers.

"I'm getting out of here tomorrow," Jeremy replied with certainty. "I thank God you came to visit today, Salina. Tomorrow would have been too late. You see, on his last raid, General Stuart captured the grandson of one of the Union's Congressmen—a Lieutenant-Some-body. A lieutenant is worth four privates in trade. General Stuart has struck a bargain to return the Congressman's grandson in exchange for me and three other Confederate privates being held here. It's all hush-hush, but it's been agreed upon, and I should be back in Virginia with General Stuart's cavalry by nightfall tomorrow. Maybe I'll be able to find Ethan and get back into the swing of things. That fever I had nearly got the better of me. There were times when I didn't feel that I was going to make it, but thank the Lord I did. If I die now, I'll die happy because I've seen you once more, and I know that you love me."

"Don't talk like that," Salina rebuked him. "You've got to live. Who knows? You might yet end up being a cavalry scout for the western campaign. You know the territory."

"That I do," Jeremy agreed. "We'll just have to wait and see. Promise me, Salina, that you'll wait to travel with Drake. Don't ride with anyone else."

"I promise," Salina nodded. She sensed her trip bothered him a great deal, but he, like Ethan and Mamma, the Reverend and the Tanners, could understand the reasons why it had to be.

"When you come back to Virginia, we'll talk seriously, Salina, about you and me," Jeremy said cryptically.

Salina looked puzzled, but Jeremy merely smiled. He decided to let her stew on that for a while. Time enough to talk about the depth of their feelings for one another when she returned from California, he thought.

Jeremy reached under his pillow. "I bought something for you, Salina. I found it in a little shop in Sharpsburg, the day before the battle. Will you do me the honor of wearing it?" He produced a dainty gold chain with a heart-shaped locket. A delicate rosebud was engraved on the top side.

"I shall wear it with pride, Jeremy Barnes." Salina fingered the necklace. "It's very pretty."

"As is its owner," Jeremy complimented.

Salina blushed again. "I have but one token to exchange with you." She eased the gold filigree ring from her finger. "This ring is a family heirloom that has been in Mamma's family for years." The emerald stone matched the shade of Salina's green eyes. "Keep this for me, Jeremy. Wear it and think of me whenever you see it." Salina put the ring on his little finger. "I don't want you to forget the color of my eyes while I'm away."

"Not a chance of that," Jeremy murmured. He looked deep into her eyes, and for a few minutes, neither one of them spoke aloud.

Salina's heart sang. *He truly loves me! Will he kiss me again before I must leave him?* She did want him to.

"I suppose it's getting to be time for you to go." He didn't want her to leave, and he didn't want to tell her goodbye. "I'll keep you in my thoughts and prayers—you can be sure of that."

Salina shyly touched Jeremy's face. Her tentative fingers curved themselves around his lean jaw. "Take care of yourself. I want you alive and well when I come back from California."

Jeremy leaned toward her again and kissed Salina a second time. Salina knew she would remember that kiss as long as she lived.

A low whistle, scattered applause, and a few catcalls came from several men around the ward. Salina's reaction was to draw away, but Jeremy didn't allow her to. He savored the kiss they shared; neither of them had any idea when they would be together again.

At length Jeremy whispered, "There's nothing wrong in sharing a kiss with someone you love."

"It's not the kissing I object to. It's the audience." Salina smiled tentatively.

Jeremy made do with placing a kiss on her forehead this time. "Heavenly Father," he prayed while clutching her hands, "confuse the Yankees. Make the way as easy as possible for the girls to get to San Francisco from here. Please God, give Salina the strength to do what she must, and bring her back safely to me. Amen."

Salina added a prayer of her own, "Dear Jesus, strengthen Jeremy's body and help him heal quickly. Keep him out of harm's way and out of hospitals like this. Thank You, Lord, for this opportunity to see one another, and thank You, too, for the love we share. Amen."

"Amen," Jeremy repeated, lightly caressing her cheek.

Grace was standing at the foot of Jeremy's cot, and she cleared her throat. "Excuse me, Miss, Ruby's out back waiting for you in the carriage."

"Thank you," Salina said. "I'll be along directly."

"Goodbye, Salina," Jeremy said, his blue eyes shining with a mixture of his love, pride, and admiration.

"Goodbye, Jeremy," Salina's voice was choked with emotion.

Jeremy used his thumb to wipe away a spilled teardrop. "Go on, now. Remember that I love you."

"I'll remember," she said to him, and she flashed a bright smile.

Chapter Twenty-Two

*C*lickety-clack, clickety-clack, *clickety-clack, clickety-clack... Whoo-ooooo!* The train whistle blew long and loud. Salina thought it a melancholy sound that most certainly matched her dark mood. For days since leaving the Union capital, she had been mentally wrestling with herself, wondering over and over if she was doing the right thing by going to California. She'd left Mamma, Ethan, and Jeremy behind her to fulfill her word to Daddy. Unaware that she squared her shoulders, she strengthened her resolve. She was honor-bound to finish the task set before her.

The train's whistle blasted again. The speed of the locomotive decreased until at last it came to a complete stop at the railroad depot.

"We're here," Taylor Sue leaned over to whisper excitedly in Salina's ear. "This is St. Joseph, Salina. The halfway mark."

Only halfway, Salina mused silently. They had such a long ways yet to go. Three weeks had passed since they had departed Washington, and the days had melded together in a great blur. It was only in her journal that Salina noted the dates, for one day was very much like the next. She had barely noticed that September had slipped into October. Perhaps their arrival in St. Joseph would help renew her purpose.

The township of St. Joseph not only represented the end of the rail line but there were many who said it marked the end of "civilization" as well. Beyond the town's limits lay the untamed wilderness. In St. Joseph adventurous souls could purchase horses, mules, wagons, and all manner of things necessary for the crossing west. Homesteaders and pioneers went in search of land in the new unsettled territories; others went to make their fortunes in the prosperous mining camps. Then there were yet others who yearned for an escape from the war-torn East and desired a fresh start on life in a new place somewhere along the raw frontier.

"Sir, could you please tell me where I might find someone who will see to our baggage?" Salina inquired as the porter assisted her down from the passenger car onto the platform.

A sneer played across the porter's mouth, and his eyes blazed as he identified her soft, Southern drawl. His disdain was evident in his rude tone, "Well, Miss Dixie, *y'all* just go on and tell the station master where *y'all* want your fine things delivered. Give him the name of the hotel, if *y'all* know where *y'all* are gonna be stayin'." He looked her over insolently from head to toe. "Don't look like no homespun to me," he added, sniffing at the quality of her traveling dress.

Salina was startled by his open disgust but bit back a sharp rejoinder. She simply replied with a polite smile, "Thank you very much, sir. You've been very kind."

"Saucy Southern wench," the porter said behind her back but just loud enough for her to hear.

Taylor Sue quickly put her arm through Salina's. "Let's catch up to Joetta and Austin."

"Do you get the feeling that he didn't much care for us Rebels?" Salina whispered.

"All too well," Taylor Sue swallowed. "We must remember that we're in Yankee territory. The sooner we get this over with, the sooner we can go home where we belong."

Salina nodded. Their first order of business was to find lodging for the night. "Joetta, if you stay here with Austin and the baggage, Taylor Sue and I will go hire some rooms and then come back. The station master will have our things delivered while we find somewhere to get a decent meal."

"All right," Joetta agreed. "It will be a pleasure to sleep in a real bed."

Taylor Sue commented, "It's so crowded here, and loud."

Joetta saw a young boy passing out handbills giving notice of show times for the circus which had recently arrived in town. "No wonder there's such a commotion going on," she showed the advertisement to Taylor Sue and Salina.

"Look, Mommy!" Austin grabbed Joetta's hand, tugging at her to follow him.

The colorful circus parade made its way down the dusty street in the center of town; the steam calliope pumped lively music as it rolled past. People cleared the street to allow the parade to go by, and Austin was enthralled with the wonderful animals. Clowns and acrobats waved at the onlookers, making people smile.

"Look, Salina, an elephant!" Taylor Sue giggled.

"I wanna see!" Austin cried in delight, and Salina hoisted the chubby little tyke onto her hip.

"See there, Austin," Salina pointed, "those are tigers and lions."

"Mommy," Austin reached for Joetta, "Mommy I wanna see those animals in the circus."

"Perhaps tomorrow, dear," Joetta deferred. "Salina and Taylor Sue are going to find us a place to spend the night, and then maybe tomorrow we can visit the circus."

Salina and Taylor Sue walked down the street after the circus parade passed by. "How do you know where you're going?" Taylor Sue asked.

"Jeremy told me where we should go, who would should see," Salina answered. "There it is, the Riverbend Hotel. That's the hotel Jeremy mentioned." Inside, Salina and Taylor Sue were met by a pleasant gray-haired woman with wire-rimmed spectacles. "Are you Mrs. Collins?" asked Salina.

The lady behind the front desk nodded. "Aye, that I am. And you are?"

"I'm Salina Hastings," replied Salina. "And this is Taylor Sue Carey. Jeremy Barnes sends his best, Mrs. Collins, and he asks that you might let me rent his old room plus an additional one. There are four of us all together who'll need lodging, two rooms will be fine, if you have them available."

"For a friend of Jeremy Barnes, I do," Mrs. Collins decided. She remembered Jeremy Barnes very well. He had been a favorite of hers as far as riders were concerned, back when the Pony Express made mail runs between St. Joe and Sacramento. Barnes was well-mannered, well-dressed, well-groomed, and didn't smoke or swear. "Sure do miss him—he could eat, that one! Kept the dining room doing good business," Mrs. Collins laughed. "Good boy, he was. Did his best to keep his nose clean, though he found his share of trouble by keeping company with Drake."

Signing the register, Salina jerked her head up quickly at the mention of the man named Drake. The sooner she could contact him, the better. "How might one go about finding Mr. Drake?" she inquired.

"That would depend on if he wants to be found or not," Mrs. Collins chuckled. "And it's not *Mr.*—it's just plain Drake. Now, why would a nice little miss like you want to associate with a young rogue like him?"

"Jeremy has asked me to convey a message to Drake while I am here," Salina replied cautiously. "Would you know where he is?"

"The girls over at the saloon usually know his whereabouts better than I." Mrs. Collins clearly disapproved. "But the freight office might know when he's scheduled to return—providing he's on a run, that is. And he might well be, considering I haven't seen him in weeks, come to think about it."

Salina sighed, crestfallen.

"There, there, miss," Mrs. Collins patted Salina's hand. "Drake's like a bad penny. He always turns up—when you least expect him, like as not."

Mrs. Collins showed them the two rooms on the third floor. The girls went back to the depot to get Joetta and Austin, and then while the four ordered dinner in the dining room at the hotel their baggage arrived.

"Well," Joetta said optimistically as she tucked Austin into bed later that evening, "at least we know this Drake character truly does exist."

"Did you doubt that he might?" Taylor Sue quizzed.

Joetta shrugged, "You never doubted it?"

Taylor Sue shook her head. "I stand behind Salina, whatever she says or does. If she says there's a fellow named Drake, then it's because she has it from reliable sources that it is so. When she says we must wait for his outfit in order that he might be the driver to take us west, then it's because Salina has a valid reason. I trust her implicitly. You can, too."

Joetta nodded. "I didn't mean to suggest that I did not believe what she said. I suppose I'm just impatient to have this journey over and done with. I don't want to delay any longer than necessary. I want to see Hank, and I want Hank to see Austin. He's grown so much since Hank left for Nevada. The train ride seemed to take a small eternity—how much more so when we're confined to a stagecoach for all those miles!"

Salina came in on the last of Joetta's statement. "I dread the weeks ahead as well, Joetta. I'm impatient, too. My nerves are as taut as fiddle strings, but I'm sure we'll be fine. As soon as we can find Drake, I'll tell him that we want to be the first passengers on his next western run." She rubbed her arms to ward away a sudden chill. Instinctively she knew that to remain in St. Joseph any longer than absolutely necessary would be dangerous, and she began to wonder if Duncan Grant would come after them...

Taylor Sue yawned. "Well, I, for one, am exhausted. Now that we've had a delicious supper, I am looking forward to a refreshing bath and a good night's rest."

"We'll be right across the hall if you should need us," Salina assured Joetta. "Who knows? Drake may already be here in town."

"I promised Austin I would take him to the circus tomorrow," Joetta said. "He's never been to one before."

Salina nodded. "I've never been to one either, and I think I'd like to very much. In the morning, we'll go to the freight office and inquire after Drake. In the afternoon, we'll see the circus. Sleep well, Joetta."

"Good night, Salina. Good night, Taylor Sue," Joetta bid them.

Taylor Sue smiled and closed Joetta's door. She followed Salina into the room directly across the narrow hall. "A circus—what fun!" she giggled. Not long after her bath Taylor Sue was quickly overcome by sleep.

For a time sleep eluded Salina, however, and she lay awake thinking. Jeremy had been here in this town, in this hotel, and she was in the very same room he had once occupied. Odd, but it seemed to give her a strange sort of comfort knowing this, though she didn't understand why. She prayed, thanking God for His good favor in bringing them along this first part of their journey. She thanked Him for supplying the train tickets in Daddy's trunk, for providing a chaperone and companions in Joetta and Taylor Sue. Salina praised the Lord for the way Mrs. Collins had revealed what she knew of Drake. Her suggestion of searching for him at the freight office was confirmation of what Jeremy had said. All the pieces seemed to be fitting together so far, and Salina fell asleep at last with a smile on her lips and an attitude of worship in her heart.

☆☆☆☆☆☆☆

Sleep was interrupted when Taylor Sue yanked the quilt away from Salina sometime in the middle of the night. "Quit hoarding the blanket," Taylor Sue grumbled.

Salina tugged the quilt back, wrapping her half snugly around herself. "It's cold in here."

"Of course it's cold. It's October," Taylor Sue yawned tiredly, "and you left the window open."

"I did not leave the window open," Salina argued. She rolled over and accidentally hit Taylor Sue with her cast.

"Ouch!" Taylor Sue complained, rubbing her shoulder. "If you'd stay on your side of the bed, you wouldn't hurt me with that thing!" Rubbing her eyes, she got out of bed, her toes instantly chilled on the hard wooden floor. A wide moonbeam made a pathway from the wall to the bed, and the curtains rustled in the cold breeze. She touched the window sash, and then she felt a strong arm steal around her slender waist. A callused hand covered her mouth before she could let out a terrified squeal.

Salina lay with her back to the window, waiting for the sound of the window sliding shut, and for Taylor Sue to climb back under the quilt next to her. Neither happened. Salina turned over, lifted her head up, and discovered that Taylor Sue was being held by a man concealed in the shadows. Fear took her breath away. She tried to swallow but could not due to the hard lump in her throat. Salina's fingers curled around the handle of the pistol hidden beneath her pillow.

"Don't do anything foolish, little one," a gravely whisper cautioned. "I didn't come here to hurt you."

"Show yourself," Salina spoke softly. "Step into the light."

A tall, bronzed man with thick black hair reaching his waist stepped into the flickering light from the candle Salina lit. She could just make out a scar on the man's forehead, and she could see that the color of his eyes was an arresting bluish-green.

"Which of you is Salina Hastings?" the man demanded to know.

"Are you Drake?" Salina asked in return.

"I am," he answered, leveling his turquoise gaze upon her.

She answered, "I am Salina."

Drake impudently used his eyes to thoroughly examine the pretty face of the dark-haired girl before responding in a husky voice, "Well, well, now I can see why Jeremy Barnes would want you looked after."

"How do you know Jeremy Barnes wants you to look after me?" Salina inquired. "And how did you know where to find me?"

"I got a telegraphed message from him at the express office," Drake said. "He said you'd be here, in need of safe conduct to San Francisco. What I want to know is why?"

"Why don't you let go of Taylor Sue and sit down? We'll discuss it." Salina seated herself at the table, expecting Drake to do her bidding.

He sat down, propped his boots up on the edge of the table, and watched intently as Salina questioned Taylor Sue as to whether or not she was all right. This Taylor Sue was a fetching creature with her russet hair and golden-brown eyes, Drake acknowledged, but she didn't hold a candle to Salina. There was something about the Hastings girl which drew him to her, like a moth to flame. He cleared his throat, "Let's have that discussion."

Taylor Sue wrapped herself in the quilt and sat down in a third chair, but she remained silent while Salina did all the talking.

Salina explained to Drake, in the least amount of detail, that it was imperative that she and Taylor Sue get to San Francisco. "There's information there that may help me help Jeremy."

Drake was skeptical. "You're willing to risk your pretty little neck for some information?"

"Yes," Salina said bravely. "I wouldn't if I didn't think it was important enough to do so."

Drake nodded. "I suppose you're right. So, with Jeremy off riding with the Confederate cavalry—and you being Southerners yourselves—this must be connected to some mighty important Confederate secrets, right?"

Salina nodded slowly. She knew Jeremy trusted this man, and now she must learn to do the same. "I should tell you right off that there's a possibility we might be followed. I don't know for sure, but I'm guessing that the Yankees will send someone after us. We cannot let them have the documents I have. They are the key to the information waiting for me in San Francisco," she admitted.

"I understand that you are reluctant to tell me much, little one, but I have to know certain things so that I can protect you and Taylor Sue the best I can," Drake said.

Salina looked deep into Drake's turquoise eyes. "Jeremy said you could be trusted. I believe him."

Drake nodded. "When we rode for the Pony Express, there were times when we trusted each other with our very lives. In fact, I owe Barnes mine. He saved my hide several times. What matters now is that *you* trust me, little one."

Salina replied, "I have no alternative but to trust you with my life, Drake—and with Taylor Sue's, Joetta's, and Austin's."

"The others, Joetta and Austin, they are your traveling companions?" Drake asked.

Salina nodded. "Surely you must realize that my Mamma would never allow me to travel west all alone. It wouldn't be proper."

"A chaperone, of course." Drake was slightly amused at the observance of convention. His rough western lifestyle contained little of the refinement or convention embodied in Salina. "And what about your father? Is he off fighting in the blasted war, too?"

Sadness touched Salina's expression. "My Daddy was a Confederate agent. He was captured by the Yankees and was killed while trying to escape."

"I'm sorry, little one," Drake said sympathetically. He lifted Salina's chin, forcing her to look up at him. "I reckon he'd be proud of you."

"I know." Tears shimmered in her green eyes.

Drake was quiet, saying nothing as his eyes again scrutinized every detail of her face. His deep intensity made Salina wonder if he could read her thoughts when he looked at her like that.

"You're up to your neck in this, aren't you?" Drake asked, though he already knew the answer.

"Why else would the Yankees send men after us?" Salina queried.

"At least I know now what I have to protect," Drake sighed. "I need to sleep for what's left of tonight and a good portion of tomorrow. I think I can talk the dispatcher into letting me make the western-bound run day after tomorrow. Until then, lay low. I'll be back to fetch you when it's time."

"We'll be waiting," Salina assured him.

Drake pulled an envelope from his pocket of his buckskin coat. "That's the rest of the telegram from Jeremy Barnes."

"Is he well?" Salina asked, absently fingering the locket Jeremy had given her at the hospital in Washington.

"Read it for yourself and find out," Drake grinned. As quick as a flash, he was halfway out the window. He could fully understand why Jeremy Barnes had fallen in love with this exquisite young miss. "Stay out of trouble till I come back."

☆☆☆☆☆☆☆

White-faced clowns greeted the paying guests at the entrance of the circus. The striped canvas tents were set up on the far side of the railroad tracks with the biggest tent in the center of the colorful encampment. Admission was fifty cents for grown-ups and a quarter for children. Austin tugged excitedly on Joetta's hand, urging her to hurry. Taylor Sue and Salina both looked all around, taking in everything they could see.

Taylor Sue shied away from the snake charmer; Joetta was amazed by the fire-eater. Other side shows displayed a sword swallower, a fat lady, midgets, giants, a bearded lady, and a tatooed man. The girls followed Austin and Joetta as they looked at exhibits and went to see the menagerie.

Inside the canvas structure were caged animals, most of which Salina had never seen before except in picture books. She was intrigued by all the varieties of animals and birds: lions, tigers, leopards, baboons, parrots, cranes, owls, grizzly and polar bears, spotted hyenas, kangaroos, jackals, apes and monkeys, hippos and elephants, camels and zebras. Taylor Sue and Joetta laughed while Austin clapped his fat little hands in delight.

Joetta ushered her son and the girls toward the largest canvas tent where at two o'clock in the afternoon the circus show began. She purchased a bag of popcorn for them to share as they watched the performance.

The tuxedoed ringmaster introduced each act. The clown routines made the audience laugh, the tightrope walkers made them hold their breaths, and the equestrian feats made them stand and applaud loudly.

At the conclusion of the circus acts, they again walked past the side shows, listening to the "talkers" try to get the people to come and see each display. Salina tried to memorize all the sounds and colors, the festivity, and the exciting sights so that she could write about them to Mamma and Ethan once she reached San Francisco. She wondered where Mamma was, and if Captain Grant was with her.

☆☆☆☆☆☆☆

Lieutenant Lance Colby showed five Union soldiers in his command a tintype photograph of a dark-haired young girl. "Her name is Salina Hastings," Lieutenant Colby said. "We have reason to believe that she is a Confederate agent."

"She's just a girl," one of the men said.

Colby nodded. "That's what they said about Belle Boyd, and she was imprisoned for supplying Stonewall Jackson with information against us. President Lincoln's orders to the Secret Service are specific: Stop the information from getting to the hands of Southerners who use it to fight against us. Captain Grant has his orders from the War Department, and this is what he wants us to do. Find the girl, and bring her back to Washington. No harm is to come to her. She is to be treated with respect but caution. She is to be made to understand that she must answer to the Federal Government for her actions."

"The little traitor," another soldier said angrily.

"Perhaps she doesn't know what she's doing," yet another suggested.

Lieutenant Colby shook his blond head. "She knows what she's doing. Don't let her fool you. Her father was Garrett Hastings, and I'm quite sure he taught her well."

"How do we know that she's here in St. Joseph?" one of the men asked.

"We don't. We're acting on a hunch of Captain Grant's. Split up and search," Lieutenant Colby ordered. "Remember, she's not to be ill-treated. If you find her, bring her to me here at the Marshal's Office. In the meantime, I'll start checking hotel registers. If we can find her, we'll hold her until we can wire Captain Grant, and then we'll take her, under guard, back with us."

"Yes, sir," the five Union soldiers saluted. They went their separate ways and began to search for the pretty little Rebel.

Lieutenant Colby stared intently at the photograph that Captain Grant had the foresight to purchase from the Irish photographer. "I'm going to find you, Little Miss Rebel," he promised himself. "You can count on that."

☆☆☆☆☆☆☆

"I think we should go back to the hotel," Salina suggested. "If Drake finds out that we've come here, I don't think he'll like it much." No sooner were the words out of her mouth than she saw a blue-uniformed corporal nosing through the exhibition booths less than twenty yards away.

Taylor Sue saw the man at the same instant. She gripped Salina's arm, "Yankees!"

Joetta snatched Austin up and balanced him on her hip. "Come on, quickly. Let's go." Austin waved bye-bye to the dancing bear and let out a disappointed wail when Joetta refused to stop and let him see the organ grinder's little pet monkey.

Austin's holler attracted the attention of a second Yankee who had been wandering through the arcade. "Ssshhh!" Joetta tried to quiet Austin down. "I think we'd better hurry.

Taylor Sue, Joetta with Austin, and Salina disappeared into the crowds, evading the enemy soldiers. They kept a sharp lookout for any more Yankees. Salina's heart pounded in her chest as the quick pace of their walk put distance between them and the circus grounds. She nearly forgot to breathe until they reached the boardwalk in front of the hotel and entered the lobby.

Drake was there waiting for them. "I ought to skin you alive—all of you!" he growled lowly, clearly displeased.

"He speaks proper English for an Indian, doesn't he?" Joetta shifted Austin to her opposite hip. "No accent whatsoever."

"He's only half-Indian," Salina whispered.

Drake's cutting turquoise glare made Salina hold her tongue. "Get upstairs, now!" he ordered.

They did as they were told.

Drake halted just outside the door of the room that belonged to Salina and Taylor Sue. "Don't bother about finding your key," Drake said. "The lock's been broken." He shoved the door open.

The inside of the room looked like it had been struck by a tornado. It was completely ransacked. "Oh, my goodness!" Salina gasped. She looked up into the face of the copper-skinned man at her side. "Drake?"

"I thought I told you to stay out of trouble," he said coldly. "What possessed you to go to the circus of all places?"

Joetta spoke up, "It's my fault. I promised Austin yesterday that I'd take him there today."

"We've never seen one before either," Taylor Sue added. "It was very exciting."

Drake looked at Salina, expecting her to add her bit. She said, "You told us to lay low. You didn't say we couldn't leave the hotel. I thought we'd just blend in among the crowds of people. Until we saw some Yankee soldiers, that is."

"If you'd stayed here, this mess might not have happened," Drake countered.

Salina argued with him, "If we'd stayed here, we probably would have been taken."

Their eyes clashed. Unwillingly, Drake admitted that Salina's statement was the more accurate one "What would somebody be looking for?" he asked.

"If the somebodies were indeed Yankees," Salina said, "they were looking for these." She lifted the skirt of her dress, revealing the secret documents which were securely pinned to the underside of her crinoline. She smiled, pleased with her own cleverness. "Surely you don't think I'd leave these here, what with the possibility that something like this might occur?" With a sweep of her hand she encompassed the wreckage of the room.

"You're smart, little one, and this time it paid off. Next time you might not be so lucky. From here on out, you listen to what I say, and you follow my orders," Drake commanded. "Do you understand?"

"Yes," Salina nodded.

"And you?" he questioned Taylor Sue and Joetta.

"Yes, of course," they answered at once.

"Good. Then get packed and let's see if we can't restore some order to this place. I'm taking you with me to the saloon. You can't stay here any longer, and I need you where I can keep an eye on you," Drake told them. He nodded toward Salina.

She nodded back. She had to trust him, and she sensed that this would be the first of many times that she'd have to rely on Drake's judgment.

Chapter Twenty-Three

*T*hat will be two hundred dollars, miss, for each," the clerk at the express company's freight office informed Salina. She counted out the required gold coins, and he handed her a one-way stagecoach ticket for passage from St. Joseph to San Francisco.

"Thank you." Salina stared down at the printed ticket, and when she looked up, her gaze met the stunning turquoise eyes that belonged to Drake.

"We'll leave within the hour," Drake said curtly. "I'll see to it that your baggage is stowed safely away."

Salina nodded silently.

"When will we get to San Francisco?" Taylor Sue asked.

"It'll take roughly three weeks," Drake replied. "It can be rather monotonous, but I'm sure you'll make it just fine. We should arrive on the eleventh or twelfth of November, give or take a day."

Salina and Drake had talked together again after breakfast. She'd told him as much as she dared of the plans for the western campaign, and she felt that Drake understood the importance of her journey to visit her aunt. He told her, countless times, that she could rely on him to take care of her. Salina prayed very hard and had the faith to let God work however He chose in such a time as this.

Taylor Sue, Joetta, and Austin were already on board with four other passengers when Josiah, Drake's mulatto shotgun rider, handed Salina into the Concord coach. Taylor Sue smiled broadly while Salina settled into her seat, her merry brown eyes seemed to say, *"Here we go again!"*

It was not difficult to learn the routine of stagecoach travel. The horses, bred for strength and distance, were replaced by a fresh team at each way station along the route. The distance between the way stations averaged between ten and fifteen miles. The horses pulled the loaded stagecoach at a brisk pace of five miles per hour. Drake handled the spirited teams well, and he handled his eight passengers with an equal dose of confidence and demand for discipline.

A handful of larger towns dotted the overland route, breaking the monotony of the smaller way stations. The first principal town was Denver, in Union-held Colorado Territory, which was a collection of tents that formed the growing city situated where the plains met up with the Rocky Mountains. It was a boom town, with precious metals mined in the vicinity, and it was showing signs of permanence as the construction of lumber and brick buildings replaced the more temporary dwellings.

Drake allowed a two-hour stopover in Denver rather than the customary thirty minutes. It gave him the opportunity to get some business settled, and it afforded the girls and Joetta the chance to hire a room and order a real bath.

Salina was growing accustomed to the grit and grime from the dust the horses kicked up every mile along the way. Taylor Sue had complained at first, and Austin had been difficult to entertain, but Joetta and Salina bit their tongues, accepting the unpleasant conditions of traveling.

The scented bath proved to be most refreshing. Salina faced the looking-glass above the bureau and tied a fresh ribbon around the end of her damp, thick braid. "I feel much better when I'm clean!"

Taylor Sue readily agreed. "I never realized how I took for granted such simple things when I was at home."

Without thinking twice, Salina answered the door when she heard a loud rapping. Taylor Sue and Joetta were through with their baths, and Austin was the last one to take a dip in the tub behind the dividing screen.

"*Never* open the door without making sure you know who or what is on the other side, little one," Drake scolded, shaking his finger. "Have you forgotten so quickly that there are people who would try to get to you or your documents no matter what?"

"I remember," Salina hung her head down. "It won't happen again, Drake."

"Good," Drake said simply. "Are you ready to go?"

"We haven't eaten yet," Taylor Sue explained. "We were hoping to go downstairs to the dining room."

Drake checked his pocket watch. "Yes, I suppose there is just enough time for you to do that. Would you mind if I joined you? I have some news that might be of interest to you." He picked up Salina's carpetbag satchel with one hand and said, "I'll take this out to the stage, and then I'll meet you downstairs."

At the stagecoach, Drake tossed the satchel up to Josiah. The shotgun rider reported, "Freddie got a reply back from that telegram you sent, Drake. It's addressed to Salina."

"Freddie holding it at the office?" inquired Drake.

Josiah nodded, "Yep."

Drake went into the dining room to fetch Salina and took her over to the freight office with him. The express clerk, Freddie, acknowledged them, and held up a folded sheet of paper. Drake took the paper and continued into the private office at the rear of the building. He shut the door and motioned for Salina to be seated.

"Is something wrong?" Salina finally asked, confused by Drake's silence.

"Perhaps," Drake answered. He handed her the paper. "But first let's deal with this. It's addressed to you. Freddie must have had quite a time getting all that down."

Salina saw that the telegram was from Reverend Yates, and she smiled slightly. "I imagine he would. It's in code."

"And you know how to make heads or tails of that nonsense?" Drake raised an eyebrow in question.

"Yes," Salina replied.

"Will it take you long to decipher it?" Drake wanted to know.

"I don't think so," Salina said.

"You stay put and translate that. I'll get us a couple of sandwiches from the hotel. I need to know what that says before we leave, because I've learned something that might have a bearing on whatever is contained in that coded telegram," explained Drake. "Be quick. We haven't got much time. We've got half an hour before we're scheduled to pull out."

Salina found that Reverend Yates' message was brief yet informative:

> *Captain Grant knows where you're going. Keep pushing on. You have the head start. Don't give up on it now. Your father wouldn't have changed his course— don't change yours. Ethan is with the medics in Stonewall's army. Jeremy sends his love and encouragement. He rode with Stuart's cavalry around McClellan's army. There was a successful raid at Chambersburg. McClellan's moving the Army of the Potomac back into Virginia, at Lincoln's insistence for action. God bless and keep you...*

"What is it? What does it say?" Drake hunkered down in front of the chair she was sitting on and gripped her shoulders tightly. "Nothing's happened to Jeremy?"

"No, Jeremy's fine," she answered. "According to what Reverend Yates says, he went on a raid with General Stuart in Chambersburg. I wish I could see a newspaper and see what is being said about it. I've heard very little of the news from home since we left."

"I'll get you a newspaper," Drake promised. "What else does it say, little one?"

Salina said evenly, "Captain Grant knows where we are."

"Evidently news travels quickly where you're concerned," Drake confirmed. "An acquaintance of mine over at the saloon had heard through the grapevine that some Yankee soldiers are headed this way in pursuit of a Rebel spy. I would take that to mean you, little one."

"So he's after us. I'm putting this run in danger, aren't I?" asked Salina.

"I'm here to see that the danger does not materialize," Drake said firmly. "We'll have to make up some time, take a little bit of a shortcut that I know. I have friends, the Whittakers, who have a way station that's not on the main route. They'll put us up, no questions asked. They can help us learn the position of the men who are following you. I've decided we won't go to Granger, but we will have to stop in Salt Lake City. Here, eat this. I'll be back in a few minutes. I'm going to wire Lacy Whittaker so she'll be expecting us."

☆☆☆☆☆☆☆

Lacy Whittaker heard the stagecoach even before she saw it come around the bend headed at a breakneck speed for the way station. The sound of jangling harness and pounding hooves stirred her into motion. Hurriedly she abandoned her stacked dishpan, wiping her sudsy wet hands down the front of her apron.

She was alone in the yard when Drake halted the team of six matched horses. Josiah tipped his hat to her, but Drake climbed down instantly without a greeting.

"You got my message, then," he said gruffly.

"Yes. You can't stay here." Lacy clutched his arm. She pulled a telegram from her apron pocket. "I intercepted this when it came across the wire. It's to Papa from an Army lieutenant. It's a forewarning that he and his men will be here first thing in the morning. It came right after your telegram did, so you've no time to lose."

Drake scanned the lines of the telegram signed by a Lieutenant Lance Colby. While the Lieutenant made vague reference to a search for a suspected Rebel agent on board a westbound stage, there were no specific details implicating Salina directly. "Have you got any horses available, Lacy?" Drake asked.

"A fresh team, and four others," Lacy told him. She looked beyond him, and her eyes singled out Salina's face among those peering from the windows of the coach. Lacy swallowed the bitter taste of envy in her mouth. "Is *she* the reason you're putting yourself at risk, Drake? Or don't you remember your last brush with the Army and the law as well as I do?"

"I know what I'm doing," Drake growled a low voice.

Lacy challenged, "Is she worth it?"

Drake glared at Lacy, a hard glint in his turquoise eyes. "Jealousy does not become you, Lacy, though I'm flattered. I'm simply paying off an old debt that I owe to a friend. He's asked me to keep an eye on her. Catch is, she's the one the Yankees are after."

Lacy nodded, choosing to believe his words of explanation, as she always did. She took the telegram from Drake's hand and stuffed it back into her pocket. "Eventually, I'm going to have to let Papa know that the Yankees intend to have breakfast here. So what do you want me to do?"

Drake thought for moment, then said aloud, "It's only a few hours to Kincaid's place. We'll stop there. I'll need a fresh team, though. And I'll take you up on the offer of three of the other horses. I want to send Josiah on ahead. He can take the two girls out of here with him. It'll be safer for them. We'll meet up again in Salt Lake City."

"That's four days from here," Lacy reminded him.

"I know, but it should give us time to shake the persistent bluebellies," Drake said between clenched teeth. "You'll not tell your father?"

"Have I ever told him anything that you asked me not to?" Lacy answered with a question.

Drake smiled down at her. "You're a good woman, Lacy Whittaker."

"I wish you'd remember that more often." she turned on her heel, heading for the kitchen. "I'll pack some provisions for them. You and Josiah can take your pick of horses from the corral. I want you to get going, and be quick about it."

Drake grinned behind Lacy Whittaker's back, and then his focus settled once more on Salina Hastings.

Five minutes later, Salina and Taylor Sue were upstairs in Lacy's bedroom, shedding their traveling suits and donning red woolen long johns, flannel shirts, and sturdy denim trousers.

"You've been kind to help us out of the scrape we're in," Taylor Sue said to Lacy, pulling on a pair of boots. "I'd be honored if you'd accept one of my dresses as a token of my appreciation for all you've done."

Lacy hesitated, "You don't have to do that to thank me."

But Taylor Sue had seen Lacy eyeing the fashionable gowns in the trunk with a certain longing. "Please, I insist. And I won't take no for an answer."

Salina selected a burgundy watered silk dress from the traveling trunk. "I think this one would look beautiful on you, Lacy."

Lacy held the dress against herself and stared at her reflection in the cheval mirror. "Where on earth would I wear something as fancy as all this?" she argued.

"You could save it for a special occasion," Taylor Sue suggested. "Or perhaps for when company comes to call?"

Salina smiled. "I'm sure Drake would say that you looked lovely in such a dress."

Lacy tilted her head to one side, her wheat-brown hair brushing past her shoulder. "I wonder if he'd even notice," she whispered to her reflection.

"He'd have to be blind not to," Taylor Sue said matter-of-factly. "You keep it, and you'll just have to wait for the right time to see what his reaction will be."

Lacy reluctantly agreed to keep the gown. She didn't care if these two girls could see right through her to know that she was pleased beyond words, but she was suddenly uncomfortable. She was unaccustomed to such kindness. She cleared her throat. "I've food downstairs and canteens already filled with spring water. Josiah knows the land between here and Salt Lake City well. It has been cold as of late, but so far no snow. It will be a hard ride for you both."

"We'll make it," Salina said confidently. "There's a promise in the New Testament that says *'I can do all things through Christ Jesus who strengthens me.'*"

"Good," Lacy said simply. "You'll need to believe that with every fiber of your being to make it through to Salt Lake—no doubt about that."

☆☆☆☆☆☆☆

Josiah made a small fire, in the back away from the mouth of the cave, where others before had obviously done the same thing. The cave had several "rooms" branching off from the main entrance. Salina supposed this would make a very good hideout for an outlaw...like herself, and now Taylor Sue as well.

"Come on, Miss," Josiah beckoned to Salina. "Come on and have a bit of Miss Lacy's stew. She's a good cook, she is."

"Yes, she is," Salina nodded, knowing it to be fact from experience. "She's a very good friend to Drake, too, isn't she?"

Josiah nodded. "Lacy Whittaker would never let anything happen to Drake, if it was within her power. And she won't let no harm come to any of his friends, either. If she acted a bit... reserved...well I suppose it's probably because..."

"Because of the styles of our dresses and the drawl of our voices," Taylor Sue suggested diplomatically. "She seemed very pleased when I offered her one of my dresses in trade for our flannel shirts, long johns, and trousers. We're indebted to her for her help."

"If she hadn't told Drake about the telegram she'd intercepted..." Salina shivered at the thought. "If it hadn't been for Lacy, we might have been caught."

Josiah smiled, a knowing gleam in his black eyes. "Lacy's a fine woman, always eager to lend a hand. But personally I think she was more or less afraid that Drake had become taken with you, Miss."

"Drake is protecting me—us—" Salina objected, "because Jeremy asked him to, that's all. Drake should have made Lacy understand that."

"He tried," Josiah chuckled. "I heard him myself."

Salina had finished her stew, which was tasty, warm, and filling. "Is there any more coffee?" she asked abruptly.

Taylor Sue filled Salina's tin mug. "That's the last of it." She, too, had sensed that Drake had taken a personal interest in Salina. A few days ago, she had whispered to Salina the very idea that Josiah hinted at now. Salina had refused to believe it, maintaining that Drake's interest in her did not go beyond his loyalty to the friendship he shared with Jeremy Barnes.

"We'll be in Salt Lake tomorrow," Josiah said with a nod. "We should have enough food and water to last us until we join up with the stagecoach again." The girls both looked tired with dark circles beneath their eyes. He knew this detour on horseback had been rough on them, but they didn't complain about the primitive conditions or lack of niceties, and both obeyed his commands without question. He had completely agreed with Drake when they'd discussed separate routes. It was better to be safe than sorry where the girls were concerned. As long as the girls were in their care, Drake and Josiah would do whatever they must to keep them safe from the Yankees.

Salina jotted a few lines down in her journal by the light of the small fire.

> *The third day: very cold, but thankfully no snow, which we have seen on some of the higher mountain peaks. Josiah says we're lucky. I argued that "blessed" was a better word. The cave provides more shelter than the lean-tos he's built for us the past nights—those were little more than tree branches propped against the side of the mountain where Taylor Sue and I crawled under and napped. I don't think Josiah has slept at all since we left Lacy Whittaker's way station. Perhaps tonight, here in the safety of the cave, he'll be able to get some rest.*

Hours later, Salina woke to sounds of horses and a foreign language. Josiah was near the mouth of the cave, but hidden in the shadows, rifle in hand.

"Stay back, Miss," the shotgun rider ordered. "They must've seen through my attempts to hide our tracks, and they have to know we're here, but I don't think they're going to bother us."

"Soldiers?" Salina whispered the question.

"No, Indians—Utes. On occasion they've made it rather clear that they don't like whites in their territory, even half-whites like me. Maybe they know we're just passing through..." Josiah's voice trailed off. He failed to mention that there was the distinct possibility that the

Utes might be employed as Yankee Army scouts. "You should be asleep. We'll leave at first light."

"Have you slept at all since we left Lacy's way station, Josiah?" Salina asked.

"Can't afford to," Josiah shook his head. "I have to keep watch."

"I'll keep watch," Salina volunteered. "You just lay right there and close your eyes for a spell. I'll wake you quick enough if I think there's any trouble."

"That's mighty tempting, Miss, but Drake's gone and entrusted you to me," Josiah argued.

"Just do as I say," Salina ordered softly. "If the Indian scouts should wait until we ride out, we'll need you alert, not dog tired."

Josiah chuckled, "Yes, Miss." He stretched out on a thin blanket, using a stone for a pillow, pulled his hat over his face. "Know how to shoot a rifle?"

"No," Salina answered.

Josiah peeked out from under the brim of his hat.

Salina smiled at him. "But I know how to shoot this."

Josiah noted the silver pistol in her hand. "I reckon you do at that, Miss. G'night." He fell asleep to the Southern melodies Salina hummed softly.

At daybreak, they set out riding as hard and as fast as they could. A Ute arrow, shot by one of the band who were chasing after them, found its mark in the rump of Salina's horse. She nearly fell when the horse stumbled, but Josiah somehow grabbed her and swung her onto the back of Taylor Sue's horse. And they kept on riding.

Salina's heart beat fiercely in her chest. Her breathing was laborious, as was Taylor Sue's, and they held onto each other in fear. After several miles, the Utes mysteriously gave up the chase.

"You two all right?" Josiah questioned. He, too, was out of breath. "Can you keep up?"

They nodded without the slightest hesitation. "We don't want to stay here another minute!" Taylor Sue exclaimed. "Are we far from Salt Lake City?"

"At this pace, we should be there before dark," Josiah told them.

Dusk was falling when they arrived at the express office in Salt Lake City. Drake hugged both of the girls to him tightly. His turquoise eyes questioned Josiah gruffly, "Where have you been? You should have been here over two hours ago!"

Josiah told Drake about the chase. "If the Indians had really wanted to, they could easily have captured us. They seemed content enough to frighten the living daylights out of us instead. Remember back awhile when you got offered a position as an Army scout?"

"Yeah," Drake nodded. "What of it?"

"Like I said, if the Utes had wanted to see us dead, we would be—which leads me to wonder if they work for the Army. Suppose it could be that their orders were merely to give us a good scare?"

"Which they did," Taylor Sue spoke up.

"Hmmm, Army scouts." Drake rubbed his jaw in a thoughtful manner. "I've been raking myself over the coals for the last four days, thinking that I never should have sent the three of you off alone like that. But then this morning was I ever glad you weren't with me." Drake shook his head and his long hair swung like a black curtain from side to side. "If you'd been with me, you'd most definitely have been captured. I reckon you'd be locked up right over in that jail as Yankee prisoners of war."

"They stopped the stagecoach?" Salina asked.

"Not only stopped, but searched—everything and everybody," Drake said.

Salina paled noticeably, touching his arm for support. "Drake, what about my trunk?"

"The soldiers broke the lock and emptied it—the dresses, petticoats, pantalets, your doll, books. They dumped it all right onto the ground. Broke your looking glass and a perfume bottle or two. Then they stuffed it all back in, tied it up with rope, and ordered me to put it back in the boot," Drake concluded.

Salina sagged against Drake in relief. She let out the breath she'd been holding, and then she started laughing. She harmlessly punched his arm. "You enjoy frightening me, don't you?"

"I told you I'd take care of you, little one." Drake touched the tip of her nose. "I just wanted you to see that I can be trusted. I asked the Lieutenant in charge what they were looking for. He wouldn't answer me, so I asked him if the Yankees issued special warrants for pawing through ladies' personal items in broad daylight in mixed company, or would just a general warrant do? That's pretty much when he ordered the search to be abandoned."

"What about my satchel?" Salina inquired.

"That I had hidden under the drivers' seat," Drake winked. "It's still there. They never even bothered to check. Most of them don't, and that's how things are successfully smuggled when need be."

A nagging thought hit Salina. "Drake, did you catch the name of the Lieutenant by chance?"

"Said his name was Lance Colby," Drake replied. "You know him?"

"I haven't had the pleasure of making his acquaintance formally," Salina said with a touch of sarcasm in her voice, "but I know he works for Duncan Grant. I'm of the opinion that he was assigned to follow Jeremy because Captain Grant thought Jeremy would be the one to take over the Network in my daddy's absence. Since the Yankees know that it isn't Jeremy, Lieutenant Colby's assignment now is to get after me." There wasn't much she could do about Lieutenant Colby—except stay out of his way. "I'm hungry. Is there someplace we can get something to eat around here?"

Drake nodded. "Come on. Joetta and Austin are anxiously waiting for you to get here. She's been worried sick—keeps saying over and over that your mammas trusted her to be a chaperone for the two of you. Go tell her you're all right—but you might want to leave out the part about being chased by the Indians..."

"Most certainly," Salina giggled. "We'll be right back."

When Salina returned to the stagecoach, Drake insisted that she bundle up warmly so she could ride up top between himself and Josiah for the next leg of the trip. "I want to talk to you."

☆☆☆☆☆☆☆

Lance Colby paced the wooden floor of the adjutant's office. He was beginning to feel like a failure as far as this mission was concerned. The orders were simple enough: Stop the Hastings girl from getting to San Francisco. He couldn't seem to do it.

In St. Joseph, she managed to slip through their fingers at the circus and boarded the stagecoach west. Nothing had been discovered through the search of her room at the hotel prior to her departure.

The driver of the stage had opted for the route to Denver rather than to Laramie, but either way, he had bypassed the way station at Granger altogether. Somehow that driver must have known Colby was there, waiting with his men—and a warrant for Salina's arrest.

Just outside of Salt Lake, Colby had overtaken the stage, forced the half-breed driver to stop and then conducted another fruitless search. Salina Hastings hadn't even been on board. The Ute Indian scouts he had hired came back with their report of a long chase.

As a last resort, Colby wired a report of his own to Duncan Grant, and now he waited impatiently for a reply. As the wire began to tap, the telegraph operator jotted down the message. "Here you go, Lieutenant."

The girl is as elusive as Hastings himself. She certainly inherited his skills as an agent. Stay on the trail. Go to San Francisco directly. Don't bother with detaining the stagecoach again. Hollis will board at Carson City in Nevada. Perhaps we'll be able to come up with something from that angle. Chin up, Lieutenant. We're working against some of the best, but we will prevail, I trust.—
Capt. Duncan Grant, U.S.A.

In one hand, Lieutenant Colby held the tintype of Salina; with his other hand, he folded the orders and stuffed them in his pocket. He went out to address his men. "We ride to San Francisco."

Chapter Twenty-Four

*H*ow long will we stay here, Drake?" Salina asked when the stagecoach pulled up in front of the Carson City express office in Nevada Territory.

"Long enough to change horses, drop off the mail, and eat. Don't go wandering too far. We've still got a ways to go yet before I'll consider you safely delivered to your destination," Drake told her.

"We won't go far, I promise," Salina nodded.

Hank Warner stood on the boardwalk waiting to meet Joetta and Austin when they descended from the stagecoach. The little boy shyly studied the big, burly man who was his father.

"I reckon he's forgotten me," Hank said with a catch in his voice. "I've been away from him—and you, Jo—for far too long. I can't tell you how glad I am that you're finally here with me." He squeezed his wife in a one-armed hug and then knelt down on one knee to put himself on Austin's level.

Austin glanced up to Joetta for approval, and when she nodded,

Austin hurled himself into Hank's waiting arms. "Daddy," the four-year-old said with a happy little smile.

"Maybe he hasn't forgotten you after all," Salina noted.

Hank looked up to find the daughter of Garrett Hastings being helped down from the driver's seat of the stagecoach. He touched the brim of his hat. "Well, Miss Salina, what a surprise! How do you do?"

"I'm just fine, Mr. Warner," Salina nodded.

"What brings you out west?" Hank asked.

"Taylor Sue Carey and I are on our way to visit relatives in San Francisco," Salina answered. "Joetta was nice enough to let us tag along with her on her way here to meet you."

Hank nodded, "I see." *Something has gone wrong*, he thought to himself. He had a gut feeling that plans for the western campaign must have changed since he had received no word from either Captain Hastings or Jeremy Barnes in several weeks. Salina's presence here in Carson City confirmed that.

"Miss Salina and Miss Taylor Sue," Hank rubbed his whiskered chin, pondering. "Well, I'll be jiggered. But I must thank you. I'm sure your company helped Joetta pass the long hours of the journey."

Joetta nodded, "Believe me, I don't know what I'd have done without their help in keeping Austin entertained."

Taylor Sue smiled. "He's a delightful little boy, really."

Hank invited the girls to dine with his family, knowing he must arrange a way to speak to Salina in private.

The opportunity presented itself when Salina wanted to check at the express office for any messages containing news from Virginia.

"And I need to go see if my latest catalog order has arrived," Hank said to Joetta. "If you'll take Austin and Miss Taylor Sue over to the restaurant, I'll accompany Miss Salina to the express office. We won't be but a few minutes."

Joetta nodded, taking Austin by the hand. Taylor Sue followed.

"I think you know why I'm here," Salina said softly, when they were out of earshot of anyone close by.

"Frankly, I was plumb shocked to see you, Miss Salina. I can't imagine why your father would send you across the country. Are things so bad in Virginia that he wanted you out of the way?"

"They're not good as we would have liked," Salina replied. "There were several successful battles that ended in our favor during the summer months, but that was before Antietam. The reason I'm here is because Daddy is dead, and I'm to see that his plans for the western campaign are delivered to the proper contacts."

"Garrett Hastings is dead?" Hank brooded. "I'm so sorry, Miss

Salina. I had no idea. I haven't heard anything from the Network in weeks—and now I understand why."

"Did you receive the documents from Daddy that were sent in a letter from Joetta?" Salina inquired.

"Yes," Hank confirmed. "That was your doing?"

"It was," Salina nodded her head affirmatively. "When I get to San Francisco, there should be a package waiting for me there at my aunt's house. I don't know what's inside yet, but I have a good idea that there will be details concerning the campaign."

"I would suppose," Hank nodded. "The last time I saw your father, I was under the impression that the campaign was to get underway before the year was out." He glanced down at the girl beside him. "You're a very brave little lady, Miss Salina, truth be told. I'm sure the Captain would have been very proud of you for what you're doing."

"I haven't completed the task yet," Salina shrugged aside his words of praise. "I've been followed, and I won't feel like I'm out of danger until I've made sure the information is in the right hands."

"I'd feel the same if I were in your shoes. I know the name of the San Francisco contact, and you'd be wise to get in touch with him just as soon as you possibly can. He's a doctor—Ben Nichols. He'll know what to do with the information. That cast of yours will provide a perfect reason to go see him," Hank indicated Salina's broken arm.

"And hopefully arouse no unwanted suspicion," Salina agreed. She recognized the name of the doctor from one of Daddy's lists.

"We're ready here," Hank whispered to Salina. "All we're waiting for is the word to make the strike. I've been in contact with some of the other leaders in their respective towns, and like me, all they need is the order to attack."

Salina swallowed and nodded her head gravely. "I wonder if the information in San Francisco includes the date on which the campaign is to start. Hopefully it will. Otherwise, I have no idea. Perhaps Dr. Nichols might."

"Perhaps," Hank conceded.

They reached the express office. No messages were addressed to Salina, but Hank did have a crate waiting for him. "I'll be back shortly to pick that up," he told the express agent.

At the restaurant, Salina ate a hearty bowl of chicken soup and a piece of fresh-baked bread. She had the uncanny feeling she was being watched, but after scanning the room, she could find no blue-clad Union soldiers.

Taylor Sue must have felt the same way. She leaned over to Salina and whispered, "That woman in black has been watching you from the minute you and Mr. Warner walked in."

Salina shivered slightly. All she wanted was to get to San Francisco and be done with this whole affair. When they had finished eating, the girls said their goodbyes to the Warners, and as Salina shook hands with Hank one last time, she felt him slip a folded note beneath her fingers.

He said, "Goodbye, Miss Salina, Miss Taylor Sue. Y'all have a safe trip. I'll be bringing Joetta and Austin out to San Francisco within the next few weeks to buy some supplies and anything else Joetta finds she might not be able to purchase in Virginia City. We'll make it a point to visit. You take good care, now, you hear?"

"Yes," Salina nodded. "Thank you." Outside the restaurant, Salina paused on the boardwalk and quickly read the brief note: *Be careful where you place your trust. As we have our eyes and ears, so does the enemy.* She paid little heed to the numbers in the bottom right corner of the piece of paper: 11-15. She tucked the note into her cast, between her palm and the plaster, and quickly walked with Taylor Sue across the street to the express office.

Drake and Josiah were waiting impatiently for the girls' return to the stagecoach. "You took your own sweet time," Drake muttered helping her up the step and into the coach. "You all right?"

Salina nodded, "Fine, thank you. Just fine. Why, what's wrong this time?"

"Nothing—that I'm aware of," Drake said curtly. "I've simply fallen into the habit of worrying about you, little one."

Salina smiled. "I'm sorry to be so much trouble to you, Drake."

A throaty grunt was the extent of his reply.

Three new passengers replaced Joetta and Austin, and now the coach was full up to capacity. One of the passengers was the woman from the restaurant, dressed severely in her black widow's weeds. A dark elbow-length veil partially concealed the woman's face, and black leather gloves encased her hands. She introduced herself as Mrs. Irene Hollis, but said no more.

The second newcomer was an anvil salesman. He kept to himself and seemed to sleep the better portion of the time away, as the majority of the other passengers did. The third newcomer was a woman, much younger than the widow, and she shared the same Southern accent that Taylor Sue and Salina possessed. "My name's Esther Nichols. I'm pleased to meet you both," she said with a smile at both Salina and Taylor Sue. "Are y'all headed as far as San Francisco?"

"Yes," Salina nodded. The stagecoach lurched forward and momentarily put an end to conversation. She wondered if this Esther Nichols was in any way related to the doctor Hank had told her about, and she remembered Hank's written words cautioning her not to trust anyone.

☆☆☆☆☆☆☆

The Widow Hollis had introduced herself to the Southern girls on board, but then she kept to herself during the miles between Carson City and Stockton. She sat quietly, listening to their scattered conversations, but there was little information to be gleaned from their words. They merely spoke of the contrasts between the West and their homes in the South.

Lieutenant Colby had been given a good dose of trouble trying to track down this Miss Salina Hastings. Sources in the east belatedly discovered that it was *she*, and not the Barnes boy, who filled the hole left by the death of Confederate Captain Garrett Hastings. The Widow Hollis was secretly amused. How typical of the men to overlook the female gender when it came to spying and transmitting intelligence regarding enemy forces—and now they had to make up for lost time because of it. This girl made an ideal secret agent. In truth, the Widow herself had aroused very few suspicions and had managed to break into the outer circle of an organized group of Southern sympathizers dwelling in San Francisco.

Now that Miss Hastings was here, the Widow intended to use her to gain entrance into the inner circle. The Widow was certain that was precisely where the girl was headed.

If she couldn't gain access to the conspirators themselves, the Widow was determined to find the information the pretty little Southern belle reportedly carried with her instead. She had a job to do, and the Widow was rather good at doing her job.

She leaned over and casually asked the older girl, Taylor Sue, what they planned to do once they arrived in San Francisco.

"We're going to visit some relatives," Taylor Sue answered carefully. "Have you ever been to San Francisco before?"

"Oh, many times. My husband, God rest his soul, and I lived there for quite a while before his accident..." the Widow's voice trailed off in contrived sorrow. After a few moments of silence, she said, "I'm sure you'll adore San Francisco. It's a wonderful city," and she proceeded to tell the girls stories of the opera and the theater, the grand balls and the lifestyles of the wealthy folks who built their mansions up on Russian Hill, Telegraph Hill, and Nob Hill with the proceeds of the gold strikes.

"I'd be more than happy to give you a guided tour of the city when we arrive," the Widow offered.

"Thank you," Salina said politely, "but I'm sure my aunt will show us around when we arrive."

The Widow nodded. She was thankful for the veil shielding her eyes from the penetrating green gaze of Miss Hastings. She was quick, the Widow unwillingly admitted. But she was young, and she was bound to make a mistake. It was only a matter of time.

☆☆☆☆☆☆☆

"No, Salina, there isn't enough time for a bath at this stop. You can take one in San Francisco—we're only twenty miles away. If you're hungry, go on and grab something to eat," Drake told her.

"I'm not hungry," Salina wrinkled her nose. Sometimes food at the way stations was wonderfully tasty, though none of the food had been as good as at Lacy Whittaker's. At other stops along the way they'd suffered due to rotten meat and moldy bread.

"Well, I am hungry," Drake said. "If you don't want to eat, then why don't you go change? If you ride up top with me and Josiah, you'll get to see the bay before the rest of the passengers." He tossed Salina's satchel down to her. "Be quick. We're leaving in five minutes."

Those five minutes stretched into ten, and then fifteen. The blacksmith was working on a loose shoe of one of the horses, and it was taking longer than Drake had anticipated or had patience for.

Salina went into the kitchen and helped herself to a mug of rich, hot chocolate. As she sipped at the steaming brown liquid, she noticed that only one of the other passengers was with her. "Hello, Esther."

"Hello," Esther returned. "I see you're back in britches. Will you be riding up top then?"

"Yes," Salina answered.

"You and the stagecoach driver seem to have much to talk about," Esther mentioned.

Salina gave a wary shrug. "We have a mutual friend back east who we talk of, mostly. Besides, it's a lot less stuffy than inside the coach."

Esther admitted, "I'd be frightened by the height of it."

"It is rather high, but you can see for miles," Salina said. "It's a spectacular view." The truth of the matter was that it was Drake's idea for Salina to sit up on top in the driver's seat. It was his way of shielding her from the new passengers. He didn't trust any of the passengers aside from Taylor Sue, and Drake preferred to keep Salina from having to associate with them.

"Esther, you wouldn't happen to be related to a Dr. Ben Nichols, would you?" Salina dared ask.

"Ben's my brother," Esther replied. "I've been to nursing school in Chicago, and now I'm on my way home to help Ben in his practice in San Francisco. I had wanted to ask you about your arm, but I always feel like the Widow Hollis pays too much attention to whatever it is that we're talking about."

Salina had felt that way as well, and so had Taylor Sue. Taylor Sue confided that she wouldn't trust the Widow a stitch, and Salina had echoed the sentiment. Esther was another matter. Yet Salina continued to act cautiously, and she trusted no one but Taylor Sue, Josiah, and Drake. Even though Esther's brother might be a Southern sympathizer and involved with the western campaign, it didn't necessarily mean Esther would hold the same convictions concerning the South's Cause.

"So, you're going to be a nurse," Salina said. "My brother apprenticed with the doctor back in Chantilly. He's the one who put this cast on me after I broke my arm." For the moment she refrained from explaining that Ethan was currently a surgeon's assistant in the Confederate Army.

"It's a very good one," Esther nodded. "And it's endured your journey quite well by the looks of it. How long have you had it on?"

"About six weeks," Salina replied. "My brother said I should be healed by this time."

"When we arrive in San Francisco, you should come to Ben's office. He'll have you out of that cast in no time," Esther invited. "Will you be staying with your aunt?"

"Yes," Salina answered. "She is Genevieve Dumont. Her husband, my uncle Henri, owns and operates Dumont's Lumber Mill."

Esther smiled. "I know the Dumonts very well. I went to school at the Young Ladies' Academy with their daughter, Marie, before Ben sent me to the nursing school in Chicago. I understand Marie is married now to an officer stationed at the Presidio."

"Really? I didn't know that. Actually, I don't remember my cousins. I was only four when we lived here once, a long time ago, while my daddy was assigned duty here after the War with Mexico. I don't remember much about San Francisco at all."

"Well I don't suppose you would. San Francisco is an interesting place. Ben and I moved here after our parents died about six years ago. I've spent the past year in Chicago, and I didn't think I'd miss the City by the Bay so very much, but I have. Perhaps while you're in town we can have lunch together or go on a shopping excursion," Esther suggested. "But first, we'll have Ben take care of that cast of yours. I hope you'll like San Francisco."

"I think I might," Salina said non-commitally. "Well, I suppose we should see if Drake's ready to start yet."

"I'll be along in a minute," Esther confided. "I've got to make a quick trip to the necessary. Don't let them leave without me."

"All right," Salina nodded. She slipped her arms into her over-sized jacket and was on her way to collect a buffalo skin robe from Josiah. She came upon the Widow Hollis, and the woman was obviously looking for something. Salina didn't care for her snooping around the unattended stagecoach.

"Were you looking for something in particular?" Salina asked abruptly.

The Widow jumped, momentarily startled, but she retained her cool expression. "Why, I...I was merely looking for my valise."

"That's odd. I distinctly remember you asking Josiah to store it up top, *not* in the boot where it might be easily crushed," Salina countered. The Widow was standing far too close to the traveling trunk for Salina's liking. "Shall I ask him to fetch if for you?"

"Oh, well," the Widow smiled, "I guess there's really no need for all that. I understand we'll be leaving soon, and we'll be in San Francisco in a few hours. It can wait, but thanks just the same for offering to help."

Salina returned the Widow's forced smile with one of her own. She again recalled Hank's note of warning, and the feeling she had that this woman could not be trusted was stronger than ever. Could the Widow be working for the Yankees? Salina did not rule out that possibility. And what of Esther? Salina wasn't completely sure about the doctor's sister. *Be careful where you place your trust. As we have our eyes and ears, so does the enemy...*

"I suppose we should board by now," the Widow said. "I believe the stage driver is a little anxious for us to get back on the trail."

"I suppose so," Salina nodded, following the Widow around the side to the stagecoach door.

"What was she up to?" Taylor Sue whispered as she stood next to Salina.

"Just snooping around," Salina answered. "Have you talked to her much?"

"Not really. Esther and I pretty much keep to ourselves," replied Taylor Sue. "But I can tell you this: The Widow has been reading a lot, and the book isn't of the standard variety. It looks much like the little leather-bound one you found inside of Celeste, remember? It's full of codes and jumbled words. I think she's a Yankee spy, Salina."

Salina nodded in agreement. "The thought had crossed my mind. See if you can find anything out that might tip off what she's really after."

"I'll see what I can do," Taylor Sue nodded. "In the meantime, you be careful riding up there. I don't see how you can bear being so high off the ground."

Salina smiled. "I enjoy it. It's exciting to see the power of the horses and the open landscape all around. Drake handles the horses with such strength, and Josiah's eyes are always searching for the slightest hint of danger..."

"Won't it be a treat when we're not in danger anymore?" Taylor Sue asked quietly.

Salina touched Taylor Sue's shoulder. "We're going to make it, you know. What ever happened to being strong and courageous?"

Taylor Sue shrugged, "That was a few hundred miles ago."

"You have been my encouragement when I questioned why we were here," Salina pointed out. "Maybe this will encourage you: *Yea, though I walk through the valley of the shadow of death, I will fear no evil; for Thou art with me; Thy rod and Thy staff, they comfort me. Thou preparest a table before me in the presence of mine enemies; Thou annointest my head with oil; my cup runneth over. Surely goodness and mercy shall follow me all the days of my life; And I shall dwell in the house of the Lord. Forever.* We are in God's hand, Taylor Sue. He'll protect us and see us through."

Taylor Sue hugged Salina. "I know He will. But as I said, please be careful up there."

✰☆✰☆✰☆✰

Salina sat wedged between Drake and Josiah, singing songs to pass the time and the miles. Josiah told jokes, and Salina recited some of her favorite poems. She even told a few stories about her life at Shadowcreek before the war had come.

"Tell me about the Pony Express, Drake," Salina requested. She loved the way he told stories. "Tell me about when you and Jeremy used to ride together."

Drake obliged—for the umpteenth time. He told her several

hair-raising tales, and even told her about the times Jeremy had actually saved his life. He delighted in her laughter, her curiosity, and her refreshing innocence.

Salina's breath caught at her first glimpse of San Francisco Bay. The water glistened like a million diamonds against a gray-green background. "We're almost there!" she cried excitedly. In her mind she thought, *It's almost over!*

It was Josiah who put into words the things Drake was thinking. "It sure won't be the same traveling without you, Miss. Drake and I have both grown fond of having your company. Haven't we, Drake?"

"Yeah," Drake admitted bluntly. "Never a dull moment with you and Taylor Sue on board—even when you weren't on board."

Salina smiled tentatively at Josiah, then looked up into Drake's turquoise eyes. "Well, I've grown fond of the two of you as well. I'm sorry that I've been such a bother, but I'm very grateful Jeremy insisted we wait for your run, Drake."

Drake grumbled something that Salina couldn't understand.

"Beg your pardon?" she asked, but Drake refused to repeat whatever it was he'd said.

Josiah told her, "He's gotten attached to you, Miss, that's why he's so surly. He's going to miss you more than he'd care to admit when you aren't with us any longer."

"Josiah, you talk too much," Drake snapped.

Salina grinned, hiding her eyes from Drake's intense blue-green glare by lowering the wide brim of her hat. She looked out over the bay and wondered about the islands she saw there. "What are those islands? Have you ever been there?"

"One is Angel Island, one is Yerba Buena Island," Drake answered. He pointed, "That one there between the two points of the Golden Gate is called Alcatraz. There's a United States military fort there and a military prison to go along with it. Some of the soldiers call it 'The Rock.'"

"Oh," Salina said lowly as a sudden chill crept along her spine. She pondered the name of the island, Alcatraz, and then she rubbed her arms to generate some warmth. "How much longer until we arrive at the express office?"

"Hold your britches on, little one," Drake nodded. "You'll be there all in good time."

Chapter Twenty-Five

*F*rom the driver's seat high upon the stagecoach, Salina instantly spotted the woman who must be Mamma's sister, Genevieve Dumont. Her facial features looked like a combination of Aunt Priscilla and Mamma rolled into one, though slightly older.

"Mrs. Dumont—hello!" Esther Nichols came down out of the stagecoach with a smile and hugged Genevieve in greeting.

"Esther Nichols, why I had no idea you were returning to San Francisco. Ben hasn't made any mention of it," Genevieve said, "or we would have planned a reception to welcome you home."

"Ben didn't mention it because he doesn't know. It's a surprise," Esther giggled. "I wrote and told him I was going to graduate from the nursing school in Chicago, but I deliberately didn't tell him when I was coming home, because I know Ben. He doesn't like a lot of fuss about anything. How is Marie? Does she enjoy being the wife of an Army officer?"

"Yes, I believe Marie is quite content in her marriage to Lieutenant Everett. Malcolm treats Marie as though she were a princess," Genevieve laughed lightly. Her stern eyes briefly rested on each female passenger as they disembarked, but none of the faces looked even remotely familiar. Genevieve was troubled. She had received a wire from a woman named Tabitha Wheeler that stated Salina Hastings—a niece Genevieve hadn't seen since the child was four years of age—was due to arrive Wednesday, the twelfth of November.

"You're looking for Salina," Esther assumed.

"Yes, as a matter of fact, I am. Do you know her?" Genevieve inquired.

"Oh yes," Esther nodded. "She, Taylor Sue Carey, and I have become friends since I boarded this stage at Carson City. There's Taylor Sue now," Esther indicated the russet-haired girl in a navy blue traveling suit.

"It's a pleasure to meet you, Mrs. Dumont," Taylor Sue curtsied slightly, her brown eyes and smile filled with warmth. "We're going to be in-laws soon. I am engaged to be wed to Ethan."

"Is that so?" Genevieve arched an eyebrow in question, "I hadn't heard, but of course I've not heard much from either of my sisters since the war began. Am I to understand that you traveled all the way from Virginia with Salina?"

"Yes," Taylor Sue nodded affirmatively.

"Well, where is she then?" Genevieve wanted to know, a trace of impatience in her tone.

Esther pointed to the top of the stagecoach. "Salina's right there."

Genevieve looked up and saw what she deemed a frightful sight. She stiffened her already straight back and pursed her lips together in a tight line as she watched an agile ragamuffin climb down, assisted by the rather rough-looking Indian stagecoach driver. Genevieve swallowed what might have been a shocked gasp when Salina stood before her, dressed in denim trousers, boots, and a flannel shirt. She wore a fringed buckskin jacket, obviously several sizes too large, and she had her hair stuffed into a wide-brimmed hat. A smudge of dirt graced the girl's cheek and another the bridge of her nose.

"Hello, Aunt Genevieve!" Salina said with a bright smile. "I knew who you were at once. You look very much like my Mamma—or should I say she looks like you? Oh, I can't tell you how happy I am that we've arrived at last, and I should hug you, except that I'm so dusty and dirty and you're so clean..." Salina brushed trail dust from her sleeves. As she looked back toward Aunt Genevieve's face, Salina's smile faded under the withering glance she encountered. She shivered beneath the cool look. "Perhaps we should see to our luggage..." Salina suggested weakly.

Genevieve said softly, but directly, "Gerard, your cousin, will fetch any baggage you might have on his way home from the mill."

Drake moved forward, half a step between Salina and Genevieve Dumont. "It's no trouble for me to deliver Salina's trunk, Mrs. Dumont. I can bring it out in about an hour or so."

"That really won't be necessary." Genevieve's smile was chilling. "My son will be here shortly. He will collect Salina's trunk and anything that Miss Carey or Miss Nichols might have. No need to concern yourself with the matter a moment longer," she commanded. "Come along, girls. We'll take Esther to her brother's office, and then I'll take you both home with me."

Salina looked to Drake, his features unreadable. She felt angry. How could Aunt Genevieve dismiss him so coldly like that? "Drake..."

"Salina," Genevieve called her name, expecting her niece to obediently get into the Dumont carriage.

This was not a new situation for Drake; it had happened far too often in his twenty years. He had grown accustomed to not being accepted by either the whites or his tribe, and he did not trouble himself with their misconceptions about him anymore. Salina, however, did not fully understand, and Drake meant to diffuse the tension. "Go on, little one. I'll see you soon," he promised.

Impulsively, Salina went to him and hugged him fiercely. "Thank you for everything you've done, Drake," she whispered hoarsely, looking up into his turquoise eyes.

Drake could see as well as feel the intense displeasure in Genevieve Dumont's sharp glare. He quickly set Salina away from himself, holding her shoulders firmly. "This isn't over yet. You be careful, and watch your back. Go on with your aunt, but take great care, little one."

Salina nodded. "I will." As she turned to go to her aunt's waiting carriage, she was somehow not surprised to find the Widow Hollis standing nearby. "Good day, Mrs. Hollis," Salina waved pleasantly.

"Good day, Miss Hastings. I trust you'll enjoy your visit here in San Francisco," the Widow replied, a bit ominously.

"Come along, Salina," Genevieve said impatiently. She hoped that no one of her acquaintance would see the ill-dressed girl getting into the finely upholstered closed carriage. Taylor Sue and Esther were already inside.

Genevieve fumed inwardly, a muscle along her jawline jumping in agitation. How Garrett Hastings could have the nerve to send his only daughter over thousands of miles of hostile country was beyond belief. Genevieve had heard such horrifying stories of Indian raids, holdups by lawless bandits, harsh weather, and the like. This latest in Garrett's long string of scandalous exploits served only to reinforce Genevieve's opinion that her brother-in-law must be mad.

The last time Genevieve had seen Garrett Hastings had been while she was taking tea one afternoon at the Tehama House in mid-July. He'd known better than to approach her at her home. She'd told Garrett then, in spite of his attempted persuasion, that she wanted no part of his plans. Yet he'd *deliberately* gone against her wishes—the arrival of that bothersome package was presently followed by the arrival of Salina and Taylor Sue. Genevieve's anger simmered over the fact that Garrett had drawn her unwillingly into the intrigue that surrounded him. If only he weren't Annelise's husband, Genevieve thought wistfully, but he is and that's that. She focused her attention on Salina and decided then and there that the girl was too much like him for her own good. Genevieve considered it her duty to take Salina in hand, the sooner the better.

The door of Ben Nichols's doctor's office had a note tacked to the frame stating that he'd gone on a house call and would be back presently.

"Well, I certainly can't leave you here by yourself, Esther," Genevieve determined. "I'll simply take you home with us and leave word here for Ben that he is to join us for dinner. That way, you may still surprise him with your homecoming."

Esther nodded in agreement. "If you're certain it's not too much trouble to have two unexpected guests for dinner."

"Nonsense, it's no trouble at all," Genevieve waved aside Esther's concerns. "We'll have a regular dinner party now as Marie and Malcolm are coming over as well. Marie will be as pleased to see you as Ben will be."

On the way to the Dumonts' house, Esther pointed out the carriage window, showing her new friends various sites and places she thought might interest them. Salina and Taylor Sue tried to look at everything all at once—from the grand mansions and houses dotting the hills to the wharves and docks where sailing ships and steam ships from foreign countries were anchored. The girls could certainly smell the salt on the ocean breeze. There were so many people here—so many different cultures and different customs.

"Over there is the Presidio," Genevieve indicated the military compound which was undergoing various stages of reconstruction. "That's where your father was stationed, Salina."

"Mamma mentions it every now and then," Salina replied with a nod. "She told me that we all lived with you while Daddy was here on duty after the War with Mexico and the Gold Rush."

"Yes," Genevieve confirmed. "It was a very long time ago. San Francisco's much bigger than it was then. Times and people have changed in the years gone by." She asked sharply, "Whatever could your father have been thinking when he sent you out here to me?"

"He had his reasons," Salina answered softly.

"Doesn't he always," Genevieve returned with a caustic reply. "We're going to have a talk, you and I, once we get you settled and into some decent clothes. You have some explaining to do, young lady. I have questions, and I expect answers."

The carriage turned onto a long driveway belonging to a house situated halfway up one of the many steep hills characteristic of San Francisco. It was not a stately Victorian structure as many of the other mansions were, but a large Spanish-style house—an elegant two-storied adobe complete with red-tile roof and a double porch surrounding the rectangular building. Taylor Sue glanced furtively at Salina. They had indeed arrived, but they clearly weren't out of trouble yet.

☆☆☆☆☆☆☆

"Ohhhhh," Salina sighed, almost contentedly, as the hot, lavender-scented bubbles tickled her nose and chin. She was submerged up to her neck in soothing, soapy water—all except for her plaster-encased arm which she balanced on the side of the copper tub. She longed to be rid of the thing once and for all. Perhaps Aunt Genevieve would allow her to pay a visit to Dr. Nichols's office first thing tomorrow morning.

Resting her head back on the edge of the tub, Salina pondered over how distant and cold Aunt Genevieve seemed. Mamma seemed to believe that Aunt Genevieve would welcome Salina and Taylor Sue into her home, but Salina didn't feel very welcome. She wondered if there was something she had done to provoke her aunt's anger, but she couldn't think of what it might be. *"Dear God,"* she prayed, her eyes shut and lips moving silently, *"Thank You for bringing us all the way to San Francisco safely. You've led us here, by Your faithfulness, and now I'm certain I'm very near to completing the task set before me. Please, help me to be patient and wait on You. Show me whatever it is*

I need to know, and let Your Holy Spirit guide me each step along the way. I know, Lord, that I can do nothing in my own strength. I want to rely on You completely. Please, keep me hidden from those who would search me out. Dear Lord Jesus, I do want to be faithful in finishing the work Daddy left to me..." Salina's prayer was interrupted by a knock at the guest room door.

"Who is it?" she asked.

"It's me, Taylor Sue," came the answer. "Can I come in?"

"It's not locked," Salina called.

Taylor Sue crossed the room and peeked around the side of the dressing screen. "Aren't you out of the tub yet?" She was already dressed for dinner. "If you don't hurry, you'll be late."

"I know it, but it feels so good to be still and not moving," Salina sighed. "And especially to be *clean* again. I will never again take for granted such a simple thing as a bath. I've learned that on this trip, and more." Salina had used the coarse sponge to scrub away the grit and grime that clung to her skin. "In truth, I was sitting in here wasting time and prolonging having to be laced into my corset again. Now that we're back in proper civilization, we'll be expected to behave as the young ladies we are—and that means dressing like them."

"You've only got two gowns, Salina. We'll need to get you some more clothes while we're here," Taylor Sue pointed out. "It's no secret your aunt didn't approve of your wearing trousers. I wonder if she or Esther might know of a dressmaker where ready-made clothing can be purchased."

"We'll ask," Salina nodded. "How long before we eat?"

"Less than half an hour," Taylor Sue replied, drawing an envelope from her pocket. "I saw this sitting on a silver tray in the entry hall, and I took the liberty of bringing it up with me. It's addressed to you, Salina. Would you like me to read it to you?"

"Please," Salina nodded eagerly. "A telegram? Is it from Reverend Yates? Or from Jeremy?" she asked expectantly.

"No," Taylor Sue replied when she opened the envelope and saw the signature. "It's from Captain Grant."

"He already knows we're here?" Salina cried.

Taylor Sue nodded. "Evidently." She cleared her throat and read:

> *To Miss Salina Hastings—*
> *I am most grateful to learn of your safe arrival in San Francisco. Your mother has been very worried about you, as I have been myself. We both thank God that no harm*

has befallen you or Taylor Sue. You are a courageous young lady, Salina, truly your father's daughter. Your cleverness, I admit albeit grudgingly, is admirable. Your determination unbelievable. Although, I suppose if I had an arrest warrant issued for me—as has been done for you—I might have been driven to act in much the same manner.

On the night I visited your father in the prison, before his attempted escape, I made a solemn promise to him— that should his escape fail, I would do whatever I could to see to the well-being of you and your family. I gave him then, as I give you now, my word of honor that I will do all in my power to fulfill that vow. You must understand that it will not be an easy thing for me to do in light of the fact that we are at war with each other. I believe I told you the night of the fire, but I want to tell you again so that you have no doubt—I will honor the trust that your father placed in me, regardless of our being on opposite sides.

Your mother sends her love.
Signed, Captain Duncan Grant
United States Army

"Captain Grant's word of honor," Salina whispered. "That should be good for *something*, wouldn't you think? Even if he is a Yankee?"

"I honestly don't know, Salina. You've more experience in dealing with the Yankees than I have," Taylor Sue shrugged.

A brisk knock sounded on the door, and before Salina could reply, Genevieve entered the room. She saw Taylor Sue standing near the dressing screen and deducted that Salina was lingering in her bath. Genevieve said, "Dawdling in the tub? Well, I imagine it would take some time and rather vigorous scrubbing to rid yourself of the grime and filth acquired in traveling." She went out into the hall and gave an order, "Gerard, just set that trunk down outside the door. Taylor Sue and I will carry it the rest of the way in. Tell your father I'll give the order for dinner to be served in forty-five minutes. I have something to discuss with Salina, and quite obviously she needs the extra time to dress for dinner."

"Taylor Sue can help me with the buttons at the back of my dress," Salina said. She heard the trunk land with a thud on the wooden floor just on the other side of the screen.

"I'm sure she can," Genevieve nodded, "but I will assist you instead. I would speak with you alone, Salina. It is a... family matter."

Salina responded quickly, "Taylor Sue is going to be part of this family. She can listen to whatever it is you have to say."

"Not this time. I'll speak to you alone," Genevieve reiterated. "You may go to your room and wait for Salina if you'd like, Taylor Sue, or you may go down to the parlour and wait with Esther. It is your choice."

"I'll be in my room, Salina." Taylor Sue retreated to the adjoining bedroom.

Salina stepped from the copper tub and dried herself quickly with a thick towel. That was the second time in the very same afternoon that Aunt Genevieve had *dismissed* one of her friends. Salina took offense at that, and she angrily pulled on her pantalets and wiggled into her corset. She wrapped her dark curls in the towel, squeezing as much water from them as she could with her good hand. Coming out from behind the screen, she bravely said, "I get the impression that you don't quite approve of my friends, Aunt Genevieve, or of me for that matter. May I be so bold as to ask you what have I done?"

"What have you done?" Genevieve repeated incredulously, "You honestly don't *know*? My dear child, have you no upbringing? No manners? No sense of propriety whatsoever? I am *astounded*—no, *appalled*—to learn that you have traveled across the entire country and without a chaperone! Well-bred young ladies do not do such things! And as for the clothes you were wearing—I was almost ashamed to acknowledge that you were the one I came to meet at the stagecoach. I hurried you into the carriage for fear that someone of our acquaintance might see you in that getup. And why on earth did you go and embrace that *savage* right there in front of everyone at the express office? None of *my* daughters would ever *dream* of doing such a thing—or be severely reprimanded if they had! When I think of the irreparable damage that might be done to your reputation by such actions... Do you never stop to consider what other people might think? Your poor mother must have her hands full raising you. You're just like your father!" exclaimed Genevieve. "It pains me to think of how he went ahead and embroiled me in one of his half-baked schemes by sending that package here when I *expressly* ordered him not to. Well, I declare this is a fine kettle of fish he's put us in! What have you to say for yourself, child?"

Genevieve's lashing tirade caused tears to well up in Salina's eyes. She was undeniably hurt by her aunt's cutting, accusing words, but she willed herself not to cry. Her bottom lip trembled, and she replied with a slight catch in her voice, "If you'll permit me, Aunt Genevieve, I can explain. Taylor Sue and I did not travel from Virginia without a chaperone. Mrs. Joetta Warner served as our chaperone until we reached Carson City in Nevada Territory. Carson City was Joetta's destination, but that's where Esther boarded, and we three looked after each other until we arrived here." She took a deep breath and continued as calmly as possible, "Drake is *not* a savage, he is a trusted friend of mine, and I believe it's mean of you to treat him like he's less than a human being. Without Drake's assistance, Taylor Sue and I might not have made it here. And as far as what other people think—I don't care what they think! The other passengers in the stagecoach, *if* they paid me any mind, realized that I could not wear a dress while riding up in the driver's seat. Besides, I have only two dresses to my name and I didn't want either of them ruined." She took another long breath and said honestly, "Evidently, you don't think much of me, do you? I am a little confused as to why you make it sound as though Daddy were a criminal of some sort. But I take it as a high compliment that you think that I am like him. He had good cause for sending the package here to you. He must have felt he could trust you to keep it until I could get here to collect it. May I have it, please?"

"It will keep until after dinner," Genevieve replied evenly, startled that Salina would stand up for herself. "If your mother had married Beau Jefferson, as our papa had originally arranged, instead of becoming the wife of Garrett Hastings—well, circumstances would be different, I can assure you! I'll tell you plainly that I have never held any regard for your father. He is reckless and unpredictable, thinking only of his precious honor, and pity the poor soul who might stand in his way. Where is he now? I suppose he's off playing soldier again..."

"Daddy's dead," Salina said abruptly. "He was killed by Yankees following his capture after the Battle of Antietam."

"What?" Genevieve covered her mouth with her hand, horrified. "Dead? You should have warned me, child! Don't you know one should not speak ill of the deceased?"

"Would your opinion of him have changed if I told you he'd been killed? I think not," Salina shook her head. "And no matter *what* you think of him, I'm still very proud to be his daughter."

Genevieve put her hands on her hips and pursed her lips. "Well, I declare you are an impudent child. You're positively impertinent with deplorable manners—talking back the way you do to your elders. Children should be seen and not heard, I've always said."

"I'm not a child, Aunt Genevieve. I'm sixteen years old," Salina caught herself before she stamped her foot in anger. Making a great effort, she stated mildly, "I have made choices, and I intend to honor them. The only reason Mamma felt better about our coming to San Francisco was because she believed your house would be safe and that you would welcome us here. Taylor Sue and I will find lodging elsewhere since you dislike me so much."

"Nonsense," Genevieve immediately rejected Salina's suggestion. "You will stay here. I will shelter you for the sake of my sister. Besides, I will not have people think that I turned you out on the streets. After all, we are related... If you will not consider your own reputation, consider mine!"

"We appreciate your gracious hospitality, Aunt Genevieve," Salina tried in vain to keep the sarcasm from her words. "Taylor Sue and I will not tread long upon your kindness and rest assured we will not stay here a moment longer than we must."

"Naturally I agree that is probably best for all parties concerned. My young Sophie is quite impressionable. I wouldn't want her to be shocked by your antics, Salina. I would appreciate it if you would refrain from talking about your adventures in her presence."

"I'll do as little talking as possible," Salina vowed, her eyes shiny with tears.

"Yes, that might be wise. Though I grew up in Virginia, I have adapted to the way of life here. California is a free state, governed by the Federal government, and the other members of my family are staunch supporters of the Union—Henri, of course, but especially Gerard. You'll find no one here sympathetic with the misguided Rebels, their Cause, or their Confederacy—and your father knew that. Your being here is like a sheep among wolves," Genevieve warned with a nod. "The less said will indeed be the better for all involved."

Salina bit her tongue to keep from protesting as Genevieve tightened her corset stays with a hard yank. Salina put on her corset cover and then tied on a stiff crinoline and two petticoats. Genevieve inquired, "Are things so bad at Shadowcreek that you only own two dresses?"

"Shadowcreek was burned to the ground by Union soldiers," Salina answered, slipping her arms through the sleeves of the blue, green, yellow, and white plaid gown as Genevieve dropped it over her head. "Everything was destroyed. When I left Virginia, Mamma was staying with Aunt Priscilla at Ivywood."

"Burned down! Land sakes—and poor Annelise a homeless

268 / *Word of Honor*

widow!" Genevieve lamented with the barest hint of compassion. "I often forget about the war going on in that part of the country since we are so removed here. Nonetheless, I shall be glad when they've finished with it. All this killing over secession, Union, States' Rights, and slavery. I wonder if in the end it will be worth all the senseless bloodshed." Genevieve inspected Salina from head to toe. She was displeased that Salina had to wear boots rather than proper shoes, but at last Genevieve decided Salina was acceptably attired for dinner and would be presentable to the company which had been invited. "Just keep your feet under your gown," she commanded. "At least your dresses are made of darker-colored fabric. It wouldn't be proper for someone in mourning to go around in bright colors." Genevieve looked down her nose at the once-white plaster wrap encasing Salina's broken arm and noted the frayed gray edges around Salina's fingers. "We'll have to see about that cast of yours. I'll speak to Ben this evening about examining you tomorrow, and to Marie about your wardrobe. She might have a castoff or two that she would be willing to part with since the two of you are about the same size. Come along, child, or we'll be later than we already are."

Salina bristled again at being referred to as a child but said nothing. She was still smarting from the repeated reproaches, and she thought Aunt Genevieve was as condescending as Lottie was so often capable of being. Perhaps that's where Lottie inherited the trait. While Aunt Priscilla might be a stickler for propriety and tradition, at least she treated the people around her with respect and didn't talk down to them. More than ever, Salina wanted to get home.

☆☆☆☆☆☆☆

In the spacious dining room, Salina was presented formally to her cousins—Gerard, Marc, and the impressionable Sophie—along with her uncle, Henri Dumont. Her cousin Marie was seated with her husband, Lieutenant Malcolm Everett, just across the table from Esther and Ben Nichols. Taylor Sue had met everyone while Salina was still upstairs.

The food was plentiful, and the company would have been more pleasant if Salina hadn't perceived such a sense of malevolence from nearly every corner of the room. She felt the eyes of the Dumont men resting heavily upon her, as if they resented her for some reason. But both Ben and Malcolm were anxious for news of the battles in the east. Salina relayed few details for time and again she met with Genevieve's look of stern disapproval.

"I read a newspaper account of the raid that brash Southern cavalry leader, Jeb Stuart, took his men on in October. The Rebels wreaked havoc as far north as Chambersburg, Pennsylvania, while Stuart had the audacity to ride his men in *another* circle completely around McClellan's Army of the Potomac," Malcolm's consternation was evident. He firmly believed McClellan should have learned *something* from the first time Stuart successfully circled him earlier in June.

Salina's heart thudded in her chest. She recalled Reverend Yates's telegram telling that Jeremy had been with Jeb Stuart during that raid into Pennsylvania—and knowing Jeremy, he would have been participating wholeheartedly in such a daring adventure. Salina could only hope and pray that Jeremy was safe, but she had no way of knowing for sure until she could get back to home and find out for herself.

"President Lincoln was rather disturbed with McClellan's slowness—or unwillingness—to pursue the Army of Northern Virginia following the Battle of Antietam," Ben explained carefully for the benefit of Salina, Taylor Sue, and Esther. "On November the fifth, Lincoln issued orders to make Ambrose Burnside the commander of the Army of the Potomac. There are rumors that Burnside's primary objective will be a march toward the Confederate capital at Richmond."

Malcolm nodded, seemingly pleased about the action considered. "Things should be different for the Army of the Potomac now that General Burnside has been placed in command. I've heard he's at Warrenton, Virginia, and certainly he is our best chance right now for a direct blow to the Rebel army."

Salina was starved for news of Virginia, but she dared not ask in the company she found herself in. Instead, she listened intently for any scraps the men might speak of. She would simply have to wait to ask Dr. Nichols more about the situation at home just as soon as the opportunity presented itself.

Genevieve repeatedly steered the conversation away from the war, interrogating Taylor Sue with questions about her engagement to Ethan and any plans in the making for their upcoming wedding.

"We haven't decided on an exact date yet," Taylor Sue replied. "But Ethan has promised that as soon as I get back, we'll have Reverend Yates conduct the ceremony."

"Malcolm and I had a lovely church wedding followed by a grand reception out in the courtyard. It was the happiest day of my life," Marie gushed, casting a loving glance at her husband. "If you need any suggestions or ideas, Taylor Sue, I'd be more than happy to show you the most modern dress styles and fabrics in *Godey's Lady's Book...*"

"Thank you, Marie," Taylor Sue said politely, then asked, "Would you happen to know of a place where ready-made dresses might be purchased?"

Marie thought for a moment, then replied, "Of course! Madame Lucy's Boutique would have some lovely dresses. They might require a few alterations, but she's very good, and she is quick about her work. I'm sure she could fix up a dress or two for you in a days' time, at the most. There are some other lovely shops that I frequent downtown, too."

"If you'll permit us, Mrs. Dumont," Esther said, "we could go shopping tomorrow. I would be delighted to have Salina and Taylor Sue as my guests."

Genevieve immediately assented, "With the condition that you'll allow me to bring Sophie along with us. She's in need of a new gown for her recital."

Twelve-year-old Sophie was pleased with the prospect of the shopping excursion, but she dreaded her forthcoming performance on the piano.

"You'll pass by my office to get to Madame Lucy's Boutique," Ben pointed out. "If you could spare a few minutes away from the dress shops, Miss Salina, I could examine that arm of yours. Esther tells me it's about time to have the cast taken off."

"Yes, it is. My brother put it on six weeks ago, and Ethan told me that I would need to find a doctor here that could get me out of it." Salina said purposefully, "It seems to me that I have no need to look any further for help."

Ben winked at her. "It will be my pleasure to assist you in any way that I can."

Dinner dragged on interminably. Genevieve inquired about the rest of the family back in Virginia with the intent of keeping the subject from drifting back to the war. Salina told of being a bridesmaid in Mary Edith's wedding, of Lottie's return from the finishing school in London, of Ethan's apprenticeship with Dr. Phillips. She decided it was wiser *not* to say anything about Uncle Caleb's funding a privateer which ran the Northern blockade of the Southern ports, though she did end up telling them about the battle near Chantilly despite Genevieve's dominant control of the conversation.

"I had no idea the fighting was so close to Shadowcreek and Ivywood," Genevieve interrupted Salina's tale, much to Malcolm's disappointment. He would have liked to hear more of what Salina had to say about the fighting, even if it was from the Southern point of view. He reluctantly acknowledged that Salina seemed to be rather well-informed for a girl.

Genevieve continued, "If everyone is through with their dinner, why don't we retire to the drawing room, ladies. Gentlemen, please feel free to stay here and enjoy your brandy and cigars."

Salina could scarcely contain her relief when at last the guests were gone and she returned upstairs. Taylor Sue came in through the door that connected their two rooms. "Each minute down there seemed like an hour!" Taylor Sue flung herself across Salina's bed. "They are so stuffy and so polite—and *so* suspicious of us! I felt like I was on display with your uncle, Malcolm, and Gerard studying me so carefully. If that's what high society is all about, I want no part of it. I'd rather be back home and mind my manners at a barbecue or a ball but not be subjected to another dinner party like that!"

Salina sat at the vanity, taking the pins from her hair with one hand. Her dark curls escaped their confines and tumbled down her straight back. "I couldn't agree with you more, Taylor Sue."

"What did your aunt say to you?" Taylor Sue wondered aloud. She stood behind Salina, catching the reflection of her eyes in the mirror. She took Salina's silver-plated brush and pulled it gently through her friend's dark curly hair. "When you finally came downstairs after your bath, you looked so hurt and forlorn—as if you're pride had been wounded, or your heart had been crushed. I could tell something was very wrong, and I wanted to reach out to you and comfort you, but we were seated on opposite sides of the table so quickly that I didn't have the chance."

"Was it that evident?" asked Salina.

"No, not really. It's just that I know you so well. Talk to me, Salina," Taylor Sue coaxed.

"Aunt Genevieve doesn't like anything about me, Taylor Sue, and she did not mince her words as she told me all about it. It was a first-rate scolding. I don't dress right, act right, associate with the right people, fight for the right side..." Salina conveyed the details of her aunt's tongue-lashing in low whispers. "According to her, my reputation is ruined, and she's in a rage because Daddy involved her by sending that package here. I wonder if Gerard or Uncle Henri know about the package. I don't think Marc's old enough to figure out what's going on."

"Gerard frightens me," admitted Taylor Sue. "There's something about him that makes me feel that he wouldn't hesitate an instant to turn us in to the authorities, or even Malcolm, simply because he's so suspicious of us."

Salina shivered. "Unfortunately, I get the very same feeling."

Genevieve came to Salina's room. "I promised you that package," she remarked stiffly, handing a box wrapped in brown paper and tied with twine to Salina. "I've never been one to break my word. I'll send one of the maids to wake you both in the morning. We'll all drive to town after breakfast, and I want you to be on time."

"We will be," Taylor Sue answered for both of them. "Good night, Mrs. Dumont. It was a very delicious dinner."

"I'll be sure to tell the cook you thought so. Good night, girls. Sleep well," Genevieve nodded curtly.

Chapter Twenty-Six

Salina's hands shook as she undid the knotted twine and unwrapped the package. She inhaled sharply when she discovered Daddy's cherry wood lapdesk beneath the brown paper. She traced the initials GDH carved in the center of the glossy, varnished cover. The letters stood for his name: Garrett Daniel Hastings. The lapdesk had been a Christmas gift from herself and Ethan nearly three years ago, before the war.

Taylor Sue sensed Salina's unspoken desire to be left alone. "I'll be right next door. When you need me, you just call."

"I will," Salina nodded gratefully.

She gathered up her skirts and sat down on the Oriental carpet, leaning against the traveling trunk with the lapdesk across her knees. Slowly she opened the lid and was not surprised in the least to find a sizable stack of papers bound together with string, covered with rows and rows and rows of coded words. Salina set the pages aside on the floor. Next she found an envelope bearing the nickname Daddy used to call her. The letter was addressed the same way, and judging from the date, it was written not long after she had seen him at the Tanners' in Alexandria—two weeks before he died.

My Darling Sally-girl:

If you are reading this letter and these words pass before your eyes, it can only mean one thing: I must be dead. You have arrived in San Francisco—taking my place—and you are now in a position to complete work on the plans for the western campaign. Enclosed you will find the instructions as to what to do.

But before I get into all of that, I want to tell you how much I love you, and how proud I am that you carried on in my absence. I don't want you to mourn for me, Sally. I live my life with all that I have to give. I am not afraid to die. I willingly volunteered to pledge my life to the Rebel Cause, but more importantly, my life belongs to Jesus Christ, and I know that my name is written in the Lamb's Book of Life. The apostle Paul wrote that to be absent from this body is to be present with the Lord. That is my hope, and He is my Salvation. I have always tried to take one day at a time, come what may. Commit your days to the Lord, Sally, and He will bless you for it. Let His Holy Spirit work through you, and He will keep you in His righteous hand. Trust in the Lord with all your heart and lean not unto your own understanding. Sometimes even I do not understand all that this war entails, but I acted on what I believed, and I did so knowing full well there was no turning back.

So, you are there in San Francisco. I can imagine your sparkling eyes being round with curiosity to see such a place as the city by the bay. You were too young to have any recollection of your first visit, I'm sure. While you are there now, you must find a way to make contact with a doctor named Ben Nichols. Genevieve is acquainted with him, and she can take you to see him. Genevieve might not show it on the surface, but she can be trusted. The rest of her family, however, cannot. And that is where the danger lies. I'd just as soon you do what you need to and then go back home. I don't know what will be happening as far as the war is concerned, but I know that you'd be safe enough with Mamma. Reverend Yates will see to your welfare if Jeremy and Ethan have gone and joined the Army of Northern Virginia. I suspect Jeremy will make his intentions of courting you known—if he hasn't done so already. I have given him my permission, and my blessing. I pray the two of you will have a love for each other like your Mamma and I have shared. I pray the same for Ethan and Taylor Sue.

On to the business at hand: Use the code hidden in the false bottom of the traveling trunk to decipher the documents you'll find in the lapdesk. You'll find the code between the wooden side and the lining. I had to send these documents west, as these are the papers that the Yankees covet so earnestly. They could cost me my life, Sally, or—I am ashamed to admit—they could cost you yours should Union sympathizers find them in your possession. Destroy everything except the translated pages once you've finished. These pages should be given to Dr. Nichols at your earliest convenience. The time frame is crucial, Sally. I must assume that you managed to see Hank Warner on your way to San Francisco. He should have indicated to you somehow the starting date that he has arranged with the contacts there in the West. Everything should be in place, and the campaign operations should be launched on the day that Hank has selected. If the plans I've drawn up are executed properly, then the Confederacy will extend from Texas to the Pacific Ocean, and San Francisco itself will answer to the Southern government by Christmas. This is an expanded version of the plan that failed at Glorieta Pass—revised now, and much more carefully prepared. You have all the names of those who are the leaders in each town and which territory they will be operating in. The maps will tell where the arms and ammunitions are stored, where the food supplies are hidden, the location of horses, clothing, and schedules for gold and silver shipments. You are familiar with how to use the code. It shouldn't take you but a few hours to get it all written out. Nichols will distribute the orders to the proper places. That is the extent of your involvement. I don't want you in any deeper than you already are. Go home, Sally, and try to pick up living where you left off, if that's at all possible. If it isn't, I want you to go someplace safe where you can start over.

Be on your guard, and be extremely cautious. It will be over one day. The war can't last forever. Somebody's going to win this conflict, and somebody's going to lose. When that happens, we'll see where we stand when the dust settles. God help us all.

I love you, Sally, and you should be proud to have done the Confederacy a great service. I have mentioned you to President Davis and to General Stuart. They both appreciate the risk you've taken to help us in our quest.

Be strong for me, my little Rebel, and smile whenever you think of me.

> *Your adoring Daddy,*
> *Captain Garrett Hastings*
> *Confederate States of America*

P.S. If Duncan Grant and I have a confrontation, which seems inevitable, I am going to ask him to look after you, Mamma, and Ethan if I am unable to do so myself. He's not such a bad sort, even though we're fighting against one another. Should you ever be inclined to ask him, Sally, he would help you for my sake. Remember that, if need be.

Tears that Salina had been holding in check for most of the day rolled freely down her cheeks in salty streams. From the next room Taylor Sue heard the sobs that wracked Salina's slight frame, and her heart went out to to her friend.

"Ssssshhhh..." Taylor Sue sat down on the floor beside Salina and put her arms around her, rocking her back and forth. "It's going to be all right, you'll see. You'll see." She let Salina keep on crying until her tears were spent. "I was reading after I left you alone in here. I read this passage in Isaiah." She turned to the place she had marked in her Bible:

> *Hast thou not known? Hast thou not heard, that the everlasting God, the Lord, the Creator of the ends of the earth, fainteth not, neither is weary? There is no searching for understanding. He giveth power to the faint; and to*

*them that have no might he increaseth strength. Even the
youths shall faint and be weary, and the young men shall
utterly fall: But they that wait upon the Lord shall renew
their strength; they shall mount up with wings as eagles;
they shall run, and not be weary; they shall walk, and not
faint.*

"The Lord has been our strength, Salina, and He will continue to
be. He can see us now, and He knows we're tired of running. He knows
we are worried about staying here for any length of time. And He
knows it will take all night to decode all of these pages," Taylor Sue
touched the documents from the lapdesk. Let's pray and ask Him to
keep us from being weary."

Salina felt much better after they had prayed together. She wiped
her eyes dry and blew her nose. Taylor Sue had already changed into
her nightgown, and she helped Salina out her plaid dress so that she
could get changed, too.

"I've got an idea," Taylor Sue said suddenly.

"What?" asked Salina.

"Let me help you, Salina," Taylor Sue offered. "There's a warrant
out for my arrest because I'm guilty by association, so what difference
would it make if I really was involved?"

Salina had been afraid that she wouldn't be able to get all
translating done alone, and here the Lord was providing yet another
answer to her prayers, and she mentally thanked Him for it. "You'd
risk that, Taylor Sue?" Salina raised an eyebrow in question.

"I already have in a way," Taylor Sue smiled. "I'm here, aren't I?
Besides, I know that you would stand by me if I were in your shoes.
What else are friends for if they can't support each other and be true in
hard times as well as the good times?"

Salina managed a weak smile and readily accepted Taylor Sue's
assistance. "I'll teach you how to decode the documents using the
cipher. You're sure you want to do this?"

Taylor Sue nodded. "Together we can get this done, but you'll
never manage it alone."

Salina realized there was no point in denying it. "All right, then.
Let's see what we've got here."

Taylor Sue thought it best to take some precautionary measures, so
she went back to her room and arranged the pillows in her bed to look
like a body was sleeping in the four poster—just in case a nosy
someone might peek in to see if she was truly there. She returned to
Salina's room and hung a blanket over the window to prevent the

candlelight from showing through should anyone be watching them from either the courtyard below or one of the rooms at the far end of the outdoor corridor.

Salina took all the pages—of which the count totaled thirty—and spread them out on the desk. She collected the remainder of the documents that had been smuggled beneath the false bottom of her traveling trunk. They certainly had their work cut out for them.

Long hours passed as the girls worked diligently and as speedily as they possibly could. Fresh candlesticks replaced the old ones whenever they burned too low. An occasional soft whisper and the rustle of pages were the only sounds in the quiet room.

The clock on the wall indicated the hour to be quarter past four when Salina leaned back in her chair and stretched. She rubbed the sides of her temples and squinted her eyes. "It's all becoming a blur to me," she said in frustration.

"I know what you mean," Taylor Sue nodded. "We haven't got much time left before sunrise. I was thinking about sneaking down to the well and getting some water to drink—unless you want to go. Seems to me you could probably use a breath of fresh air. I'll stay here and keep working. I'm not nearly as adept at translating as you are, and it takes me longer."

"You've picked it up so rapidly, though. We really haven't got all that much more to do, have we?" Salina stood and stretched again. "But now that you've mentioned it, I am thirsty. I'll go down to the well and get us some water. Take a break, Taylor Sue. Give your eyes a rest, and your back, too. I'll be back in just a minute."

☆☆☆☆☆☆☆

Malcolm Everett was decidedly late to the meeting being held at the Miner's Daughter's Saloon—but Gerard Dumont was just as tardy. Lieutenant Lance Colby was impatient. "Where have you two been?" Colby wanted to know. He'd finished his steak more than an hour ago and was on his third bottle of sarsaparilla.

"Dinner," they both replied. "You don't know my mother," Gerard added. "Especially when she's being the formal hostess."

"I had to take my wife home. You know I couldn't bring her along," Malcolm explained.

Colby nodded. "Very well," he spoke in a tone that was barely able to be heard above the tinny-sounding piano and the general overall din of the rowdy saloon. A thick haze of bluish smoke hung above the gaming tables and clouded one's view of the stage where the dancing girls were high-kicking a can-can. Colby leaned across the table. "I was hoping one of you might have been present when the stagecoach arrived this afternoon. There was supposed to have been a passenger on that coach—the one that I'm in search of. Here is a photograph of what she looks like." Colby pulled the black-and-white tintype of Salina from his breast pocket and handed it to Gerard. "Her name is Hastings—Salina Hastings."

Malcolm snatched the photograph from Gerard's fingertips. "Salina!"

"Keep your voice down!" Colby warned. "Yes, Salina Hastings. Did you see her?"

Gerard grinned, shaking his head in disbelief. "She is my cousin, Lieutenant Colby. She has indeed arrived and is staying in one of the guest rooms at our house."

"Who else knows about this?" Malcolm wanted to know.

"Why?" Colby asked.

"If word of this gets out—if people in the social circles that Marie and I have a habit of moving in were to find out that Marie's own *cousin* is the daughter of that Rebel spy—well, I wouldn't want my wife's reputation tarnished in any way. It could cast a dark cloud of suspicion on my otherwise exemplary military record."

"That's why this assignment is considered *undercover* work," Colby reminded Everett. "There's no need for anyone to know who she is. All we have to do is get our hands on the documents she has in her possession."

Gerard knew precisely where Salina would be for at least the morning hours of the following day. "First they're going to Dr. Nichols's office, then they're going shopping."

"Who is *they*?" inquired Colby.

"My mother, my sister Sophie, Esther Nichols, Salina, and Taylor Sue Carey," answered Gerard.

"Marie's not going?" Colby asked Malcolm.

"No, she's got a ladies literary meeting or something or other..." Malcolm didn't quite remember, but he was sure his wife had mentioned it several times, and he knew tomorrow was the day of the event, whatever it was.

Colby said, "This is a big town. Do you know where they plan to shop?"

"Madame Lucy's Boutique," Malcolm recalled. "If only I'd known who she was, I'd have paid more attention to what was being said. Garrett Hastings's *daughter*. No wonder she knew so much about the war and was so interested in learning that Burnside had replaced McClellan."

Gerard commented, "When Malcolm mentioned Stuart's Chambersburg raid, that certainly captured her attention."

Colby replied, teeth clenched, "I imagine it would when you consider that her beau rides with Stuart. Naturally she'd be anxious to know if there was any news of him."

"What do you want us to do, Lieutenant?" Gerard asked.

"Correct me if I'm mistaken, but you sound as though you'd be willing to turn her in, Gerard. Would you do that?" Colby questioned directly.

"Look, I've told you before—just as I told Mrs. Hollis—I've no loyalty to anything but the Union," Gerard said seriously. "Salina Hastings might be a relation through my mother's bloodline, but she's a Rebel by geography and a spy as far as I'm concerned. I don't agree with anything she stands for."

"I don't either," Malcolm remarked. "I just don't want Marie to get involved. Promise me she'll not get dragged through all this."

"I'll do my best," Colby answered, unable to make a firm commitment. "With any luck, our actions won't even be officially reported to the War Department. No press, no publicity—no ruined reputations to consider. I'll speak to Mrs. Hollis tonight. She'll give us our orders by first light. I'll meet you at the Occidental Hotel on Montgomery Street at eight o'clock."

"Eight, then," Malcolm nodded.

Gerard nodded affirmatively. "I'll be there, Lieutenant Colby. On time."

Colby waited until the others left before he made his own exit. He left enough bills on the table to cover the cost of the meal and the beverages. He glanced curiously at the next table to where an intense poker game was being played over a hefty pot of money. His gaze inadvertently caught the startling turquoise eyes of a half-breed Indian, and instant recognition crackled between the two men. Colby saw it was the stagecoach driver—the very same one whom Colby had stopped just outside of Salt Lake City a few days ago.

The stage driver nodded brusquely. Colby returned the gesture. Had the half-breed overheard anything he'd been discussing with Malcom and Gerard? Colby wondered. If he had, then Colby was positive that the Indian would find a way to warn Salina Hastings.

Instead of leaving as he originally intended, Colby went to the bar for another sarsaparilla. He would wait awhile and keep an eye on the stage driver. It looked as though he had been lucky enough to have a good winning streak. Colby took a long swallow from the brown glass bottle, then turned to keep watch on the poker table—but the Indian was already gone.

☆☆☆☆☆☆☆

Without a sound Salina made her way down the stairway that led below to the cobbled courtyard. The rectangular area surrounded on all sides by the adobe house was filled with wispy gray fog, and if a gentle breeze hadn't parted the translucent mist, she wouldn't have been able to see the well at all. The clinging dampness and shadows lent an eeriness to the inky night. Neither moon nor stars shone through the fog, and the darkness seemed tangibly thick. Salina choked back a terrified scream as strong hands gripped her shoulders the exact moment she heard a familiar gravely voice say, "It's just me, little one. I'm here."

"Drake!" she exclaimed in a whisper. "Oh, Drake, I'm so glad to see you!"

He held her for a minute, stroking her dark curls, offering whatever comfort she might have need of. Drake had a deep desire to want to protect her from whatever menace was here in this place.

"What are you doing here?" she finally asked.

"Keeping watch," Drake answered directly. "You're not safe here—do you know that? You've gone from the frying pan into the fire, little one."

"Yes, I realize that now," Salina stepped out of the circle of Drake's arms.

"I want to take you and Taylor Sue out of here—tonight," Drake said with determination. "Let's go upstairs and get your things. I've got a buckboard. We'll take the trunk..."

"We can't, Drake. Taylor Sue and I aren't finished with the documents yet. We're still working on getting them translated from the code into plain English. Tomorrow morning I plan to take them to the Network's contact."

"All right—fine," Drake sighed. He didn't like it. "The Yankees know you're here, little one, and they know what you're about. Once you've delivered the documents, I want you to come back here, pack, and I'll come fetch you and Taylor Sue. I'm taking you back to St. Joseph with me first thing on Friday morning. I've got the east-bound run on the fourteenth, and you *will* be on that stage," his order brooked no opposition. "Understand?"

"Yes," Salina did not argue with him. "I don't want to stay here, Drake. I want to go home. Do you think we might make it back in time for Christmas?"

"That would depend—it would be cutting is awfully close," Drake shrugged. "I wouldn't count on it too much. And here, I've got something that might want to make you go home even worse," he handed her a small envelope.

"Is this from..." Salina's eyes expressed her hope.

"From Jeremy Barnes? Yes, it is. Take it back to your room with you. The way I figure it, he must have wired a letter to St. Joe and then had it forwarded to the express office here. Otherwise it couldn't have gotten here so quickly. I picked it up earlier this afternoon, along with this telegram. It's from Virginia, too."

"Maybe it's from my Mamma," Salina whispered. "Drake, could you send a message for me? Could you wire Tabitha Wheeler at Fairfax Court House and tell her to let Reverend Yates know that we've arrived but will be returning home? That way, at least they'll know we're safe."

"I'll take care of it," Drake assured her. "Read those things later, little one. Right now you've got to listen to me. That widow that boarded the stage at Carson City is a Union agent."

Salina nodded, "I thought so, but how do you know for sure?"

"I was playing poker at the saloon, and was doing rather well for myself I might add, when I saw that Lieutenant Colby come in. He met with two men—one of them was your cousin, Gerard, and the other was an officer, your cousin's husband, I believe."

"Malcolm Everett?" Salina asked. "He's in league with them, too?"

"It seems so." Drake continued, "Colby has a tintype of you, little one, and he showed it to Gerard and Everett. That's how he's been able to track you. He must show it whenever he goes to ask someone if they've seen you. He must have had it when he ordered the search party for you at the circus in St. Joseph—and then at every stage stop along the route west between here and there."

An icy chill stole down Salina's spine, and she pulled her shawl closer around her body. "How would Colby get a picture of me?" she mused aloud. Then she belatedly remembered her birthday, the day of Mary Edith's wedding, when she sat for the Irish photographer. "Sean Patrick O'Grady took *three* portraits, and I only saw *two* of them. Colby has the third in his possession—but how?"

"It doesn't matter how he got it, just that he does. Colby was going to meet the Widow Hollis after he met with Everett and your cousin," Drake told her. "I've no doubt that you'll be the topic of their discussion."

Salina swallowed. "I'm afraid, Drake. This has gone so far beyond what I ever imagined it would..."

"Do what you came to do, little one," Drake encouraged her. "I'll be close by, but it wouldn't hurt for you to sleep with that pistol of yours beneath your pillow. I'm staying at the Oceanfront Inn. You send for me if you need me before I come to collect you tomorrow afternoon. Josiah will know how to find me."

Salina nodded, "Thank you for the warning, and for watching over us again—still."

"I'll do what I can, little one, for your sake," Drake said softly as he rested his forehead against hers. She should have backed away, but something in the way he looked at her didn't allow her to move a muscle. Drake lowered his head, and his mouth brushed across hers in a mere whisper of a kiss. His arms went around her, and his intense turquoise eyes blazed. He pressed his lips against hers.

Salina was startled by the warmth and desire she tasted there. Her arms were between them, and she firmly pushed him away. "Drake, don't, please. It's not right. You know I love Jeremy very much."

Drake nodded solemnly, caressing her cheek with his long fingers. "I know." He watched a blush creep along Salina's cheekbones, and he chuckled softly. "You're a beautiful lady, little one, and I can't help but admit that I've been wanting to kiss you for quite some time now. I won't ask your forgiveness because I don't want it. But I can promise you that I won't let it happen again. I envy Jeremy your love for him, and his for you. He is a lucky man, and I hope he realizes it." He squeezed her hand, pressed something into her palm, and let it go.

"I hope so, too," Salina whispered, not brave enough to meet his penetrating eyes. "I'll see you tomorrow afternoon, then?"

"Count on that," Drake said comfortingly. "Until then, little one, it is imperative that you be on guard every minute."

Salina finally gathered the courage to look up at him to assure him that she would be careful, but Drake had disappeared, and she stood all alone in the mist.

☆☆☆☆☆☆☆

Pouring herself a mug of water, Taylor Sue listened intently to Salina's abbreviated account of her meeting with Drake in the court-yard. "He gave me a letter, a telegram, and this..." Salina unfolded the item Drake had pressed into her hand. It was clipping from the *Daily Alta California* dated November 12, 1862.

"Yesterday's newspaper," Taylor Sue commented, "considering today is soon to dawn. What does it say?"

Salina read aloud the brief paragraph Drake had circled with a pencil:

> *Look on the map and see what a ride Stuart's cavalry took from Hancock to Chambersburg, entirely round McClellan's army, and back east of the mouth of the Monocacy. That he didn't go to Washington and take what cavalry horses we have there is explained by the fact that the rebels don't use that kind.*

"The reporter seems to be implying that if Stuart had wanted to, he could've ridden directly into Washington and captured all the horses there before the Yanks knew what hit them. And he probably could have done *just* that if he had a mind to." A light shone in Salina's green eyes and a smile appeared.

Taylor Sue nodded. She, too, knew that Jeb Stuart's exploits were legendary throughout the South. "I imagine so. I wonder where Ethan is."

Salina shrugged. "Wherever Stonewall Jackson's troops are, no doubt mending the wounded." She opened the telegram which wasn't from Mamma but from Reverend Yates. It was a few lines of reassurance, and his suggestion that the girls come back home as quickly as they could.

"I would interpret that as another confirmation that we shouldn't linger here in San Francisco!" Taylor Sue exclaimed softly. "God guided us here, and we know He'll guide us back. What does Jeremy's letter have to say—or is that one private?"

Salina blushed. "I don't know. I'll have to read it and find out."

"Do that," Taylor Sue sipped her water. "I'll keep working. There's only four or five pages left. The handwriting has changed. It's different, larger than that on all of the other pages, so what appears to be quite a bit of writing might actually be less translation than it seems. Go on and read your letter and I'll show you what I mean afterwards."

October 14, 1862
Cavalry Hdqtrs. at The Bower

My Darling Salina:

    I apologize for such a brief note, but I trust this finds you in good health and successful in the purpose for which you made your journey. I beg you not to stay in San Francisco any longer than you must, Salina, for I'd rather you come back home. It would make me feel better to know where you are. I miss you very much.

    In the last three days we've covered 130 miles with 80 of them coming in the last twenty-four hours. We raided between here and Chambersburg, Pennsylvania, following to the letter our orders to cut telegraph wires, obstruct the railroad, confound the Yankee soldiers, and capture much-needed supplies of food, clothing, arms and ammunition, and horses. I'm of the opinion General Stuart lives for such orders. He thrives on risk, danger and glory—and for having a good time. Rumor has it that we are to have a celebration ball in honor of our triumph. If you were here, Salina, you might come visit me, and we could spend some time together. General Stuart keeps an open camp and visitors are welcome and frequent. It seems that there is always music and entertainment of some sort. Our bivouac is spread on the lawn of a plantation, and before we left on the raid there were dances in the hall practically every night. I've no doubt such things will resume now that we've returned.

    My tent mate, Corporal Weston Bentley, is a poet, and he writes beautifully though you wouldn't know it to look at him. He has challenged me to make a try, so I'm sending you this copy of my feeble attempt. It is about our mission, as you will quickly discern, but the next time I try my hand, I intend to use you, Salina, as my inspiration.

    ~ Poem of a Cavalier ~

    Confederate hoofbeats muffled by sucking mud
As a cold autumn night grows even colder still
Beneath the eerie gray light of a distant moon.

Hunger growls in the pit of every comrade's gut
   threaten
To drown the hushed whispers of leaves overhead;
We ride with orders to hasten our pace to reach our
   target by noon.

No warmth of a campfire will ward off
   the cutting chill
That penetrates our tattered uniforms
   and threadbare blankets
While some try in vain to use rags to
   replace the lack of shoes.
Miles begat more silent miles
   while we go trotting along
Not a one dare sing for fear of
   certain discovery by enemy pickets;
Others give their mounts their heads
   and in their saddles snooze.

Thoughts of home far away and those
   of loved ones missed
Tend to dampen the spirits of many
   a brave and gallant man
Who in days have not chanced to taste
   the thrill of a good fight.
Risky is our mission: circling the perimeter
   of the Yankee forces
That are oft too slow in following when we strike,
   and thankfully
They seem unwilling or unable to give us
   chase in the dead of night.

In closing, I'll tell you again: I love you, Salina. I
dream of holding you in my arms, sharing a kiss between
us. Hurry back to your horse soldier.

                                  Affectionately yours,
                                  Private Jeremy Barnes
                                  1st Virginia Cavalry — C.S.A

               ☆☆☆☆☆☆☆

"Forgive me for breaking into your reverie, Salina, but I think you should take a look at this," Taylor Sue said softly. "Here."

Salina took the last translated pages from Taylor Sue's outstretched hand. She began reading the lines, and the more she read, the wider her eyes grew as a result of her utter disbelief at the contents. "This is..."

"Frightening," Taylor Sue readily supplied the adjective. "Downright frightening."

"Where are the original pages?" asked Salina. She set Jeremy's letter aside for a moment and went to the desk where Taylor Sue collected the four pages. "These are not in Daddy's handwriting."

"No, they're not. It's a different slant altogether, and the letters are larger in size. But look, here in the margin are notes in your father's writing. He wrote: *I cannot bring myself to pass along such a diabolical scheme. The Washington connection has done all the research, and I suppose it would work if carried out as indicated, but I refuse to be party to blatant murder. The western campaign is one thing, but even I have my limits as to what I will or won't do in the name of the Confederacy...* This is an assassination plot, Salina. It's designed to kill Abraham Lincoln."

Another chill ran the length of Salina's spine. She reread the pages slowly horrified. Every detail was taken into consideration, and there was a descriptive schedule of the daily routine of the Union's president. This was followed by an outline of the plan with an explanation of the best time and place to eliminate him altogether. It concluded with a path of escape and the name of two contacts for whoever was assigned to carry out the ghastly scheme.

"Killing and bloodshed are inevitable in war when one fights against his enemy, but Daddy's right. This is a deliberate, calculated plan for an unspeakable crime," Salina shuddered. "Evidently, Daddy couldn't bring himself to forward this information because he didn't feel it was right. I don't think it is, either."

"I agree with you," Taylor Sue nodded. "Your father mentions a Washington contact. Only someone familiar with inside workings of the government in Washington would be able to draw up something as sinister as this so precisely..." She swallowed. "You don't think this is one of your father's assignments, do you?"

"No," Salina shook her head. "It sounds like his assignment was to give it to someone, but he intentionally intercepted it. I won't forward it either." Impulsively Salina tore the pages containing the assassination plot into small pieces. She tossed them into the grate without noticing that some of them fell through. She quickly gathered the remainder of the coded documents and put a match to them and the cipher, destroying them as Daddy had instructed. "Now it's done. Tomorrow we'll smuggle the translated pages out of the house and deliver them to Ben Nichols."

"Then we'll be free, Salina. We'll have peace again, at least within ourselves. It will be out of our hands once and for all," Taylor Sue said with relief.

"How I pray you're right," Salina said softly.

☆☆☆☆☆☆☆

The girls were able to catch a half-hour's worth of rest. Taylor Sue fell asleep instantly, but Salina's rest was haunted by a strange, bizarre dream.

She envisioned herself on a rocky, windswept island with no way of escape. She saw faces—of Jeremy, Daddy, Drake, Duncan Grant, and the Widow Hollis. Each of them was trying to get to her somehow, but the water between them was far too deep, and she was left all alone. She cried out, over and over, but the only reply was the sound of harsh, mocking laughter. As Salina looked around, all she could see was hundreds of pages blowing in the wind, swirling around her and then sinking into the depths of the dark water...

Salina sat up in the bed, panting hard and trembling, not realizing she had called out, and Taylor Sue had heard her. Tears streamed down Salina's white face.

Taylor Sue held Salina's hand between hers. "It's all right, Salina, you must have had a bad dream. I'm here with you. You're not alone."

Salina nodded, wiping her tears away with the sleeve of her nightgown. Her whimpers subsided, and she fell back to sleep, but fitfully.

Taylor Sue almost didn't have the heart to wake Salina when the sun made too early of an appearance, yet she did rouse her because she didn't want Salina to risk Genevieve Dumont's wrath if they were even a *minute* late to breakfast.

Chapter Twenty-Seven

*I*f Genevieve Dumont noticed the dark circles beneath the eyes of both her niece and Taylor Sue Carey, she did not make mention of it. The girls had seen their own reflections in the vanity table looking glass, and they knew how exhausted they appeared. Repeated yawns were not much of a reward for staying awake all night, and Salina's eyes were still puffy from crying so hard the day before.

Sophie was eager to get underway with the prospect of the shopping excursion. She practically inhaled her breakfast before Salina and Taylor Sue were served.

Salina was quiet, contemplative. Everything was just as Daddy said, except for one important detail. There was no indication of a starting date anywhere in the translated documents. Salina had reread Daddy's letter and found he mentioned that Hank Warner was to have known the date and told her when, but he hadn't done that. At least not that she was aware of.

Hank had given her the note, warning her about the enemy having eyes and ears everywhere—which was proving to be an undisputed fact. *The note...* Salina vaguely remembered that there had been numbers written on the bottom corner of the note from Hank. 15-51...no, that wasn't it. 11-51...no, that wasn't it either. Suddenly she seemed very sure that the numbers meant *something*, but she had to see them again before she could figure out what. Perhaps Dr. Nichols would know...

She dabbed the corners of her mouth with her linen napkin and made an excuse to return to her room, "I've forgotten my gloves. It won't take me but a minute to get them." Upstairs she shut the door behind her and sat down on the bed, relieved to have a moment out from under Genevieve's ever-watchful eyes. Salina tried to retrieve the note, which she had tucked into her cast for safekeeping, but she couldn't manage. The note must have slipped too far down between her arm and the side of the plaster cast to enable her to reach it.

Salina heard footsteps on the stairway, and she went to the traveling trunk to get the gloves Taylor Sue had given to her for her birthday. She closed the trunk, locking it, and absently caressed the brass-edged lid. She felt the scratches in the metal, but for some reason the travel-inflicted gouges seemed to be too deep to be accidental.

"That's got to be it!" Salina whispered lowly. She knelt down to examine the markings more closely and to her delight discovered that they were *not* mere scratches but deliberate carvings. The markings were the same numbers as those that had appeared on Hank's note, of that she was positive: *11-15*. Salina shivered. She recalled the day when Reverend Yates had brought the trunk to Shadowcreek, the day he informed them of Daddy's death. Salina had known then that there was something more to the trunk than just the false bottom. The carved numbers had to be significant. The question remained, *How?*

All the way to Dr. Nichols's office Salina pondered. *11-15*. The more she thought about it, the more probable it seemed; after all, she was looking for a starting date. Suppose the numbers 11-15 represented a specific day? Could it mean the fifteenth day of the eleventh month? *November 15?* Salina's heart raced. This was the thirteenth day of November. If that was the true meaning of the numbers, then the western campaign was scheduled to start in two days' time. Salina sighed with relief, knowing Drake would be taking them home tomorrow—on the fourteenth—and they should be well out of the way by then.

"What are you thinking, Salina?" Taylor Sue whispered when Genevieve and Sophie were talking among themselves. "You've got that gleam in your eye that tells me something is going on that I don't know about."

A small smile lifted the corners of her mouth. "I'll explain it to you later," promised Salina.

☆☆☆☆☆☆☆

Dr. Nichols's office was lined with bookshelves on one wall, counters and cabinets on two of the others, and on the remaining wall hung framed pictures of a plantation in Mississippi, anatomy charts, and a diploma from the university where he had studied medicine. A faint odor of turpentine, dried herbs, and some other chemicals permeated the air. A bony skeleton stood propped in one corner, and the leather-topped examining table was centered in the middle of the room.

Esther was already there, with a smock tied over her dress. She was going to assist her brother with the removal of Salina's plaster cast. "Good morning!" she smiled brightly at Taylor Sue, Salina, Sophie, and Genevieve. "Ben's just finishing up with his breakfast. We stayed up and talked most of the night away, and he overslept this morning."

Ben joined them. He wore a white coat over his dark suit. He rolled up the sleeves of his shirt and those of the white jacket to his elbows. "Good morning, ladies. Beautiful day today—the fog of last night burned away exceptionally early, and the sun on the ocean is breath-taking. Unfortunately, I missed my customary walk down by the beach this morning because I didn't get up on time," he grinned. "So I can only imagine what an awesome sight the sunrise must have been."

Genevieve, Sophie, and Taylor Sue seated themselves in the waiting area at the far end of the room near the windows overlooking the street while Ben led Salina to the examining table. She used the step stool to climb up and sit down as Ben insisted that the only form of payment he would allow for services rendered was the story of how Salina had broken her arm.

Esther withdrew a small saw from Ben's instrument case, handed it to her brother, and Salina cringed visibly. She sat as brave and still as she possibly could, telling as calmly as she was able about the day Peter Tom had spooked Starfire in the woods near the burned remains of Shadowcreek. Ben had his head bowed over his work, and Salina whispered softly, so that only he could hear, "I hid a note from Hank

Warner in the space between the plaster and my arm. We'll need to save that if we possibly can."

He nodded almost imperceptibly, whispering under his breath, "I'll certainly try." Unhurried, Ben methodically continued sawing away the plaster cast, finally freeing of Salina's arm from its long confinement. Some of the chalk dust got in her nose, and she sneezed twice.

"Bless you," Esther grinned. "It's all done now, Salina. How does it feel?"

"Sort of warm... tingly," Salina answered. "But mostly stiff."

"The more you use it, the less awkward movement will be for you," Ben said stuffing the rescued note into his pocket. He rotated her arm and moved her wrist in a circular motion. "Exercising it like this might help." Then he had her wiggle her fingers. "You'll be as good as new in no time."

"Is there someplace I can wash up?" Salina frowned, gently touching her grayish, scaly-looking skin and brushing off the chalky dust.

"The roughness will go away in time, too," Ben smiled kindly. "I'll have Esther get some lotion for you. It will help ease the dryness and make your skin soft again." He led her to the washroom, which was down the hallway between the examining room and his pharmacy.

Salina seized her chance. She whispered quickly, "Hank Warner told me to contact you. I have information that you need concerning the Confederate takeover of the Western states and territories."

"Have you got it with you?" Ben asked quietly.

Salina nodded. "Yes. My Daddy forwarded everything, and Hank said that you would know what to do with the documents I've been instructed to deliver into your keeping."

"Salina *Hastings*—of course! Why didn't I put the pieces together last night? I had wondered why you looked familiar when I met you at dinner with the Dumonts!" Ben gently patted her shoulder, "Please accept my condolences for the loss of your father. The Cause will miss him greatly. As for the documents you have, I'd prefer not to have them stored here. It's too dangerous. Esther has told me of her plans to accompany you this afternoon, to the dressmakers' shops, I believe."

"That's right," Salina said. "Do you want me to leave the information with Esther?"

"No, no," Ben immediately shook his head. "Esther doesn't know of my involvement with the western branch of the Network. She's been away in Chicago, and I'd rather she not learn of my dealings with other

Southern sympathizers. She has too many Union friends like Marie Everett. If Esther's kept in the dark, she won't be a security risk either." Ben fell silent, deep in thought. "At dinner last night, there was mention of visiting Madame Lucy's Boutique. Make sure you go there. Find a dress, any dress, and ask to be fitted. You can leave the documents in the dressing room."

"The dressing room at Madame Lucy's Boutique," Salina repeated. "But where?"

"Hide them in the bottom left drawer of the vanity table," Ben instructed. "Madame Lucy is an old friend of mine. She'll ask no questions."

"All right," Salina nodded. She stepped into the washroom and poured water from the pitcher into the basin. Ben gingerly scrubbed her arm and then patted it dry with a hand towel. It still looked odd to Salina, like it wasn't quite her own skin, but she was sure it would be back to normal very soon. "Did you manage to save my note?"

Ben took it from his pocket. "Here it is."

Salina unfolded the scrap of paper. "Taylor Sue and I translated the documents that were in code. It took us almost all night. Everything is accounted for as far as times and places and people go—but there was no date to start with. This morning, I discovered some markings carved into the brass edge on the lid of my trunk—which at one time belonged to my daddy. The markings match the numbers on this note that Hank gave me."

Ben studied the note. "It's good advice he's given. I second it." He looked again at the numbers. "Eleven-fifteen?"

"My guess is that it stands for the eleventh month, fifteenth day," Salina shrugged.

"November fifteenth—brilliant!" Ben nodded. "You, Salina Hastings, are to be commended on a job well done. The western campaign will go on just as your father planned for it to—on schedule, even—due to your courage. You're an exceptional young lady. You may rest assured that I will pick up the documents from Madame Lucy's this very afternoon and preparations will be launched for Saturday's action. Will you be staying in San Francisco long enough to witness the outcome?"

"No," Salina shook her dark curls. "I've been followed here and am still being followed. The Yankees are highly suspicious of me and in pursuit of those documents. Once they are out of my hands, I want nothing more to do with it. I just want to get back home to Virginia so they will leave me be. You must be very careful, Ben. I can attest to the fact that these particular Yankees are the personification of persistence and determination."

Ben nodded with an air of certainty. "There's nothing for you to worry your pretty little head about, Salina. We Rebels will strike and succeed before the Yankees realize what hit them."

"For all of our sakes, I do hope so," Salina said wistfully.

Ben and Salina returned to the examining room. Esther offered a bottle of lotion to Salina, saying, "Rub a little of this on it and see if it doesn't make your skin feel a bit softer."

The lotion did help, more than just a bit. Salina smiled. "It works." She continued rubbing her arm until the lotion absorbed into her dry skin. "See? It's much better than it was at first."

"Good." Esther smiled back. "Now we can get on with our shopping. We'll go to Madame Lucy's Boutique first thing. She has the most beautiful clothes, and I'm sure you'll be able to find something there that you'll absolutely adore." She untied her smock and hung it on a nail behind the door. "You're sure you won't mind my deserting you, Ben?"

"I've no appointments for this afternoon—yet anyway. You ladies go on and have a good time," Ben encouraged. "And thank you again for the delicious dinner last night, Mrs. Dumont."

Genevieve smiled politely. "You're quite welcome. It was my pleasure to aid Esther in surprising you by her homecoming. You were surprised."

"I certainly was." Ben winked at his sister.

"Come along, Sophie," Genevieve said. "If you're ready, girls?"

"Do you want me to bring back some lunch for you, Ben?" asked Esther over her shoulder on the way out the front door.

"I have a better idea. Why don't I meet all of you in Chinatown for lunch? We must treat Taylor Sue and Salina to Chinese food at Chin Li's."

"That's a fine idea," Genevieve agreed. "As long as the girls are here, they might as well learn something from their experiences."

"It's wonderful food," Esther said to Taylor Sue and Salina, who both had wrinkled their noses in uncertainty. "Sweet-and-sour chicken with rice is my favorite. I'll teach you how to use chopsticks, and for dessert there's always a fortune cookie..."

☆☆☆☆☆☆☆

Madame Lucy's Boutique boasted gowns of first-rate quality. Each dress, made up of the finest materials available, was of her own design, and she had established quite a reputable clientele who often made a social statement by wearing one of her originals. Custom orders were her specialty, but as of late, Madame Lucy ventured to cater to San Francisco's fast-paced lifestyle. She had begun to construct gowns in various sizes and have them on hand for display. These gowns, which would need only simple alterations—a hem, an extra layer of lace on a sleeve cuff, or a slight taking in—could be done up easily for customers who wished to have something new to wear within a few hours' time.

"Look at this one," Esther said to Salina. "This would be lovely on you. That green would accent your eyes beautifully. Don't you think so, Taylor Sue?"

Taylor Sue nodded. "There's another in the window you should see, right over there."

Salina touched a sleeve of the emerald green gown. It had a solid colored bodice edged with black velvet trim. The wide skirt was also dark green but had a contrasting pattern of black paisley print.

Genevieve left Sophie in the dressing room with Madame Lucy to be fitted and measured for a gown to wear at the piano recital. She stood directly behind Salina and remarked dryly, "It would do you well to remember that you are in mourning, child. I will ask Madame Lucy if she has anything ready-made in black."

"She hasn't forgotten that she's mourning her father, I can assure you," Taylor Sue said defensively against Genevieve's reproach. Like Salina, she was looking forward to when Drake came to take them away from Genevieve Dumont's reluctant hospitality. "I feel certain that any other dark-colored dress might be substituted in the event that there aren't any black ones here. Wouldn't you agree, Esther?"

Salina smiled as Esther nodded. Salina said, "Thank you, Aunt Genevieve, for taking the time to remind me of the rituals of mourning. It's very common at home for there are many women in mourning due to so many killed in the battles. And just so you know, I did wear a proper black dress to Daddy's memorial service."

"I should think so," Genevieve said in a clipped tone. She still shook her head in despair, and Salina had no doubt that whenever her aunt looked at her, the word "incorrigible" came to mind.

Taylor Sue led Salina over to the deep plum-colored dress displayed in the shop's front window. "I had to bite my tongue in order to keep from telling her to mind her own business. She's almost as bad as Lottie!"

Salina laughed at that. "I thought so myself." She looked at the plum dress, admiring the simplistic style. She had enough money for both gowns, and she certainly had need of them. "I need some shoes, too. Maybe after lunch we could find a pair for me."

"We're really going to eat Chinese food?" asked Taylor Sue.

"We have to at least give it try. Ethan will tell us we have no sense of adventure if we don't," Salina giggled.

"I suppose you're right," Taylor Sue admitted. She complained in a low whisper, "The documents beneath my corset are scratching me, Salina. Hurry up and try something on so we can get this business over with, would you?"

That made Salina laugh even more. She turned away from the window, deciding to try the green dress first, and missed the sight of Lieutenant Lance Colby on the plank sidewalk across the street.

Sophie came out of the dressing room with Madame Lucy right behind her, scribbling measurements and notes rapidly on a tablet with a pencil. "You take a look at the fabrics and tell me which you like the best," Madame Lucy told Sophie. She introduced herself to Salina and Taylor Sue. "What can I do to be of service?"

Salina pointed to the green gown. "I'd like to see if that one will fit me first, and then the plum-colored one in the window, if I may."

"But of course," Madame Lucy returned Salina's smile. "You go on back into the dressing room. Perhaps one of your lady friends can help you out of what you have on, and I'll bring these lovely dresses back for you."

Taylor Sue went with Salina, and they both hurried just as fast as they could. They knew they did not have much time. Salina shed her dress and stood barefooted in her pantalets and chemise. She had to work at it, but she finally managed to pull the transcribed documents from where she'd hidden them beneath her stays without having to unlace them.

Taylor Sue had smuggled her documents the same way, pressed against her ribs under her corset. She scratched her side to alleviate the itch, and she handed the remaining pages to Salina. Her heart hammered furiously. "Hurry, Salina! You've got to help me get back into this dress of mine."

"Let me put the pages away first!" Salina's heart was pounding hard, too, as she located the hiding place Ben Nichols had indicated. "Get your dress on, and I'll button you up," she said over her shoulder. Salina put the documents in the bottom of the drawer of the vanity table and piled yards of lace and ribbons on top of them, praying that no one would disturb them until Ben came to collect them. Quickly she shut the drawer and then went to work on the buttons on the back of Taylor Sue's dress, fumbling with shaking fingers. "I'm hurrying. I'm hurrying!"

Taylor Sue sat on the vanity bench when Salina finished with the buttons at the back of her gown. She put her hand over her heart and shook her russet head. Their eyes locked conspiratorially, and they both sighed, unspeakably relieved to have accomplished the task just before Madame Lucy brought the new dresses in to Salina.

The emerald dress was a perfect fit as it was, with no need of any alterations. "I believe this was made just for you, mademoiselle," Madame Lucy declared. "It is a very smart-looking outfit on you."

Salina turned to study her reflection in the full-length mirror. "I do like it."

"Very elegant," Taylor Sue complimented, then added with a giggle, "Jeremy would heartily approve, I think. That neckline sets off the locket he gave you perfectly."

Salina lovingly touched her golden necklace. "So it does." She then tried on the second gown, which was just as lovely, but needed to be taken in and have the hem raised at least an inch, maybe two. "Not a problem," Madame Lucy assured her. "I can have the alterations completed and the dress ready by tomorrow. If you like, come back at this same time and it will be waiting for you."

Salina nodded and paid for the garments in advance. "Thank you very much, Madame Lucy."

"It is my pleasure helping girls look beautiful," the dressmaker smiled. "Your Jeremy will indeed like the green. I'm sure of it."

"I think I'll wear it now," Salina smiled.

Taylor Sue grinned and predicted, "Aunt Genevieve won't approve."

"Today, I don't care," Salina told her friend. "I just don't!"

They were laughing together when Salina came out of the dressing room in her new emerald dress, but the laughter vanished the instant they saw that the Widow Hollis was standing very near the dressing room door. Taylor Sue's hand clutched Salina's behind the folds of her skirt, gripping tightly.

Salina recovered herself, putting on a forced smile and chatting gaily, "Hello, Mrs. Hollis. How are you today?"

"Very well, thank you," the Widow nodded stiffly.

Salina's mind screamed, *She knows!* But in her heart she stood steadfast, believing firmly that God was in control of this entire situation. *Trust in the Lord with all your heart... In all thy ways acknowledge Him and He will direct thy path...* She mentally cried for

God's help while she attempted to extract her hand from Taylor Sue's before she had no feeling left in her fingers.

"Have you come to look at the dresses? They're gorgeous," Salina rambled. No, the Widow probably didn't know anything. Salina heard the bell on the front door ring only a moment ago, so the Widow couldn't have been in the shop for more than the last few minutes at the most. "I saw a very becoming black straw bonnet with a dyed ostrich feather near the front counter..."

"Actually I came to see the mourning jewelry," the Widow replied evenly. "I had heard Madame Lucy had some fine pieces."

"I see," Salina said, meeting the Widow's scrutinizing eyes without flinching. "Well, good day to you. It's been a pleasure to see you again."

The Widow smiled deliberately, her eyes penetrating even through her black veil. "It might be that we will see each other again while you're here in town."

I certainly hope not! Salina thought to herself, but she said aloud, "We'll have to see about that, won't we. At present we're off to do some more shopping with Esther, my cousin, and my aunt. Would you by chance know of a good shoe store nearby?"

The Widow Hollis recommended one that she knew on Market Street, and Salina thanked her for the information. She followed Taylor Sue to where Esther was waiting with Genevieve and Sophie, and she whispered, "Don't forget to breathe, Taylor Sue."

"Breathe?" Taylor Sue shot back. "My heart caught in my throat, and I honestly didn't know if it was going to start beating again. Oh, she gave me a fright! Do you think she's following us or it's just a coincidence?"

Salina shrugged, then smiled. "Don't worry, Taylor Sue. It doesn't matter anymore. We're out of it, and we're going to be just fine," Salina said confidently.

"I'm so glad you're so sure of yourself," Taylor Sue remarked, still shaking like a leaf.

"That's a beautiful dress, Salina." Esther was pleased with Salina's appearance. "I'm so glad I picked it out for you."

"So am I." Salina nodded and turned around for full inspection.

"You'll have to be careful that you don't spill anything on it," Genevieve mused. "Eating with chopsticks can be very tricky..."

Salina paid no mind to her aunt's condescending tone, refusing to be bothered by it anymore. She winked at Taylor Sue as they were climbing into the carriage. Shopping for shoes would have to wait, as it was nearly time for them to meet Ben in Chinatown at Chin Li's restaurant, and she suddenly discovered that she was very, very hungry.

She said little on the way to Chinatown, and she didn't quite see the colorful banners blowing in the breeze, the bright Oriental decorations, or the words on signs painted in what appeared to be a foreign alphabet comprised of unreadable symbols rather than familiar English letters. Salina was lost, deep in her own thoughts, and praying silently again. *"Dear God, if You see my daddy, could You please let him know that I've kept my word of honor. The task he left me is complete. Thank You for being my strength, Lord. "* A strong sense of peace washed over her as she felt her burden lifted from her shoulders, and Salina relaxed for the first time in weeks. Under her breath she hummed *Dixie*, and she was anxious for tomorrow to come quickly so that she and Taylor Sue could be on Drake's stagecoach first thing in the morning. A serene smile touched her lips, a loving warmth stole around her heart, and she absently fingered her golden heart-shaped locket. Heading home to the war-torn East was preferable to staying here in the far-removed West, Salina had no doubt on that point. Besides, she knew Jeremy Barnes was waiting for her there.